may

Are these ... about to ... child.

By Request

maybe baby!

HONEYMOON BABY
by
Susan Napier

RICO'S SECRET CHILD
by
Lucy Gordon

THE UNEXPECTED BABY
by
Diana Hamilton

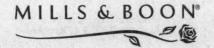

MILLS & BOON®

*MILLS & BOON and MILLS & BOON with the Rose Device
are registered trademarks of the publisher.
Harlequin Mills & Boon Limited,
Eton House, 18-24 Paradise Road, Richmond, Surrey, TW9 1SR*

MAYBE BABY!
© by Harlequin Enterprises II B.V., 2002

Honeymoon Baby, Rico's Secret Child and *The Unexpected Baby*
were first published in Great Britain by Harlequin Mills & Boon Limited
in separate, single volumes.

Honeymoon Baby © Susan Napier 1998
Rico's Secret Child © Lucy Gordon 1999
The Unexpected Baby © Diana Hamilton 1999

ISBN 0 263 83162 0

05-1102

*Printed and bound in Spain
by Litografia Rosés S.A., Barcelona*

Susan Napier was born on St Valentine's Day, so it's not surprising she has developed an enduring love of romantic stories. She started her writing career as a journalist in Auckland, New Zealand trying her hand at romantic fiction only after she had married her handsome boss! Numerous books later she still lives with her most enduring hero, two future heroes – her sons! – two cats and a computer. When she's not writing she likes to read and cook, often simultaneously!

Look out for more of Susan Napier's fantastic stories. Coming soon in Modern Romance™!

HONEYMOON BABY
by
Susan Napier

CHAPTER ONE

JENNIFER was filling a vase at the kitchen sink when the sleek, low-slung dark green car came gunning around the tree-lined curve of the driveway, almost fish-tailing into a bank of ferns as the driver belatedly realised the bend was a lot sharper than it looked. She frowned out of the window as she watched the unfamiliar car recover from its near-skid and continue at a more cautious pace up the narrow, rutted gravel drive to park in front of the low dry-stone wall which enclosed the cottage garden in front of the house. With the heavy dust coating the tinted windscreen she couldn't make out the driver, but the lone pair of skis strapped to the moulded black roof-rack suggested a stray single hoping for a bed.

Whoever it was would be out of luck. Jennifer disliked having to turn custom away, but all her rooms were currently occupied and—she unconsciously crossed her fingers—apart from a few odd days, booking was fairly solid for the rest of the month…providing the mountain minded its manners.

She glanced out of the corner window at the billowing, dirty grey mushroom-cloud of steam and ash which boiled up from the snowy summit of Mount Ruapehu, blotting out the formerly blue sky. The scenery was spectacular but living on the borders of a National Park, within twenty kilometres of an active volcano, had its drawbacks. Although there had been no major eruption here for thousands of years, the 2797-metre-high mountain itself was a powerful reminder of man's vulnerability to the forces of nature, and lately a series of minor eruptions had put a serious crimp in the local economy of one of New Zealand's premier ski resorts.

Jennifer's wide mouth turned down at the corners at the thought of another disappointing winter. Vulcanologists and government scientists had been closely monitoring the mountain since it had exploded back into life just over a year ago, coating the ski fields with successive layers of brown ash for months, causing the closure of the mountain to skiers, sightseers and climbers, and creating great financial hardship for the local businesses who were heavily reliant on a good ski season for the greater portion of their annual income. There had been no loss of life or property, but the damage in terms of adverse publicity had been considerable.

Now, just as the public alert level had finally been dropped and early snowfalls presaged a long ski season that would enable the local tourist industry to recoup some of the previous year's losses, Mount Ruapehu was rumbling again, sending steam and sediment from its crater lake streaming into the atmosphere. Although the scientists claimed there was no indication that the new eruption would be any bigger than last year's, casual skiers were already cancelling their holidays in droves. Only the hard-core snow-junkies seemed willing to gamble on parts of the ski fields remaining open for the duration of their stay.

Fortunately a small, quiet bed and breakfast establishment like Beech House appealed more to mature tourist couples and lone travellers than to groups of avid skiers, so Jennifer hoped to weather the crisis better than some of the other, larger moteliers and resort operators, whose advertising was focused on pre-packaged ski deals. Some of her guests were even booked in *because,* rather than in spite of the possibility of a more fiery eruption.

Jennifer's mouth curved up again, tawny brown eyes glowing in a secret smile of contentment behind her tortoiseshell spectacles. At least this year she didn't have to suffer the black panic of wondering whether she was going to be able to meet the next mortgage payment…

The sound of a car door opening switched her attention back to the new arrival as a slight figure glided into the kitchen to place some garden produce and a bunch of brilliant yellow chrysanthemums on the bench.

'Snazzy car. Who is it?' asked Susie Tang, going on tiptoe to peer out of the window.

Even so, her glossy black head barely came up to Jennifer's collarbone. Although five feet ten wasn't much over average height for a woman, she always felt like a veritable Amazon next to her diminutive part-time employee. 'My guess is foreign, lost or illiterate…or maybe just someone who doesn't believe ''No Vacancy'' signs.'

'Uh-oh!' Susie clapped her hand over her mouth, her almond-shaped eyes widening under her jet-black fringe. 'I said I'd hang it out for you when I left yesterday, didn't I? Sorry, Jen, I forgot…' The mournful mobility of her expression banished any illusion of oriental inscrutability. Susie's every thought and mood registered on her face.

A masculine hand splayed on the roof of the car as the driver hauled himself out of his bucket seat. 'Never mind—if he gets a look inside and likes what he sees, maybe he'll come back and stay another time,' said Jennifer, reaching for the flowers. A lot of her custom came from repeat business or via word-of-mouth recommendation.

'Wow!' Susie was nearly falling out of the window. 'He's even snazzier than his car! Since there's no room at the inn do you think *I* could interest him in bed and breakfast?'

Jennifer's laughing reply died in her throat as the man lifted his head in a quick, predatory motion to stare up at the house. The sun flared off hair the colour of old gold and the black wrap-around sunglasses couldn't disguise the distinctive jut of his high cheekbones and the hollow cheeks bracketing the unshaven chin. A wave of nauseating disbelief washed over her, making her knees sag against the kitchen cupboards.

Surely fate couldn't be so cruel!

She clutched the vase to her stomach, slopping water onto the tiled surface of the bench, praying that her eyes were deceiving her.

Gravel crunched under his feet as he strode around to the back of the car and opened the boot. Faded jeans moulded long legs and lean hips, and a cream woollen jumper under the black hip-length leather jacket studded with snaps and zips completed the image of threatening masculinity. He hefted a suitcase out of the boot, moving with the easy confidence of a man in the prime of his life, at the peak of his virility...

And definitely no wild illusion.

'Oh, *God*—!'

'Jen, what's the matter? You look as if you've seen a ghost?'

Worse than a ghost. Much, much worse! She was staring into the face of grim reality. A nightmare complication to an already convoluted existence. A living, breathing reproach to her unquiet conscience.

She had thought him safely ensconced in London. What hellish coincidence had landed him here, in her own private little corner of the world?

Oh, *God*!

'Jen, you're not going to pass out on me, are you? *Jen*?'

Susie's sharp anxiety penetrated her ringing skull, beating back the icy chills of disbelief which had frozen her brain. She shook her head violently, self-preservation screaming to the fore as she jerked back from the window.

'No, I'm fine,' she lied, grabbing the bunch of chrysanthemums and haphazardly stuffing them into the pottery vase.

'Is it him? That man? Do you know him?' Susie angled herself against the glass to watch him vanish around the corner of the sprawling bungalow, in the direction of the front porch. 'If he's bringing in his bag perhaps he's not just cold-calling. Maybe there's been a mix-up in the bookings. If he spoke to Paula on the phone—you know she's not big on writing things down...'

At the mention of her mother Jennifer's heart leapt in her chest. Thank goodness she wasn't here! She and Aunty Dot had driven over to The Grand Château for a Gourmet Club luncheon at the hotel restaurant; they should be away for at least another hour.

There was a welcoming bark and the loud scrabble of claws on the wooden porch, and seconds later the harsh grind of the old-fashioned doorbell reverberated in the entranceway. To Jennifer it sounded uncannily like the knell of doom.

'Uh, shouldn't you go and see what he wants?' suggested Susie when the bell rang a second time.

If the newcomer got impatient and tried the door, he would find that it wasn't locked. He could just walk in, and then, and then...

Oh, God!

'You do it,' she blurted.

'Me?'

Guests and potential guests were always dealt with by either Paula or Jennifer at their own insistence—the personal touch was a hallmark of Beech House. Susie's job was only peripheral to the bed and breakfast business—helping run Paula's afternoon cooking classes and delivering the jams, pickles and jars of edible and decorative

preserved fruit, which she sold to stores as far away as
Taupo.

'I have to put these flowers in the Carters' room. Mrs
Carter complained that the vase of daphne that Mum put
in there was too highly perfumed,' babbled Jennifer,
conscious of the feebleness of her excuse.

She couldn't blame Susie for looking bewildered at
her urgency over the floral arrangements. Mr and Mrs
Carter had gone on a cruise on Lake Taupo for the day
and wouldn't be back until late evening.

'Are you sure you're feeling all right?'

The doorbell rang again and Jennifer flinched, splashing water from the crammed vase down the leg of her
fawn trousers.

'I do feel a bit sick,' she admitted bluntly, grabbing
at the straw. 'Look, all you have to do is say that we
don't have any vacancies for the foreseeable future, and
direct him to another B&B or one of the hotels. Don't
go into details. And don't give him one of our new advertising leaflets; I haven't decided how to use them yet,'
she tacked on hastily, remembering the glossy reprints
that her mother had ordered as a surprise, with *'Jenny
Jordan and Paula Scott, proprietors'* in flowing bold
type on the front.

'But, how—?'

'For goodness' sake, Susie, I'm only asking you to
answer the door, not perform brain surgery!' she
snapped.

Susie blinked, more surprised than offended by the
implied insult. In the three months that she had worked
at Beech House she had never known Jennifer be anything but kind, considerate and polite, if a little wicked
in her sense of humour. Perhaps, though, a little moodi-
ness was only to be expected from now on…

'OK, OK—don't get your hormones in a bunch.' She
grinned. 'I'll go…but, uh, what if he asks—?'

'Just get rid of him!'

Jennifer bit her lip as Susie shot out of the kitchen, propelled by the low-voiced shriek. She was going to have to apologise, but later—when the immediate danger had passed and she had control of herself again.

Not wanting to compound her sins by being caught out in another lie, she forced her shaky legs into action, slipping through the dining and living rooms and sneaking out along the sweeping back verandah, leaving a faint trail in the thin mantle of volcanic ash. She let herself into the large double bedroom which was considered the best in the house for its unobscured view of Ruapehu. Closing the French doors on the icy southerly wind, she picked up the crystal vase with its artfully arranged sprays of daphne and replaced it with the flung together chrysanthemums.

She looked blankly around the room that she had tidied earlier. Should she wait in here until she heard his car leave? She eyed the door to the passage, which was slightly ajar. She longed to creep up to the sanctuary of her bedroom and bolt the door, but the narrow staircase to the converted attic was in full view of the front door.

She turned away, catching sight of her glazed expression in the old-fashioned mirror atop the dressing table. No wonder Susie had looked at her with such concern! She had never considered herself a beauty, but right now the too-square face with its too-sharp nose and slightly asymmetrical mouth was starkly plain—her dark brown hair, tumbling in careless waves to her shoulders, contrasting with a complexion as pale and waxy as the daphne blooms that she held in her hand. The bright red jumper that her mother had knitted the previous winter further accentuated her pallor, and snugly defined full breasts which trembled as if she had just run a marathon. With her left eyebrow twitching above the thin amber curve of her round spectacle frame, she looked like a woman on the verge of a nervous breakdown.

Which was exactly how she felt.

The cloying sweetness of daphne clogged her nostrils as she paced. Why on earth was Susie taking so long to get rid of him?

A vivid picture of golden male confidence sketched itself in her head and she halted on a silent moan. What if Susie couldn't handle it?

What if he chose to flex his insufferable arrogance and argue?

What if he exercised his brutal charm and insinuated himself over the threshold?

And what if his being here wasn't simply a rotten piece of malignant bad luck?

She stared out at the smouldering mountain, so busy agonising over the possibilities that she didn't notice the door to the hall swinging open until a squeak of the hinges made her stiffen.

'Playing hard to get, *Mrs Jordan*?'

Jennifer's quickened breathing hitched to an uneven stop as she slowly turned around, to be impaled by green-gold eyes which were every bit as cruelly condemning as she remembered. But now their contemptuous coldness was super-heated to a vaporous fury that made her wish he hadn't taken off his sunglasses.

Her face was on fire while her hands and feet felt like lumps of ice. Black dots prickled across her vision and her tongue suddenly felt too big for her dry mouth.

'R-Raphael. What a surprise. Wh-what are you doing here?' she managed threadily.

Raphael Jordan advanced into the spacious room, shrinking it to the size of a jail cell, his cynical smile oozing pure menace.

'What do *you* think, *Mrs Jordan*?'

She swallowed, trying to work moisture into the dryness of her throat, wishing that he would stop sneering her name in that ominously insulting fashion.

'I don't know,' she said, meaning she didn't dare speculate. 'Are—are you just passing through on holiday?'

He bludgeoned aside the frail hope. 'Not a holiday— a hunting expedition.' He kept on moving, forcing her to back up until her calves hit the dressing table drawers. 'For certain very valuable—and very elusive—kiwis...'

Jennifer's stomach lurched sickeningly at his use of the plural. 'K-kiwis are a fully protected bird,' she stuttered stupidly. Although she knew he was only just over six feet, he seemed to loom for ever. 'It's against the law for people to hunt them.'

His feral gaze gloated over her white face. 'In their native habitat, yes, but what happens to greedy kiwis who venture where they don't belong and violate the laws of nature...? I'd say that makes them fair game, wouldn't you?'

He made no attempt to touch her, yet she sensed his straining muscles yearning to do physical violence. Her heartbeat thundered in her ears, her eyes sliding away from his grim expression to search the empty doorway behind him.

'Where's Susie? What did you say to get her to let you in?' Her cold hands were suddenly as clammy as her brow and her voice sank to a horrified whisper. *What have you told her?*

His shrug was a ripple of expensive leather. 'About our relationship? How about the truth?'

She fought against the bile rising in her throat. 'What *truth*?'

His full-lipped smile was cruelly taunting.

'Why, that you're my father's wife, pregnant with my child!'

The heavy vase slipped through Jennifer's nerveless
fingers, smashing to pieces on the polished hardwood
floor as she tumbled headlong into the smothering
darkness.

CHAPTER TWO

'JEN? Hello! Are you in there?'

Jennifer's eyes fluttered open to find Susie's round face filling her vision.

'Thank goodness! How do you feel?'

Jennifer moistened her dry lips, momentarily disorientated by the discovery that she was lying flat on the living room couch, with Susie kneeling on the floor beside her.

'OK...I think,' she wavered, remembering her awful anxiety dream. Had she been taking a nap? Was her guilt now going to pursue her even into sleep? 'What happened?'

'You fainted. Switched out like a light, apparently. Luckily your husband caught you before you fell face first into all that glass.'

'Husband?' she echoed feebly.

'I guess you were too busy feeling rotten to really look at our visitor, huh?' Susie suggested with a wry grin. 'I felt horribly embarrassed when I found out who I was giving the bum's rush to, but fortunately Rafe seems a forgiving kind of guy.'

'My *husband*?' Jennifer struggled up onto her elbows, her whirling head causing her to sink back against the padded arm of the couch. '*Rafe?*'

'Yeah—he said not to worry about it, that he knew you weren't expecting him. He wanted to surprise you, but I suppose it wasn't such a hot idea when you were feeling so wonky...'

So it hadn't been a dream!

'He's really here?' Jennifer cast a hunted look around

15

the room, her eyes skipping over the comfortable, well-used furniture. Everything was still fuzzy around the edges. She groped at her face.

'My glasses—where are my glasses?' She needed a barrier, however flimsy and transparent, to hide behind.

Susie picked them up off the coffee table and handed them to her to fumble on.

'Now, don't fret,' she said, misunderstanding Jennifer's panic. 'He'll be back in a moment. I got him to carry you out here because your clothes got splashed and I knew you wouldn't want the Carters' bedclothes all damp when you'd just made all the beds. He's just in the kitchen getting you a drink. See, here he is back!'

Susie scrambled to her feet to allow the tall, whipcord-lean man to weave around the coffee table and perch sideways on the broad couch. He wedged his right hip against Jennifer's side as he braced one arm on the cushioned back and leaned over to offer her a sip from the glass of water in his other hand, effectively caging in her body with his chest.

Satisfied that her employer was in good hands, Susie backed away. 'I'm going to leave for home before this volcanic fog gets any worse, but don't worry about that mess in the Carters' room, Jen, I'll clean it up for you before I go. That way you two can just concentrate on each other...'

'Thanks, Susie.' Rafe's deep, warm tone cut off Jennifer's spluttering objection as he pressed the glass to her pale mouth. He threw a burnished smile over his shoulder. 'You're a sweetheart, but...' He trailed off, raising silky brows.

Susie laughed, as if she had known him for years rather than merely minutes. 'I know, I know—three's a crowd. I guess I'll see you later then...much later!'

Jennifer pushed at the glass which had been used to

gag her as Susie scampered away. 'Take it away! I don't want a drink.'

Trust Jordan to have suborned her ally while she was unconscious. As a former male model, and former editor of a raunchy men's magazine, he was no doubt used to women falling over themselves to be friendly.

There was no smile for her. Just a probing look. 'Too bad. You need extra fluids to counteract shock—and don't tell me you're not shocked to see me. Drink!'

The glass clinked against her resistant teeth, forcing her head back against the arm of the couch, and, knowing his stubbornness, she took a single swallow, defiantly tiny.

'Again,' he insisted.

Another, even tinier sip. 'Bully,' she muttered, wondering if she dared spit it in his face.

'Cheat. Gold-digger,' he retaliated softly. *'Thief.'*

At the heavy significance placed on the last insult she almost choked on the small mouthful, the blood surging up into her face.

'Good. You've got a little of your colour back,' he said, studying her clinically. The simmering violence with which he had confronted her in the bedroom was gone, superceded by an implacable air of purpose that was even more threatening. He had taken advantage of her unconsciousness to firmly establish himself in her household, leaving her no option but to fight a rear-guard action.

Close up, his lightly tanned face revealed the imprint of thirty-three years rich with experience, fine lines fanning out from the corners of his knowing eyes and cynical curves bracketing the corners of his sensual mouth. The slight stubble softening the hard line of his jaw sparkled like gold glitter on a Christmas card, and the short, spiky tufts of deep blonde hair, sun-bleached almost white at the tips, created an improbable halo above the narrow temples. However, apart from his name, any similarity to an angel was purely illusory—no angel possessed Raphael Jordan's decadent past!

'More?'

He tilted the glass, ignoring her sullen resistance, and a trickle of water repelled by the compressed seam of her lips skated down from the corner of her mouth.

To her intense shock Rafe bent his head and licked the droplets off her chin before they could drip into the cowl-neck of her angora jumper.

'Stop it!' she gasped, wiping the back of her hand over the spot where his moist tongue had lashed her tender skin with fire. 'What do you think you're doing?'

She gulped as he lifted his head, just enough for her to see the sexual taunting in his emerald eyes.

'Just my husbandly duty, *Mrs Jordan*…'

She hated the ease with which he could disrupt her senses. From the first time Sebastian had introduced her to his son she had been deeply aware of the dangerous undercurrents, and was secretly grateful for the strained relationship between the two men which had kept their association to a minimum.

'You said you told Susie the truth,' she said, her voice ragged with the effort of controlling her fear.

He placed the barely touched glass on the beechwood coffee table without releasing her from his tormenting gaze. 'Actually, she didn't give me the chance,' he admitted with a cool lack of remorse for the fright he had given her. 'I told her my name and before I could say that I was looking for my father's wife—'

'His *widow*!' It was a distinction that was vital to Jennifer's bruised sensibilities.

He inclined his head, his eyes glinting as if her fierce correction had accorded him some kind of important victory.

'Whatever… As soon as I said I was Raphael Jordan,

she began talking as if *I* was your husband. She seemed so certain that your husband's name was Rafe, and so positive that you'd be over the moon to see me that I thought it best not to argue with her romantic delusions.'

Best? He meant most useful to his own purposes!

Jennifer clenched her hands at her sides, hating the helplessness of her position but knowing she would be no match for Rafe in a physical tussle. He clearly had no intention of letting her up until she was intimidated into giving him some answers.

She would have to rely on her wits to extricate herself and somehow persuade him to leave before he encountered loose-tongued Susie again, or—God forbid—her mother!

'It seems funny that she should get so mixed up,' he mused perilously, 'because she seemed otherwise a fairly intelligent and switched-on young woman. Could it be, dear stepmama, that you've been purposely vague about the whereabouts of your husband? Haven't you let on that he's no longer in the land of the living? Been keeping your widow's mite secret from your impecunious friends and relatives?'

Her stomach roiled at his clever guess. But not clever enough!

'Don't call me that! And how can you be so flippant about the death of your own father? I know you two didn't get on, but you might at least have some respect for his memory—'

'If you'd bothered to hang around for the funeral you would have seen me paying my respects,' he ripped at her. 'I even shed a few tears for the stiff-necked old bastard. But don't expect me to elevate him to sainthood just because he's dead. He was a good doctor and a brilliant businessman, but he was a poor husband and a rotten father; his ambitions always got in the way of his relationships and he never stopped trying to force me into his own mould. So don't preach to me about my filial duty, Stepmama—'

Worms of horror squirmed across her skin. 'Stop *calling* me that!'

'Why, isn't that what you became when you married my father?'

'Because it's—it's…'

His eyes followed the inarticulate workings of her crooked mouth.

'Ridiculous? Distasteful?' A lethal pause before he leaned forward and added insinuatingly, *'Obscene?'*

He was close, too frighteningly close. She steadied herself and got her tongue to shape her choppy breath into a crisp, 'Definitely ridiculous.'

'But technically correct. And Sebastian was always big on getting the technicalities right, wasn't he? That's how he was able to create such a truly unique inheritance for us to share…'

She could feel the warmth of his breath swirling around her face, causing the blood to sing in her cheeks. Hadn't she read somewhere about a predator which breathed on its trapped prey before tearing it to pieces? The animal version of a ritual act of gloating possession…

'I didn't expect Sebastian to leave me anything in his will—he told me he wouldn't,' she said, in the desperate hope that he was referring to the money. She silently cursed Sebastian for breaking his promise. His God complex at work again. Even from the grave he couldn't resist trying to get his own way! If he had stuck to their original agreement there would have been no reason for anyone from the Jordan family to search her out.

'I don't want to cheat anyone in the family out of their inheritance,' she told him, her light brown eyes owlishly earnest behind the little round spectacles. 'When Sebastian's lawyers wrote to tell me about the shares and bonds, I wrote back and said I didn't want them, that I'd sign a waiver of claim so they could be returned to the estate—'

His crack of cynical laughter cut her off.

'Sure, why bother with the petty change when you've already got your hot little hands on the main prize, right?' he growled, abruptly dropping his arm from the back of the couch and planting his hands on the arm of the couch, on either side of her head.

'I—I don't know what you mean,' she said warily, excruciatingly aware of his thumb-tips brushing the straining cords of her neck and the metal zip of his open jacket sawing at the soft wool over her breasts as the heavy sides enfolded her like black leather wings.

'No? Apart from all the hard cash you gouged out of him while he was alive, under the terms of the Jordan family trust, as my father's legal wife at the time of his death you've inherited his position as trustee of a multi-million-dollar investment fund! I notice you're not offering to waive *that* family privilege!'

She bit her pale lower lip. 'That's only a nominal title—the trust is still going to be run by the three professional trustees, exactly as it was when Sebastian was alive. And if you're familiar with the deed then you must know that as a named trustee I have no legal access to *any* of that money.'

'Not for yourself personally, I agree,' he said silkily, 'but any *child* conceived during your marriage to Sebastian would be a blank cheque in your hands…'

'No…! Never!'

Her appalled cry of rejection was followed by a short, electric silence.

Jennifer felt the hairs rise on the back of her neck and a metallic taste flood her tongue. How could he have found out? she thought hysterically. Sebastian had assured her that his exclusive London clinic guaranteed total confidentiality and that his staff were well trained in protecting the anonymity of both donor and recipient. Ethics had obliged him to hand over her case to one of his senior colleagues, and Sebastian's rapidly failing health had meant he rarely visited the clinic himself, but he had promised to sequester her case-notes amongst his own inactive files as an extra precaution.

Of course, those staunch ethics of his—which had been so vital to her trust—had in the end turned out to be tainted by self-interest. Maybe he had been unforgiveably lax in other ways, too... Or maybe Raphael was just making guesses based more on his cynical certainty that Jennifer was a greedy bimbo out for everything she could get than any real hard evidence.

Her hands instinctively crept to protect her flat abdomen.

Rafe's eyes flickered down as he registered the movement and returned to hers, gleaming with yellow fire.

'Scruples, Jennifer? From a woman who married a dying old man for his money?'

He was making it all sound so *sordid,* when in fact it had been an eminently practical arrangement on both sides.

'It wasn't *like* that—'

'You're not trying to claim it was *love*?' The word was uttered with a deep contempt that seemed to sum up Raphael Jordan's views on relationships in general, and Jennifer in particular.

She flushed and tried to cling to her fast-dwindling courage. She recognised his interrogation technique. He was harrying her in ever-decreasing circles, slipping under her defences to nip painfully at his target and then retreating to prowl around another topic before darting in for another bite.

Somewhere in the background she heard Susie carol out a goodbye, and the front door bang, and a little of her tension eased. At least now if there was a messy scene there would be no witnesses.

She would have liked to fling Raphael's cynicism back in his teeth with a passionate declaration of emotion, but instead chose the dignity of the literal truth. 'I liked Sebastian from the time I first met him. I had a lot of respect for him—'

She broke off, for that respect had taken a severe beating the day he died...

'And I'll bet you liked him a whole lot more when you discovered he had inoperable cancer, hmm?' said Rafe crudely. 'He told you about it, didn't he? When he was staying here?'

'Yes, but—'

'So—out of pure altruism, of course—you instantly agreed to abandon your home and business and travel back to England with Sebastian as his—now how did he introduce you to the family?—ah, that's right, his *"nurse-companion"*...the one with a murky past and no credentials!'

A sunburst of anger overrode Jennifer's guilt. She still vividly remembered the humiliation she had suffered at the hands of three of Sebastian's bickering ex-wives and his numerous, spoiled, grown-up stepchildren when they realised that an Antipodean nobody was threatening their future access to the Jordan gravy-train.

Only Raphael, Sebastian's eldest son and sole natural child, had remained aloof from the outpourings of spite which followed. Never having allowed his father to bankroll his lifestyle, he was immune to the bribes and rewards by which Sebastian had manipulated his greedy brood of dependents-by-marriage. Although Rafe had bluntly disapproved of his father's precipitous marriage to a woman thirty-six years his junior, in keeping with his own history of rebellious independence he had not disputed Sebastian's right to make a bloody fool of himself.

'I *did* train as a nurse—I just never got to complete the practical part of the course for my formal qualification,' she flared now.

'Yes, well, you were obviously better qualified as a *companion* than a nurse, because lo and behold, only a month after you land in England you're married to your patient—and three weeks after *that* your very wealthy new husband, whose heart was never a contributor to his health problems, has a heart attack in his own bed and is dead within days. And what does his doting bride do to mourn his passing? She skips out on the funeral, leaving only a post office box on the other side of the world as a forwarding address...'

Jennifer gasped. 'If you're trying to imply that I had *any*thing at all to do with Sebastian having heart failure—!'

'Oh, no, I've read the autopsy report and spoken to his doctors...I have to absolve you of murder,' he conceded, with what she thought was insulting reluctance.

'Kind of you!' she snapped recklessly.

He raised silky eyebrows. 'It does happen: energetic, lusty young wife entices her elderly, ailing husband to prove that he's still a man...'

Her tawny eyes flashed up at him, her fingers itching to slap his face, but before she could act out the impulse his eyelids drooped and he purred, 'Only we both know how unlikely *that* scenario is...since my father's cancer treatments had made him impotent well before he ever left on that round-the-world trip. Your marriage was never actually consummated, was it, Jennifer—?'

Her fingers curled into her palms. 'You have no right to—'

'I saw his medical records after he died...I *know* that

claim of paternity you got him to sign isn't worth the paper it's written on!'

'I don't know what you're talking about—'

'I'm talking about the "bargain" you made with Sebastian, the one that you're going to use to unlock the trust.'

She clapped her hands over her ears. 'I refuse to listen to—'

His strong fingers wrapped around her wrists, wrenching them away from her head. He pinned them against the centre of his chest with one hand and used the other to cup her chin, forcing her to acknowledge what he was saying.

'Oh, no, you're not getting out of it that easily. If you won't tell this story, then *I* will—and you're going to listen to every single, solitary word!'

While his eyes, feasting on her every reaction, were no doubt going to be her judge, jury and executioner! Jennifer tried to congeal her expressive features into a stony mask.

'It's one of life's little ironies that my father the fertility specialist discovered not long after his divorce from my mother that he'd become sterile himself,' Rafe said harshly. 'But typically he never reconciled himself to it. Practically from the time I hit puberty he was nagging at me to find a steady girlfriend. As far as he was concerned my sole purpose in life was to become a doctor like him and marry early so that I could have lots of little Jordan brats. When I told him I didn't intend to do any of those things—ever—he began taking wives with children of their own, and when that proved unsatisfactory he started throwing genetically desirable women in my path, offering bribes to the first one to get pregnant and to the altar.'

His voice hummed with remembered fury, his pupils smouldering coals ringed with green fire. Ignoring the curiosity that was eating away at her outrage, Jennifer pushed ineffectually against his thick cabled sweater as she tried to twist her wrists out of his unyielding grasp. He responded by adjusting his grip on her chin, his long thumb sliding under the point of her jaw to dig into the soft flesh and find her furious pulse.

'Finally, last year, I figured out the perfect way to get him off my back. I went to his clinic's IVF sperm bank and made a generous donation to his fertility programme. Afterwards I told him that now he could populate the whole damned world with his precious genes— I was out of the loop!'

Jennifer's struggles were momentarily eclipsed by a wickedly inappropriate desire to laugh. Sebastian's telling had differed greatly from Rafe's, and no wonder! Sebastian had regarded his work with an almost religious seriousness, and his son's act of cheeky irreverence must have been a grave offence to his pride.

'Funnily enough, he was furious at what I'd done,' confirmed Rafe sardonically. 'It turned out that mere genetic reproduction wasn't his aim, it was the *family* connection that was the vital requirement—another legitimate Jordan heir to perpetuate the name along with the genes. Then his cancer was diagnosed and he suddenly seemed to lose interest in the idea.

'I should have known better than to think he'd given up his pet obsession. He just went off on his annual world trip and did what he'd done so often in the past— he bought himself what he wanted. He bought himself a wife: a strong, fertile, healthy woman who would pander to his sick fantasies and allow him to father his own grandchild—'

'*No!*' Jennifer began to struggle again, kicking out helplessly with her legs as she squirmed in his hold.

'He paid you to undergo artificial insemination at his

clinic, in a new IVF procedure with a high rate of success: my sperm injected directly into your egg—'

'*No!*'

'—and re-implanted in your body. Of course, this all happened in the weeks before your wedding, because there was no point in him marrying you until you had been confirmed with a viable pregnancy.'

'You're mad!' she panted. 'I don't know where you get your *bizarre* ideas from but you know what you can do with them. I'm *not* pregnant.'

He had to believe her. He *had* to!

'No?' He let go her captive hands, sliding his palm down to rest firmly on her lower belly.

'No!'

She blinked defiantly back at him, confident that there wasn't even the hint of a swell under her waistband. Against her silence he could prove nothing. *Nothing!*

He splayed his fingers and applied a light pressure, just enough to make her aware of the heat of his hand seeping through the damp-splashed woollen fabric.

'Do you always faint like that—at the drop of a hat?' he asked, his thumb discovering the front placket that concealed her zip.

'It wasn't a hat you dropped, it was a bombshell,' she pointed out. 'An ox would have fainted!'

He smiled, that full-lipped smile of bitter scepticism. 'Aren't you even going to ask me how I know all the gory details?'

'Since there are no details to know, gory or otherwise, I'm not in the least interested in your speculations,' she bluffed wildly, jerking her chin from his hand. 'I think *you're* the one who has been having the sick fantasies.'

For some reason he seemed to find that genuinely amusing. 'You could be right.'

She pounced on the faint lightening of his mood. 'So,

would you mind letting me up? I can't lie around here all day. I have work to do.'

His smile faded. 'Actually, I do mind. I still haven't finished my examination.' His thumbnail tauntingly flipped the tiny metal tab of her zip and her hand slapped down over his.

'Don't you dare!'

It was the wrong thing to say to a man who lived life strictly on his own terms, and who, according to his disgruntled father, cared nothing for history or tradition or polite behaviour. A man who flaunted his vices before the world without the least consideration for the embarrassment he had caused his family.

He gave the tab a sharp little downward tug, and when Jennifer screeched and clutched at her gaping zip with both hands he swiftly transferred his attention to her heaving breasts, cupping and lifting them for his bold appraisal.

'Is it just my imagination, or are these a bit more lush than they were three months ago?' he baited her, fluffing the red angora with his swirling fingertips as he traced her generous contours. 'Mmm, I certainly don't remember them being a D-cup, and there are plenty of people who can testify that I'm an infallible judge of a woman's breast size...'

He also was the most despicable man she had ever met!

Jennifer yanked up her zip with shaking fingers, hunching her shoulders to try and evade his provocative touch. 'You, you—'

'Oh, yes, definitely bigger,' he decided, cuddling the firm mounds together so that they were plumped into even greater prominence. 'I understand pregnancy makes them more sensitive, too...' He rubbed his thumbs goadingly across the soft tips, and to her horror Jennifer felt them tingle and begin to push against the lace constriction of her bra. In a few moments he would be able to feel her treacherous response for himself.

Shame and fear exploded the last of her caution. She slapped his mocking face, hard, his gold whiskers rasping like sandpaper against her furious palm.

'Take your hands off me! How many times do I have to say it? *I am not pregnant!*' she shrieked at him. 'I'm *nothing*. Can't you get that through your thick head? Yes, I was your father's wife for a very brief time but now he's gone and it's *over*. It's *history*. I came back here because this is my *home*. This is where I want to live my life. I don't care what you *think* you know about me, unlike you and your paranoid family of snobs, I don't happen to enjoy living in a world where everyone is judged by how they dress and what they own rather than who they are and what they've achieved. I *told* you I won't interfere with the estate, so why can't you just go back to where you came from and *leave me alone*?'

His blond-tipped head had snapped to the side, his cheek scorched by the outline of her angry fingers, and now he slowly turned back, working his jaw cautiously to and fro in his hand.

At least he had stopped touching her. Jennifer pushed herself up on stiff arms, scooting backwards with her hips so that she was half sitting, no longer helplessly submissive to his will. She had never struck anyone in anger before, and was miserably conscious that this man was responsible for a number of unfortunate firsts in her life. An apology was edging forward on her tongue when she caught sight of the punishing expression in his eyes.

'So, you're saying that my father couldn't even be honest with me on his deathbed? That the last words he ever said to me in this world were an ugly, pointless lie?'

Her blow had been a butterfly kiss in comparison.

Jennifer felt as if she had been hit on the head with a brick.

'Your father?' she croaked, devastated by this latest betrayal. If she hadn't been already sitting she would have keeled over again. 'I— I don't believe you... *Sebastian* told you those things?'

'In hospital on the night he died. The night *you* did your moonlight flit.'

She winced at his clipped contempt, utterly incapable of defending herself. There was no denying the fact that when she had angrily fled the hospital that afternoon she had made herself deliberately inaccessible. And later, when she had phoned the hospital and learned that Sebastian had died...well, she had been extremely distressed, confused and frightened—because she had still felt so angry with him for abusing her trust. Running away from an untenable situation had seemed the best and safest option.

'He deteriorated suddenly and became agitated and disorientated. He kept saying your name, but no one could find you or knew where you'd gone, and by the time I got to the hospital he was in a bad way,' said Rafe, making no attempt to spare her the brutal details. 'He was pretty heavily sedated but he knew what was going to happen, and I guess he realised it was his last chance to clear his conscience—so it all spilled out, how you had leapt at his cash-for-a-kid deal.

'He kept asking me to forgive him as he drifted in and out of consciousness, kept saying that he'd made a bad misjudgement about you, that he was worried about what you might do, what might happen to the baby if he wasn't around to protect it, babbling about betrayal and blackmail...'

'And you *believed* him?' she forced herself to say steadily. 'You didn't think it might have just been the wanderings of a drugged mind?'

'Yes. That's why I checked to see whether you'd ever been treated at the clinic.'

Her heart clenched. 'There's no way you could have had legal access to that kind of information—'

His smile mocked her naïveté. 'Who said my access was legal?'

'You—'

'Legal or not, I know to the exact minute how and when our baby was conceived.'

'*My* baby—'

The cry was out before she realised it, never to be taken back. All her protests, all her stonewalling had been futile. He had known all along and he had enjoyed watching her twist and turn until she had tangled herself up in her web of lies and evasions and more lies. She felt sick, but also oddly liberated.

'So, Jennifer…you and I are going to be parents in a little under six months.' He stroked his faintly marked cheek, and then touched hers with a gentleness that was far more blood-curdling than his former aggression. 'We're practically strangers, we've hardly spoken and barely touched, let alone made love, but we've engaged in the most intimate act two human beings can share… the procreation of life.'

His knuckles touched her chin and then ran down the centre of her jumper between her breasts, dissolving away one or two faint pearls of vase-water still nestling amongst the strands of wool, gliding down to stop in the folds at her waist. This time she made no effort to stop him, so stunned was she by his lyrically soft words. It almost sounded as if…

She shivered. 'We haven't *shared* anything—'

'I beg to differ. My seed is growing in your womb. I'd say that made us pretty damned intimate, wouldn't you?'

She blushed. 'That was a medical procedure. You had nothing to do with it.'

He laughed, and for once she couldn't detect a single cynical note in his amusement. 'I had everything to do with it—me and my little jar and my wicked stock of fantasies.'

Her blush deepened, her hands fisting on her thighs. 'You know what I mean.'

He sobered. 'Yes, I know exactly what you mean. And you're wrong. I may not have been a partner in the highly questionable deal you and my father struck but I *am* involved. You're a rich, pregnant widow because of *me*. If I'd thought about it at all I presumed that my sperm would go to help happily married infertile couples have the children they desperately wanted…not to a self-ish, egotistical old man and a soon-to-be-widowed wife with extremely questionable values. As I see it, I have a responsibility here.'

'Responsibility?' Jennifer echoed, her eyes widening in horror.

'To my father—may God have taken pity on his ma-nipulating soul—and to you.'

'But you don't have to feel responsible for me. I don't want you to!'

'And of course to my son or daughter,' he said calmly, as if she hadn't spoken. 'I suppose it's too early to tell which?'

She nodded her head dumbly. 'You can't—you told your father that you never wanted brats of your own,' she accused shrilly.

'But you and Sebastian took that decision out of my hands. Instead of giving my gift of life to some anony-mous couple, Sebastian took it for himself, and in asking me to forgive him for it—the first time I've ever heard him admit he was wrong about *any*thing—he was trust-ing me to repair the harm he might have done. I'd be a despicable bastard if I turned my back and ignored his dying wish.'

'But I *want* you to turn your back!' she wailed. He was tormenting her again, that's all, she told herself. He was just saying those things to wind her up. He just wanted to make sure she wasn't going to try and hold the family to ransom over child support. 'I told you, I don't need anything. I'll even sign a paper saying so, if that's what you want!'

'You're very emotional, aren't you? I never noticed that when you were in London. You always seemed very quiet and practical, very restrained…a colonial country mouse in the big city. So maybe all the extra hormones flooding your system are making you touchy.'

His hand had crept under the band of her jumper while he was talking, and found the silky skin of her belly.

She jumped. 'What are you doing?'

'I just want to see if I can feel my baby.' He pushed up the band a little way, so they could both see his tanned hand contrasted against the white skin of her stomach.

His use of the word 'my' made her nervous. 'Well, you can't—even I can't feel anything yet. Stop it. I don't like you touching me.' She wished it were true. The pads of his fingers were surprisingly soft, while his palm was faintly dry and abrasive. Just below the cuff of his jacket she could see silky threads of dark blond hair dusting the back of his wrist.

'You're very pale here,' he murmured, his thick lashes masking the glitter of his curiosity. 'Don't you wear a bikini in the summer?'

'No.' He was running his finger around and around the rim of her navel, making her skin feel too tight for her body. 'Do you mind? You're making me queasy.'

He stilled the movement, but left his hand where it

was. 'Have you been having morning sickness?' he asked, studying her flushed face.

'No, I've been as healthy as a horse,' she said. 'Another reason why you're not needed.'

'Well, we'll wait and see, shall we?' He began to withdraw his hand; and whether by accident or design his middle finger slid into the indentation he had been lazily circling.

Jennifer sucked in her breath and his finger snugly rode the sudden movement of her diaphragm.

'Perfect fit,' he murmured wickedly, glancing down, then up again, catching the streak of sinful speculation in her startled gaze.

His lids drooped as he slowly withdrew his finger, and to Jennifer the whole world seemed to darken and shiver in awareness.

She knew then that the devil had green eyes and an English drawl. How else could he offer so much temptation with so little effort?

'What did you mean, wait and see?' she asked belatedly.

'Why, you don't think I came all this way just to turn around and go home again, do you?' he said, pulling her jumper back down over the top of her trousers. 'I think I need to know a great deal more about the mother of my baby before I make any decision about whether to trust her with the raising of our child. And what better place to plumb the depths of her character than in her own home?'

Her jaw dropped. 'You can't mean you intend to stay in New Zealand!'

'Not just New Zealand. Here. In this house. With you. I'm sure you could put me up for a few days, or however long it takes. You could put me in the room my father had…'

However long it takes?

Just as Jennifer was about to shoot him down in flames she heard the sound of the front door opening and two female voices mingling with excited barking, one rising to a familiar contralto lilt.

'Hello, Jenny darling, we're home! What a nightmare, I hope you've got the kettle on…'

'It's my mother! Oh, God—' Jennifer clutched at Rafe's jacket.

'Good. I'm looking forward to meeting her.'

'You can't!' She looked around, wondering frantically where to hide him. He was too big to stuff under the furniture. 'You can't let her see you.'

'I think it's too late for that,' said Rafe, rising politely to his feet as a stocky grey-haired woman in a baggy beige suit marched into the room, followed by a slender, bird-like woman in a wheelchair, whose thin face lit up at the sight of the hovering man.

'*Rafe!* How wonderful that you could come! Oh, Jenny darling, why didn't you tell me—or did he surprise you, too?' Paula Scott didn't seem to notice Rafe's dazed expression as she coasted forward to hold out her delicate hands. 'Oh, come down here, you wonderful man, and give me a kiss. I can't tell you how pleased I am to meet my daughter's husband at long last—I was beginning to think you didn't exist!'

CHAPTER THREE

JENNIFER sat tensely upright on the soft couch, balancing her cup of tea on her lap while Raphael sprawled comfortably beside her, his jacket discarded, his long legs tucked under the coffee table and his arm extended along the back of the couch so that his fingers could idly play amongst the tousled waves at the nape of her stiff neck.

'Yes, I flew into Auckland yesterday, shortly before they closed the airport because of the spreading volcanic smog,' he was telling her mother. 'I had been going to catch a connecting flight here, but when the airline said it had no idea when any of the local airports might be reopened I decided to hire a car and drive down. And I'm glad I did—it gave me a chance to see something of your wonderful countryside.'

He was certainly turning on the friendly charm, thought Jennifer sourly, brushing at the faint damp patches which still lingered on her trousers.

After being briefly disconcerted by Paula Scott's words of welcome, Rafe had quickly summed up the situation and deftly turned the scenario to his advantage. And her mother had fallen for him like a ton of bricks, leaning forward in her wheelchair, her blue eyes sparkling with animation, as Rafe described his drive and his dramatic first view of the rumbling mountain with its ash column rising thousands of feet in the air, casually comparing it with some of the world's other active volcanoes which he had witnessed in action.

Even Aunty Dot, an eccentric elderly spinster who generally treated all males with brusque impatience—being of the opinion that there were no 'real men' left in the world—was looking at him with grudging interest. An amateur naturalist and inveterate shoestring traveller, Dot was a semi-permanent resident of Beech House, living there between her long trips abroad, and anyone who brought news of fresh vistas for her to explore would be welcome grist to her mill.

'Well, thank goodness you came when you did! That was what I wanted to tell you when I came in, Jenny,' said Paula excitedly. 'We just heard on the car radio that they've upgraded the volcano alert level to three. That's on a scale of five, and it means they're classing it as a hazardous local eruption,' she explained in an aside to Rafe, before switching her attention back to her daughter.

'They've closed the mountain completely, and with the ash cloud blowing this way they're issuing a general warning for residents not to go outside without masks and to stay off the roads unless absolutely essential. Driving conditions are awful on the main road already, aren't they, Dot? We had to crawl along and the headlights didn't seem to help at all. Did you feel that earth tremor just as we arrived? That must have been another massive ash blast going up!'

Earth tremor? Taking a sip of her untasted tea, Jennifer instinctively glanced at Raphael and found him looking back, a knowing quirk at the corner of his mouth. He knew that neither of them had been aware of any external shocks. She remembered that moment of shattering temptation. A volcano had been erupting outside her window and she had still assumed it was *Rafe* who had made her world shudder!

Her cup rattled in her saucer as she replaced it with a trembling hand.

'Careful, darling,' said Rafe, leaning over to still the teetering crockery. He had already drunk half of his own tea, *and* eaten two of her mother's feather-light scones while inveigling his way into her good graces.

Jennifer's eyes told him she would like to dump the contents of her cup over his head. She wasn't fooled by his amiable air of relaxation. He knew now why Susie had made her apparently inexplicable mistake and had accepted his assigned role as her husband purely for some nefarious purpose of his own as smoothly as if he had planned it for himself.

He was relishing seeing her hoist by her own petard, knowing that he now had her precisely where he wanted her—totally at his mercy. One word and the whole elaborate charade she had created to protect her sweet, unworldly mother would come tumbling down.

If she had been the crying type she would have burst into tears. But then she doubted that even a Niagara of tears would soften Rafe's cynically hardened heart.

'I've got it, *darling*,' she responded through her beaming teeth.

'It's so lovely to see you two together,' her mother sighed, getting back on the subject that her daughter had spent the last fraught fifteen minutes trying to obscure with meaningless small talk. 'Poor Jenny has been missing you so dreadfully since she got home; she could hardly bear to talk about you—I had to base most of my impressions of you on her letters and phone calls before your marriage, and your photograph—so I hope you won't mind if I'm rudely inquisitive.'

'Of course not, Paula. If you don't mind the reverse.' Rafe's hand massaged Jenny's neck under her veil of hair, a possessive, lover-like caress that didn't go unnoticed by the two older women. 'Jenny and I didn't seem to talk about anything other than ourselves when we were together. I just hope that photo was a flattering one...' He trailed off invitingly.

As anticipated, Paula Scott glided innocently into the

trap. 'How could it not be? Having been so often in front of the camera when you were a model, I suppose it's second nature to show it your best side—not to say your other sides haven't turned out to be very attractive too,' she added, looking him over with a twinkle. 'Actually, it was your wedding photo.'

Rafe stiffened slightly, although his voice remained casually amused. 'Oh? Which one was that?'

Jennifer considered herself lucky he hadn't asked which *wedding*…

'Would you like to see?' Paula bent and felt in the tray under the seat of her wheelchair, pulling out her handbag. Her long battle against the debilitating effects of a back injury might have worn her frame thin, but not her valiant spirit. 'I hope you don't mind, Jenny—' she smiled a trifle guiltily, her gamine grin making her look more like a girl than a fifty-five-year-old woman '—but I had a copy taken off for my wallet. A mother has to have something to boast over!'

'Of course I'd love to see it,' said Rafe, with a gentle courtesy that Jennifer would have appreciated if she hadn't known he was merely sucking up for more information.

'I'm sure Rafe isn't really interested—'

'Oh, let him speak for himself, girl,' Dot chipped in, creaking heavily in her chair as she scooped another scone off the plate. 'The man has a mind of his own, doesn't he? Maybe after three months apart he needs to remind himself that he's married. I notice you don't wear a wedding ring, young man.'

Jennifer nervously fingered the heavy gold band on her left hand. 'Aunty Dot—'

'I don't believe in them, Mrs Grey,' said Rafe without turning a hair.

Dot's deep voice broke on a crack of laughter. 'Neither do I, sonny, neither do I. Never could abide a man

wearing jewellery. Namby-pamby, I call it. And you
may as well call me Dot, seeing as we're as near as
dammit related. Jenny calls me Aunty, but I'm really just
an old friend of the family.'

'A very valued friend, I'm sure, Dot.'

This time Rafe's smoothness backfired on him. 'No
need to butter me up, young man. I've already decided
you'll do. Jennifer's always had a good head on her
shoulders. If she chose you then that's good enough reason for me to like you.'

'Thank you,' Rafe chuckled, proving that unlike his
father he had no problems admitting his own faults. 'I
suppose a backhanded compliment is better than an insincere one.'

'Here you are!' Jennifer's mother finally produced the
result of her rummaging in her untidy bag.

Jennifer had one more lame attempt at deflecting the
inevitable. 'He probably already has that print anyway—'

'We ex-models are terribly vain; we can never resist
drooling over shots of ourselves,' Rafe interrupted her
coolly, half rising to take the slim leather pocketbook
from Paula's deceptively fragile fingers. He settled back
beside his rigid companion and inspected the small coloured photograph displayed under the plastic window.

'Oh, yes, I remember that moment *very* vividly,' he
murmured, causing Jennifer to shift uneasily on the
cushions and rub her neck, which strangely seemed to
still feel his phantom fingers. She didn't have to look to
know what Rafe was seeing: a study in deception.

In deference to Sebastian's insistence that their wedding appear as normal as possible, to subvert any potential future threat to the legality of Jennifer's position, she
had worn an expensive white silk suit, paid for by
Sebastian, and had carried an exquisite bouquet of white
roses and baby's breath, and afterwards they had posed

for the register office photographer. She had been wearing her contact lenses, and a visit from a hairstylist and make-up expert had prettied her unconventional features, but it was the secret which she happily carried inside her which had made her truly bloom like a genuine bride.

To Jennifer's extreme discomfort, and Sebastian's startled satisfaction, Rafe had turned up to hear them exchange their brief vows—the only one of the extended family to attend. Although he had refused to act as a formal witness, his father had insisted on him joining them for a photograph. He had broken off one of Jennifer's white roses and thrust it through the button-hole on the lapel of his son's grey suit, lining them up with Jennifer in the middle.

In hindsight she could appreciate the irony of the pose, but at the time only Sebastian had known that the man on the other side of his wife was in fact the true father of her child. As far as Jennifer had been aware, her baby's father was irrelevant, a number on the label of an anonymous test tube of frozen sperm, chosen from hundreds of others. The anonymity was a necessary part of general fertility programmes, she had understood, to prevent genetic parents launching bids to reclaim the off-spring created from the sperm or eggs they had previously donated…or birth parents trying to sue donors for maintenance!

While in the originally posed photograph she and Rafe had been wearing identical fake smiles, a few seconds later the accidental triggering of the photographer's remote control had caught an informal shot of Sebastian nudging Jennifer into accepting Rafe's polite kiss on her cheek. Frozen on film in embarrassed mid-stumble, she had been pressing her bouquet-filled hand against Rafe's dark jacket to steady herself, and in profile it seemed as if she was looking up at him, pink-cheeked and adoring, while the three-quarter angle of his head showed clearly his smiling intent to kiss her as his arm encircled her silk-clad waist.

What *didn't* show up in the photograph was the angry pride in Jennifer's eyes and the sardonic contempt behind Rafe's teasing smile...and the gaunt, elderly groom, neatly excised from the negative she had taken to the camera shop to be reprinted.

'Jenny has a larger, framed version up in her bedroom,' said Paula fondly, wheeling over to retrieve her wallet. 'Since all our living areas are used by our guests, we like to keep our private things to ourselves.' She looked down at the photo and smiled. 'I thought this looked so lively, full of warmth and fun. It was such a relief to know that Jennifer had found someone wonderful—and for it to be Sebastian's son of all people! Your father was such a pleasant guest, so helpful and undemanding.'

Jennifer bit back a nervous giggle when she saw Rafe's eyes widen at this description of his exacting, imperious father.

'Mum always sees the best in everyone,' she said, obliquely warning him against trying to shatter her mother's rosy illusions.

'A rare and admirable quality,' Rafe murmured, looking thoughtfully from Jennifer to her mother, obviously racking up more evidence for the prosecution. 'Of course, people often act quite differently from their usual selves when they escape the pressures of their normal environment. Some of them see it as an excuse to go wild and do dangerous things that they'd never dream of doing at home...and later live to bitterly regret it.'

Jennifer knew the message was explicitly aimed at her, but as usual Paula took the words at face value.

'Oh, your father came here for the peace and quiet we could provide, not to go adventuring. But he was so very exhausted by the time he got to our section of his holiday that I was rather worried for him. Thank goodness Jenny was on hand, with her home-nursing experience, because Sebastian refused to see a doctor or alter his plans for the rest of his trip. I encouraged her, you know, to accept his offer to accompany him back to England after he said he didn't like the idea of employing a total stranger. I thought the travel would be a good chance for Jenny to broaden her mind a little—she'd never been overseas before...'

From the cynical heft of an eyebrow Jenny could see Rafe thinking that she had been plenty broad-minded by the time she had married his father.

'I was *so* sorry when she arrived back and told me that he had died,' Paula continued. 'You have my very deepest sympathy, Rafe. But at least he had the chance to see you happy first,' she added, always ready to stress the positive. 'Jenny never said, but I supposed his being in such a precarious state of health was the reason why everything happened in such a rush between the two of you...' She paused delicately.

'Thank you,' said Rafe in simple acceptance of her sympathy, warmed, as people usually were, by Paula's natural empathy. 'But the rushing part was just as much Jenny's idea. Your daughter is one determined lady once she's made up her mind about something.'

Jennifer almost choked on her tea. A lady was the last thing that he considered her to be! Coughing, she let Rafe whisk her cup and saucer out of her hands and pat her on the back with what she felt was unnecessary firmness.

'I know. She was very stubborn as a girl,' said Paula. 'And very quiet. She never seemed to need a lot of friends. Always daydreaming and scribbling and inventing her own private games with her own rules that nobody else could follow.'

'She hasn't changed much then,' said Rafe, and the tiny blade of sharpness concealed in his words made a small nick in his carefully presented image of a totally besotted husband.

'I expect you still have a lot to learn about each other,' Paula said mildly. 'It was a pity you had to dash off up the Amazon, Rafe, so soon after the wedding, and your father's death, but Jenny said that invitations to join an expedition like that are few and far between, and you had to grab the opportunity while it was offered. She said it had been a secret dream of yours for years to help the indigenous peoples of the rainforest, and she didn't want you to sacrifice it for her sake...'

Now it was Rafe's turn to choke, on nothing more than his own astounded tongue. 'The Amazon?'

'She said you'd be away at least four months, possibly six. I hope nothing went wrong that you're back early? Jenny said it could be dangerous working so far out of contact with civilisation.' Paula's head tilted in motherly concern.

'Fascinating place, the Amazon,' commented Dot, washing down the last of her scone with the dregs of her tea. 'Been there myself a few times. Marvellous specimens. Going to go back some day, I hope. Like to talk about it with you some time.'

'Uh, well, I...' It was the first time Jennifer had ever seen Raphael Jordan speechless, but unfortunately she couldn't afford to enjoy the sight of him floundering in his own witlessness.

'He just got a little unexpected R&R,' she said hurriedly. 'He had to catch all sorts of odd flights to get here, and now he has virtually to go *straight back* to be able to rejoin the team in time. *Don't you*, Rafe?'

He looked at her, her heavy-handed emphasis wiping the stunned glaze from his green eyes, replacing it with a wicked admiration that made her creamy pale cheeks pinken. How she wished she had never embarked on this agony of deceit!

She nervously brushed non-existent crumbs from her lap, and her hand touched her stomach and stilled, acknowledging that she was fiercely glad her wish could never be granted. She had what she wanted and nobody, *nobody*, was going to take it away!

Rafe folded his arms over his chest, the thick cabling on his sweater pulling tight over his shoulders, letting his silence stretch until Jennifer was on the verge of panic before he drawled, 'Actually, *darling*, I can take longer if I like. Everything's been going so well we've pretty much done what we originally set out to do…and various members of the team are already splitting off to take up other projects. It won't be a problem if I send a message that I've decided not to return…'

'I thought there was no way to get communications in or out of your area of the rainforest?' said Paula innocently.

Rafe pursed his lips to disguise his amusement. Jennifer had thought of everything.

'Before, no—but I made special arrangements at every step along the way on my trip out,' he replied with bland aplomb.

'Well, that's wonderful news!' Paula beamed. 'Isn't it, Jenny?'

Her mother's joyful exclamation was punctuated by a low rumble and a shimmer of windows in their wooden frames. Mount Ruapehu obviously had the same opinion as Jennifer.

Dot got up and crossed to the glass doors, peering towards the mountain through a fine haze of grey powder interspersed with swirling, fingernail-sized ash flakes.

'It's pretty black up over there now,' she said. 'There's hardly a glimpse of clear sky left. I bet the colour of that plume means most of the crater lake has gone. We could see some real pyrotechnics soon.'

She rapped at the dust-coated glass with a stubby finger. 'I hope the wind changes again, or I'm going to lose some of the plants to this damned ash. I've covered the most delicate ones, but at this time of the year they need as much sunlight as they can get.'

In spite of the fact that she travelled for about four months of every year, Dot had put herself in charge of the flower and vegetable gardens, and whenever she was in residence she worked with a passion amongst her beloved plants and planned all the new plantings. Over the years she had built up the grounds of Beech House to the point where they were regularly featured in 'open gardens' tours during local festivals.

Rafe went to join her at the window, the seams of his close-fitting jeans whitening as he stepped across Jennifer's legs, dragging her unwilling attention to his taut backside as he moved away. To her chagrin, her mother caught her looking and grinned, miming a silent whistle.

Jennifer smiled weakly in return as she began stacking the tea things on the tray. If her mother had never met her 'husband', the discreet long-distance 'divorce' that she had been planning to blame on their extended separation could have been achieved with minimum fuss. Now it would be that much more difficult.

'Are we likely to be in any danger at this distance?' she heard Rafe ask Dot.

'Not from molten material. In an eruption the size they're predicting the danger zone for that is only a few kilometres.' Geology was another of Dot's hobbies. 'But the radio said that there'd already been several big lahars through the ski fields, and once the mud-flows reach the river systems they can cause havoc downstream. There was a big train-wreck in '53, when a rail bridge over the

Whangaehu River got washed away and a hundred and fifty people were killed. But our main problem will probably just be the ash flying around and clogging things up, and then you get water shortages when people try to clean it up. And it can be toxic when it's breathed in, of course, so we'd better make sure the animals come inside…'

'Oh, dear,' said Paula. 'Do you want to put a canvas over your car, Rafe? We have some spare covers in the garage that we bought after last year's big blow. I know it's only a rental, but heaven knows what this dust might do if it gets into the engine.'

Jennifer stopped what she was doing, aghast at the tacit invitation contained in the suggestion, but before she could think of an objection Rafe turned from the darkening view and strolled back to smile down at his eager hostess.

'I suppose that would be a good idea, but I don't want to impose, Paula.' His diffidence was a beautifully calculated pre-emptive strike. 'I know you weren't expecting me, and Susie told me when I arrived that you had a full complement of guests. Actually, since I wasn't quite sure of the set-up here, or what Jennifer's immediate plans were, I *had* made a reservation at a hotel…'

'Rafe! Of *course* you'll stay here with us!' Paula was visibly shocked by his offer. 'We always have room for *family*, no matter how full we are. Jenny has a lovely big bedroom which takes up the whole of the upstairs, with *en suite* bathroom and outside access via the balcony, so you can both have tons of privacy. Goodness!' she laughed, as the loaded tea tray crashed back down onto the coffee table. 'Jenny would never forgive me if I tried to chase you away—look at her face, she's horrified at the very thought!'

Rafe knew full well what she was horrified by, and it wasn't the thought of their separation.

'But, Mum…' Jennifer was fast running out of spontaneous inventions. A contagious disease? A fear of heights? What reason could she dredge up for her pretend husband not sharing her room? She wracked her brain for inspiration. How about a pathological fear of being murdered in her bed?

Bed? A wave of heat flowed over her body. Oh, God, her mother expected her not just to share a room but to *sleep* with him, in the euphemistic as well as the literal sense. Her breath began to labour in and out of her lungs, as if she was outside, inhaling the smothering ash. She looked at the tall man in his stylishly casual clothes, the easy stance and confident set of his shoulders, the careless good looks, and simmered with hot resentment.

He had apparently earned a small fortune as a model when he was in his late teens and early twenties, enough to subsequently set himself up in the publishing business without using a penny of his father's money or a shred of his influence, and it was obvious why he had been so favoured for spreads in *GQ* and *Vogue*. He oozed a kind of universal sex appeal, attractive to both men and women. And that was with his clothes on!

Jennifer's knees weakened at the impossible task her mother had unknowingly set her. She was supposed to go to bed with *that* and *not* think of sex?

'Now, Jen, I know what you're going to say, but Dot and I can handle the guests.' Her mother interrupted her scurrying thoughts with unaccustomed decisiveness. 'You don't seem to like to admit it, but we managed perfectly well for ourselves during those two months that you were in England. You just devote yourself to getting to know your husband again. After all, considering how little time you've spent together as a married couple, you're still practically honeymooners…'

'Why, so we are,' purred Rafe, moving over to Jennifer and sliding his long arm around her waist, hugging her to his side while he nuzzled the side of her head, lowering his voice to a murmur.

'Just think of it, darling—the two of us up there all alone in your lovely, cosy eyrie, exploring each other's wants and needs...' His warm breath hummed in her ear, lapping at her senses and teasing her overheated imagination. 'Rather like the fantasies I used to weave for myself during those long, languid, steamy Amazon nights...when I'd lie awake, staring into the velvet-black darkness, aching with loneliness, yearning for the touch of a passionate woman...*my* woman...'

He nipped suddenly at her ear and laughed softly as she gave a little squeak, furious with herself for being momentarily seduced by his evocative words into forgetting who and what he was. She, of all people, should know better than to get carried away by his technical mastery of a few seductive phrases. Taken individually, they weren't even particularly *clever* ones...

Jennifer wriggled out of his grasp and found her mother and Dot exchanging silently satisfied looks. She hoped they hadn't caught the substance of Rafe's words, although they had undoubtedly understood the context.

'I'd better clean these up so the kitchen's clear for you to think about dinner, Mum,' she muttered, bending for the tray.

'Here, let me help you with that; you don't seem to be having much luck with crockery today.' Rafe hefted the tray and swivelled it on one flat palm, high above Jennifer's safe reach. 'I was a waiter, too, during my misspent youth,' he told the two older women with a grin. 'Anything to thwart my father's attempts to send me to med school. So, if you need a silver service while I'm here, I'd be delighted to go through my paces.'

Out in the kitchen, Jennifer wrenched on the hot tap and bundled the cups from the tray into the sink with some liquid detergent. 'Did you *have* to play up to them like that?' she sizzled, under cover of the running water.

'Would you rather I bit and snarled and knocked you around so they'd pity you for the brute you married?'

'Yes!'

'Liar. That would horribly upset your mother and that's the last thing you want. This whole charade is to stop her worrying about you. She has absolutely no idea what you're really like, has she?'

Jennifer ignored the comment. It was far too apt, in more ways than he would ever know. She concentrated angrily on the dishes, damning him for being so perceptive. For good or bad they were now co-conspirators, and she would be cutting her own throat if she was *too* antagonistic.

'How did you find me?' She and Sebastian had deliberately avoided mentioning exactly where they had met, and when asked where she was from Jennifer had merely said she was born in Auckland. She had wanted a permanent barrier between her New Zealand and English lives.

'My father's credit card receipts. I found one from Beech House amongst his things a few weeks ago, and recognised your signature from the register office,' he said, revealing he had not only sharp eyes but an excellent visual memory. 'Why did you tell Paula it was *me* you'd married?'

'Believe me, I wish I hadn't,' she said fervently as she rapped a foamy cup upside down onto the tiled bench.

'Careful, you'll chip them if you throw them around like that,' said Rafe, whipping a teatowel off the wall-hook beside the oven and beginning to dry with the comfortable ease of a man used to doing his own domestic chores.

There was a strained silence for a few moments, and

just as it began to get on Jennifer's overstretched nerves he chuckled.

'The Amazon? Couldn't you think of anywhere more remote and inaccessible to send me?' His amused sarcasm drifted into teasing provocation. 'I suppose your ultimate aim was to have me eaten by piranhas during my morning swim in the river.'

'Actually, we were just going to slowly drift out of love under the pressure of the long separation,' she gritted. 'But I must admit that the thought of having you swallowed alive by a giant anaconda had a certain tempting appeal!'

This time his laugh was full-throated. 'Well, you'd better tell me what I was supposed to be doing on this famous expedition, just in case anyone starts asking me for details.'

'You won't be here long enough for them to ask,' she argued.

'Well, I'm certainly not going anywhere while this lasts.' He nodded out of the window at the gritty fog which was continuing to darken the afternoon. His parked car was already coated with a thickly stippled layer of grey-brown volcanic dust. 'I know you'd prefer me permanently out of the way, but even you can't expect me to ignore traffic warnings and risk *real* death for the sake of your personal convenience.'

Reluctantly Jennifer described the fictitious trip she had created, and the function that her 'husband' was supposed to fulfil.

'Photographer! I don't know a thing about cameras!'

'You modelled—you ran a magazine—'

'Neither of which actually involved me getting behind the camera and taking the shots!'

She was irritated by his condescending amusement. 'Well, I know you run several companies now, but I don't think Sebastian ever said what it is you actually *do* every day.' Only that it was very profitable. And Jennifer had resolutely avoided showing any curiosity in that direction. 'So I just drew on your background—I said freelance photography was a sideline of yours.'

'I see. I'm the artistic type. Currently respectable...but with plenty of potential to turn out to be a selfish, self-absorbed swine, constantly pursuing my own goals at the expense of yours,' he guessed shrewdly. 'What else did you make up about me that I should be warned about?'

'Nothing,' she said sullenly. 'I knew the less I said the better.'

She finished the last teaspoon and pulled the plug out of the sink.

'Do Paula and Dot know you're pregnant?'

She angled her stubborn chin at him. 'Of course they do.'

With a genuine wedding ring on her finger, Jennifer had had no hesitation in telling her mother the good news, and, as she had anticipated, Paula had been frankly delighted for her, knowing that her daughter's romantic daydreams had always included a family of her own.

'No "of course" about it, where you're involved,' said Rafe drily. 'Do they think *I* still don't know? Is that why neither of them congratulated me on my impending fatherhood?'

She nodded briefly. In abstract she had accepted that this man was the progenitor of her child, but the concrete reality was still something she avoided. 'I said I didn't find out until after you'd left.'

'So at least you didn't make me the kind of cad who'd run out on his *pregnant* new wife to pursue his own dreams.' He tossed the damp towel onto the bench and leaned one hip against the tiles, his mocking gaze darkening as it ran over her body, lingering on her breasts and reminding her of his earlier outrageousness.

'Well…go ahead, do your duty. Tell your husband he's going to be a daddy…'

A heavy tread made them both turn towards the door. It was Dot, carrying two disposable protective masks.

'I'm just going out to check my plants and call the cats. Do you want to come and get that car-cover with me first, Rafe? Then Jenny can show you around and you can settle in.'

'Sure.' He straightened, taking one of the masks. 'Would you like me to help you look for the animals?'

Dot took a can of fishy catfood from the fridge. 'They'll come pretty quick if I give them a whiff of this; it's so potent we should always wear a mask when we dish it out!'

'See you soon, darling.' Taking Jennifer by surprise, Rafe chucked her under the chin and brushed a light kiss across her startled mouth as he exited, leaving her glaring after him, scrubbing furiously at the tingling brand. The fleeting kiss he had given her at her wedding, when that embarrassing photo had been taken, had been equally disturbing, and after that she had been even more careful to avoid his company. Now there would be no avoiding him, and by her own words she had condemned herself to allowing him to touch her whenever he liked…at least in public.

His suspicion, his bitterness, his contempt she could fight with reciprocal fierceness, but her defences were proving alarmingly vulnerable to his mocking humour, his quick intelligence and his sheer physical attractiveness.

Frowning, she quickly put the dried crockery away and went back to the living room, to find her mother unwinding the draught excluders that would stop the windblown ash from seeping in through the doors and windows.

'I see Rafe's bags are still out in the hall. Do you

want to tidy your room before you take him up?' Paula asked, adding teasingly, 'Just in case there's anything lying around you don't want him to see. I know there are always *some* cosmetic secrets a woman likes to keep beyond the first few weeks of her marriage—'

The words were hardly out of her mouth before Jennifer dashed out of the room and up the stairs, her heart pounding. How could she have forgotten?

The sloping ceilings of the converted attic framed the friendly clutter of the room. Two dormer windows and bi-folding glass doors opening out onto a wooden balcony facing the mountain let in plenty of light to counteract the effect of dark wooden plank walls and ceiling. A squat double bed, an old-fashioned mirrored wardrobe and matching dressing table, a big bookcase and a large battered desk and chair were the main pieces of furniture.

Jennifer ran over to the desk on which her budget computer had pride of place. She knew she couldn't rely on Rafe not to snoop and pry into every corner of her existence if he felt like it, so she quickly sat down and turned on the computer, mentally calculating how long it would take him to tie down a loose tarpaulin over his car as she deleted large chunks of her hard-copy files, safe in the knowledge that they were already doubly backed up onto floppies.

While the computer was chomping its way down the list she emptied all red-labelled floppy disks from the plastic box beside the screen and bundled them into her underwear drawer, wrapping them securely in an unattractive woollen spencer before pushing them deep to the back of her bras and undies. Then she gathered cardboard hanging files out of the bottom drawer of her desk and stuffed them, papers, files and all, into the slit between the wall and the back of the heavy oak wardrobe. Heaven knew how she was going to get them out again!

Fortunately she had formed the cautious habit of always cleaning up very thoroughly after herself every time she worked at the computer, and personally burning the contents of her wastepaper bin in the outside incinerator, so it wasn't long before all that remained on her computer and desk was information regarding the running of Beech House that would probably bore Rafe to tears.

She stood for a moment in the centre of the room, nervously shifting from foot to foot, double-checking that there was nothing else she had forgotten, her roving eyes deliberately avoiding the big, soft feather bed.

The books! Even if Rafe wasn't much of a reader himself he was clever enough to know that he could learn something about her character from the type of books she kept.

She swept a section from the middle row off the shelf, and one or two others at random, and dumped them into her wicker laundry basket, heaping her soiled clothes over the top. With luck Rafe would be gone before the next wash. If not—*no*, she refused to even contemplate not being able to persuade him to leave.

There!

Not a sign that the bedroom was inhabited by anything other than a normal, ordinary, twenty-seven-year-old woman of average, everyday tastes who had nothing to hide.

She just hoped that Raphael Jordan could be persuaded to believe the evidence of his own eyes!

CHAPTER FOUR

JENNIFER tried to look relaxed as Raphael dropped his soft-sided suitcase and expensive leather roll-bag under the dormer window and circled around her bedroom, his head tilted and eyes half-closed, almost as if he was tasting the air. He made her aware of the soft mingling of subtle feminine scents—lavender from the perfumed paper with which she lined her clothes drawers, a woodsy sweetness from the dish of dried petals on the bookshelf, rose from the lingering fragrance of her morning shower and hints of a darker, more sensuous floral tone from a spilled perfume bottle on the dressing table.

He ran his finger moodily along the outer edge of her pristine desk, lifted frosted make-up bottles on the dressing table, opened her wardrobe to inspect the contents and stepped into the adjoining bathroom, with its polished rimu cabinetry and deep, claw-footed white bath, with a modern, hand-held brass shower spray hooked high on the wall above the vintage brass taps.

On the way back out he passed the laundry basket, and in her nervous state of heightened anxiety Jennifer half expected him to lift the lid and rummage inside to find the evidence of her secret notoriety.

As she had expected, he stopped before the bookcase for the longest time, absently toying with the dish of petals as he studied the titles, an eclectic array of fiction and non-fiction, classic and contemporary, treasure and trash.

'You like to read,' he pronounced with faintly surprised satisfaction, stroking the flowing gilt inscription on the spine of a vintage cloth Bible. 'Have you read this?'

She was wary of the innocuousness of his question. Nothing about Raphael Jordan was harmless. 'Most of it. My father was a minister—'

'Was?'

'He drowned when I was nineteen, saving the life of a young boy who was swept off rocks at a surf beach.' Her quiet pride in her father's impulsive act of self-sacrifice was evident in the soft lilt of her voice. 'He worked amongst the local parishes here. We grew up helping him search out his readings and themes for his sermons.'

Rafe turned. 'We?'

'My brother, Ian, and I. He was a year younger than me. He was killed in a car accident seven years ago. That was when my mother damaged her back…'

She looked away from the penetrating green stare, remembering the tragedy of that day and the added anguish six months later when her fiancé, who had been the driver of the car in which they had all been travelling, had been unable to handle his guilt and had broken off their engagement.

Rafe saw the tightening crook of her wide mouth, and the distant, unfocused look in her brown eyes as they suddenly evaded his, and wondered with a renewed burst of savage frustration what else she was holding back. He wanted to stride over and seize her by her soft shoulders and shake her until she rattled, spilling out all her secrets, but he had already decided that guile was more effective than force where she was concerned.

The more he found out about this infuriating woman the less he felt he knew her. His angry preconceptions had begun to crumble from the moment that he had held her, soft, limp and helpless in his arms. Unconscious,

she had been totally vulnerable, unable to protect herself
or the baby nestling inside her ripening body.

His baby.

Ignorance no longer protected him from the consequences of his impulsive act of reckless defiance.
However artificial the method of conception, thanks to
his father's unethical revelation there was no retreating
from the knowledge that part of Raphael was now part
of Jennifer, and vice versa.

So, who was she?

Was she a cunning, money-grubbing, conscienceless
bitch? Or a foolishly misguided innocent? A hard-
hearted, clear-thinking opportunist? Or an impulsive
woman who had confused wealth with security and panicked when her rash decision landed her in over her
head? Or perhaps she was a combination of all of those
things.

It would have suited him to have her as black as she
had been painted by his rampaging ex-stepmothers and
their ravening hordes. By the time he had finally tracked
Jennifer down he had been in a killing black fury, the
blade of his rage honed and sharpened by three months
of torrid internecine warfare amongst the various competing Jordan factions trying to overturn Sebastian's
will.

There had been threats of injunctions and court orders,
and unseemly scuffles in the lawyers' offices, until it was
made clear that the old man had sewed everything up
watertight, even to the point of having an independent
psychiatric report done which attested to his mental
health at the time he had amended his will. Any legal
challenge to his final wishes and most of the estate
would go to charity. So the scavengers had finally settled
for their assigned portions—which had been fair, even
generous, if not as lavish as they would have liked.

As the only blood heir, Rafe was unable to avoid be-

ing tainted by the ugliness, and even though he knew
that the same scenario would have been played out by
his rapacious relatives *whatever* had been in Sebastian's
will, he had focused his anger on Jennifer. She had become the repository for his deeply conflicted feelings
about his father. When he had set out from London he
had been headed towards a confrontation with the past,
and now that he had run slap-bang into the future he was
still groping to reconcile the two.

He watched Jennifer nervously brush at the fringe that
feathered her pale forehead as she realised he was still
staring at her. She got very uneasy if he looked at her
for any sustained length of time. When he had first met
her in London he had thought it was shyness, but when
he had seen her coolly out-staring some of his obnoxious
stepbrothers he had realised that her uneasiness was a
much less innocent form of awareness.

He pulled his wandering thoughts back into line, calculating the facts. Her father had died when she was
nineteen, and a year later she had lost her only
brother...and been left with a disabled mother. That
gave him an inkling as to the reason Jennifer had never
finished her nursing training. He already knew how protective she was towards her mother.

'And she's been in a wheelchair ever since? Is she
completely paralysed from the waist down?'

Jennifer looked at him in surprise. 'Oh, no—Mum can
walk...some of the time she doesn't even have to use
her stick. But she still has bad bouts of chronic pain and
weakness in her legs, and at those times it's easier to
use the wheelchair. It gives her back a rest and it's safer
than her staggering about, risking a fall. Sometimes it
happens when she's overdone things, or is tired, and at
other times for no reason that she can explain.' A
shadow passed over her expression. 'She's had several
operations over the years, but there was so little im-

provement after the last two that the doctors say it's no use trying any more corrective surgery. At least there's no sign of progressive degeneration of the spine, so it shouldn't get any worse than it is now. Not that that's much consolation for Mum...'

'She seems a very happy, well-adjusted person.'

She thought he was still talking about her mother's injuries. 'She is.'

'So why bother with all the complicated lying?' he continued in the same even tone. 'Why not simply tell her that you were marrying Sebastian?'

'Because she would have known it wasn't for love!' Paula would have been deeply shocked by the idea of her daughter marrying Sebastian, and even more appalled if she'd discovered the reasons behind it.

'Then why mention getting married at all?'

'I was going to have a baby, that's why! I couldn't arrive home pregnant *and* unmarried after only a couple of months away,' she said, exasperated by his blank look. Of course, in the trendy circles in which he *had* moved, unmarried mothers were probably the norm. 'I couldn't do that to Mum. This is small-town New Zealand. People gossip and they have long memories. She and Dad always set a very moral tone, and Mum is still very active in the local church...'

'Well, if you didn't want her to know it was for the money, you could have told her you were doing it out of compassion for a dying man, that it *was* going to be a marriage in name only—which I take it was part of the agreement?'

'And then how would I have explained getting pregnant?' she argued, her question a tacit affirmative to his question.

'What was wrong with the truth? That Sebastian so desperately wanted another child that you entered a programme for infertile couples.'

'Mum doesn't approve of assisted reproductive technology,' she admitted starkly, aware that she could be handing him yet another weapon against her. 'I told you—she has very traditional moral views. She and Sebastian had arguments about it. She thinks it's going against God's will to try and manipulate life. She would have been very hurt and disappointed to think that I...I—'

'That her sweet little girl had decided to go into the lucrative rent-a-womb business?'

After his preceding mildness the harsh interruption was like a dash of acid in Jennifer's face. Before she could summon an equally searing reply he had turned away, as if uninterested in her response, moving over to sit testily on the edge of the bed.

'Well, well...feather mattress?' he asked as he sank down into the deep softness that lay atop the slatted wooden frame. His laced suede walking boots planted firmly on the floor, he let himself fall back, spread-eagled, onto the smooth, cream duvet, staring up at the rimu ceiling.

'The last time I lay on one of these was in Switzerland, at a tiny little country inn. Best night's sleep I ever had in my life,' he gloated.

The bed had puffed up around him, almost swallowing him from sight, so Jennifer's view of him was reduced to a pair of spread thighs angling to a V at the centre of his body, where the denim ridged over a firm bulge. It was a disturbingly erotic image of anonymous male sexuality.

Did he *have* to flaunt himself like that? she thought furiously. Did he think she didn't already have *enough* proof of his fabulous virility?

'Well, don't get too excited about it because *you're* sleeping on the floor,' she informed him.

He pushed up onto his hands, catching the direction

of her offended glare. His green eyes mocked her flustered expression as he casually hooked one foot behind his other knee, widening his thighs in an even more blatant display of his undisputed manhood.

'Maybe I won't feel like sleeping at all tonight,' he murmured with an insinuating smile.

She stiffened. She knew she shouldn't but she had to ask. 'What do you mean?' she burst out aggressively.

His spiky blond hair provided a ruffled halo to his exaggerated expression of innocence. 'Only that if the mountain blows its top I'd like to see it happen. We'll be able to keep watch all night from up here, won't we? From where I am now, the summit is in a perfect frame.' He nodded towards the glass doors parallel to the bed. Having positioned the bed in precisely that place so that she could lie there in the mornings, dreamily contemplating the sheer majesty of nature, Jennifer didn't even have to look to check that he was right.

Rafe had already turned his attention to something else. He was sliding open the drawer of her small bedside table and peering interestedly at the jumbled contents. She hurried over but she was too late. One eyebrow quirked and he lifted out a wood-framed photograph, shaking off a sprinkle of elastic hairbands and clips that had littered its surface.

'So this is where you keep me. I'm sure your mother implied I was prominently on display…'

'She hardly ever comes up here—the stairs are too difficult for her,' snapped Jennifer. 'Anyway, *she* respects my privacy too much to pry.'

'So I was relegated to out of sight, out of mind, hmm?'

If only it had been so easy! Jennifer watched in frustration as he dusted the glass with the edge of his sleeve and propped the photo on the table, between the small shaded lamp and the cream telephone.

'I don't remember seeing you wear spectacles when you were in England,' he mused, glancing from the photograph to her annoyed face.

'I usually wear contact lenses, but with all the volcanic dust in the air right now…' She shrugged, her average looks never having given her much cause for vanity.

'They make you appear quite bookish…but then you are, aren't you? I can't figure you out. Your wardrobe here is full of home-made clothes, but in London you wore smart labels—abandoned along with your husband. Over there you were always demure and polite, no matter what the provocation; here you lash out. In London you only admitted to being an unqualified nurse; in New Zealand you're an experienced inn-keeper. Which is the *real* Jennifer, I wonder?'

'Everyone has different facets to their personality that are revealed in different situations,' she said stiffly, thinking that even *she* wasn't sure who the real Jennifer was any more.

'So they do. I look forward to exploring more of your…revealing facets.' Her watched her mouth prim, her eyes flash, and flicked a finger at her blushing cheek in the photograph.

'Amazing how deceptive appearances can be, isn't it?' he said drily. 'How it must have bruised Sebastian's ego to see himself edited out of his own wedding picture…or didn't he know about this little game of musical husbands you played for your mother?'

'Of course he did; it was his i—' She stopped and Rafe's eyes narrowed.

'Idea,' he finished slowly, when she showed no signs of going on. 'My *father* suggested you use me as a substitute?' By the end of the sentence his incredulity had risen to sharp suspicion.

Alarmed, she tried to step back, but he caught her

narrow wrist, bending it back until she was forced to
sink to her knees in front of him to relieve the uncomfortable pressure on her arm.

'He— He thought that it would be easier to borrow
an identity than to invent a completely new one and then
have to make up a whole lot more lies to remember,'
she stammered, as he eased the pressure just enough to
act as a leash. 'He said that if I used you I wouldn't
have to lie about my new surname. A-and he said that
it would reassure Mum to know that I hadn't been swept
off my feet by a complete stranger, but someone whose
background she was aware of...'

It had seemed such a good idea at the time, and one
that Sebastian had claimed had very little risk of discovery. Part of their infamous bargain had included
Jennifer's mother being kept strictly in the dark. They
had both known that Paula would have been deeply worried by her daughter's marriage to Sebastian, and equally
appalled if she had ever learned the reasons behind it.

'Since I'd always planned to come straight back here
after Sebastian died, there was no reason why you and
Mum should ever have had any contact,' she finished
weakly.

'And then a fictitious divorce from your fictitious husband and everybody's happy!' he grunted. 'I take it your
mother has more liberal views on divorce than she does
on marriage and procreation?'

'Well, even the church recognises irretrievable breakdown,' she muttered. Her mother would have been disappointed but, with a long, gentle tapering off, hardly
devastated.

'And what about the baby? The unfortunate bargaining chip in all of this? What was it agreed you would
do with *my* baby after Sebastian died?'

'Nothing... I mean, he knew I was going to bring it

up here, of course,' she said huskily. 'He knew that I'd
be a good mother—'

'And a *father* didn't matter? What if something happened to *you*, for God's sake!' he exploded, jerking her
wrist and leaning forward to thrust his face fiercely close
to hers. 'Don't you think Paula would have wanted to
contact me *then*? Even if I'd never demonstrated a shred
of interest in the child before, your mother still might
have considered that I had the right to know. Or
wouldn't it have mattered what a bloody mess you left
behind you, as long as you had everything you wanted
while you were alive?'

Jennifer blanched. She had never even considered the
possibility. Under the rules of donor IVF programmes
the biological parents had no legal access or responsibility, and, anyway, in her own mind the baby had always
been hers and hers alone. Both the nominal and the biological father had been irrelevant. If anything happened
to her she vaguely assumed that her mother would have
sole legal guardianship—but of course Paula thought
that it had been an entirely natural conception...

'Oh, God,' she breathed, her free hand moving to her
stomach. She couldn't believe how short-sighted she had
been—no, how utterly blind in her pursuit of her goal.

The movement dragged Rafe's eyes away from her
face, and he suddenly cursed virulently under his breath
and dropped her wrist as if it was hot coal. She sat back
on her heels, rubbing at the faint red weals on her tender
skin. He got up and paced, running a hand down the
back of his neck, and Jennifer got shakily to her feet,
uncertain of her next move.

'What a mess! What a crazy bloody mess!' Rafe
ground out. 'I still don't understand it! If everything was
going as planned, why did you have to run away like a
thief in the night? That certainly put a kink in your image as a caring wife. What were you afraid might happen

after he died? Everything was legal. You had the money.
And you had no way of knowing that he'd told me the
baby was mine, because I was the last one to see him
alive.'

She jumped as he prowled back to stand in front of
her, hands on his hips, streaks of temper across his hard
cheekbones.

'Tell me this one thing straight at least: if Sebastian
hadn't suffered his deathbed crisis of conscience, would
you ever have told me that my ''half-brother'' or ''half-
sister'' was in fact my own child?'

'I— I don't know—'

'You don't know.' It was repeated with such contempt
that she knew he didn't believe her. 'Come on, you must
have *thought* about it. Maybe you figured that if you
ever milked the trust dry you could turn up and blackmail *me* for child support.'

'No! I never thought— Maybe if— Oh!' She raised
her hands and covered her distraught face. She didn't
know how much it was safe to admit. How much to trust
him.

'Oh, I don't know *what* I was going to do! How could
I know? How could I possibly have known that—' She
put her clenched fist to her mouth, biting down on the
words, her brown eyes dark with anguished doubt.

'How could you have known—what? Jennifer?' He
pulled the gag from her mouth, encompassing her entire
fist in his warm hand. *'How could you have known
what?'*

But the moment of revelation had passed. Jennifer had
herself under control again, albeit very shaky control.

'That it was all going to come apart at the seams like
this,' she whispered.

The dark gold stubble on his lower cheeks glinted as
his jaw muscles clenched. He lifted her fist and pressed
his mouth to the tiny indentations created by her teeth,

his lips brushing in a mocking salute across the gold wedding band on her third finger before letting her go.

'Lies usually do, especially the kind of whoppers you've been telling.'

'Oh, right, and I suppose you've never told a lie in your life,' she said sarcastically, wiping her fingers on her trousers to try and rid herself of his lingering touch. 'You were doing pretty well there downstairs, for an amateur…'

'I'm reasonably proficient with a social lie, but, no, until I met you I'd actually considered myself to be quite painfully honest—especially in my relationships with women.'

He bent to his suitcase, unzipping the top and flinging it back, pawing through the neatly packed clothes. He threw a pair of black jeans and a thin black knitted jumper over the back of her desk chair and pulled his cream sweater over his head, dumping it back on top of the unzipped suitcase. Underneath he was wearing a white silk shirt with pearlised buttons, which he began to flick open with one hand. As the shirt parted she could see that the hair on his chest was one shade darker than that on his head. It grew in flattened swirls around his dark, masculine nipples and created a thick mat over his rippling pectorals. His evenly tanned skin was sleek and glossy, glowing with health.

'What are you doing?' she asked, her eyes darting nervously past him to the bed.

He dealt with his cuffs and divested himself of the shirt before he spoke, now bare to the low-slung belt of his snug jeans.

'I've been travelling non-stop for over twenty-four hours. I'm grimy, I'm tired and I'm angry—and I can do something about at least two of the three. I'm going to strip, shower, nap and change into fresh clothes—in that order. If you want to stand there and watch, feel free. Or you can join me, if you like...'

His eyes fixed on her, he unclipped his flat gold buckle and stripped his leather belt from its denim loops, folding it to a strop in his hand, which he then struck lightly against his other palm.

He saw Jennifer's eyes widen behind her glasses and growled, 'You needn't look like that; I don't beat my women.'

'I never thought you did,' she defended herself, wondering if he realised what he looked like, standing there stripped to the waist, golden head cocked, his green eyes stoked with insolent challenge, the lean muscles of his arms and torso rippling as he flexed the leather strap. He looked like every woman's fantasy of a dangerous lover. Jennifer's fingers itched for her keyboard, her protection against the pangs of forbidden lust.

'Unless they consider it a stimulating form of fore-play, of course,' Rafe added, with a sultry smoulder designed to get under her creamy skin. 'Then I'm perfectly willing to indulge in a little light bondage and discipline to enhance the lady's pleasure...' He slapped leather to palm again. 'How about you, Jennifer? Do you like your sex strictly straight—or with an intriguing twist?'

She was shattered by the question and it showed. Shattered but not shocked, Rafe's keenly developed sexual instincts told him, and he felt a hot throb of curiosity thicken his loins. Then his anger kicked in, snarling through his veins. Dammit, he *wanted* her to be shocked. He wanted her to feel tormented, as the thought of *her* had tormented *him* for the last few months. He wanted her to be eminently shockable, so that he could have the satisfaction of making her pay in some small measure for all the trouble that she had caused him, and *would* cause him...

'Maybe you just like to watch, hmm?' He dropped his

belt and boldly unzipped his jeans. 'Is this what you're waiting for, Mrs Jordan?' he jeered, sliding his hands inside the denim to cup himself.

That got her!

She gasped, blushing furiously, and backed away, almost stumbling over Rafe's roll-bag and losing a flat shoe. He withdrew his hands and bent to toss his bag out of the way while she frantically nudged her loose shoe back onto her foot and continued to skitter towards the door.

'Not going to join me in the shower, then?' he said, sauntering after her fleeing figure, his unsnapped jeans peeled back to reveal silky white briefs which brazenly outlined the contours of his semi-arousal.

'I'm told I give *incredibly* good showers...'

Jennifer was *incredibly* proud of herself for keeping her eyes firmly at chest level.

'In that case I'm sure you'll remember to wash your mouth out with soap while you're in there!' she said, as her hip bumped the door handle and she grabbed at it, spinning to safety and slamming the door behind her.

She might have had the last word but it didn't feel like it as his mocking laughter, muffled by the solid door, followed her down the stairs. He had routed her from her own private territory and he knew it!

It took a good hour of solid dusting and stuffing of draught excluders into every structural chink and crack that she could find for her to cool off. It didn't help that while she was doing the kitchen her mother, chopping vegetables for dinner on a specially lowered section of bench, wanted to rhapsodise about how nice he was, how intelligent and articulate, interesting and amusing, and terribly, terribly sexy...

'Mum!'

'Well, so he is, darling. I'd have to be blind not to notice.' Paula heaved a sigh. In her softly draped blue dress, with spiral tendrils of her long brown hair escaping from the plump chignon at the back of her head, she looked exactly what she was—a hopeless romantic.

'And that secret smoulder in his eyes whenever he looks at you—as if he's longing to pounce on you and eat you up!'

Jennifer shivered. Chew her up and spit her out, more like!

Dot brought in the cats—Maxie, the lazy white Persian, looking extremely disgruntled at the disruption to his afternoon snooze as he was carried off to the laundry for an extra grooming of his long, grit-laden fur, and Milo, the short-haired Burmese-cross, sneezing when the panting golden Labrador which had bounced in at Dot's heels thumped down on the floor and began scratching vigorously, raising a cloud of dust around the disdainful chocolate nose.

'Bonzer!' Jennifer tugged him to his feet by his brown leather collar. 'Go into the laundry with Dot and she'll give you a brush. *Then* you can scratch.'

Since they were fed in there, 'laundry' was a word both animals associated with food, and they responded with amusing alacrity, as usual Milo getting there first by taking a shortcut under Paula's chair while Bonzer, whose enthusiasm outran his intelligence, took the corner too fast and surfed the mat into the wall before rebounding out of sight with a sheepish bark.

Jennifer got out the vacuum cleaner to whisk across the kitchen floor, and then figured she might as well do the rest of the ground floor. Anything to take her mind off the man upstairs.

The temperature continued to drop rapidly as the afternoon moved into evening and the mountain continued to push more dense clouds of black ash high into the atmosphere, blotting out the remaining warmth of the sun. Wearing a mask that couldn't obscure the sour smell of sulphur in the air, Jennifer went out to the woodshed behind the garage and brought in several loads of split and round logs and a scuttle of coal. She restoked the small pot-belly stove in the dining room and lit the fire she had reset that morning in the grate of the huge stone fireplace in the living room.

Dot took her camera out onto the verandah and took several shots of the new cloud formations, part of her project to document the progress of the eruption in her daily journal. Then she helped Jennifer disconnect the pipes from the roof to the concrete water-tank, to make sure that their water supply didn't get contaminated if it rained and the compacted ash in the gutters washed into the system. Fortunately the tank was fairly full, and Jennifer was confident that with careful usage they wouldn't run out before the crisis passed.

The phone shrilled several times as the local grapevine swung into action and friends and acquaintances passed on information and gossip about the latest developments, and Jennifer was unsurprised when the Carters phoned to say they'd heard the warnings on the radio and decided to remain in Taupo for the night and drive back the next day, conditions permitting.

Jennifer's brief flare of elation died as she realised that there was no way to suggest Rafe use the unexpected extra bed without raising awkward questions about her marriage. And she couldn't see him meekly agreeing to sneak down under cover of darkness—or allowing her to do it. He had no intention of making things easier for her.

She went to tell her mother about the Carters and found herself quizzed about Rafe's food preferences as Paula pondered over the next day's menu.

'What about chicken? He must like chicken,' Paula said as the list of 'don't knows' grew. She leafed through the recipe book she had open on the dining room table.

'*I* never saw him eat it,' Jennifer said truthfully. She had dined with him a few times in Sebastian's company, but had always been too self-conscious, too tensely aware of his cynical gaze, to pay any attention to what they were eating. The atmosphere between father and son had been none too conducive to digestion, either. Their relationship seemed to be based more on tolerance than affection, and although there was a certain mutual respect it was strictly man-to-man rather than father-to-son. They held opposing views on almost everything, and Sebastian's habit of hammering endlessly at his point in order to prod a reaction out of Rafe only served to make his son withdraw deeper into the cynical indifference that infuriated the father.

'I think he likes sweetbreads, brains, liver, ox-heart—things like that,' she said, in a burst of malicious inspiration.

Paula's brow wrinkled. 'Offal, you mean?'

Jennifer grinned. 'Yes.'

Her mother tapped her pencil against her greying temple, looking dubious. 'Are you sure, dear? He just doesn't look the offal type.'

'What type do *you* think he is?'

'Oh…hot and spicy, sharp and crunchy—he looks as if he'd enjoy Thai food and pickles.'

The comparison made Jennifer's tastebuds tingle. He had certainly been hot and spicy earlier. 'What a weird combination!' she joked, to hide her chagrin.

'Speaking of which, have you told him about the baby yet?'

When Jennifer hesitated, Paula sped happily on to her own answer. 'No, of course not—you wouldn't want to hit him over the head with the news while he was still groggy from jet lag. You want to savour it…set the mood. Maybe tonight, when you go upstairs together…'

Later, as early dusk set in and Jennifer was setting the table, Paula fretted.

'Don't you think you've let him sleep long enough? I know he's travelled a long way but they say the best way to combat jet lag is to try to keep as closely as possible to your new destination's time frame. Anyway, that leg of lamb will be ready soon, and I'm sure he'll be hungry after all that plastic airline food. Why don't you go and wake him up?'

Because Jennifer infinitely preferred him solidly unconscious. She wasn't looking forward to the four of them sitting down to a cosy family dinner. And she *especially* didn't want to go upstairs and see him lying like an arrogant lord in *her* bed. Probably nude. Oh, yes, he would love it if she went upstairs to wake him up—it would give him another chance to embarrass and humiliate her by flaunting his brazen sexuality.

'Um, he said to let him sleep until he wakes,' she said, adding another lie to the long list that had already imperilled her soul.

'If he wakes up *too* rested he won't want to sleep tonight,' her mother pointed out, then realised what she'd said. Her eyes crinkled. 'Oh! Is *that* why you're letting him sleep!'

'He said he'd like to watch if the volcano goes up,' said Jennifer severely.

'Well, of course, dear, that's what I meant,' said Paula blandly, handing her the table napkins from the sideboard. 'He's very well travelled, isn't he, your Rafe— all those other volcanic regions he's been…I know you said that after he got the Amazon thing out of his system he wanted to settle down here in New Zealand, but sometimes once that sort of adventuring gets into the blood…well, just look at Dot—sixty-five and still backpacking her way to far-flung places!'

Another lie coming home to roost. But Jennifer saw a chance to turn it to her advantage.

'Rafe knows that this is where I want to bring up my child.' That much at least was true. 'He knows that you and I run this place as a team, and that I would never leave you in the lurch...' She owed her mother the reassurance that she would not be left alone in the twilight of her life. If not for Jennifer's former fiancé, Paula would probably have had a daughter-in-law and other grandchildren by now.

'The best time to travel with children is when they're little, and you don't have to worry about regular schooling,' Paula said wistfully. 'I would have liked to have been able to do that. I sometimes think it would have been nice if your father had been a missionary, rather than a parish minister. Not that I regretted marrying him for a moment—there's no substitute for love.'

Jennifer only vaguely registered what her mother was saying as she timidly began to lay the groundwork for future disillusionment.

'I sometimes wonder if—Rafe being so...so sophisticated and so much more *exciting* than me—if—well, he might end up finding me boring. I mean, when I look at us together I wonder what a fantastic guy like him sees in someone as ordinary as me...'

Paula clicked her tongue reprovingly. 'Jenny! You're not ordinary—you're unique—the only you in the entire universe. You're a warm, loving, loyal, compassionate and caring young woman, and *any* man would consider himself fortunate to have you in his life!'

'Believe me, I do.'

Jenny's heart leapt into her throat as she saw Rafe standing in the doorway, clad in the black clothes he had draped across the chair, the long sleeves of the V-necked sweater pushed up his strong forearms to bunch at his elbows.

'I can't tell you how *fortunate* I feel to have found Jenny,' he said, moving into the room with an easy stride. He looked well rested, alert and dangerously determined as he rounded the table and homed in on his target. He reached for Jennifer, sliding firm hands around her narrow waist and pulling her towards him until their thighs clashed, bending his head so that his mouth slowly approached hers.

'And before tonight is over I'll make very sure that she knows exactly where she belongs in my life!'

CHAPTER FIVE

RAFE'S lips were only a breath away when a burst of activity in the hall rescued Jennifer from her mesmerised state. She quickly turned her head aside so that his mouth landed on her ear.

He nuzzled it softly, his fingers tightening on her waist as she stiffened.

While her mother manoeuvred her chair to investigate the raised voices, Rafe took shameless advantage of the chance to tease his 'wife'.

'Sophisticated, exciting, fantastic…?' he whispered mockingly into the depths of her sensitised ear. 'I had no idea you found me so impressive, darling. You can be sure I'll do my best to live up to my billing!'

Jennifer jerked her head back, glaring at him through stony eyes, fighting her vivid awareness of the iron-hard thighs pushing against her lower body. But before she could utter the words that sizzled on her tongue the cause of the commotion trooped into the room.

It was Dave and Celia Wright, the young couple who were renting the front bedroom. They were freelance documentary-makers making a tourist film about New Zealand ski resorts, and had revelled in the profit to be made from grabbing dramatic news footage.

They were grimy but exhilarated, having come from the east of the mountain where, they reported, the Desert Road, the main arterial route south, had now been closed by the lethal combination of falling ash and black ice forming on the snow-banked road. They had stopped in for a quick shower and change, and to pick up some of their extra gear, before they headed on to tiny

Whakapapa Village, the closest settlement to Ruapehu's
northwestern ski slopes, where they had heard rumoured
a 'lahar party' was being held in the pub by some of the
hundreds of ski workers who had been laid off their
seasonal jobs as a result of the closure of the mountain.

When Paula expressed concern about their being on
the road at all, let alone at night, Dave shook his shaggy
ginger head and pointed out they had the same kind of
big four-wheel drive equipped with chains and fog-lights
that the rangers and emergency services were using.

'And, besides, we can't afford to let the competition
get the jump on us. The place is crawling with press.
The TV networks have all got crews roving around out
there, but if we get the best pictures, we can beat them
out with their own networks, and maybe even CNN.'

Dave's dark blue eyes suddenly focused suspiciously
on Rafe, who still had one arm around Jennifer's tense
waist, preventing her from easing away.

Rafe grinned, reading his mind. 'It's OK, I'm not a
member of the Fourth Estate. Your story lead is safe.'

There was a small, expectant pause, and Jennifer
forced a smile. 'Dave and Celia, this is—' How to de-
scribe him? She simply couldn't push out the words, and
settled for a lame, 'Uh, this is Raphael...'

Rafe had no such qualms. As he shook hands with the
couple he paraded the outrageous truth as a silly joke.
'Rafe Jordan—since this delicious hussy claims to be my
wife, I guess that leaves me no alternative but to admit
that we're related by marriage.'

A faint puff of air punctuated his last word as Jennifer
discreetly jabbed a warning elbow into his solar plexus.

'Oh, sorry,' she said, levering herself away with the
elbow as he rubbed the tender spot. 'Did I hurt you?'

'Winded rather than wounded, darling,' he said, his
tigerish smile carrying a warning of its own. 'And I'm

rapidly adjusting to your wicked knack for taking my breath away.'

Celia commented on the heavenly aroma of roast, and, on learning that the Wrights hadn't eaten since they had gulped a hamburger on the run around noon, Paula persuaded the pair to join them for dinner before they rushed off again. It was with relief that Jennifer heard them agree, on the understanding that they would pay extra on the tariff.

At least with Dave and Celia present the conversation wouldn't get too personal, she thought, as the pair went away to clean up and she set two extra places, while Rafe was roped into carving the lamb.

The reality was somewhat different.

Paula explained as they all sat down at the extended oak table, to a succulent roast with all the trimmings, that although Beech House operated as a bed and breakfast, they were willing to negotiate for the provision of other meals, as long as the guests concerned didn't mind eating *en famille*.

'So, if you want a packed lunch, or to eat here in the evening, Celia, you only have to let us know in time to organise it.

'Your father used to have most of his dinners with us, Rafe,' she reminisced, putting Jennifer's nerves immediately onto alert. 'Right from the first time he came here—which was what, Jenny? Just over five years ago now? I suppose she told you the story.' Her thin face softened with her gamine grin as she told the Wrights, 'There was some mix-up at the expensive hotel Sebastian was booked into so he stormed out in a huff and we were the first place he'd phoned that had a vacancy—it was the height of the season.

'I don't think he'd ever stayed at a B&B before, he usually went everywhere first-class, but he really appreciated the personal touch and what he called our "homespun charm''.' She laughed, with a rueful look at Jennifer. 'The surroundings *were* a bit shabby in those pre-renovation days, but he said he liked being made to feel he was part of the family.' She preened faintly. 'He even used to say that it was my fabulous cooking that kept him coming back year after year!'

'Five years?'

Sitting beside Rafe, Jennifer was able to avoid his hard stare, but she couldn't help feeling the tension that entered his body as he sipped from his glass of water—having declined, on the grounds of jet lag, Paula's offer to open a bottle of wine.

As far as anyone in London, including Rafe, had been concerned, she had met Sebastian only weeks before she had married him. He had asked her not to mention their previous, intermittent acquaintance, smugly enjoying the notion of thwarting all attempts to discover any motive in his apparent madness. Since the whole point of his annual month-long overseas holiday had been to get completely away from the stresses and strains of his daily life—including his demanding, dysfunctional extended family—he had always refused to leave a fixed itinerary behind. And Rafe had been unfairly included on his father's information blacklist not, Jennifer suspected, because he had been curious to know where his father went on his trips, but because he so resolutely *hadn't*.

'I don't remember you telling me you'd known him quite *that* long, darling,' Rafe said with studied casualness, and under the table Jennifer felt his long legs shift, his knee brushing up against hers. When she tried to angle her leg away she suddenly felt his hand curling over her wool-clad knee, clamping it to his.

Above the tablecloth he serenely continued to wield his fork, and it became a matter of pride to show that she was unmoved by his threatening touch.

Jennifer shrugged, strands of her silky hair catching against the red angora sweater. Much to her mother's dismay she hadn't changed for dinner—not only because she hadn't wanted to go into her room while Rafe was still there, but because she didn't want him to think she was doing it for *him*…and she would have been, for in the casual tradition of Beech House they rarely dressed for dinner.

'Don't you? I'm sure I must have,' she said off-handedly, taking a sip of her own water, half wishing it was a hefty slug of whisky, except she knew that she needed an exceptionally clear head when dealing with Rafe.

Her punishment was to feel the warm, heavy weight of his hand slide further up her thigh, and she hastily pressed her legs together, unfortunately trapping his fingertips between the tender cushions of her upper thighs. He wiggled his fingers, sending ripples of sensation thrilling up her legs, and when she tried relaxing her muscles just enough to let his fingers slip free he insinuated his touch even higher, so that she quickly had to lock them tight again.

She casually put her hand under the table to fend him off, but even the gouge of her neat, short fingernails into the tender joints of his wrist didn't make him flinch.

Nobody else at the table seemed aware of her impotent squirming, but Jennifer could feel herself beginning to glow like a beacon with anger and embarrassment.

'Gravy, Rafe?' She snatched up the steaming boat and hovered it above the edge of his plate—and his vulnerable lap.

'I already have some, thank you,' he said politely, his green eyes meeting her silent challenge, his hand remaining firmly in possession.

She tilted the gravy boat fractionally but his gaze remained steady, showing not even a flicker of concern that his manhood was in imminent danger of being scalded. What made him so damned certain that she was bluffing?

Maybe the fact that they both knew he held all the cards.

With a sigh she put the gravy boat down and he immediately removed his hand and picked up his knife again, a smile ghosting around the corners of his mouth.

She scowled at him, and he tilted his head in mocking acknowledgement of her unwilling surrender.

'No disrespect to the dead, but I don't suppose you can claim that we really *knew* Sebastian,' Dot said in her usual brusque fashion, her short helmet of grey hair gleaming under the overhead lights as she leaned over to pass Paula's home-made mint sauce to Dave. 'I mean, think of it—a week a year for five years is only five weeks out of nearly three hundred. For the other two hundred-odd weeks he could have been an axe-murderer for all we knew.' Dot had been too strong-minded and opinionated to get along well with Sebastian.

'Dot! Sebastian was a *doctor*!' Paula cried.

'So was Crippen,' Rafe pointed out drily.

'Rafe!' Paula reproached him with a reluctant smile.

'Who was Crippen?' asked Celia, whose blank, fresh-scrubbed face showed her lack of years as well as her lack of knowledge of forensic history.

'He was famous as the first criminal to be caught by police using a radio-telegraph,' supplied Rafe. 'Hanged in 1910 for poisoning his wife. No, you're right, Paula, I guess there's no similarity—Sebastian's method of getting rid of his wives was strictly legal. Divorce may be more expensive than murder when you're wealthy, but it's a lot less risky in the long run.'

Celia looked intrigued at the mention of wealth. 'How many wives did your father have?'

'Let's see…' From the corner of her eye Jennifer was

infuriated to see him pretend to count on his fingers, knowing he was deliberately tormenting her when he suddenly shook his head and started counting all over again.

'Four,' Jennifer interrupted flatly, deciding to take a leaf out of Rafe's book and mislead with the literal truth. 'He was divorced four times.'

'No kidding!' Dave and Celia exchanged looks, and Jennifer could see them wondering, from the supreme confidence of their youth, how anyone could screw up that many marriages.

With a pang she wondered whether, if her engagement hadn't collapsed under the weight of her brother's death and her mother's long convalescence, she and Michael mightn't have been divorced by now, too. She had loved him, and had passionately committed herself to the belief that their love would last a lifetime, but Michael's feelings had withered in the face of early adversity, leaving her nothing but false dreams and empty hopes.

'What's it like having that many mothers?' Celia wondered, her journalistic curiosity tweaked.

Jennifer went cold as she realised what could happen if Celia got wind of the bizarre story that was happening right under her very nose. Would she be able to resist the lure of another profitable scoop?

'TEST TUBE FATHER IS STEPBROTHER OF HIS OWN CHILD!'

It was the kind of story that tabloids and talk shows could play up for weeks—years, even. The second most precious gift that Sebastian had given Jennifer, after her baby, had been privacy, but that would be well and truly blasted into smithereens if anyone in the media got hold of the details.

Rafe didn't seem to find Celia's question intrusive, but then he asked some unnervingly intrusive questions himself.

'My own mother divorced Sebastian when I was four, and he didn't marry for the second time until I was in my teens, by which time I'd long since lost the desire to regard any of his changing guard of consorts in a maternal light.' He gave a quick glance at Jennifer that brought a little sting to her cheek. 'Fortunately for me, as it turned out, because all *their* motherly instincts were already focused on their own children.'

There was a neutrality in his voice that spoke volumes to Jennifer.

'So were you brought up by your mother or Sebastian?' wondered Paula.

Jennifer's eyes lowered to her plate as she tried to conceal her interest in his reply. Although Sebastian had often spoken about his son, it had usually been in the form of some grudging boast of his achievements, or a complaint about Rafe's refusal to show proper filial respect. Suddenly she wanted the knowledge she had previously rejected. While the father of her child had been anonymous it hadn't mattered, but now that he had become a force in her life she needed to know the things that had shaped his personality, if only to enable her to correspondingly shape her defences.

'My mother, thank goodness—she's Italian and has very firm feelings about mother-son bonding.' Without looking at him, Jennifer knew he was smiling. 'My father, on the other hand, worked hard and he played hard. He liked to bask in the image of himself as a family man, but the reality was that he couldn't hack the boring, everyday routines of parenthood. He couldn't be bothered with children until they became old enough to behave like real people. He liked the world ordered to his own liking, and children, of course, are notoriously allergic to order...'

A distant low boom made them all look towards the window, where the brooding hulk of volcanic rock and ice that was Ruapehu was still just barely visible against the spreading inky stain of night. A little earlier the thick mushroom cloud of ash and steam haloing the summit had looked like boiling red dye, the falling particles of ash absorbing the refracted rays of the setting sun and diffusing them into a brilliant red-orange haze that had made the whole mountain look as if it had caught fire, the permanent ice on the highest ridges blushing a fluorescent orange-pink while the lower snow-clad slopes dropped away into deep violet-blue shadows.

Another faraway crack and Dave, who had busied his mouth with food rather than conversation, pushed his plate away, wiping his beard with his napkin as he jumped to his feet, crackling with energy.

'I think that's our cue. They must be pretty huge blasts if we can hear them all the way down here. I hope you don't mind if we take off.'

'We have no idea what time we'll be back,' said Celia, running a hand through her bubbly blonde hair. 'I mean, it depends on what's happening out there...'

'We'll leave the key in the front door for you,' said Jennifer, smiling up at them. 'So you won't have to worry about waking us up when you come in.'

Rafe looked startled at the suggestion. 'Isn't that a bit risky?' he asked as the couple departed. 'Leaving the place unlocked at night.'

'This isn't London,' Jennifer told him with a superior sniff. 'We're a small community; we prefer to trust people to behave decently rather than to live in a perpetual state of siege against potential muggers and burglars.'

'I'd like to trust people too, but experience has taught me that it's painfully unwise.'

Jennifer would have liked to argue against his cynicism, but she was hardly in a position to talk to him about trust.

'Of course, in the season, when there's a big influx of

tourists, we do get an increase in petty crime and vandalism, that kind of thing,' Paula chipped in. 'But being a little off the beaten track, as we are here, we don't worry about it. Why, when we first moved in we didn't even have a lock on the door!'

That led to a discussion about the origins of Beech House, a blessedly safe topic as far as Jennifer was concerned, and she happily left the three of them talking as she cleared away the plates and went to fetch the rhubarb pie from the oven.

But when she came back the conversation had turned to the renovations that had been carried out over the past three years, and how Jennifer had been so clever at handling the business side of things that she had recently been able to pay off the substantial mortgage and medical bills, and take out medical insurance that covered one hundred per cent of any care that Paula might require, so that she wouldn't have to be reliant on the badly overstretched public hospital system.

Jennifer pushed rhubarb pie and cream at her mother to try and stop her singing her paean to the wonderful, supportive daughter she had, but Paula refused to be diverted.

'She probably didn't tell you because she tends to hide her light under a bushel, but after the accident life was such a struggle for the two of us. We had managed to scrape enough to put a deposit on this house, but there was nothing left over and Jenny had to give up her nurse's training to care for me. Once I was a bit more mobile she got several part-time home-caring jobs, then decided to start the bed and breakfast for the extra income. But I think that was mostly for me at first, wasn't it, Jenny? She was desperate to jolt me out of my depression and get me interested and involved in life again. Pain does tend to turn one in on oneself terribly...

'Anyway, then Dot came along and decided she

wanted to more or less have her room permanently, and she started doing the grounds—' she gave her friend a beam '—and I started giving some cooking classes, and soon we had so many regular guests that Jenny was able to give up her other jobs and run Beech House in a more businesslike way, so that she could borrow the money to invest in the renovations. I insisted one of the first things she do was expand that attic of hers so she had some more space for herself, and somewhere to do her paperwork. She's so meticulous about her records and files, she spends hours up there most nights, tapping away at that computer...'

'Girl's a genius with money—seems to be able to stretch it like rubber,' said Dot, cutting herself another fat slice of rhubarb pie. 'Of course, thrift is a forgotten art to most people these days, and someone like you probably never had to learn it—'

'Oh, I know the value of a pound,' said Rafe drily. He also knew something about business and building costs, and his shrewd eye had estimated that tens of thousands of dollars must have gone into the remodelling of Beech House...a great deal more money than any bank would have been justified in loaning to such a small-scale business. Jennifer wasn't just a genius, she was a magician, and Rafe had a burning ambition to discover the source of her mysterious magic.

'I may have had what you would class as a privileged childhood, but I worked for my own living from the time I was seventeen,' he told Paula and Dot, bemused by his nagging desire to make a good impression, even though he knew that by the time he left the two women would probably have every reason to despise him. 'My father offered to pay me an allowance if I went to medical school, but I chose art school instead and dropped out of that when modelling turned out to be so lucrative. Apart from what I inherited a few months ago, everything I have I earned through my own blood, sweat and fears!'

'You mean tears.' Jennifer was unable to resist correcting the misquoted cliché.

He turned his head, the skin slanting over his high cheekbones as he smiled. 'I mean that without any business training, every time I expanded into some new venture it was hands-on, trial and error stuff that had a huge potential for disaster—I take on small failing enterprises and turn them around; that's nail-biting stuff.'

'So you're an entrepreneur,' said Dot, pleased to have discovered where he fitted in the scheme of things. 'You take the initiative, you take the risk, and then you sell and take the profit.'

'Oh, I don't sell,' said Rafe. 'I keep. When I make a success of something, I'm possessive. I do what I do for *me*, and I pick and choose my targets because they interest me, not just for their profit potential. Maybe I should hire *you* to work for me,' he aimed across Jennifer's bows. 'Then you could teach my accountants some of that incredible thrift...'

'You're the *last* person I'd ever work for,' she said hotly, before remembering their audience.

'You don't believe in husbands and wives working together?' Rafe smoothly covered her gaffe.

'Uh, n-no, I think it's asking for t-trouble,' she stammered.

'God forbid we do that!' he murmured, his green eyes declaring that they had plenty enough of that already.

'Your father and I worked together for twenty-five years in perfect harmony,' protested Paula. 'Though I admit we weren't shut up in an office together, and of course he was the one with the real job while I was an unpaid accessory, but still, I was pretty essential to his ministry.'

'I should imagine you made a wonderful vicar's wife,'

said Rafe, with a frank sincerity that made Paula pinken in pleasure. 'I don't really work in an office, either. It's more a case of have laptop will travel, because I like to keep a close eye on my favourite projects. I have a company that handles personal management for celebrities, several art galleries, a theatre production company, a few publishing ventures—'

'Publishing?' Dot's broad forehead creased with interest.

'Oh, Jenny, you made Rafe sound like a boring businessman when you said what he did, but now I know why you two felt such an instant affinity. Jenny is an inveterate reader and loves to write!' Her mother clapped her hands together.

'The reading I know about—but, writing?' Rafe's golden eyebrows rose at Jennifer's trapped expression.

'Just a hobby,' she said quickly, aghast. 'Dot's the one who's the writer…'

After a thoughtful hesitation, Rafe's gaze was reluctantly diverted. 'Oh, what are you doing, Dot?'

The older woman waved a dismissive hand. 'Been doing it for years. Travel book…all the places I've been…personal journey, that kind of thing. I'm not in any hurry to finish it, though—I haven't done all my travelling yet!'

'There's a big market for travel books,' Rafe said, and he and Dot proceeded to pick apart some of the offerings they had read in common.

Rafe cleverly lured Jennifer into the discussion as the talk broadened into books and writing in general, and by the time they moved into the living room with their tea and coffee she had forgotten her agonised self-consciousness, forgotten to guard and examine every word before she uttered it and was arguing as warmly as the other two, her body relaxed yet simmering with vitality, her brown eyes glowing with passion, her capable hands darting to illustrate her words.

She didn't even care that she had to sit close to Rafe on the couch to satisfy her mother's expectation of marital bliss. No longer stiff and repressed, she flowered under the fierce cut and thrust of ideas, her animation flowing like wine through her veins, bringing a luminous warmth to her pale features and softening the square of her face as she ardently defended her point of view with wit and humour.

Although Jennifer loved Paula and Dot, and had planned to be utterly content with her future at Beech House, the strange double life she lived—of wild, passionate flights of daring imagination on the one hand and intensely practical, down-to-earth respectability on the other—had its drawbacks. She maintained a careful separation of the two starkly opposing sides of her personality, and at the moment they were revelling in their unexpected outing together!

Only when her mother mentioned that Jennifer had once taken some creative writing courses did the barriers slam back into place.

'Sebastian was very intrigued—wasn't he, Jenny?—that first time he stayed here.' Paula laughed. 'He found a scrap of something you'd written and you were horribly mortified when he said he'd read it and thought it was good. I remember how amused he was when you came over all shy, Jenny, and blushed like a tomato when he tried to talk to you about it. She hates people to read what she's done,' she confided, to Rafe's intense interest. 'I think that was why she was so keen on getting a computer for the bookings and accounts, so she can write to her heart's content without leaving embarrassing scraps of paper floating about for all and sundry to see.'

'Because it's just private scribblings,' said Jenny desperately, feeling her colour inexorably rising. It would be her mother who would die of mortification if she ever found out exactly what it was that her daughter was writing, and how sinfully successful she was at it!

She got up to take a jab at the cheerfully blazing logs on the fire with the cast-iron poker, hoping her blush would be put down to her proximity to the heat. The way Rafe was looking at her she felt as if the guilty truth was written in scarlet letters on her forehead.

'What sort of things do your companies publish, Rafe?' she heard Dot say as she pretended to be engrossed in the sparks that were flying off the blackened surface of the logs.

'Oh, there's a couple of high-class fashion magazines, and one or two aimed at, uh, the sophisticated male…' Jennifer smiled maliciously to herself at his revealing euphemism. 'Then I have one publishing house that specialises in children's books and another that prints general and genre fiction. I also have a couple of niche publishers under the wing of a company I bought a majority interest in from my father a few years ago, after he'd rescued it from one of my stepbrothers, who'd driven it to the verge of bankruptcy with his incompetent management. One produces medical text and reference books and the other publishes series fiction for women.'

'What kind of women's fiction?' Paula asked, having become an avid reader of wrenching emotional sagas during her convalescence. 'Do you have any famous female authors?'

'Not famous outside their narrow field, no. As I said, it's a niche market. I guess you could say that Velvet Books are sort of educational—'

There was a sharp clang as Jennifer dropped the heavy poker on the hearth, nearly impaling her foot with its viciously barbed end.

She stared at Rafe in glassy-eyed horror.

Velvet?

Rafe owned the English company that was fast becoming the leading international publisher of female erotica? *He* was behind those elegantly sexy paperbacks which had tapped into the gap in the market between steamy sensual romances and crudely sexual romps?

The whole picture suddenly leapt into ghastly focus in her head—Sebastian's vague publishing 'contact' all those years ago had been a member of his own family!

She felt a hot burst of maniacal laughter building up inside her.

Velvet novels were a lot of things: sinfully smouldering, intensely exciting, wildly romantic and exquisitely erotic.

But 'sort of educational'?

Jennifer put a hand over her mouth to hold in her hysterical giggle.

Rafe had sprung up, misunderstanding her horror, sliding his cupped hands supportively under her elbows as she swayed in front of the fire.

'Jennifer? Are you all right? Did you hurt yourself?' he murmured into her owl-eyed confusion. When she didn't immediately answer he knelt to run his hands over her feet, assuring himself that they were undamaged.

She blinked back to life, staring down at his blond head, conscious of how close she'd come to needlessly giving herself away. Thank God she'd never used her own name, not even in the earliest correspondence. She would never have even considered taking Sebastian's advice if she hadn't been able to wrap herself in complete anonymity. Only her lawyer and the tax department were aware that she was two people.

Certainly not the man kneeling at her feet.

Like a pleading supplicant, she thought, and felt another dangerous bubble of laughter form as she contemplated the awful irony of the situation.

'I'm s-sorry. Uh—it was just the shock,' she said with

perfect truth, regretting it when he rose, regarding her with a glimmer of suspicion.

'It slipped out of my hand,' she added, laying it on. 'I nearly spiked myself.'

He pushed her gently back towards the couch before bending to pick up the fallen poker, weighing it for a moment in his grip before dropping it back into its guard.

Bonzer, who was sprawled on the sheepskin hearthrug, lifted his head for a throaty growl as Rafe moved past his line of vision.

'Pipe down, Bonzer!' said Dot, tossing him an afterdinner mint which he snapped up not at all lazily.

'Sharp reflexes, old man,' said Rafe, crouching to give the dog a pat and a lazy scratch on his tubby belly. Bonzer whined and squirmed with delight, his tail thumping against the rug.

'How long have you had him?' Rafe asked Jennifer.

She had almost recovered her equilibrium. 'Three years. I found him out on the road in a ditch. He'd been hit by a car and had a broken hip, and for a while the vet thought he might have to put him down. But he got better and nobody claimed him, so I brought him home. I think he was about four when we got him, and obviously nobody had ever tried to train him so he didn't take to discipline too well. He's still a bit boisterous and dopey, but he's very friendly and he loves children...'

She had said the words without thinking, but when Rafe looked up at her she had a vision of a little green-eyed, golden-skinned, tow-headed boy, shouting with laughter as he had his face licked by his doggy friend. Her lips curved dreamily, unconsciously inviting him to share in her fantasy, and Rafe's pupils expanded, darkening his eyes to a moody jade as he stared with a peculiar kind of hunger at her tender expression of delight. The delicate silence lasted until Rafe looked away and caught sight of Maxie, sharpening his claws against the logs in the basket.

'And what about your cats, are they former strays too?'

'How did you guess?' grinned Paula. 'And Fergus.' She pointed at the cage in the corner where an overly plump budgie listed drunkenly on a perch. With an incredulous look at Jennifer, Rafe scrambled up to take a closer look.

'Good God, that's why it's on a slant.' Rafe peered into the cage. 'It's only got one leg!'

'But, as Jenny pointed out to the vet, it's a very *sturdy* leg,' laughed Dot.

Jenny braced herself for more jokes about her rescued menagerie, but Ruapehu had a more dramatic subject in mind.

A low roar and a series of deep sonic booms had them rushing for the verandah, standing spellbound in the freezing night air at the sight of the incandescent fireworks spitting arcing streamers of molten fire hundreds of metres above the mountain crater. Even knowing that they were at a safe distance, Jennifer shuddered at the awe-inspiring, raw power unleashed by the volcano. She felt like a small, lonely, insignificant dot in a vast universe, and welcomed the strong arms that closed about her, pulling her back against the warm, solid body of another human being.

'Now I know why Dante calls nature "the art of God",' said Rafe quietly over the top of her head, his words forming as steam in the icy air, his arms tightening around her waist. 'Magnificent and terrifying, and powerful beyond our comprehension.'

It was hypnotically fascinating watching the fiery jets of super-heated liquid rock, propelled by the violent eruption of gases, fountain continuously over the rocky outline of the cone. Huge, flaming orange 'bombs' were flung out amongst the cascading rivulets of white-hot fire, and through Dot's binoculars some could be seen tumbling and melting down the snowy west face of the mountain like giant fluorescent tears. Dark ash blotted out more of the stars as it streamed up into the atmosphere, creating a huge black void above the brilliant pyrotechnic display.

Eventually it was the cold that drove them back inside, and while Dot and her mother elected to stay in the living room, wrapped in blankets with hot toddies on their knees, to watch the continuing fireworks as long as they could manage to stay awake, a few yawns and coy hints from Rafe had led to Jennifer being shooed upstairs to bed for the sake of her ostensibly tired 'husband'.

As she'd suspected, when they got up to her room Rafe's tiredness miraculously fell away, as did the cloak of relatively civilised restraint he had worn in company. He was back to the restless, hostile, suspicious and openly aggressive enemy he had been on his arrival. Only now there was an added element, a primitive possessiveness in his insulting gaze that made her spine crawl with apprehensive excitement.

He watched calmly, arms folded across his black chest, as she busily folded spare double blankets from the glory box at the foot of the bed to form a narrow mattress on the floor and covered it with a thick quilt, tucking a fat pillow at the head.

Then, just as calmly, he stalked over and tore her work apart, tossing the blankets and quilt in opposite directions and kicking the pillow under the bed.

'You're not doing me out of my feather bed,' he told her, his body language spoiling for a fight—legs astride, hands on hips, shoulders tense, stubborn jaw thrust slightly forward.

Laboriously, silently, Jennifer collected all the discarded pieces and constructed the makeshift bed all over again.

'This is for *me*, not for *you*,' she announced haughtily, completing her statement by ramming the pillow back into position. It galled her, but she knew she didn't have a hope in hell of keeping him out of the big bed, if that was where he wanted to be.

He grunted and pulled off his shoes, not the laced walking boots this time, she noticed, but elegant, black, hand-made Italian jobs. Any moment now he would start the strip, and Jennifer was not going to be put through *that* humiliation again!

She hurried over to her nightwear drawer and blindly grabbed a handful of garments. Then she slammed into the bathroom and locked the door. Maybe if she took an age to shower and clean her teeth and brush her hair and—and…hell, and give herself a manicure, pedicure, perm, the whole works!—maybe by then he would be harmlessly asleep.

He'd better be asleep, she groaned silently as she looked at her choice of sleepwear. Of course there was no prim flannel nightdress or practical passion-killing pyjamas. She didn't own any. Although Jennifer plumped for comfort over fashion in her clothes, her underwear was a different matter. There she felt free to indulge her private fantasies, and sexy bits of nothing featured large in her lingerie drawers. As for the slinky, sensuous things she slept in—they were intended to inspire the kind of wicked dreams that swept her to fresh heights of passionate creativity!

With Raphael Jordan in her bed, she needed a soporific, not an aphrodisiac!

CHAPTER SIX

MUFFLED up in the old pink towelling bathrobe that she
never used, Jennifer crept past the sunken lump in the
bed. Rafe had turned off the overhead lights and only
the lamp beside the bed shone, throwing a rich glow over
the golden head on the pillow. He was lying on his stomach, face half buried to one side in the pillow, one
smooth-muscled naked arm thrown up around his head
as if to shield himself from the intrusive light.

Jennifer glided across the cool floorboards, the shivery
thrills goosing over her skin having nothing to do with
the temperature. In fact the room, well-insulated in walls
and ceiling, was quite toasty warm, thanks to the ther-
mostatically controlled convection heater in the corner.

The hush of the night was disturbed by the muffled
crump of faraway explosion, and she was irresistibly
drawn to the balcony doors for another look at the
fireworks display. After nearly two hours the powerful
forces were showing no sign of diminishing, and now
lightning bolts were crackling around the summit,
threading zig-zag patterns of brilliant white through the
black ash-clouds roaring into the night sky.

'You're blocking the view.'

She turned quickly, almost tripping over the drooping
hem of her robe. The first thing she saw was Rafe
propped up on his elbow, the cream duvet sliding away
from his bare chest to settle at his waist.

The second was that her meagre bed on the floor had
vanished. And this time there were no scattered bedclothes or assaulted pillow.

'I thought you were asleep.'

He made a negative movement with his head, abrading his whiskers against the knuckles that were propping up his jaw as he contemplated her deep dismay.

'Did you really think I was going to make it that easy for you?' he said, with menacingly softness.

Easy?

Jennifer had no illusions on that score. But she *had* hoped to put off another devastating confrontation until she had had time to repair the weaknesses in her buckled defences, particularly in view of this wretched new complication. She just hoped to God that Rafe wasn't involved in the editorial side of Velvet Books!

She ignored his taunting reply and flung open the glory box. It was empty. With a furious glance at Rafe's innocent expression her gaze hunted around the room for the missing blankets.

'This is just childish!' she burst out.

'I agree, so stop behaving like a sulky schoolgirl. Come to bed and we'll talk about it like mature adults. You know what they say—a husband and wife should never let the sun go down on their anger...'

She let the lid of the box fall with a sharp crack that echoed her snapping nerves.

'We are *not* married and I'm *not* getting into bed with you!'

'Claiming the moral high ground? That's pretty shaky territory for a compulsive liar...'

'*You* can talk about morality?' she scorned fiercely. 'You've had more women than you've had hot dinners!'

His mouth took on a cynical slant. 'I presume you got that spicy tidbit from my father. Well, maybe that's what I wanted him to think, when rebelling against his hypocritical version of morality was my chief aim in life, but in fact I've always been extremely selective where women are concerned—certainly more sexually discriminating than *he* ever was. Sebastian was congenitally

incapable of being faithful to one women, yet he persisted in making vows of fidelity, while I, on the other
hand, never made any promises and never once betrayed
a lover.'

'I'm not in the least interested in your sex life,'
Jennifer bit out.

'Yes, you are. Or you wouldn't constantly stroke me
with those hot little looks from under your lashes.'

She immediately flashed her eyes wide. 'I do not!'

'Did you think I hadn't noticed? I spent a good few
years in front of the camera, learning how to attract that
particular look from women—I know exactly what it
signals. There was never any hint of sexual awareness
in the air between you and my father, but you and I…we
were a different story, weren't we?' His voice deepened
as his eyes swept her from head to foot, mocking her
scruffy armour. 'Even if we chose not to acknowledge
it, that delicious sting of mutual curiosity was always
there, wasn't it? You might even say that the atmosphere
between us was pregnant with possibilities…although at
the time I didn't realise how literally true that would
turn out to be!'

Jennifer yanked the belt on her robe cuttingly tight,
trying to separate herself from the wicked sensations
shimmering through her lower body as Rafe rolled onto
his back, exposing more of his torso, folding his arms
provocatively behind his head as he said boldly, 'You
know, at one stage it did occur to me that I could seduce
you away from Sebastian, but then I figured, Why should
I do the three witches' dirty work for them…?'

He meant Lydia, Sharon and Felicity, the bitchy tri-
umvirate who, unlike Rafe's mother, had remained
firmly within Sebastian's orbit, playing on his spasmodic
guilt and pandering to his obsession that they should all
be one, big happy family. Sebastian's regrettable habit
of throwing money at problems to make them go away

had only served to multiply the problems of his ex-wives and their children.

'Besides, the old man was dying—all his riches couldn't protect him from that—so why shouldn't he spend them going out with a bang, so to speak, rather than a whimper?' Rafe continued, with an insultingly careless tilt of one gilded shoulder. 'So I resisted the temptation to respond to your subtle invitation—'

'There *was* no invitation!' she hissed, stooping to peer under the bed. 'Where have you put my damned blankets?'

'I threw them off the balcony.'

She popped up again, her face furiously flushed.

'You didn't!' she gasped, clutching her lapels, imagining what her mother and Dot must have thought when bedclothes had suddenly come raining down in front of their eyes.

'For a consummate liar you're incredibly gullible yourself,' he jeered. 'No, I didn't—but even if you find them it's not going to get you anywhere. I'm not going to let you sleep on the floor. Apart from anything else it won't do the baby any good…'

'What the hell do you care?' she snarled unwisely, recoiling from any hint of potential interest in her pregnancy.

His eyes narrowed as he sensed her fear. 'Why don't you come over here and find out?' he invited, with silken insolence. 'You might be surprised to find what we care about in common…'

Her heart jittered. Oh, no, she wasn't falling for that one. She wasn't going to get within striking distance of that lithe golden body. As long as he didn't touch her she could maintain her defiant front.

She tossed her head in an unconsciously challenging gesture of contempt. 'Forget it!' she said, flouncing over to the door. 'The Carters' room is empty tonight, I can sleep downstairs in *their* bed.'

Braced for an explosion of thwarted anger she was disconcerted when he remained relaxed against the pillows, a look of boredom on his face.

She soon found out why when the door refused to open to her touch. She rattled the handle in frustration, realised what was wrong and whirled around.

'What have you done with the key?'

He unfolded his arms and spread them wide, boredom replaced by a smug smile. 'I'll give you a clue. It's somewhere in this bed. Why don't you feel around and I'll let you know when you're getting warm?'

She was very warm now, and getting hotter by the moment. If only she could *melt* through the door at her back. 'You're the most hateful person I've ever met!' she dredged from the depths of her helplessness.

His smile vanished. 'If that's the way you feel, maybe I'm right to worry about how carefully you're looking after your pregnancy. Have you changed your mind about having my hateful baby? Are you hoping your body might reject it?'

Jennifer was stricken to the core. 'That's a vicious thing to say,' she choked, welcoming the pain of her shoulderblades digging into the door as a distraction from the searing pain in her heart. 'I'd *never* hurt my baby! And I'd never blame an innocent child for the acts of its parents, either. Children don't have any choice about who their parents are going to be—'

'And parenthood often isn't a matter of conscious choice either, but it was for *you*,' he pointed out ruthlessly. 'On the day you agreed to be inseminated with my sperm you made a choice. You accepted Raphael Jordan as the father of your child. You accepted me!

'Now, are you going to come over here and get into bed or do I have to come over there and fetch you?'

He sat up and began to peel down the duvet, revealing more and more naked flesh.

Jennifer squeezed her eyes tight shut against the threatening sight, throwing up her hands to ward off her invisible panic. 'No, wait. Look, can't we just…?'

She heard the rustle of sheets, his bare feet hitting the floor, his quiet padding across the room towards her. And then nothing. Silence.

She swallowed, her nostrils quivering at the scent of danger. He was close, standing directly in front of her; she could feel his proximity with every nerve in her body. Her imagination went into overdrive. If she moved her hands even a fraction of an inch she would touch his hot, smooth, satiny skin…

'You can look now.'

The sardonic humour in his voice warned her to ignore him.

She licked her dry lips and was ashamed of the slight whimper that slipped out. 'Please…'

He took her resistant left hand and placed it on his hip. Her eyes flew open and she looked down in blessed relief. He was wearing a pair of black silk pyjama trousers, loosely tied by a drawstring. They had settled low on his lean hips, dipping on his hard belly at the point where the arrow of hair below his navel began to spread into a dark blond thicket. But at least he was respectably covered.

She snatched her gaze back to his face. It was all hard angles and brooding shadows, his lower lip pushed out in a sombre, sexy pout.

'Disappointed?' he smouldered, and massaged her hand in slow circles on the fabric, shaping her palm over the jutting hardness of his hip-bone.

There was another electric silence, and he picked up her right hand and put it on his right hip. Then he removed her spectacles, folded them, and tucked them snugly into the breast pocket of her robe.

'Wh-why did you do that?' she said light-headedly, as he withdrew his fingers from the pocket, his knuckles scraping briefly against her towelling-padded breast.

'You won't need your glasses in bed. Everything you see there is going to be in close-up,' he murmured, his forehead briefly resting against hers as he looked down for the belt of her robe. 'You won't need this, either.'

'Don't…' she uttered weakly, stopping him, her toes curling against the bare floorboards.

'You won't be comfortable all bundled up like this.' He tugged gently at the trailing bow.

She tipped up her face to protest and, shockingly, her mouth met his. His lips were firm and resilient, his tongue limber as it slipped moistly past the guard of her teeth and stroked her silky interior. Shock turned to violent craving and she moaned, her mouth opening to receive him. His head tilted, his mouth slanting to deepen the kiss, deepen the penetration of his tongue into her willing depths. He broke off and bit at her lips, licking and sucking at the juicy pink flesh, his hands twisting in the loops of her belt, dragging her closer into the hot, wet embrace of mouths.

His whiskers rasped on her delicate skin, the small pain intensifying the oral pleasure as she savaged him in return, and he groaned, plunging himself even more recklessly into her inviting moistness, the ragged sound of his desire vibrating seductively in her arching throat. His tongue flickered over hers in a dance of erotic compulsion, rubbing at her, teasing her with addictive skill, saturating her overloaded senses with his unique taste.

Her body tightened, her breasts swelling against the rough towelling as he seduced her tongue into his mouth so that he could suckle her in a slow, hard rhythm that matched the sensual undulation of his hips.

Only when she felt his hands move at her waist, fumbling again with the now impossibly knotted belt, did Jennifer drag herself back from the brink of terrifying surrender.

'No, oh, no, we can't…' She tore her mouth from his, the words breaking clumsily from swollen lips, her tortured lungs struggling for the breath he had stolen.

'Can't what?' he muttered, his mouth seeking across her averted cheek, his voice richly clotted with passion.

She had to force herself to think logically. 'Can't—can't go to bed together…' She groaned. That was where they were headed, wasn't it?

He raised his head. His eyes, sultry and heavy-lidded, were glittering slits of molten green. 'Why not? It's what we both want.' His voice roughened to a guttural scrawl. 'And there's nothing to stop us any more…'

Why not? The words whispered seductively in her brain. Why not take what you want…and pay for it?

But no, not like this. It was too dangerous, the gamble too great, the stakes too high.

'We just *can't*…' she whispered.

There was a heartbeat's pause before he responded, brushing his mouth across her feathery fringe. 'Would you do it if I paid you?' he urged softly, the golden shadow of his beard capturing several strands of her hair, sliding them across his mouth as he turned his face to breathe his sin against her temple. 'Would you strip for me if I gave you money, darling? Would you take off your clothes, slowly…and touch yourself for me?' His creamy voice curdled into brutal cynicism as he went relentlessly on. 'How much for your body, Jennifer? How much would it cost me to do whatever the hell I liked with it? How much do you charge to have a man's stolen sperm planted inside you?'

By the time he had uttered the last bitter word he had her thrust against the wood, his hands trapping her shoulders, his thigh pressing across her legs, his searing questions battering at her horrified emotions.

'It wasn't *stolen*; you *donated* it,' she protested wildly, pushing at his bulging biceps as she fought an avalanche of undeserved guilt. She wasn't going to be blamed for *his* mistakes as well as her own. 'You went there voluntarily—you said so yourself—and you weren't at all bothered about the consequences *then*. You didn't care about any potential babies *then*. All you cared about was getting back at your father! It was *your* idea, so if there's any blaming to be done you have to take a fair share for yourself.'

'Anonymity was intrinsic to the whole process,' he tore at her savagely. 'And if my sperm wasn't stolen then why is it I feel *raped*?'

Jennifer went slack against the door, her defensive anger shattered by his tormented bewilderment. Her fingers relaxed on his straining muscles, and she began unconsciously soothing him with tiny movements of her fingertips. Her mind reeled at the knowledge that her selfish attempts to protect herself had caused him such pain. She couldn't bear it.

'No, oh, no, no, no…' She shook her head, the blunt-cut ends of her hair fluttering across his white knuckles. Her eyes were dark with empathy. 'Please don't say that, don't even *think* it; it's not that way at all—'

'No? So tell me the way it is, Jennifer,' he said harshly. 'Make me feel less violated. Tell me how a woman who makes a living out of caring for other people, who sacrifices her career for her disabled mother, who spends her own money building up a business so two old people will feel secure and needed, who's a sucker for a wounded stray…tell me how a woman like that could knowingly exploit a sick old man's obsession for what she could get out of it. Did the money really mean that much to you?'

It was the 'knowingly' that did it. Jennifer's own sick sense of betrayal came rushing back.

'*Will you stop talking about the money?*' she said fiercely. '*Yes*, Sebastian gave me a marriage settlement, and, *yes*, I took it. But I *didn't do it for the money.*'

'Then in God's name *why*?' He shook her shoulders in a violent fit of frustration. 'What else did you hope to gain from it? His name? His power?'

He was so smart, yet he still couldn't see it! Because it hadn't mattered at all to him, while to her it was *every-thing*.

'A *baby*!' She yelled her contempt for his blind stupidity. '*That's* what I had to gain! I made a bargain to marry Sebastian because I wanted to have a baby!'

His hands fell away. He looked utterly thunderstruck, and, perversely, that gave her the courage to carry on.

'I did it to have a baby,' she admitted painfully, crossing her arms under her breasts. 'All right? I did it because I wanted a baby of my own and Sebastian promised to give me one if I helped him secure the trust against the witches.'

She saw his expression change from one of stunned incomprehension to raging incredulity. Next, she was certain, would be disgust.

'Well, what was I *supposed* to do?' she cried. 'I'm twenty-seven, single, not in a relationship—not even *interested* in getting married....there was no way I was going to get pregnant naturally, unless I was willing to pick up a man just for sex...and I didn't want my baby to be born out of some sordid liaison that I would be ashamed of—not to mention the risks of doing something like that. But I did want a child of my own so much...'

She turned her face aside so that he wouldn't see the sheen in her eyes as she remembered her fierce yearning for a dream that had seemed to be slipping further and

further out of her reach. A hand under her chin forced
her to look back at him. The humiliating look of disbelief had gone from his eyes, but it wasn't disgust that
she saw in its place; it was a dawning wonderment.

'Th-then Sebastian came back to stay,' she said huskily. 'And it seemed natural to talk about it with him—
he'd spent his life helping people to have children. We
talked about options, and then he told me about his pros-
tate cancer, and said we could help each other. He…he
offered a way for me to get pregnant that would be completely clinical and safe…and free. It was like a miracle.
All I had to do was have my doctor do some tests, accompany him to England…a-and marry him—'

'*All…?*' Rafe's hand smoothed her towelling lapel,
creased by her anxious kneading.

She flushed at his sarcasm. 'It was so that Felicity
wouldn't get her hands on the trust,' she said flatly. 'He
said there was a loophole, that she'd be able take over
as trustee when he died, or before that if he got very ill
and was judged incompetent, because she was his most
recent wife.'

Rafe opened his mouth as if to protest, then closed it
again, and after a brief hesitation said drily, 'He must
have trusted you to the hilt.'

'He knew I only cared about the baby,' Jennifer said
with touching naïveté. 'Under our bargain we *both* got
what we most wanted—I had my baby and he got my
name on all his legal documents…'

'And a grandchild to bear his name,' he reminded her
heavily. 'So it never made you feel queasy that it was
my baby he was bargaining with? You never wondered
if maybe *I* had a right to know he was putting his grandchild into your womb…'

She whirled away towards the windows, putting her
hands to her hot cheeks.

Tell him.

He knew his father, knew the lengths he'd been willing to go to get his own way. Why should she protect Sebastian any longer when he hadn't protected *her*?

Tell him.

She could feel Rafe on her heels, pursuing her for an answer, but she couldn't turn, couldn't face him.

'It wasn't supposed to be yours,' she whispered wretchedly.

'What?' He circled in front of her, catching her by the sleeve. '*What* did you say?'

But she didn't have to repeat it. He stared at her anguished embarrassment, the echo of disillusionment in her shimmering eyes, and she saw it all come together in his mind, saw the precise moment when the intuitive leap of his intelligence suddenly made sense of all the confusing contradictions.

'My God…he didn't tell you,' he breathed, the realisation transformed into instant, utter certainty. He peeled her hands gently away from her scalding cheeks. 'The manipulating bastard didn't tell you that the donated sperm was mine. Did he? *Did he?*'

She shook her head, the tears that had been in abeyance for months spilling over—tears for her tarnished miracle.

'I—I didn't know whose it was; I didn't *want* to know,' she cried. 'You just fill in a questionnaire about the physical characteristics you'd like the father to have…I did put down tall and blond, and—but I never— it wasn't… He didn't tell me until that awful afternoon at the hospital, the day he died.' Another sob tore from her aching chest. 'He…he s-said that he'd been wrong not to tell me from the beginning, but that it didn't change our bargain, it didn't have to matter… But it did, oh, *it did!*'

She closed her eyes in memory of the devastating shock. 'I didn't know he was going to tell you as well.

I know I shouldn't have run away from the hospital like that, but, oh, God—how could I have stayed? I didn't know what to do, what to think…I felt so alone. How could he expect me to see you, to talk to you, to act naturally around you knowing…knowing that…?'

'Ah, don't, Jennifer…don't!' Rafe gathered her against his bare torso, rocking her with his strength, sinking his fingers into her soft brown hair and combing it soothingly against the back of her skull, letting her sob out her repressed anger and betrayal.

Her damp face buried in the crisp curls on his chest, her arms wrapped around his solid waist, Jennifer couldn't help but become aware of the growing tension in his body as her storm of emotion eased and he continued to stroke her back and nuzzle at her hair, murmuring nonsensical words of reassurance, acknowledging that they had both been victims of his father's hidden scheming.

He wiped her face with her towelling lapel and then proceeded to erase the evidence of her tears with kisses, his lips moving down over her tangled lashes to her pink nose and the salty traces on her cheeks. Her lips, still rosy from his previous kisses, were tasted and savoured anew.

'Rafe…'

His hand, tangled in her hair, wouldn't let her evade his sensual assault.

'Tell me what it feels like to have me inside you?' he whispered into her mouth.

She groaned.

'You love it, don't you?' He sipped the husky sound from her lips. 'In spite of everything that's happened, you love the feeling that your body is changing, ripening, stretching itself to fit around my baby…'

His long, languorous kisses and sinuous words made

her feel exquisitely feminine, earthy and voluptuously sensual.

'Share the feeling with me, Jen. Let me make love to the mother of my child…'

Shaken by the intensity of need in his voice, she leaned back to look into his face and was surprised when he instantly let her go.

She put a hand to her breast and took an uncertain step back, her face flushed with a mingling of guilt and desire as she realised he was giving her the freedom to choose.

'We shouldn't…'

Rafe's body surged into full arousal as he recognised the implicit surrender in her thready protest. The guilty fascination with which her eyes furtively caressed him was a fierce turn-on. It made him want to tear off her clothes and thrust inside her without preliminaries, staking his claim and slaking his raw lust before she could change her mind. But even stronger was his greedy desire to draw out the process of sensuous discovery as long as possible, to spend a long time exploring, arousing, tasting, teasing…making her moan and thresh with orgasmic pleasure before he finally granted them both release. He wanted to be the lover she would never be able to forget.

'You want me,' he said, deliberately thickening his voice, permeating it with a gravelly sexuality, simultaneously both rough and smooth.

Jennifer could no longer deny it, to herself or to him, but she found she couldn't look him in the face as she admitted one of her most private fantasies.

She turned and looked out across the balcony, to the mountain whose eruption symbolised the irrepressible forces of nature. Like the force that ensured the survival of a species, the overpowering urge of male and female to mate, to reproduce…

'Yes. But just for tonight,' she added quickly, thinking that at least she could circumscribe her sin. Wrapped in her own doubts, she didn't consider she might be insulting his male ego.

'Just one reckless night of forbidden love,' he agreed softly, attuning himself so perfectly to her thoughts that her shoulders slumped with relief. She would not have been so relieved if she had glimpsed the grim amusement with which he had accepted her unconscious challenge

He stepped up behind her, sliding his palms from her shoulders down over her breasts to her waist.

'Shall we begin?'

In the glass doors Jennifer could see his reflection, his naked chest rising behind her shoulder, his green eyes glinting mysteriously, his hands graceful as they slowly untied her belt, knowing that this time she wasn't going to stop him.

Her robe fell open, revealing the shimmering wisp of thin forest-green silk that skimmed her body to the tops of her thighs. The shoestring straps supported a plunging scooped neckline that exposed most of the upper curves of her full breasts, the undarted bodice stretching provocatively between the two concealed peaks and then falling away to follow the indentation of her waist and smooth over her rounded hips to flirt around the V of her legs.

She found she was trembling as he looked down over her shoulder at what he had uncovered. She heard him suck in his breath at the sight of her firm creamy breasts straining against the watery silk, their faint tracery of blue veins guiding the way down to her barely concealed nipples.

'Sexy,' he growled, fingering the pure silk hem where it lay against her hip, but otherwise touching her with only his eyes as he lifted the robe from her shoulders

and let it fall in a hush to the floor, leaving her exposed
to his reflected view. Very exposed. She was suddenly
conscious of her overripe breasts and broad hips. Her
breath quickened, tugging at the silk.

'You wore this for me,' he said, still not touching her.
'You knew all along you were going to say yes...'

She licked her lips. 'No—I—all my night things are
s-sexy...'

'S-sexy...' he teased, and shivers ran up and down
her spine as she watched his hands come around her
waist to settle on her belly and begin to inch the silk up
from her thighs.

'What am I going to see next?' he whispered, nibbling
at her shoulder. 'Are you wearing anything underneath
this little bit of nothing?'

'Y-yes.'

'Spoilsport.'

He ravelled the silk higher with his gathering fingers
and sighed when he saw the reflection of a tiny stretch-
lace G-string.

'Or maybe not...' He ran his fingers down the lace
edging that splayed over her hip, down between her legs
to a place that made her gasp. His fingers fluttered with
unbelievable delicacy against the plump folds pouting
against the lace while his other hand moved up from her
waist to languorously fondle her breasts, sliding beneath
the silk to find her soft, velvety nipples.

'Do you like watching what I'm doing to you, darling?'

She did. It was wilder even than her reckless imagination. Fierce thrills cascaded over her in waves as she
revelled in the wanton sight of the big, half-naked man
standing behind his lover, his hands moving on her,
pleasuring her, enslaving her with his skill.

He pulled aside her G-string and bit her ear as his
fingertips teased inside her slippery heat and he whis-

pered, 'Would you like me to take you here, like this, from behind, so that you can see it happen to you?'

Her mind exploded in a riot of sensation which had her crying out and jerking so violently that she twisted out of his grasp, surprising them both.

The fantasy interrupted, Jennifer floundered for a few breathless seconds. After what Rafe had just been doing to her she felt unbelievably, stupidly shy. She had been wildly aroused, but what about him? Wasn't she supposed to be giving *him* pleasure, too? All her stories and fantasies were conducted from the female point of view; she'd never had to consider the *man's* pleasure. And one lover followed by more than six years of celibacy hadn't exactly equipped her with confidence for the real thing!

She glanced at Rafe, to find him locked in his own world, his head tipped back and his eyes closed, his chest rising and falling as if he'd been running, his arms hanging tense at his sides, the curled fingers of one hand glistening with a faint slick of moisture that it made her blush to see it. He looked as if he was praying to some pagan god, and out in the darkness a molten fireburst accompanied by another crackle of silver brilliance seemed to be his answer.

'Oh, l-look—have you seen the lightning over the mountain...' Jennifer babbled, putting her hands against the glass doors and pushing them open. The wind must have shifted, for there was only a slight grittiness in the air as she stepped out onto the balcony. She immediately realised she was being gauche and foolish, and looked back over her shoulder. Rafe had opened his eyes and she could see the laughter in them as he slowly followed her out onto the wooden planks, but her silly nervousness vanished as she saw that, rather than mocking, his amusement was indulgent.

His thick lashes lowered and she realised he was hungrily watching the way the dark silk clung to the cheeks of her bottom as she moved and revealed flashes of the lush white globes left bare by her G-string. Feeling her confidence return in a ripple of wicked delight, she gripped the cool balcony rail and leaned forward slightly, her face still turned mischievously towards him to assess his reaction.

'Minx,' he said, studying the charmingly provocative pose with a connoisseur's approval. 'But I thought we came out here to look at a volcano erupting.'

'I'd rather watch you,' she dared confess.

'Watch me erupting?' His smile sizzled through her senses as he moved closer and cupped her downy bottom underneath the flirty hem. 'Do you want to see me lose control?' he murmured as he handled the peachy softness, tugging at the G-string to create an intimate friction between her legs.

Her fingers tightened on the rail as she unconsciously arched her back and bowed her head. 'Yes, I think I do.' She shuddered. She didn't want to be the only one...

'Then come to bed,' he purred into the nape of her neck. 'You're cold.'

She felt she would never be cool again. 'No, I'm not...'

She gasped as his hands slid up to cup her breasts, rounding them, his thumbs rubbing at her stiffened nipples.

'Then I guess you must be aroused.'

He bent his head and bit the tender curve of her neck, between nape and shoulder, his teeth grating gently against her flesh while his hands moved lazily on her breasts, his hips pushing rhythmically against the crease of her bottom, letting her feel the length of swollen shaft.

He spun her around and kissed her, hard and fast, hooking his fingers under her slender straps, pulling them sharply down her arms so that the slithery silk was dragged below her breasts, spilling their pale bounty over the shadowy fabric, an erotic contrast in colour and texture. He shaped the creamy curves and stroked the darkened tips, rolling them gently between his fingertips before bending to take them in his mouth, suckling each one in turn until they were unbearably sensitised.

His hand swept under her bottom and he lifted her in his arms, his mouth buried in hers as he carried her back inside and over to the bed, pushing her down, down, down into the feathery depths. He stripped the silk slip down over her hips and thighs and threw it off the bed, then he did the same with her G-string, his hands kneading her belly and breasts, his mouth stealing across the hidden delta of her womanhood to nuzzle into the musky darkness, his tongue lapping at the tiny budded erection there until she was racked with helpless convulsions.

Only then did he kick off his black drawstring trousers, drawing her hands down to his hugely jutting manhood, groaning thickly in ecstasy as he showed her how he liked to be touched and found her inventive enthusiasm more than he could handle and stay in control.

To Jennifer it was a dazzling revelation, beyond anything she had imagined, to have this sleek, powerful, sexy, sophisticated lover shuddering in her arms, lavishing her with his sensual praise, begging for her touch and responding to the lightest stroke of her mouth with savage abandon.

Finally he rolled over onto his back, his sweat-slicked muscles bulging as he lifted her to straddle his hips, his green eyes smouldering at her strangled cry of surprise.

'Yes…like this,' he said, his hands tightening on her hips as he teased himself against her satiny moistness. 'This way you can control how much of me you take inside you.' He gritted his teeth, finally remembering to ask, 'Is this safe?'

'If you mean will I get pregnant,' she said giddily, 'I already am.'

He shuddered, the tip of his broad shaft slipping inside her. 'No, I meant for the baby?'

'Yes, it's safe. As long as you're not too rough...' Her fingers raked through his chest hair, her hair tumbling over her feverish face as she leaned eagerly over him, her voluptuous breasts swaying towards his mouth. She wanted him and she wanted him *now*!

His eyes darkened as he eased her gently down, stretching her, sheathing himself tightly within her clinging warmth. 'I'll take good care of you, darling, I promise,' he told her. 'I'll make sure that every single orgasm is mellow and sweet and strong...'

CHAPTER SEVEN

JENNIFER stretched luxuriantly as she felt sunlight across her closed eyes, arching her back and pushing her toes towards the bottom of the bed, a delicious sense of well-being permeating her awakening body. Suspended half-way between waking and dreaming, she nestled on her side in her downy hollow, a slow smile curving her lips as she continued to drift on the lazy wings of her favourite erotic fantasy. She had Raphael Jordan at her mercy, his glorious, nude, aroused body tied to her bed, leashed for her pleasure. He was fighting against his silken bonds, his green eyes blazing fiercely as he begged—but he wasn't begging to be set free; oh, no, he wanted her to keep him, he wanted her to keep him for ever because he knew she was the only woman in the world who could satisfy his craving for love...

Jennifer sighed as the sensuous warmth in her belly moved up to her breasts, exploring their relaxed shape, insinuating into the soft cleft between the pillowed mounds and encircling them with—

Jennifer's eyes popped open and crossed to find Rafe nose to nose with her on the pillow.

'Good morning, darling,' he purred, and kissed her as if he had every right to, taking his time, enjoying the muffled sounds she was making as she struggled to separate fact from fantasy.

'What were you dreaming about? You looked like the cat that got the cream,' he murmured, slowly withdrawing with a series of little pecks around her sleepy mouth.

She could feel her temperature go up, and the give-away flutter of her lashes made him offer her a sultry,

116

knowing grin. 'You were squirming and rolling your hips, and making those sighing little moans you make when you have a man between your thighs...'

She flushed at the wanton image of herself. 'You were touching me!' she accused, looking down at his hands, which were still cupping her breasts. She noticed the faint red marks marring the creamy roundness, patches of whisker-burn and little pink crescents where Rafe's mouth had feasted greedily on her succulent flesh.

'I couldn't resist,' he said, snuggling closer, his lower legs entangling with hers under the bedclothes, which she discovered had been pushed down around their hips. 'You're so sexy when you're asleep, all soft and pliant and innocently arousing. Are you going to breastfeed?'

'Wh-what?'

Her sleep-deprived brain found it difficult to cope with the sudden switch from sexual banter to questions of maternity. Rafe had kept his promise with spectacular success, and mellow, sweet and strong had taken them far through the night. Long after the mountain outside the window had died back into a quiet smoulder, the molten passion had continued to seethe and pulse in the confines of the wide feather bed. Somewhere, also in the dark reaches of the night, they had talked about what Sebastian had done, comparing their versions of the truth, tacitly avoiding any mention of the future. Now he was back to the future with a vengeance.

'The baby? Are you going to suckle our baby at your breasts?' His hands contracted, her soft nipples slipping between his fingers. 'A mother's milk is important for a newborn baby's immunity; it's full of antibodies and guards against all sorts of infections later, even some chronic diseases. If you want to give your baby the best protection, you should breastfeed for at least six months, even a year or more...'

He was looking at her breasts as if they were miracles

of wonder, and she could feel them begin to firm under his possessive gaze. 'How do you know?' she asked hoarsely, stunned by his command of the facts.

'I bought a book. I read it coming over here on the plane.' He lifted his eyes to hers, his expression faintly defiant. 'That's how I know you can't feel the baby move inside you yet; it's still only about ten centimetres long.'

He had been reading up about pregnancy and childbirth? Warning bells began to clang in Jennifer's mind as his attention returned to her breasts and a faint frown marred his tanned forehead. He traced around her dark areola.

'Your nipples are already quite large, and they're going to grow bigger as you become more heavily pregnant…you don't think they might get to be too much of a mouthful for a tiny baby?'

Jennifer forgot the bells. Ever conscious of her robust figure, she was prepared to hit back at him until, incredulously, she realised that he was genuinely anxious. Mr 'I bought a book' had gaps in his learning!

'Of course not.' Her tremulous reply was torn between laughter and anger. 'God doesn't make those kind of design faults. Breasts are expressly *designed* to feed babies, whatever their respective sizes.'

He heard the hint of hurt in her tone and shrewdly guessed its source, the planes of his face tautening. 'And to give pleasure,' he added huskily, his thumbs pressing lightly over the stiffening tips. 'I love your womanly proportions. I love the roundness of your bottom and the size of your breasts. And I especially like the way your nipples fill my mouth when I suck them. Last night you loved me doing that…'

His sexual frankness had its usual devastating effect. 'L-last night was last night,' she said shakily, remembering the caveat she had issued before their lovemaking.

He was remembering it, too, and his rebellious reaction. His thumbs continued to brush back and forth as he watched the lambent glow in her brown eyes grow. His thighs moved against her and she felt the brush of his heavy loins. 'I'd like to watch you feeding our baby.'

She wished he would stop calling it *our* baby. 'Well, you can't, you won't be here. You'll be back in England when the baby's born...'

'I could visit you.' His potent arousal was growing against her belly.

The suggestion crept like a thief into her soul, rifling her treasury of dreams.

'C-come all this way just t-to watch me feed the baby?' Jennifer stammered, watching him edge closer and closer, knowing that she was playing with fire, but unable to resist the lure of the heat.

'That and...other things.' He bent his head and showed her what those other things were, and in a slow, tender, lazy coupling, vastly different from the sizzling passion of the night before, Jennifer learned a new appreciation of her lover's sensuous skills.

Later, lying weak and dewy in the aftermath of his magnificent possession, Jennifer suddenly noticed the angle of the sun in the sky.

She sat bolt upright, dragging the duvet with her.

'What time is it?'

Rafe yawned, scrubbing his fingers through his streaky gold hair. 'I don't know; I took off my watch last night.'

Jennifer had left hers in the bathroom. She hitched up the duvet and lunged across his supine chest to squint short-sightedly at the small digital clock on the bedside table. She let out a little squawk when the blurry numbers swam into focus.

'Oh, no, it's after eleven o'clock!' she discovered, sinking back onto her knees. 'What about the breakfasts? What will everyone be thinking?'

'Maybe they'll think you stayed up late watching Ruapehu erupt and then slept in because you were tired,' suggested Rafe, with a rakishly innocent air.

She hugged the duvet to her breasts, her brown eyes stormy at his teasing.

'Or they could think that you spent all night making mad, passionate love with your husband and then lingered in bed for his morning wake-up call. Everyone knows that most men are inclined to be amorous in the mornings, especially ones who've just come back from a sex-starved excursion to the Amazonian jungle.'

Jennifer's glare became a dignified scowl. She shook her hair behind her shoulders and looked down her sharp nose at him. The disdainful effect was rather ruined by the ruffled nipple peeping at him from the crook of her arm, but he was enjoying the view too much to point it out.

'I know I often wake up with an erection,' he confided cheerfully, for the pure, wicked pleasure of seeing her blush.

She did, her haughty pose completely disintegrating as he continued silkily, 'Of course, having a voluptuous nude threshing about next to me in the throes of an erotic dream probably had something to do with this morning's delectable awakening.'

Pink and flustered, Jennifer massed the duvet around her, preparatory for a dive towards the puddle of pink towelling on the floor, knowing that Rafe was probably going to hang onto his share of the bedclothes so that she would be forced to abandon her cover just short of her goal.

In the event she was wrong; Rafe let go of the duvet as she made her half-spring, half-tumble, and she was able to hurriedly struggle into her bathrobe under the modest shroud, only to emerge and find him lying bold, bare and beautiful on the rumpled white sheet in a disconcertingly similar manner to the love-supplicant in her dreams. Even the slightly out of focus softness around the edges of her vision were vaguely dream-like.

Averting her eyes, she threw the duvet over him and hurried to snatch up the scraps of green silk and lace from the floor.

'I'm going to have a shower—'

'Is that an invitation?' He was rearranging the bed-clothes over himself, obviously in no hurry to abandon his—*her*—sybarite bed.

'No!' She made an effort to calm down, nibbling her lip and discovering it felt uncomfortably tender. 'Last night—well, it happened, and I accept my share of responsibility for it, but it's not going to happen a second time...'

'Just a one-night stand,' he agreed blandly, turning the top sheet down over his chest and folding his hands on it in an attitude of deceptive piety.

She felt terrible. She was reducing the most enravishing experience of her life to the status of a fleeting encounter. And she had told him that she hadn't wanted to be involved in any sordid liaisons!

'Tonight things are going to be different,' she announced, tacitly acknowledging that he wasn't simply going to fade out of her life, that the ties between them had become too complex to sever quickly or easily.

He looked at her stubborn face and smoothly preempted her argument. 'Of course they will be. Now that we've made love every which way, and got the uncomfortable lust for each other thoroughly out of our systems, we can relax into physical indifference.'

Since he had taken the words right out of her mouth, Jennifer had no right to feel so disappointed. She hid her chagrin behind a tight smile. He made it sound so…so boringly *commonplace*. Perhaps it was—for *him*. Surely nobody got that mind-blowingly good at making love without a lot of practice.

'I'm not in the habit of having one-night stands,' she pointed out.

'Neither am I, although I must admit to a few in my testosterone-driven modelling years. Now I prefer more satisfying relationships. And I'm very careful of my health, so you needn't worry on that score.'

She was embarrassed to realise that it hadn't even entered her head. Her pregnancy had seemed to make a condom superfluous, and with a shock she realised that she had also subconsciously harboured a bone-deep trust in Rafe's regard for her physical well-being.

'If I hadn't already guessed that you hadn't had a great deal of sexual experience, I would have known it as soon as I entered you,' he continued. 'You were very tight. You weren't a virgin by any chance?'

She would never get used to his blunt way of approaching delicate topics.

'No, of course not!' she said, rattled that he should have thought so. Had she been clumsy, inept? 'I think even Sebastian might have drawn the line at arranging a virgin birth!'

'Then it must have been a while for you—I remember you saying you had no prospect of getting pregnant naturally…'

He was obviously angling to know, so she certainly wasn't going to tell him.

'And for you, judging from your hurry to get me into bed,' she snipped.

'My last long-term companion dumped me ten months ago when she decided that I meant what I'd said all along about not ever marrying her.'

Jennifer's eyes widened. 'You haven't had sex in ten months?'

'I've been busy.' He grinned at her expression, teasing, 'I know you think of me as your rampant sex-god, but I do perform other functions in life. Just because I'm good at it doesn't mean I'm profligate with my talent. If anything it's the reverse—once you've experienced how intense sex can be with the right person, you get bored with bonking the fluff.'

'You weren't bored last night,' she accused hotly, incensed at being reduced to a casual 'bonk'. That was even less meaningful than a one-night stand!

His grin widened. 'But you're not a piece of fluff, darling, you're my wife.'

She slammed the bathroom door on his smirking face and then had to go back out and fetch her clothes, attempting to ignore the way he rolled over to watch her, his green eyes following her from wardrobe to drawer, to dressing table and back to the bathroom.

'Don't use all the hot water, honey,' he sang out after her in a parody of domestic affection.

If it wasn't for the need to save water she *would* have run the *en suite* bathroom's small hot water cylinder cold, but she had to settle instead for rifling the toiletries he had placed on the shelf next to her things and maliciously running the battery of his expensive electric razor flat by shaving her legs with it and then leaving it to buzz on a towel while she had her quick shower.

Having washed and blowdried her hair the previous night, she was forced to linger over cleaning her teeth until the razor gave its last, sick cough and puttered into silence. Now he would have to recharge it before he gave that designer stubble a graze, and her petty sense of revenge had her smiling as she returned to the bedroom warmly dressed in a green tartan skirt and pale yellow blouse.

Rafe had gone out onto the balcony, and she was relieved to see that he had donned his drawstring pyjama trousers.

'Looks like the mountain has gone back to belching just steam and ash,' he said, coming back inside and shutting the doors against the strongly sulphurous smell, the skin on his torso puckered from the southerly chill. 'The wind seems to be pushing the plumes higher, but it's difficult to tell because the sky is pretty grey and there's still a low haze drifting this way.'

His bare feet made slight tracks on the floor, and Jennifer remembered that after their sizzling little piece of foreplay on the balcony the glass doors had stood open for some time before Rafe had got up and closed them during the night. Fine ash had sifted over the polished floorboards by the doors and she hoped that it hadn't drifted as far as her desk. Her computer, inclined to be a little bit temperamental, would not take kindly to volcanic dust clogging its cyberpores.

A loud thump against the door to the stairs made Rafe glance at her with a droll expression.

'Someone come to complain about their breakfast, do you think?'

Another thud made the door shake, and she hurried across the room.

'It's just Bonzer, head-butting the door,' she explained. 'He usually comes up in the mornings.'

But when she opened the door it wasn't only Bonzer, but Milo, too. The cat strolled under the dog as he bounced forward and his paw accidentally clipped her ear. With an offended yowl Milo took off, springing onto the bed, and, ecstatically responding to the unexpected game, Bonzer followed.

'No, Bonzer, no!' cried Jennifer ineffectually as cat and dog careered around the room, barking and yowling.

'Catch him!' she yelled to Rafe as Bonzer shot past

him for the third time, but he was laughing too much, for it was obvious the nimble cat was taunting her clumsy pursuer by sticking to the high points of furniture while the dog dashed a parallel course at floor level.

Finally Milo made a mistake, leaping onto the top of the woven laundry basket, which looked stable enough for a doggy brain to figure it would support a more substantial weight.

Cat, dog and laundry basket went flying, and the last Jennifer saw of the two guilty animals they were racing down the stairs, Bonzer trailing a shocking-pink lace demi-bra from the buckle on his collar and with a transparent stocking flying like a flag on his tail.

'Anyone who sees him is going to think he's a decadent dog who's come off a hard night on the tiles,' chuckled Rafe as he crouched to pick up the overturned basket. 'Hello…what's this? Do you usually wash books along with your sexy under—'

He stopped, rocking on his haunches as he picked up one of the slim paperbacks and recognised the familiar black-edged cover.

'Well, well, well…' His stunned eyes rose speculatively to her appalled face. 'I see you're a fan of Velvet Books…apparently a *big* fan,' he added, stirring the betraying pile.

'I—I—'

'Why keep them in with your dirty laundry? Is that supposed to be an ironic commentary on their contents?'

Thank God he didn't realise that the books *were* her dirty laundry!

'Or were they hidden away for my benefit?' he guessed shrewdly. 'I noticed a few gaps on your bookcase. You don't have to be ashamed that you enjoy erotic stories, Jennifer…nobody should have to apologise for their leisure reading. And I can attest to the fact that Velvet Books are well crafted and well written, and they're specifically written *by* women *for* women. I'm the one who developed the line from a small, under-staffed, under-invested part of the company into a major publishing success.'

'I— I'm not ashamed,' she lied.

'Then why care whether I see them or not?' he said. He began to stack the slender books in a pile, noting the titles. 'I see Lacey Graham is your favourite. I guess you've realised from the setting of her books that she's a New Zealander? We have two Kiwis writing for us and five Australians—about two hundred and forty regular writers worldwide, and more unsolicited manuscripts than we can handle since we moved up-market and began establishing a mainstream readership. Lacey's one of our hottest sellers, and I'm grooming her to be number one...'

'*You're* grooming her?' Jennifer grabbed the oak slats of the curving bed-end, her legs feeling like wet noodles as she watched Rafe carry the books over to the bookcase and begin plugging the gaps.

'I've been her editor ever since I took over Velvet Books and started revitalising the line.'

'*Sariel?*' All oxygen had vanished from the room, leaving her lungs only a breathy wheeze.

He looked up sharply. 'What did you say?'

'I said, seriously? Are you really?' Jennifer improvised shrilly, slurring the words.

There was only one way she could possibly know that the name of Lacey Graham's editor was Sariel.

He tapped one of the books against his chin, studying her wilting figure thoughtfully. She hated that look; it seemed to reach deep down inside her and plunder her mysteries.

'What's she like?' she asked, hoping to throw him off the track. 'Is she attractive?'

'Her mind certainly is; I don't know about the rest of

her.' He slotted the book into place and watched her nervous smile flutter as she tried to act like an eager fan.

'Why not?'

'Because we've never met. All our dealings with each other are by letter, via a firm of lawyers in Auckland.'

Her legs began to regain some of their strength. 'What about her voice? Haven't you ever spoken to her on the telephone?'

'She prefers the written word. She lives somewhere fairly isolated and says she resents the encroachment of modern technology on her privacy. If I ever need to communicate with her urgently I send a fax or an E-mail to the lawyer.'

Who then promptly faxed or E-mailed it on to Jennifer!

She had never meant her writing to be taken seriously. It had just been a secret pleasure, a stimulating hobby with which to relieve the boredom and tension of every-day life when she had been struggling to support her slowly convalescing mother. Abandoned by her fiancé, missing dreadfully the brother to whom she had been so close and coping with several emotionally demanding jobs, as well as constantly presenting a cheerful front to Paula's frightening fits of depression, Jennifer had desperately needed a harmless way to let off steam.

Her mother had probably believed her young daughter was going to the altar as a virgin, but Jennifer and Michael had been unable to restrain their ardour, and after their engagement had been broken Jennifer had found herself missing those private lovemaking sessions at his flat, where she had been able to give her passionate nature free rein, secure in the knowledge of their loving relationship. She had been shocked when her physical desires didn't fade away after she relinquished her love. Not wanting to risk going through the same agony of rejection with another man, she had thrown herself into creating safe fantasies about wildly passionate heroines and impossibly sexy heroes who *never* rejected each other.

Writing erotic stories had proved enormous fun. The secret vice had made her feel dangerously naughty while at the same time allowing her to remain totally in control of the events she was describing. The adrenaline rush of writing them also conveniently sublimated her sex drive. As her inhibitions over seeing her words in print loosened, her brief sexual fantasies grew longer and more involved, the writing more explicitly erotic, her characters more complex and plots more complicated until she'd realised that she had the equivalent of two short novels stored on her computer.

She would never have plucked up the courage to do anything with them if, one day, the wind hadn't whisked away one of the discards she was burning in the garden incinerator and been fielded by Sebastian. He had teased her that the scorching words hardly needed a match to ignite them, but instead of betraying her secret or scoffing at her efforts he had told her he could recommend her to a contact at a London publishing house which specialised in women's erotica.

Jennifer had been far too timid to take him up on it, but Sebastian, after he had got back to London, had sent her the publishing house's address and told her that she could deal in complete anonymity if she chose—even the publisher need not know her real name if she cared to go to the bother of concealing it through an agent or lawyer—and that a number of Velvet authors chose to similarly protect their identities for both personal and professional reasons.

Four years later Jennifer had nine books to the credit of 'Lacey Graham' and two more in the works, and still hadn't figured out a way to admit to her mother that the majority of her income was now coming from something other than the bed and breakfast business. The last six-monthly payment of royalties had been the most substantial yet, and her editor had been encouraging her to be even more prolific.

Her editor.

Her interest had been piqued three years ago, when her previous, female editor had left Velvet and a witty letter had arrived from the new one, jokingly introducing himself under the pen-name 'Sariel', a play on Jennifer's persistent refusal to provide any personal information about herself. She had replied in similar vein, saying that a fantasy editor was the perfect choice for a fantasy writer, and that she appreciated the added buffer from reality since she found the idea of working with a male rather inhibiting. That exchange had set the tone for their diverting professional relationship. Lacey had remained Lacey and Sariel had remained Sariel ever since. The fact that he was male had been less important than the fact that he proved a superbly inspirational editor and an extremely entertaining correspondent.

She realised that Rafe was wearing 'that look' again, and hastily said, 'Well, I guess she has good reason for avoiding interruptions. Most writers are rather solitary by nature, aren't they?'

'Mmm? Oh, yes, I suppose so.' Instead of placing the last book on the shelf with the others he began to idly thumb through it. From the title she realised it was one of her earlier works, written before he had become her editor.

'Do you, uh, work with many other writers?' She wanted to know whether her 'special' relationship with Sariel was so special after all.

'Not directly. I selected a few I thought had special potential to work with when I first took over as editorial director, but I'm mainly in a consulting role now that Velvet is strongly established. I kept Lacey, though, because we're such a successful combination it would be a shame to break us up, and working with her still gives me an enormous kick...' He smiled down at the page, whether at something he read or at his own thoughts she couldn't tell.

So now she was a kept woman. Kept by Raphael Jordan. Father of her child. Goodness, he was already paying her child support and he didn't even know it!

Far from being a stranger, in some ways Rafe knew her almost as well as she knew herself. No wonder they had been so attuned to each other in bed—they had been sharing erotic fantasies for years!

Although she knew he must be very familiar with her work, and was probably regarding it with a serious professional eye, it gave her a shivery feeling of vulnerability to see him leafing through her book.

'Here, I'll put that back if you want to go and have your shower,' she offered, attempting to slip it out of his hand.

He waited until her fingers were almost touching it, then snapped it closed and tucked it under his arm. 'No, thanks,' he said. 'I think I'll re-read it. I did read Lacey's backlist when I took over as her editor, but I only vaguely remember what this one was about.'

He watched her seethe in thinly veiled frustration, intrigued by the definite tinge of urgency in her haste to get him off the subject of Lacey Graham. She was embarrassed, certainly, but there was something more...

'I'm sure there are other books here that you *haven't* read that you'd find interesting,' she was lecturing him. 'Ones that were written for *men*...'

He bit back a smile at the unspoken 'real' hanging in the air before 'men'. She *must* be desperate if she was standing there, pregnant with his baby, her body barely cooled from their hot night of love, trying to hint that he was less than masculine.

'I'm sure there are, but I'm not sexist in my reading habits. I want to read this one.' He patted the book under his arm. 'In fact, while I'm here I might re-read the whole set of Lacey Grahams.' He paused. 'Does that bother you, Jennifer?'

She bared her teeth at him. 'Of course not. But doesn't that make it a bit of a busman's holiday?'

'Not if I read them for *pleasure*,' he told her, effectively securing the last word as he sauntered off to the bathroom, still carrying the book.

Jennifer stumped downstairs to track down her dog-napped underwear, then had to hear her mother's fond assurances that naturally they hadn't expected the honeymoon couple to join them for breakfast.

'We're not on our honeymoon, Mum,' she protested, firmly shutting the door on memories of last night.

'No, but you can pretend,' said Paula, using her stick to limp back and forth across the living room floor as she sorted out cartons of clothes and magazines for the church bazaar. 'Anyway, the Wrights didn't get up for breakfast, either. They said they didn't get in until gone three a.m., but they got some marvellous footage of the eruption. I gave them some muffins and pikelets and a flask of coffee in lieu of breakfast, and they went off to see if the Department of Conservation would let them film some of the lahar sites. Do you think you'll ever wear this again, Jen?'

Her mother held up a crocheted orange mini-dress and Jennifer couldn't help smiling. She had been a schoolgirl when she last wore it. Her mother was a sentimental pack-rat. When Jennifer had converted the attic to a bedroom Paula had insisted on moving everything to the garage, and only when they had been unable to get the car in far enough to shut the door had she consented to winnowing out the chaff.

'I don't think so. Certainly not in the next six months,' she said drily.

'Did you get a chance to tell Rafe about the baby?'

Jennifer busied herself with sorting and folding. 'Yes.'

'I'd bet he was surprised.'

'You'd lose; he'd guessed already.' She felt mean when her mother's face fell.

'Oh.' She rallied. Once having conquered her depression, Paula had been resolute in finding silver linings. 'But I'll bet he was pleased.'

'He was...' She looked at her parent's brightly expectant blue eyes and sighed. 'He was pleased. It's just—being an only child and not having a very good relationship with his own father, I suppose he's a bit wary of what it entails.'

'Well, he strikes me as being a very determined man,' said Paula. 'I think that if he wants something badly enough he'll succeed in achieving it through sheer force of will if necessary.'

Jennifer had ample evidence of that. He had badly wanted her last night and he had certainly achieved *that* goal, though not, she admitted, purely from force of will. He had succeeded because, in spite of her insistence to herself that she was only interested in sex, Rafe already had a piece of her heart. Attracted as she had always been to him physically, it was the deeply sensitive man that she had glimpsed beneath the mocking cynic who had truly exerted the most powerful appeal. As soon as she had learned that he was the father of her baby she had felt a shocking sense of recognition, of inevitability, of jealousy and possessiveness that had sent her shooting off in the opposite direction. But she hadn't been able to outrun either Rafe or her own confused feelings. And now that she knew he was also Sariel he had unknowingly established another claim on her emotions—he was someone she liked and respected, and as Lacey Graham she knew her respect was reciprocated.

Respect and liking, however, were the last things she felt when Rafe came downstairs in jeans, white shirt and a shearling-lined corduroy jacket to receive her mother's lavish congratulations on his impending fatherhood. For he was still carrying her book, tucked visibly in the side pocket of his jacket.

He acknowledged her furtive glare with a grin as he told her mother that, no, he didn't care if it was a son or daughter, as long it was healthy and had Jennifer's beautifully expressive brown eyes.

Then he charmingly offered to help with their task.

'Oh, you don't have to do that, Rafe. You sit down and relax. You're on holiday. You deserve some rest after your marathon experience in the jungle. Dot says it's very physically draining, working in that type of climate.'

'I do feel rather physically drained after my recent experiences,' said Rafe, his mocking glance at Jennifer leaving her in no doubt as to the exact experiences he had in mind. 'But once you acclimatise yourself to a place or activity it's amazing how quickly you re-energise and find yourself ready for action again. Really, I'd like to help.'

'Well, you can do the magazines, then, since you're in the publishing business. Jen, you help Rafe—I'll do the clothes.'

'These are all at least ten years old!' discovered Rafe as he dug down to the bottom of the box.

'The box has been in the garage for years. Mum probably picked them up second-hand herself,' said Jennifer, with a sudden qualm. 'Some of these things are endlessly recycled around the various charity bazaars. Let's just put them all in—'

'Hey, I was featured in some of these.' Rafe's unshaven face was boyishly eager as he unearthed a few dusty copies of English *Vogue* and riffled through the pages. He looked ludicrously disappointed when he failed to find what he was looking for, and frowned as he ran his finger up the centre fold.

'The pages've been cut out!' He sounded as outraged as if someone had removed the frescoes from the Sistine chapel, and with an inner smile Jennifer realised that he had wanted to show off, to display his pride like a peacock to her admiring gaze.

'We probably used them to line Fergus's cage,' she couldn't resist saying, knowing she was making a noose for her own neck.

Sure enough, her mother punished her for her mean-spiritedness. 'More likely they're in Jen's scrapbook. Maybe you didn't know, but Sebastian used to carry a picture of you from *Esquire* magazine folded up in his wallet.'

Colour ran up under the tanned skin of Rafe's face and he looked down at his hands. 'No, I didn't know. He was always insulting about my choice of career.'

'Well, he showed it to us the first time we met him,' Paula continued gently, 'and told us that you took after your mother in looks and him in brains. After that, whenever Jen saw a picture of you in any of the old magazines I bought, she'd cut it out and put it in a book to show Sebastian the next time he came.'

Rafe's flush didn't fade as he turned to look at Jennifer, an arrested expression in his eyes. 'You mean I was your pin-up years before you even met me?' he murmured, the corner of his mouth turning up.

More than he knew!

'I didn't pin you up, I taped you down,' she said tartly.

'Sounds kinky, darling. Did I like it?'

'I was young and impressionable,' she said primly. 'You were the only famous, glamorous person I knew.'

'But you didn't know me.'

'By proxy I did.'

'Our relationship obviously started the way it was intended to go on,' he said drily, and then had to reintroduce the ubiquitous Amazon when Paula wanted to know what he had meant.

Dot came in from dusting her garden and they had a casual lunch of thick vegetable soup and home-baked bread rolls. While they were eating Rafe suggested that an ideal marketing ploy for Beech House might be to take advantage of Paula's special talents and offer residential cooking classes that would enable them to charge a premium rate for the combined accommodation and lessons. That led to a discussion of other, more fanciful ideas, but when Rafe talked about the potential of the upstairs bedroom being a luxury suite for those guests who didn't like sharing a bathroom, Jennifer felt constrained to point out that it was already occupied.

'True, but what if you didn't live here any more?'

Her eyes flashed a warning at him. What on earth was he trying to do?

'All of this is speculation, anyway. Mum couldn't possibly cope—' she began sharply.

'Well, now, dear, that's not quite true,' Paula interrupted mildly. 'I coped while you were away, and Susie has indicated she could work quite a few more hours. And there's Dot, of course. And if we needed any handiwork doing there's always Fergus—and he could help with the business end as well!'

Jennifer stared at her mother in consternation. Was she going mad?

'I don't see how a one-legged budgie is going to be much help when the roof needs patching, and I doubt that he can count to one, let alone do double-entry bookkeeping!'

She heard Rafe shout with laughter as her mother said,

'Not Fergus the bird. Fergus McDonald, from the Gourmet Club. I'm sure you met him, Jen, at one of the church dinners. He's a retired builder and he says he's always looking for something useful to do.'

'And someone to do it with,' added Dot darkly.

Jennifer watched as her mother turned pink and patted her hair.

Her mother? And a *man?*

She turned her accusing gaze on Rafe. This was all his fault. He was the one turning her life inside out and upside down, and now he was dragging her family into the conspiracy!

CHAPTER EIGHT

HE KNEW.

He knew.

All day, Jennifer couldn't shake off the uneasy feeling that Rafe knew more than he was letting on. It wasn't anything he said, it was rather what he did. He trailed her everywhere, helping her make the beds and change the towels, do what laundry could go in the drier, because she didn't want to risk hanging anything out in the still hazy air, relighting the fire and washing the windows with carefully measured amounts of water.

He insisted on sweeping the ash off the verandahs and rinsing down the paths and parking area himself, with buckets of water from the garden pond, because he didn't think a pregnant woman should breathe in too much dust—'It would be as bad as smoking'—and when she wrapped up warmly and took Bonzer for a walk in the gardens, and to fetch the mail from the end of the drive, he accompanied her, asking innumerable questions about Paula and her father and, when she mentioned him, her brother Ian, managing to ferret out of her the reasons for her broken engagement.

'So your first love turned out to have feet of clay.' He dismissed Michael with a contemptuous shrug. 'If he wasn't prepared to stick around when the going got tough, what kind of husband would he have made?' he growled. 'If I was in love with a woman and we had a problem, we'd work it out together.'

Jennifer felt a frisson of hope at his words. But then she reminded herself that any woman who could make a cynic like Raphael Jordan fall in love with her would

have to be very special—and very brave! 'I didn't think
you believed in love and commitment, or making promises.'

'It's not love and commitment I have the hang-up
about, it's marriage. Watching my father ring the
changes was a great incentive to bachelorhood. And I
have no problem making promises; I simply refuse to
make any that I know I won't keep.'

'What about your mother, hasn't she married again?'

'Twice, not happily. I think she was looking for another Sebastian. He was the one she really loved, but
she had too much pride and self-respect to live with a
man she couldn't trust, and he couldn't forgive *her* for
not forgiving *him*.'

Of the three of them perhaps it was the child, Raphael,
who had ultimately been the most damaged by the break-
up, she thought as they walked the lolloping dog back
to the house, her heart aching at this new insight into
his character. No wonder he was so determined not to
marry; to Raphael, family life was synonymous with uncertainty and turmoil rather than security and happiness.
But now that he was faced with the reality, not just the
abstract of fatherhood, he was being forced to confront
issues which had shaped his adult values, perhaps realising that he had deep-seated needs that his prejudices
had hitherto refused to acknowledge.

Her tender feelings didn't stop her feeling exasperated
when Rafe continued his campaign of friendly helpful-
ness, especially when the helping always managed to
involve some kind of touching. Finally, when she was
setting up the ironing board in her usual spot by the fire
in order to do her most disliked chore in comfort, she
got fed up with his hovering and snapped at him that it
was a one-woman job.

'In that case I'll just quietly read my book while I

keep you company,' he said, taking the wind out of her sails.

Which he did. He sprawled full-length on his back on the couch and read his Lacey Graham, the shush of the turning pages competing with the angry hiss of the steam iron and the crackle of the fire. Every now and then, when Jennifer looked at him out of the corner of her eye, she would find pensive green eyes staring at her over the top of the open book, then the thick lashes would fall and she would see the rapid flickering movements under his lids as he read on down the page.

Jennifer could feel the pressure inexorably building in her skull, like lava pushing up a blocked vent.

'Do you have to stare at me like that?' she erupted at last, after scorching one of their best table napkins trying to second-guess his thoughts.

'Sorry, was I staring?' His reflective gaze sharpened as she flicked her hair behind her ear and nervously adjusted her spectacles. 'I was just wondering…'

'Well, wonder in another direction,' she said, picking up another napkin.

'Listen to this.' He put a finger to the page. '"The man in the shadows stepped into the light—"'

'Those books aren't written to be read out loud,' she interrupted hastily, certain he was going to taunt her with her boldly explicit prose.

'But listen.'

She was disconcerted when he read out a passage which was a physical description of the book's hero, a lustful billionaire, who had kidnapped the prim, unawakened heroine and whisked her to his private tropical island to ravish and seduce her into being his sex slave, only to find the tables turned when his innocent captive discovered the true sensuality of her own nature. She even tied him to the bed at one stage, Jennifer remembered.

'Well?'

She hastily wiped off her dreamy smile. 'Well, what?'

'Don't you think he sounds familiar?'

'I've read the book, so of course it sounds familiar,' she said stiffly, saying a rude word under her breath as she saw the brown mark on the crocheted edging of the napkin.

'No, I mean, don't you think the character sounds like me?'

Her scalp prickled. 'No!'

'*Very* like me.' He looked down at the page and picked out the salient points again—eyes, hair, face shape, height, build, lean athleticism... 'You'd almost think she was describing a picture of me,' he mused.

A picture of him lounging against a white pillar staring sullenly at the camera and wearing nothing but a famous brand of jeans and a sneer. At least she had had the sense to make her heroine a flaming redhead!

'Don't flatter yourself. It's an idealised generic *type*, that's all. You can't take a word-picture as literally as you can a visual representation,' she said, driving the iron across the third white linen square.

'Come to think of it, Lacey's most successful heroes have always been light-eyed blondes,' he commented.

'There's no accounting for taste,' said Jennifer, concentrating intently on her difficult task.

'Mmm.' In the periphery of her vision she could see him tuck one hand behind his head, fanning open his jacket, as he lowered the open book to rest page-down against his white shirt. 'It must be your taste too, or you wouldn't be such a fan of her books,' he pointed out.

Jennifer's eyes narrowed on the knife-edged crease she was making along the folded edge of a napkin.

'And you did say that you asked for blond sperm.'

Jennifer slammed the iron down flat. 'Keep your voice down!' she hissed, looking furtively around, even though she knew Dot had gone for a nap and her mother was baking. In her feverish imagination even Fergus seemed to be leaning a little further on his perch, in order to eavesdrop on their conversation.

'Well, you did,' he answered in a theatrical whisper. 'You asked for your ideal man, didn't you: big, blond, sexy...'

Never, never in a million years would he get her to confess to the eye-colour she had ticked on the clinical form.

'I never asked for sexy!' she spluttered.

'You needed virile, though, which amounts to the same thing. Maybe you would have got me even if my father *hadn't* interfered.'

It was a devastatingly seductive thought.

'But, since intelligence was top of my list, that would certainly have eliminated you,' she said, using acid to counteract the sweet surge in her breast.

He grinned, supremely secure in his own intellect. 'I thought you were supposed to be steaming those things, not smoking them.'

Jennifer groaned as she lifted the iron and saw the smouldering ruin of the third napkin. At this rate they were going to have no table linen left.

'You should have asked me for help after all,' he said smugly propping up the book again. 'I do all my own ironing at home.'

Jennifer had enough. 'Good, then you can do the rest,' she said, emerging from behind the ironing board and snatching the book out of his hand. 'And *I'll* do the reading.'

She was reluctantly impressed when he meekly took over the job without turning a hair, but unfortunately, just as she was about to spirit the book safely back upstairs, she was waylaid by Margaret Carter, who was taking off her padded jacket to hang on the brass hook beside the door.

'Oh, Jennifer, I hope it's not too late, but we were wondering if you could possibly do dinner for us tonight?' There was an apologetic smile on her plump, seamed face as she took off her headscarf and draped it over her jacket. 'The roads are awfully dusty—after we went through Turangi, every time we passed a car it was like being caught in a sandstorm. I don't think Ron likes the idea of navigating after sunset, and we don't want to get stranded again, as we were yesterday.'

'Of course we can,' smiled Jennifer, clasping the book behind her back in her linked hands. 'Mum is doing her famous pheasant cassoulet, with a feijoa and banana flan for dessert. Did you have a good cruise yesterday?'

'Yes, and they gave us a wonderful lunch. But it was rather cold out on the lake. And when we woke up this morning there was a layer of dirty ash all over the town. Do you think it's going to snow and make things clean again? It's getting rather nippy out there.'

She ventured into the living room, looking for the fire, as her husband came up the front steps, jingling his car keys and looking very spry for a rotund man of middle years. Belatedly Jennifer remembered Rafe, and nervously trailed Ron Carter's heels, but she found herself too late to take control of the introductions.

'You must be the bloke who's been in the Amazon,' said Ron Carter, enthusiastically pumping Rafe's hand when his wife told him that he was Jennifer's husband. 'One day deep in the wilds, the next deep into domestication,' he joked, nodding at the ironing.

Rafe's eyes had gone first to the clerical collar and then to the bluff, open face with its wide smile. 'Each has its own merits,' he admitted, with an answering grin.

'Raphael—were you named for the painter? People often grow up to bear out their names. I remember Paula mentioning you were doing the photography on your expedition,' said Margaret.

'Actually, I was named for one of the seven archangels,' Rafe said modestly. As well he might—he was certainly no angel, thought Jennifer. 'It's a tradition in my mother's family. Her brothers are Gabriel, Raguel and Michael.'

'So that leaves you Uriel, Sariel and Jerahmeel for *your* sons.' The Reverend Carter completed the set with a chuckle and Jennifer's eyes flew to Rafe's face in shocked recognition as he demurred at the idea of saddling children with unusual names.

Of course he noticed her sharply reactive look, and, thinking that it might be wise to escape his perceptive eye Jennifer began edging towards the door, only to collide with Dot and feel the book behind her back slipping out of her hands.

It bounced with a thud off Dot's sturdy brown lace-up, ending cover-up on the floor, the elegant grainy black and white photo of a male torso on the front cover seeming to Jennifer's guilty mind to shriek its contents long and loud to the room. In fact it was only a few seconds before she and Dot simultaneously bent to scoop it up.

Dot's stubby hand got there first. She perused the cover photo, her thick silver eyebrows descending over her black pebble eyes as she flipped it over and read the blurb on the back. 'Haven't read this, have I?'

'I doubt it,' said Jennifer in a strangled voice. 'Uh, I don't think it's your kind of book.'

'I'm old but I ain't *dead*,' Dot told her with a little snort that indicated she recognised exactly what kind of book it was. She handed it back. 'Everybody needs a little spice in their life now and then. I've read some pretty hair-curling things in my time...'

Since her hair was now dead straight, Jennifer guessed

that they had had no permanent effect. Murmuring a reply, she beat a hasty retreat before the Reverend and his wife decided to get in on the literary discussion.

She stowed the book back on her bookshelf and hurried over to her desk, thinking that while Rafe was chained to the ironing board she would do a little catching up on her computer. She carefully wiped down the casing with a damp cloth to ensure it was free of volcanic dust before switching it on, and entered the two bookings she had received in the mail into her files, printing out confirmation letters that she would get Susie to post. Then she brought her expenses up to date and typed out her mother's recipes and notes for the next day's cooking class.

A printer jam had her cursing, and while she was trying to clear it her mother called on the intercom phone and told her that there was a tradesman at the door offering to spray the ash off the roof and out of the gutters and downpipes using his own tanker of water. Jennifer went downstairs and after intense discussion decided she wanted to wait a few days to see what the mountain was going to do before she spent money on a job that might have to be done all over again. Several other minor distractions intervened before she remembered that she had left the computer suspended in mid-task, and by that time Rafe had finished his ironing and had inevitably ended up wherever he could cause her the most trouble.

'What are you doing?' she demanded as she walked in to find him swivelling idly in her chair, snooping through her operating system.

'I fixed your printer problem,' he said, pointing to the neat stack of papers on the desk. 'And you had an awful lot of conflicts in your system so I cleaned up the clutter on your hard disk for you. Don't you run your diagnostic programme regularly?'

'If I don't have a problem I don't see the need to go

hunting for one,' said Jennifer, silently praising her fore-thought in deleting her compromising files.

'Ah, well, there we differ. I like to seek out potential trouble and deal with it *before* it can develop into a serious problem.'

He was talking about more than computers, he was expressing a philosophy of life, and Jennifer wondered if she and her baby were classed as 'potential trouble' or 'a serious problem'. Her heart clenched in her chest as she wondered how he intended to 'deal' with it.

'I see you're on the Internet,' he added as the screen registered his arrival back at the desktop, and she reached over his shoulder and smartly tapped the escape button, shutting down the computer, grateful that her password would have prevented him browsing too close to her secrets.

'You're welcome to plug your laptop into the phone-line if you want to use a computer,' she said pointedly, having noticed the slimline case amongst his bags.

He accepted the metaphorical slap on the wrist with remarkably good grace, swinging around in the chair to face her. 'Thank you, if I'm going to be here a while, that would be useful.'

'A while?' she echoed, putting her hand to her stom-ach.

'An indefinite period,' he clarified with beguiling soft-ness, a disturbing gleam of elation in his eyes as he wooed her with his possessive look. 'A period of dis-covery, adjustment and adaptation…'

A combination of fear and uncontrollable longing scrambled her brains. 'Won't your mini-empire collapse if you're not there to run it? Don't you have important things to do—places to go, people to see?' she said, nervously pushing her glasses up her nose.

'Not at the moment, no. I think I have my priorities straight, and I've always believed in delegation—my employees are used to acting on their own initiative.' He got to his feet and looked down into her blustering confusion with a terrifyingly tender smile of understanding. 'Right now *you're* the most important thing in my life.'

He had a masterly gift with an exit line, thought Jennifer dumbly as she watched him calmly saunter out through the door. He couldn't possibly understand how she felt, so how *dare* he make her feel so...so wretchedly wonderful and stupidly cherished.

'Right now' didn't mean tomorrow, she was still reminding herself fiercely as she helped her mother with the last-minute preparations for dinner. 'Right now' was a warning, not a promise, telling her that Rafe's interest in her was only temporary. Once he had solved the 'problem' she represented, he would go back to the sophisticated life in which she could have no part.

And anyway, she wasn't a *thing*, she seethed; she was a person with her own feelings and thoughts and *plans*. Plans which she had not permitted to include Raphael Jordan. Rafe was the stuff of heady fantasy, not of practical reality. It should be enough for her to know that she would soon have his son or daughter to lavish with all her love and adoring attention—which would surely be wasted on the baby's father!

In spite of her worst anxieties, dinner was miraculously easy. Jennifer had difficulty believing that it was simply out of respect for Ron Carter's clerical collar, but for whatever reason Rafe subdued his wicked streak of rebellious mischief and was almost as angelic as his namesake as he conversed with the vicar and his wife on the subject of preserving ethnic cultures without once mentioning the tribes of the Amazon.

When Ron and Margaret mentioned that they lived in Wellington, Jennifer learned that Rafe had turned twenty-one there, on his way to a working holiday at the Coronet Peak ski fields near Queenstown in the South

Island. The skis on his roof rack had obviously not been there just for show, she thought, as he spoke of his hopes that parts of the Whakapapa or Turoa ski fields could be groomed of ash so that he could try out Ruapehu's famous slopes.

Not even when the mention of the mountain prompted Ron to say heartily, 'I understand we missed some thrillingly spectacular goings-on here last night!' did Rafe pick up the gauntlet with one of his fiendish *double entendres*, and it was left to Jennifer to embarrass herself with a nervous burst of giggles.

Dave and Celia arrived back while they all were still having tea and coffee by the fire, and they chatted for a while before the guests began drifting off to their rooms.

Rafe scraped dishes and stacked the dishwasher alongside Jennifer, and Paula leaned on her stick to tell him he was shaping up to be an ideal son-in-law.

'I must get you some brains,' she declared, startling him with one of her frequent *non sequiturs*.

'Uh, what have I done wrong?' He looked down at his stacking to discover his mistake.

'No, I mean to *eat*,' Paula laughed. 'Jenny told me you like that kind of thing.'

'I guess my preferences are changing, then,' he murmured, wiping the smirk off Jennifer's face as he continued, 'Because since I arrived I've developed a taste for something plump and juicy that I can really sink my teeth into…'

The innuendo went entirely over Paula's head. 'I'll do you a nice aged fillet steak for tomorrow night, then.' She beamed.

Plump! Jennifer slammed the dishwasher shut and jabbed the button.

Plump! she smouldered as she and Rafe partnered against her mother and Dot in a game of cards in front of the fire, losing because they kept trumping each other instead of their opponents, then watched a late news report on the television covering the eruption and its aftermath.

Plump! she brooded as she lingered to put the guard in front of the fire and the cover over Fergus's cage before she switched off the downstairs lights and followed Rafe upstairs.

But she was thinking of Rafe's teeth as she ventured reluctantly into her bedroom. His strong, even white teeth, which nibbled and raked and aroused and...oh, hell! yes, all right, she had to admit it...made her feel all plump and juicy inside...

But she had told him that tonight would be different, and for the sake of her sanity as well as her pride she had to stick to her decision. She already knew that Rafe was seriously addictive. One glorious infusion of unbridled delight was all she dared permit herself—two would be getting dangerously close to a habit. Tonight any attempt to taunt or seduce her into forgetting her principles would fall sadly flat!

She had half expected Rafe to have stripped for battle while he was waiting for her, but he was standing beside the bed still fully dressed, although his white shirt was untucked from his jeans and half unbuttoned, and his open cuffs flicked back on his strong wrists.

Jennifer opened her mouth to remind him they would not be sharing a bed, but then he shifted aside and she saw what was on the floor behind him.

She stared at it, a blood-rush of humiliation roaring in her ears. The bedclothes, which had miraculously reappeared in the glory box some time during the morning, were as deftly arranged as they had been the previous night.

'I'll sleep on the floor; you take the bed.'

She stared at his face, as cool as the flatly uninflected

words. Oh, God, had he really *meant* it about having got her out of his system?

'I—you don't have to… I—I'm sure the bed is big enough for both of us to sleep in without encroaching on each other's space,' she stammered, all her intentions of keeping him at a safe distance going up in smoke as she strove to match him for cool indifference.

'I'm sure the bed is, but unfortunately *I'm* not,' he said, his mouth adopting a cynical twist.

'I—I don't understand…' she muttered, caught up in her own agony of embarrassment. Thank God she hadn't blurted out what she had been thinking when she had walked into the room.

'I mean that if *I* don't trust myself, then you certainly shouldn't. If I get into that bed with you, Jennifer, I won't be doing any sleeping. I can't lie within kissing distance of you and think pure thoughts…'

She trembled as his voice roughened, his cool evaporating, his fists clenching at his sides. 'I'd start thinking about what we did last night and I'd get hard. I'd want to touch you, make love to you—do everything that we did together all over again, and more—much, much more…'

Her mouth went dry. 'But this morning you said—'

'I can't believe you were naïve enough to believe me. You're a woman, a sensual, passionate woman, and there was a lot more than sex going on between us last night. That's why you were running scared this morning and trying to set limits on our relationship, to restrict our contact—it was your fight or flight response to danger. And in some ways you're right to worry; I *am* dangerous to you—because I'm not going to meekly accept limits and restrictions,' he said rawly. 'I'm not going to let you push me away because I might disrupt the nice, cosy set-up you have here. I *do* want to disrupt it; I want to disrupt *you*. I need you to look at me and see *me*—not a reflection of your own fears, not Sebastian's son or your baby's father, but *me*, Rafe Jordan the *man*—your lover…'

His unconscious use of the word 'need' rather than 'want' ravished Jennifer's resistance. To be desired was a powerful aphrodisiac, but to be *needed* was infinitely more desirable. It gave her the courage to recognise and accept that her own need to love was greater than her fear of being destroyed by the loving. The blood beat heavily in her veins as she made her decision.

'As long as you realise my baby is more important to me than anything else,' she warned him unevenly, stepping forward as her hands went to the buttons of her yellow blouse. 'Whatever happens between us from now until the time you leave—my baby stays with me…'

His eyes darkened, a corona of flaring gold ringing his expanding pupils within the outer halo of green as he stilled her hands on her buttons. 'Always. I would never, ever separate a loving mother from her child; that's one promise that's easy for me to make.'

The dark intensity of his expression was suddenly slashed by a dazzling smile, a sinful, sexy challenge. 'I hope you're as hungry as I am, darling, because the appetiser is about to be served…'

Holding her gaze, he ripped open the rest of his shirt and threw it on the floor. He unbuckled his belt and unzipped his jeans, again stopping her tentative move to unfasten her blouse.

'No, let me do that.' He stepped back and rapidly stripped off the rest of his clothes. Naked, he slowly unstrapped the watch from his wrist, and dropped it on his clothes. Then, equally slowly, legs astride, he raised his arms and raked his hands through his hair, letting her watch the lift and play of lean, hard muscles, displaying himself unashamedly to her blushing fascination.

'Do you like me?' he asked. As if there was anything

about his magnificent body to *dis*like, she thought dizzily, and nodded.

'You don't mind the scar?' He pointed to an infinitesimal flaw low on the dark golden belly, just above the dense thicket of his groin, his fingers brushing across the bold thrust of his erection as if by accident. But Jennifer knew it wasn't any accident. He had deliberately drawn her gaze to his manhood. He wanted her to look at the swollen shaft, to see how much he wanted her, and to realise that soon she would feel that satiny thickness pushing up into her body again.

'You're the first woman I've ever made love to without using a condom,' he said huskily, frankly enjoying the jolt that went through her at his admission, and the sight of her nipples visibly hardening under the thin material of her blouse. 'That's why I came so fast that first time—it felt so incredibly good to be naked inside you.'

Jennifer could feel her breasts readying themselves for his touch, and a hot moistening between her thighs. In her mind's eye they were already making love, and it was with a shock she felt her hand fisting in her tartan skirt and realised that she was still fully dressed.

She looked up at his face, her eyes glazed, and he tilted his head, saying silkily, 'Does it make you feel powerful and in control, to be wearing clothes while I'm naked?'

No, but it was sinfully erotic.

Before she could answer he had picked her up by the waist and lifted her high against his chest.

'Wrap your legs around my waist,' he ordered gruffly and as she clung to his shoulders and obeyed he carried her across the room to her desk.

Wrapping one arm across her back, he swept the clutter beside the computer to the floor and sat her down on the rounded edge, pushing her thighs apart as he stepped between them, his hands sliding up under her flared skirt, a ripple of hesitation hitting him as he found that she was wearing suspenders and stockings rather than panty-hose. Then his hands were moving up to roughly snatch off her panties, and when she squeaked a protest he covered her mouth with his and stroked her with his tongue.

She fumbled with her glasses as they bumped against his nose, but he wouldn't let her take them off.

'No, leave them on. I want you wearing everything except your panties,' he growled, sending thrills ravishing through her senses.

'Still feel in control?' he murmured mockingly, his fingers touching her intimately, exploring her damp folds. 'Mmm, just how I like you,' he reminded her approvingly, 'sweet and juicy.' And then he was sliding to his knees, replacing his fingers with his mouth, his hair-roughened cheeks grazing the sensitive skin of her inner thighs. Jennifer threw back her head, her spine arching, her hands sinking helplessly into his spiky soft hair.

But no sooner had the pleasure begun to slam into her than he was rising to his feet again, pulling her hips further forward onto the very edge of the desk, ripping open her blouse to expose her transparent bra and tipping her flat on her back as he hooked his arms under her bent knees and mounted her in a single thrust.

As she gasped with shock and moaned with pleasure he dragged away the sheer fabric of her bra with his teeth and began to lick and suck at her jutting nipples in hungry rhythm with the frantic driving of his hips, grunting as her fingers and heels dug into his flexing buttocks, pulling him deeper into her fastness.

It had all happened so quickly that Jennifer had had no time to think, only to feel and react to the erotic stimuli, the familiar words that he was whispering calling forth instinctive replies until their panting cries rose to a simultaneous crescendo and died away in a shuddering of sighs.

After a few moments, without withdrawing from her body, Rafe raised himself on his braced arms and smiled triumphantly down into her drowsy, sated face.

'Well, Lacey, I guess we can both agree *that* chapter works…'

It hit her then—the wicked things he had said to her in the throes of passion, the automatic replies that had floated up from her subconscious—the whole highly charged erotic scenario: starchy secretary and wolfish boss locked in their office suite overnight…a torrid affair conducted on an interesting array of office furniture…

She and Rafe had been re-enacting a scene straight from one of her own books. One, moreover, that hadn't been published yet!

'*Oh!*' She closed her eyes, shutting out his hugely smug face.

'Yes, oh! How much longer did you think you could keep it from me?'

The protective instinct was too strong. 'Keep what?'

Warm lips covering her own made her eyes fly open. She began to struggle and he eased himself from her body and helped her to sit up, but while she tried to straighten her twisted clothes he was busy taking them off.

'What are you doing? Stop that!' she cried, slapping at his hands as he unzipped her skirt.

'I'm levelling the playing field,' he said, plucking off her glasses. 'For the purposes of this discussion there's going to be nothing between us but the raw, naked truth.'

What a terrifying thought! Aftershocks of pleasure were still rippling through her body as she wrestled with him, losing her blouse as well as her skirt to his superior cunning.

'You—you did this to me just to—just to prove some wretched theory!' she choked, hot with humiliation at the idea, hitting out at his hard chest, her fists sliding off his perspiration-slicked skin.

His hand slid around her back to unhook her bra and peel it away from her jouncing breasts. Then he tossed her over his shoulder, ignoring her furious curses and the pounding on his back as he carried her over to the bed and threw her down on the mattress, straddling his body over her squirming bundle of rosy outrage while he unsnapped her lacy garters.

'I did it in the first place because it was an incredibly arousing fantasy and I was curious to know if it would be as hot and wild in real life,' he said, pushing her stockings down her threshing legs. 'It was,' he added roughly, causing her feverish struggles to slacken. 'And secondly, I did it because it was *your* fantasy and *I* wanted to be the man who realised it for you. I'd like to explore all your sexy fantasies with you...'

He lay down beside her, propped up on his elbow, his other arm lying loosely across her waist, and she caught her breath at his sultry expression, letting it out in a huff as he admitted, 'The rest was pure bonus. I was so turned on by the time I got you flat on your back I hardly knew what I was saying—how was I to know you'd confirm your secret identity by sticking so perfectly to your own script?'

The dancing gold glints in his eyes mocked her glowering doubts. She wouldn't put it past him to have ruthlessly planned and executed every single steamy moment of her downfall.

'Come on, darling, 'fess up. It's far too late to pretend you don't know what I'm talking about.'

He wasn't angry at her deception, she realised in sudden wonder, the tight knot of wretched embarrassment loosening its stranglehold on her emotions. If anything he looked soaringly elated, immensely proud of his discovery. Proud of *her*.

'How long have you known? How did you find out?' she mumbled, reaching behind her to pull the duvet over her bare body.

He tugged it to include himself, enfolding them both in a fluffy cocoon of enforced intimacy before slinging his arm back over her waist.

'I'm no mathematician, but I can add two and two,' he told her. 'I had the feeling you were hiding something else from me, but I had no idea what it might be until the books turned up and you *really* began to act guilty— far more so than was warranted by my finding the female equivalent of a stack of *Playboys* stuffed under the mattress. Everything I was learning about you seemed to hint to me in a certain direction, but I couldn't bring myself to really believe it. Not until I happened across your E-mail. You have one, by the way, from a certain firm of lawyers—' His voice turned whimsical '—passing on a message from some guy called Sariel who would like to arrange a meeting with you while he's in New Zealand to discuss a new book contract...'

He had known all evening!

That angelic behaviour at dinner had merely been a calculated attempt to lull her into a false sense of security.

'You *happened* across my E-mail? You logged onto my Internet connection? But you couldn't have!' she protested bitterly, cursing the fact that things had been so hectic in the past few days that she hadn't bothered to check her messages. She *knew* he had been up to no good puttering around her computer. 'I have a secret password!'

He shook his head, baffled at her stupidity. 'Are you kidding? What's secret about it? Don't you know you're *never* supposed to use the names of pets for security passwords? It took me about thirty seconds to find out that it was ''Fergus''.'

'You shouldn't have been snooping around my computer in the first place!'

He grinned at her rosy-cheeked annoyance. 'I do a lot of things I shouldn't; that's why I'm so successful. Besides, around you, snooping is the only way I get to find out anything interesting. I take it my father was the one who hooked you up with an English publisher?'

She nodded jerkily.

'Lucky for you I rescued it from my blockhead stepbrother, or we wouldn't be celebrating the secret of your success today. He was letting the Velvet line sink into oblivion, but I knew that it had untapped potential.'

His eyes crinkled. 'Rather like our relationship, wouldn't you say?'

Where he saw potential, she saw complications.

'So…what happens now?' she asked warily, wondering what he intended to do with his new knowledge.

He shifted his thigh suggestively over hers.

'Now, my sinful, sexy authoress—we negotiate a new contract!'

CHAPTER NINE

JENNIFER pulled off her helmet and laughed up through her spattered glasses at a saturated Rafe, the adrenaline still pumping through her veins after the swooping ride down the foaming waters of the Tongariro River.

'See, I told you it would be easy!' she teased, flexing arms which ached from paddling under the shouted instructions of the rafting guide. Clad in wetsuits and bulky yellow padded life-jackets, they had got thoroughly wet but not cold, and Jennifer felt as if she was ready to go back up-river and do it all over again. She had rafted down the Tongariro on other occasions, but never had she felt so full of the joy of living.

'I think your "easy" work-out might require a massage with liniment tonight,' he replied wryly, removing his helmet and life-jacket, amused by her bouncing excitement. 'Or if not liniment, something equally stimulating to the circulation. Perhaps…whipped cream?'

The flaring heat in her tawny brown eyes was matched by the sudden glow drying her wet cheeks.

It amazed Rafe that Jennifer still had the capacity to blush and he couldn't resist the urge to constantly test her helpless response to his flirting. He had assumed that a writer of erotic novels would be casually blasé about sex and sexual banter—that was what had thrown him when he had begun suspecting Lacey Graham's real identity—but Jennifer's sizzling fantasy life seemed to make her more, rather than less vulnerable to blushing confusion. She was a strange mixture of sophistication and innocence, boldness and caution, soft feminine yielding and infuriating female stubbornness, and the heady combination had proved deeply alluring to his jaded soul.

'I'm afraid I have other plans for this evening,' Jennifer said, tilting her nose loftily in the air. 'I have a slave-driving editor hounding me to finish my next book.'

'I'm sure he'd want you to get all the proper research done for it first. Perhaps he'd even be willing to offer himself up to the delights of whipped cream—purely in the interests of literary accuracy, of course...'

He walked away, taking with him the immensely satisfying picture of Jennifer drenched in pretty pink.

Jennifer's smile faded as she cleaned her glasses and watched her lover pick his way down the bank to help some of the other raftees lift the big yellow inflatable rafts out of the water and carry them up the steep grade of loose stones, slippery with muddy ash, to where the rafting company's four-wheel drive and trailer were waiting to tow them back for the next group of paying customers.

Her lover.

She still couldn't believe that she, Jennifer Jordan, was having a scorching affair with a man who had threatened to cause her such grief.

Was still threatening to, for that matter.

It was four days now, since he had found out her guilty secret. Four entertaining days and three, long, glorious, passion-filled nights. Long enough for her to realise, to her delight and despair, that he was a man she could love...and *did* love...not wisely but far, far too well.

It wasn't the steady, slowly unfurling emotion she had felt for Michael. This time love was hot and strong and fierce, and it had burst upon her with the impact of a bomb—a time bomb which had lain ticking away inside as she had cut Rafe's photos out of magazines and writ-

ten him into her fantasies, as she had exchanged friendly
and stimulating letters with Sariel, and as she had silently coveted the son of her husband, and secretly
yearned for the father of her baby.

It was a love that cared nothing for logic or for reason,
and as she watched him walk down the hill Jennifer
acknowledged that it was a sight that she would have to
get used to: Rafe walking away.

She hadn't asked him how much longer he was staying, for she hadn't wanted to know, and to her relief her
mother had not pressed them for their future plans, seeming to assume that husband and wife needed time and
privacy to reassimilate their marriage and that they
would broach the subject when ready.

Meanwhile Jennifer had given herself permission to
suspend her despair and devote herself to basking in the
delight. She would sort out the emotional tangle she had
created later. In spite of the grief that opening her life
to him was storing up, Rafe *was* a delight simply to be
with, to talk to, to challenge and even to quarrel with...

He was also good at making sure she didn't take herself too seriously, as she had learned that night in bed,
when Rafe had mentioned the negotiation of a contract.

She had bristled with suspicion, demanding to know
what contract he was talking about. Looking down into
her belligerent face, he had told her it was quite simple:
as long as she continued to sleep with him, he would
keep all her guilty secrets safe.

'That's blackmail! You're trying to *blackmail* me into
having sex with you!' she had screeched at him in a
spasm of astonished outrage.

'Yes, and unless you agree to satisfy my evil lusts,
you and your mother will be thrown starving into the
snow,' he had hissed sibilantly, twirling an imaginary
moustache.

'Oh.' She had subsided, mortified by her gullibility,

as she'd recognised his wicked amusement. She would have to learn not to bite at every piece of tantalising bait he dangled in front of her eyes, she'd told herself as his grin widened.

'Wanna try it?' he had drawled provocatively, scraping his whiskers on her naked shoulder. 'Me, the ruthless deflowerer of virgins, and you, the helpless innocent, quivering and begging as I ravish you within an inch of your life?'

'No!'

But he had seen the glint of professional interest in her eye and had fallen back on the bed, shaking with laughter, until she had muffled his mirth by stuffing a pillow into his mouth. Rising to the challenge, he had romped her into giggling submission and made love to her again, in a very simple, straightforward, *very* satisfying way.

So, in the end the only contract there was any negotiation over was the one between their *alter egos*, Lacey Graham and Sariel. Rafe wanted to offer her a greater advance for her next three books, but was suggesting tighter controls on her output, and Jennifer was dubious.

'I've always only written at my own speed; I don't know if I could work to someone else's deadline,' she had said. 'How fast I write depends on what's happening around me, and with the baby coming I need to stay even more flexible.'

She had propped up her elbows on her desk, where they were discussing the draft contract Rafe had produced from his suitcase the morning after they had engaged in a very different form of negotiation on the very same battered surface!

Rafe, having discovered a miracle within his own grasp—his pet protégé, the reclusive authoress he had suspected he would never meet—was determined to make the most of his unexpected opportunity.

'I want to enjoy this baby,' Jennifer told him firmly. 'It'll probably be the only one I have, so I want to spend as much time as I can being a mother.'

Rafe frowned at the wistful inflection. 'You want more children?' He sounded faintly hostile, as if he couldn't understand such a desire.

'I would have liked some more, yes,' she said sharply. 'Michael and I planned to have three.'

The frown turned to a scowl. He tapped his gold pen, slotted between his finger and thumb, on the notepad in his lap. 'You're lucky it didn't get that far. He'd probably have ended up walking out on you *and* the kids, hooking up with someone else who wouldn't make demands on him and skimping on his maintenance.'

His cynicism struck to the heart of her beliefs. 'Just because children have no place in *your* life doesn't mean that other men don't care about their offspring.'

'I care,' he rapped. 'I'm here, aren't I?'

Just. It was on the tip on her tongue to say it, but his pen was tapping at an ominous speed.

'And what about all your other anonymous children? Do you care about *them*?' she demanded unfairly.

The pen stopped, his knuckles whitening. 'That's different, you damned well know it is! That whole process is designed to be deliberately detached. I have no involvement or awareness of their conception, therefore no emotional investment.'

'You had no awareness or emotional investment in *this* conception, either.' If only she knew exactly what was going on inside his head she might be able to put to rest her secret fears.

The tautening of his expression was an indication that he realised the futility of the argument. 'But I do have other, more concrete investments in you, don't I? Notably the one we're supposed to be discussing. Look, can we stick to the subject here—?'

'*I* wasn't the one who wandered off it—'

'We were *talking* about your *career*,' he interrupted, his pen beginning to tap again. 'I, of *all* people, should know how much motherhood means to you, but you usually write at night anyway, when the baby will be asleep.'

'Babies don't always keep regular hours, and motherhood is tiring, especially in the early stages. What you're talking about is the equivalent of working almost full-time. I just don't want to over-commit myself.'

'We can be flexible on the deadlines, as long as you give me plenty of notice if you think you're going to run over. Lots of other women authors write while bringing up their families.'

'I'm not other women; I'm me.' Under pressure of his gaze, she snapped, 'Would you mind not doing that with your pen? It's very irritating!'

'Sorry.' He folded his arms and put the pen to his thoughtfully pursed lips, which was even more of a distraction. 'You know, this wouldn't be such a problem for you if you weren't so damned secretive about what you do.'

She was instantly wary. 'I told you last night, Mum would be even more upset about the type of stories I write than she would be about my arrangement with Sebastian.'

'I think you underestimate your mother. Paula's a survivor; she's proved how resilient she can be. I'm sure she'd rise above her embarrassment for your sake. You're good at what you do; that's something for her to be proud of.'

She stiffened at the implied threat. 'If you *tell* her…'

He threw the pen onto the desk, straightening in the hard chair he had brought up from downstairs.

'Damn you, if you can't bring yourself to trust me, at least grant that I'm too good a businessman to risk killing the goose that lays the golden egg! Lacey Graham is a very valuable asset to Velvet. I want to work *with* you, not against you. Stop treating me as if I was the enemy.'

She looked at him incredulously and he ran an impatient hand through his hair. 'You know what I mean...' he muttered, his eyes faintly uncomfortable.

Yes, she did. He meant that although he had swooped down on her home like an avenging archangel, and had angrily blackmailed, lied, harassed and seduced his way into her life, he fully expected her to embrace his bone-deep integrity as a fact of life.

She leaned back in her seat, suddenly enjoying herself. Rafe had dragged her out of bed practically before she was awake to hammer out his offer. She had barely been allowed time to pull on her clothes before he was flourishing his contract under her nose and demanding her full attention to business.

'Maybe I should take advantage of the fact that I'm sleeping with my editor and hold out for a bigger percentage of royalties,' she taunted him.

His eyes narrowed as he ignored the flagrant provocation of the first half of her statement. 'The profit margin per book isn't big enough to offer authors a higher percentage of net. We make our money on volume—our sales grow; your income grows.'

'I suppose another publisher might have something different to say,' she said slyly.

He was too canny to disagree. 'Maybe. But we're the best. If you want to write for the best you write for Velvet Books. And there's another reason it wouldn't be in your interests to write for a rival publisher.'

'Oh, what's that?' she attempted to look bored.

'You own fifteen percent of Velvet Books.'

'I *what*?' She nearly fell off her chair.

It was his turn to sit back and enjoy her consternation.

'You didn't even look at the names on the shares Sebastian left you in his will, or the details of the bequest, did you?' He grinned. 'He left you his minority interest in the company that owns Velvet Books. I own the other eighty-five percent. You and I are business partners.'

Oh, *Sebastian*! Jennifer cringed inwardly. No *wonder* Rafe had been so furious with the disposition of his father's will.

'No, we're not.' She stoutly rejected the tantalising link. 'I told the lawyer I wasn't accepting them.'

'In the event of which, Sebastian provided for a nine-month holding period for you to change your mind, before they revert to the very person who put them in the toilet in the first place; Lydia's son Frank, remember him? The twerp who asked you if you had silicone implants in your breasts the first time you met.'

The significance of the gestation period of the clause escaped neither of them as he continued wryly, 'Believe me, I'd far rather it was someone with talent and imagination holding the shares than that obnoxious, over-educated cretin, who thinks a soft degree makes him God's gift to business.'

'You *want* me to accept the shares?' she asked, shaken. She had been certain that one of his prime purposes in coming to New Zealand was to ensure the exact opposite.

He shrugged. 'Under the terms of the will you can't sell them for a year after you inherit, and then only to me. There's no restriction on what Frank can do with them, and after my comments on his business acumen he'd never sell to me. So, yes, you and I would both benefit if you kept them.'

'What on earth was Sebastian *thinking*?' Jennifer fretted in exasperation.

Rafe stared at her for a moment from under flat golden

brows. 'Unfortunately he didn't see fit to leave us that information.'

But he could make a very shrewd guess.

Later, Jennifer had had to suffer the embarrassment of asking him to shift the heavy wardrobe so that she could retrieve the files containing her old contracts and letters. Amongst them was a large scrapbook, which she tried to slip casually into a drawer.

Not casually enough. Rafe smiled as he leafed through the newsprint pages, looking at her collection of faded cuttings from glossy magazines, carefully attached with double-sided tape.

'I have quite a few scrapbooks of my own at home,' he conceded off-handedly, consoling her blushes. 'At first it was just for the sake of my portfolio, but later, well…' He gave a rueful shrug. 'I guess I have a healthy streak of narcissism in my soul, and I thought it would be something to show—'

He stopped guiltily and she completed the cliché for him. 'To show your grandchildren?'

He gave her a sidelong glance. 'I *was* going to say, to show people when I'm old and shrivelled,' he lied defensively.

She couldn't imagine such a thing. She was sure that Rafe would mature like a fine wine, growing more impressive with the years. Definitely worth laying down, she thought mischievously.

He stroked a finger over a moody photograph of his twenty-year-old self. 'So, this was the Raphael Jordan who captured your imagination. Did I live up to your expectations in the flesh?' he teased.

'Actually, you lived down to them,' she said, straight-faced, and he laughed.

'Maybe you would have preferred me to remain your unattainable *beau ideal*?'

She put the scrapbook in the drawer. 'But this way I can have both,' she said smugly.

In a way she did have the best of both worlds, she'd consoled herself—at least for a while…that precious 'indefinite period' that Rafe had talked about.

As the ashfalls eased, replaced by a steady stream of sulphur dioxide rising from the empty crater lake to form a thin blue-brown haze above the volcanic plateau, and the weather stayed dry and cold, Paula had insisted that her daughter show Rafe some of the local sights, and so for a few hours each day they had acted like carefree tourists.

Although the three ski fields were closed to skiers, the no-go area had been reduced enough that they had been able to drive up the access road to the Whakapapa field, and then walk up to see the black scars that streaked the ash-covered snow where the rivers of mud from the crater had flooded perilously close to some of the ski lift equipment.

Jennifer had also taken Rafe on a bush walk through the native forest at the foot of Mount Tongariro, which, along with Mounts Ngaruahoe and Ruapehu, formed the rumbling threesome of active volcanoes that were the main attraction of the Tongariro National Park. Yesterday they had driven east to the Tokaanu geothermal area, where they'd strolled amongst the hissing steam vents and boiling mud pools, getting a hint of the sulphurous fury which had raged inside Ruapehu.

It had only been the suggestion of today's rafting trip that had caused Rafe to baulk.

'White water rafting?' He'd frowned dubiously as he padded after her into the kitchen, where Paula had been assembling the ingredients for breakfast. 'What if you fall out?'

'It's not very likely; the guides are very clued-up on safety. I've rafted this stretch before and no one's ever fallen out,' said Jennifer, surprised by his reluctance. She would have thought Rafe was a prime candidate for an adventurous experience.

'You weren't pregnant before,' he pointed out disapprovingly, stopping her in her tracks.

'It's only a Grade 3 river,' she explained. 'So it's not dangerous—just enough white water to get the adrenaline going, that's all. It's easy enough to be recommended everywhere as a first trip, and I've never heard of anyone being injured, so if you're nervous about being on the water—'

'I've been rafting before, and on some pretty challenging rivers—but you, of *all* people, shouldn't want to do anything that might endanger your pregnancy. How would you feel if you lost the baby because you took an unnecessary risk?'

'I'm not going to lose the baby,' she said, resenting the implication that she would be careless with her precious cargo. 'I'm pregnant, not ill, and the doctor says I'm fit, strong and healthy—I do a lot of walking with Bonzer, and lifting and stretching and heavy work around the house. I wouldn't go rafting or horseback riding in late pregnancy, but at this stage the baby's still very tiny and extremely well insulated.'

His eyes went to her trim waist. 'I just don't like the idea of you hurting yourself or our baby for the sake of entertaining me,' he said stubbornly, his lean jaw jutting.

Now *the* baby had become *our* baby. She always felt vulnerable when he chose to remind her of his claim. He had been regularly dipping into the book on childbirth he had bought, and had pestered her with his embarrassing frankness about the minute changes in her body, becoming a self-professed authority on what was good for her and expressing a compulsive interest in her determination to have a natural birth, without the aid of drugs. Much to her unease, he had also started blatantly referring to the later chapters, on early childhood development.

Paula, having one of her good days and moving quite freely without her stick, put in her gentle support of her daughter as she broke eggs into a large copper bowl and began whipping them with a large wire whisk.

'I really don't think there's any harm in it, Rafe. I have several elderly friends who've done the trip, and they said that though it was exhilarating they never felt in danger.'

So Rafe had allowed himself to be persuaded, but he had been very solicitous of Jennifer, insisting on being positioned behind her in the raft and double-checking all her safety equipment.

'I never realised you were such a worry-wart,' she had mocked softly as he tightened the buckles and straps on her life-jacket.

'I never was before,' he murmured, with a hint of grimness.

She touched the back of his hand. 'It's not such a bad thing, is it? To be worried for other people?'

He interwove his fingers with hers and lifted her hand to his mouth—a lover's salute.

'It can be if it gets out of control, and from evidence so far I suspect that you have the ability to make me thoroughly paranoid.' His smile was rueful as his mouth brushed her knuckles. 'I shudder to think what you might get up to when I'm not around.'

A shadow passed across the brightness of her day, but she banished it with a laugh as he added smokily, 'All these harnesses and straps are giving me ideas. Perhaps I should put you on a safety leash.'

'Is that one of *your* fantasies?' she teased, and her blood simmered at the look he gave her.

'Ask me that again tonight,' he growled, and tucked

his arm behind her back to guide her down to the flowing water's edge.

In the event, he had thrown himself whole-heartedly into the rafting experience, his concern for Jennifer notwithstanding, and now, after he had helped reload the rafts and they had changed back into their own clothes and handed in their wetsuits and safety gear, they decided to pick up some lunch at the tiny township of Rangipo and picnic at one of the scenic roadside spots on the way back to Beech House.

They ate their sandwiches and drank their cans of orange juice undisturbed at a weathered wooden picnic table out of sight of the road, the sunlight filtering through the high canopy of mountain beech and the lower interlacing of tree ferns to dapple on the undergrowth of fivefinger and broadleaf. It was cold, but Jennifer was well padded in her red parka and green woollen sweater, worn over jeans tucked securely into the tops of her sheepskin-lined leather boots. Rafe was wearing the same clothes in which he had arrived at Beech House, and Jennifer was awed to think how much had happened since that tumultuous day. The whole focus of her life had subtly shifted, the baby that she carried still unutterably precious and yet no longer alone in being central to her happiness.

Rafe's appetite was greater than Jennifer's, so she let him filch from her brown paper bag and laughingly fed him pieces of her crumbling custard tart. Her laughter died as he took hold of her hand and, holding her gaze, gently sucked her fingers, one by one, clean of their sweet, sticky sediment. Her breathing slowed and her body quickened, her brown eyes growing darker as she watched his lean cheeks hollow with the tugging suction, reminding her of his sultry absorption the previous night, when he had lain beside her in bed, suckling her breasts while his hand played idly between her thighs.

Still holding her hand, Rafe got to his feet, glancing around, then he was tugging her deeper into the fringes of the bush with a devilish grin, towards a towering totara tree whose soaring straight trunk and massive girth proclaimed more than a century's growth.

'Rafe, where are we going?' she asked breathlessly. 'We don't want to get lost…'

'We're not going far, darling, just a quick trip to paradise…'

He swung her behind the huge totara, pushing her up against the thick, stringy bark, pulling off her knitted ski hat and plunging his hands into her soft brown hair as his mouth sealed itself over hers. She moaned, welcoming the familiar wet heat of his tongue, the grate of his teeth against her lips. Her arms went around him, under the heavy black leather jacket, her fingers clutching into the thick wool of his sweater as she hugged him against her, feeling her breasts flatten against his chest.

His knees pushed between hers, levering her legs apart, and he reached down between their bodies, fumbling with the button and zip of her jeans.

'Oh, no, we can't—someone might come…' she protested in delicious apprehension, but the zip parted and she heard the chink of his belt as it was hurriedly unfastened.

'Yes—me,' he husked into her mouth, and she giggled nervously, gasping when she felt his cool hand slide into her panties, pushing them and her jeans down below the silky V of curls at the juncture of her thighs. 'Don't worry, no one will see us, and if you scream you can scream into my mouth…'

'We can't…' she moaned as he tugged at the back of her jeans and her bare bottom scraped against the matted fibres of bark. She arched against him, and with a grunt of satisfaction Rafe wrenched open the fly of his jeans and guided his thick shaft into the narrow gap between her constricted thighs, pushing himself up inside her until he felt her shudder and accept his full length in a slippery rush.

'God, I needed this…I can't ever get enough of you,' he gritted, and quickly began a tight, grinding series of jerking thrusts that he mimicked with his tongue in her mouth, his hands sliding up under her jumper to contract rhythmically on her lace-clad breasts as he brought them both to a swift, fierce convulsion of pleasure that left them weak and panting.

He pulled up her jeans and refastened their clothing as they continued to lean against the huge tree, and Jennifer slowly became aware of her surroundings beyond the warm press of his body—the muffled swish of cars out on the road, the flutter of wings and the scrape of insects, the rustle of leaves and somewhere high up in the canopy the sweet song of a white-throated tui.

'It's ironic,' he murmured, his forehead resting on hers. 'All these years I've been so very, very careful not to get any woman pregnant, not to be trapped into a relationship I didn't want. I *always* took on the responsibility for contraception every time I made love; I've always used condoms whether or not a woman said she was on the pill. And yet here I am, at thirty-three, strutting like a randy teenager at having got a girl into trouble…and finding it an incredibly erotic experience. I like not having to use any contraception with you; I like the thought of flooding more of my sperm into your fertile body; I like knowing you're lush and ripe for me because my seed is flourishing inside you…'

The first part of his speech was so shattering that Jennifer barely registered the second.

'I'm not in *trouble*,' she said tightly, looking at him through lenses which were only now clearing of the fog of their combined breath.

'Yes, you are.' He lifted his head, his eyes the same

dense, dark, concentrated green as the totara's foliage. 'You have this rosy vision of what motherhood is going to be, that once you have your baby your life is going to be complete, a charmed little circle of perfect happiness. But life isn't that neat and tidy. Motherhood is only part of being a woman. What about the rest of you? You can't live only through your child; it's not good for the child or for you. You have needs, powerful adult desires, emotional and physical, that have nothing to do with your maternal feelings. You need someone in your life who can satisfy those needs, who can give your life balance and perspective.'

His stunning words battered at her brain, filling her with such dread hope that Jennifer felt sick. She pulled out of his arms and moved over to pick up her hat, brushing off the leaves which clung to its woven surface.

'And where do I find this paragon of fulfilment?' she asked unevenly, as she turned back.

He looked away from her, his profile rigid, and for one awful instant he looked as horribly aloof as he had in London. But then he looked back, and she saw the fierce determination in his gaze as he said roughly, 'What you and I have—it's been good for both of us— I don't want it to end…'

She let out a gusty little sigh. 'Neither do I,' she admitted with grave caution, detecting the hint of resistance in his words. He didn't sound too happy about whatever it was he was going to suggest. Perhaps, like her, he was conscious of the horrendous complications involved.

But she had misjudged him, because he pounced, seizing her hands and saying eagerly, 'Then come back with me to London, Jennifer. Don't let this end here. Come and live with me and let me prove to you how happy we can be—how well we can complement each other in so many ways. As companions, lovers, partners, profes-

sional colleagues, friends…parents…' His voice deepened to urgency as he felt her fingers tense in his grasp.

'I know you were homesick last time you were there,
but this time it'd be different—I'd make sure you're
never lonely, and your life would be so filled to the brim
with new experiences you'd never get the chance to be
bored. And living with me you'd have the freedom to
truly be yourself, to be able to do and be whatever you
want. You could write to your heart's content until the
baby's born, and then, if that's what you want, you could
be a full-time mother, or let me look after our baby while
you write…'

It sounded idyllic.

Come and live with me.

With Rafe, Jennifer could do and be whatever she
wanted, he said…

But for one notable exception.

No matter how much she wanted it she couldn't be a
wife.

And she had noticed that although he had spoken very
passionately and persuasively, it had all been about the
practical advantages of her going to live with him, nothing of his own feelings. Love was obviously not one of
his fine inducements…

Jennifer's sickness heaved like hot lava into the back
of her throat, and then died away again in a burn of acid
bile.

'How long do you envisage the—arrangement—last-
ing?' she asked thinly.

His urgency dimmed, his eyes shuttering. 'I hadn't
thought about imposing any time limit. I suppose—for
as long as you were happy…naturally, I wouldn't expect
you to stay with me if you were miserable,' he added
stiffly.

Naturally. Just like his last 'companion'! And again,

no mention of *his* feelings. For a man who normally flaunted a painful frankness, it was a telling omission.

'What would people say about your suddenly shacking up with your pregnant stepmother?' she asked crudely, pulling her cold hands from his.

'Who cares what other people think?' he said, thrusting his empty hands into his pockets, cynical lines carving into his narrow face. 'The witches might try to give us a hard time, but I'm more than a match for anything they can dish out, and they're hardly going to rock the boat and risk tying up Sebastian's estate even longer, or alienating you as a Jordan trustee. If you're worried about gossip, don't be. London is very definitely *not* a small town, and I live a pretty private life these days— most people wouldn't even know, let alone care what you and I do together.'

He hunched his shoulders and tilted his head, striving to lighten a conversation which had somehow gone bewilderingly wrong, seeking an answering glimmer of amusement in her eyes as he said, 'Besides, as you took such convenient advantage of yourself, we have the same surname, so most people we meet as a couple will probably simply assume we're married to each other— we don't ever have to mention our convoluted family history.'

His attempt fell aggressively flat. 'So we'd live the lie over there, too. Although we wouldn't be married you'd be quite happy for people to think we were. Isn't that rather hypocritical of you?'

His eyes narrowed, his head jerking straight. 'Is *that* what this is all about, Jennifer? Marriage? You'll sleep with me for a few nights but you won't commit to me in any other way unless I ask you to marry me? What kind of twisted morality is that?'

'I never expected a marriage proposal from you. I never would,' she said proudly, the bitter truth of it blazing in her eyes. 'But the whole point of my getting married to Sebastian was to make having my baby respectable. If I moved in with you that would all be destroyed.'

'Being married is no guarantee of respectability these days.'

'It still is to my mother.'

'And your mother thinks we're married already.'

He was cutting away at her objections one by one. Soon he would be down to the quick. God, if he discovered how she felt about him he would know it was only a matter of time before he was able to wear her down. But no matter how much she was tempted, how could she make a genuine commitment to a man who didn't love her? And how could she project emotional security for her child if she didn't feel any herself?

'You said you didn't want to be *trapped* into a relationship by a pregnant woman,' she reminded him acidly.

He stepped forward and cupped her face, ignoring her stiff resistance, his thumbs smearing the bitter words from her lips as he replied with restrained ferocity. 'Damn you, I was speaking about the past. This is my *choice*, not a trap I'm stumbling blindly into. Getting to know you these last few days has meant getting to know my baby too, accepting that I don't want to back away from the excitement of nurturing a new life.' He slid his hands down to her stomach under her padded jacket. 'This baby is an intrinsic part of who you are, of who I am. How could I want you and not want the baby too? I'm not anything like Sebastian. I could be a good father if you'll give me the opportunity...'

So now he was admitting he wanted the baby. The old, foolish terror plucked at her heart: the fear of loss—now not just of her baby, but of herself.

'I belong here and so does my baby,' she said desperately, pushing herself free. 'You might have only your own selfish wants to consider, but I can't afford to just swan off and leave Mum to struggle on her own.' She turned and began to hurry back to the car.

'Why don't we ask Paula her opinion instead of you making the decision for her?'

She swung around, her hand on the door. 'No! She'd pretend it was all right for my sake. She'd just tell me what she thought I wanted to hear—'

'You mean, like you tell her what you think *she* wants to hear?' he said angrily. 'Who's the hypocrite now? Have you ever considered that maybe she'd *benefit* from being treated as a capable adult rather than as an invalid who always has to be protected? Stop using your mother as an excuse to cop out! If you're so worried about her being on her own while Dot's away, or not being able to handle the business, then let me pay for someone to move in—a sort of companion-cum-business manager. You don't have to worry about what you can *afford* any more, dammit. I'm not as rich as Sebastian but I can certainly support you and your family—'

'And that's typical of *your* family!' she cried at him, whipping herself up into a frenzy. 'Only what *you* want matters. You claim you're not like your father, but that's *exactly* the sort of thing he would have said. If you can't get something by fair and decent means, you buy it.

'Everything has a price as far as you're concerned, doesn't it, Rafe? Nothing is sacred, not even the bonds between mother and child.' She tossed her head at the murderous fury in his eyes, telling herself she didn't care. 'Well, *I* don't have a price, and you needn't think I'm going to let you buy a half-interest in my baby, either!'

The twenty-minute drive back to Beech House was achieved in blistering silence. When Rafe finally skidded to a gravelly halt on the driveway he unclipped his seat belt and wrenched open his door, before turning back to say thickly, 'Know this, Jennifer: whether you choose to have anything more to do with me or not, I expect to be registered as the father on that baby's birth certificate. I want my son or daughter to know who I am, to know that I'm proud to be a father, and that I'll welcome any child who wants to seek me out with open arms.'

'And if I don't do it, I suppose you'll threaten to sue me for custody?' she choked.

Rafe went pale. The savage heat in his gaze turned to green ice, and when he spoke it was through lips rimmed with white.

'When Sebastian knew he was never going to have any more natural children he battled my mother through the courts to try and get custody of me. When she was going through a bad patch with her second husband, and was ill, some moron of a judge, whom I've no doubt was a crony of Sebastian's, gave him temporary custody. I was nine years old and hardly knew who he was. I lived with him for six months and hated it. I was just a possession, to be bribed into silence when he was busy and expected to perform in front of his guests when he wanted to show off his heir. He didn't want me; he wanted what I symbolised. I was eventually sent back to my mother, but Sebastian kept petitioning the court for years afterwards, requesting changes in visitation rights, making her life a hell of insecurity.'

Rafe's voice actually shook as he said into Jennifer's now equally white face, 'So don't you ever, *ever* again accuse me of threatening your bond with your child. I wouldn't do that to my worst enemy, let alone the woman I love!'

She followed on trembling legs as he stormed out of the car and into the house. He slammed up the stairs to her bedroom and crashed the door shut with a resounding bang.

Paula came out of the front bedroom as Jennifer hovered in the entranceway, staring up the stairs in horror.

The woman I love?

'What's going on?' Paula saw Jennifer's face and dropped her armful of sheets. 'Jenny, darling, what's happened?'

'Oh, *Mum*!' Tears filled her eyes and Paula rushed to put her arms around her sobbing daughter, then led her into a vacant bedroom to sit on the side of the bed.

'What's wrong, darling? Is it Rafe?'

They both jumped as a crash came from upstairs, then a pounding clatter on the stairs and the front door slamming. Looking out of the window, they could see Rafe striding full-tilt across the lawn towards the far trees, Bonzer panting at his heels, his hands thrust into the pockets of his leather jacket, his body leaning into the wind as if welcoming the slicing chill.

'What is it, Jen? Have you had an argument?'

Jennifer stared at her mother's thin, anxious face in an agony of indecision. Her mind tracked into a future where *her* child was an adult, and suddenly there was no decision to make. It all became obvious. And there was an obvious place to start. To offer her faith in the future. She jumped to her feet, scrubbing her cheeks under her glasses.

'Just a moment. I have to get something to show you.' She ran upstairs and pulled one of her books out of the bookcase, the one with the raunchiest cover.

Back in the bedroom, her mother was still sitting patiently where she had left her, and Jennifer silently handed her the slim volume, mentally bracing herself.

'What's this?' Her mother blinked a little as she saw the cover.

'I wrote it,' Jennifer said baldly, and her mother's brow wrinkled.

'But it says Lacey Graham—'

'I know, that's the pen-name I use. I've had nine books published by Rafe's company—he's my editor. I've been writing them for years.'

Paula looked bewildered and began to open the book, and Jennifer hurriedly put her hand on it.

'They're—there's a lot of sex in them, Mum. They're erotic books for women. That's why I never told you about them. I— I make quite a bit of money on them.' She named the sum of her last royalties, which made her mother's eyes widen.

'Goodness, you must be quite good at it.'

Jennifer smiled a watery smile. 'Very good, actually. Rafe said he thought you should be proud of me.'

'Then so I shall be,' her mother said stoutly. 'Is that why you and Rafe quarrelled? Because he wanted to tell me and you were embarrassed?'

'I thought *you'd* be embarrassed.'

'Well, I suppose I might be, darling, when I get around to reading one,' her mother said, going a little pink. 'But sex is a natural part of life after all. I think I'll still want to boast about my daughter the author— except to the vicar, of course!'

'Oh, Mum!' Jennifer shook her head helplessly— she'd been so wrong about so very many things. And such a coward. She'd taken Rafe's words at face value without looking for the meaning beneath the surface, without realising that Rafe, too, was fiercely self-protective. A man so cautious of marriage would be even more cautious of love, of declaring and of accepting it in return. It had been a huge step for him just to admit that he had changed his attitude about children, and the woman he loved had thrown it back in his face!

'Rafe and I didn't quarrel about that—not exactly.' She hugged her arms around her waist. 'He wants me to go back to England with him and I was worried about leaving you.'

'Well, I didn't expect him to move in here with us, Jen,' her mother said deflatingly. 'Of *course* your place is with your husband. How could it be otherwise? You never talked about it, but I knew that after his Amazon trip was over you would fly the nest with Rafe—I thought that was why you were arranging all those medical benefits for me. I guessed when Rafe mentioned about how we could use the upstairs room as a suite that it wouldn't be long before you were leaving. It's a good idea of his about the room, don't you think? You wouldn't mind us turning it into a guestroom? Of course, we'd make sure it was kept free for when you and Rafe and the baby visit...'

Paula was full of plans, and so, suddenly, was Jennifer. Why had she insisted on making life so complicated for herself when it was really all so blindingly simple? Rafe was right—they *could* work things out, providing that she *wanted* to work things out. And she knew now that she did, that she wanted to embrace life, not hide from it or live it only vicariously, through her books.

She ran across the waving grass, listening for Bonzer's bark but hearing only the empty wind in the beech trees along the drive. Through the shrubbery around the back of the cottage garden she thought she saw a glimpse of Bonzer's waving tail, and she veered towards the orchard in so much haste she almost missed him.

Rafe was leaning against the side of Dot's ramshackle potting shed, his head tilted back against the weathered timber, his eyes closed, and as she stepped closer on the soft earth she could see a faint glister on the high cheekbones and a thin trail of silver through the stubble on the side of his jaw.

Oh, God...

The shock of fierce tenderness that pierced Jennifer's

heart nearly sent her to her knees. He had freely displayed his rage but he had come out here to hide like a
little boy with his pain, like the lonely, bewildered nine-
year-old boy he must have been in his father's house,
desperately missing his mother and struggling against a
deep sense of emotional isolation.

'Rafe…'

Her soft sigh made his eyelids flicker in alarm, but
they merely closed tighter, and he quickly raised his
forearm to rest across his eyes, his fist clenched.

Not just pain—but grief and anger. She moved around
in front of him, knowing that the measure of his hurt
was also a measure of his love. He might never be able
to bring himself to say it to her again, but she would
know…

'Rafe, darling…please, look at me.'

He didn't move, his body a rigid line of fierce rejection, and she put her tentative hands on his chest, feeling
the sharp recoil of his muscles.

She picked up his balled fist from his side and pressed
her lips to the white knuckles, then placed it between
her breasts against her heart, wondering how to begin.
It awed and shamed her to think that she had brought
the man she loved to the point of tears.

'I'm so afraid of you,' she whispered. 'So awfully
afraid of what you make me feel. You make me feel so
greedy and needy—wanting things that I thought I could
never have.' She pressed herself against the rigid wall
of his body, trapping his hand between them, resting her
cheek against his chest, absorbing the shuddering beat
of his heart as she slid her arms around his lean waist,
knowing that she was going to have to humble herself
and not caring.

'Like you…I never thought I would be able to have
you, except for this one, brief time. I couldn't let myself
even think of what a future with you would be like. I

couldn't even admit to myself that I loved you, let alone admit it to you. I was afraid it would give you too much power to hurt me…'

He didn't move, but the quality of his rigidity had changed, his tension now charged with a new stillness.

'I want— I want to be with you. I want to be allowed to love you, I want to be loved. I want to give you our child to love and be loved. I want you to have everything that you want and be happy for ever, and if I can give you any small part of that happiness I will.' She buried her face in his chest. 'So, please, ask me again, Rafe…ask me to come and live with you and be your love and prove all the pleasures with you. Or, if you won't—let me do the asking…'

The arm that was over his eyes came down over her head, across the back of her shoulders, the fist still clenched.

'Damn you! How could you do that to me?' he said rawly, his angry breath stirring her fringe, and she knew it was going to be all right. 'How could you listen to me tell you I love you and want to live my life with you, and turn me away like that, with those words?'

She lifted her head against the brace of his arm, letting him see her drenched brown eyes, seeing the bloodshot green of his. 'But you didn't tell me you loved me,' she said gently. 'You didn't say anything about love until just now, in the car.'

'I must have—I told you I wanted you, and my baby, and you kicked me in the teeth.'

'I'm sorry.' She lifted her hand and laid it along his rough cheek, her thumb stroking his jaw, feeling the dampness there. 'But I didn't know how you felt, only what I was feeling. I was so confused and it just sounded as if you wanted things convenient for you.'

'I've never told a woman I loved her before,' he said fiercely. 'I was working up to it slowly, and you jumped in and wanted to know how long it would last, as if you thought you'd get tired of me.'

Tired of *Rafe*? She looked into his grim expression and knew that they had been racked by the same uncertainties.

'I'm sorry,' she said again, meekly. 'Did I ruin your big declaration?'

Colour came into his pale face and his arms slid down around her waist, and suddenly the rich humour was back in his eyes. 'Yes, you did. So I guess I'll have to do it all over again. Jennifer, darling…?'

'Yes, Rafe?'

He smiled warmly. 'Will you come to London and marry me and have more of my babies?'

She almost slid through the bracelet of his arms, and her stomach swooped, but her love sustained her to accept his teasing.

'Rafe, I've said I'm sorry. I understand why you feel the way you do about marriage,' she said quietly. 'You once asked me to see you as *you*—well, I do. And it's *you* I love. The way you are…' She smiled back mischievously. 'Hang-ups and all. As long as I know you love me too. I don't need the piece of paper—'

'But maybe *I* need it,' he said. 'It gave me a shock to realise how possessive I felt about you and the baby, how outraged at the thought of not being allowed to be part of your life. I'm *not* going to let my father's mistakes rule my life and manipulate my thinking. I have nothing to prove any more—except my love to you.'

She put her finger across his warm lips. 'You don't have to prove anything, or to bribe me with a wedding ring. I respect your word, Rafe, whatever promise you give me is enough.'

He nipped her finger. 'Then I promise I'll love you for the rest of my life; I promise I'll never be unfaithful to you; I promise I'll never leave you; I promise I'll never abuse your trust or lie to you, or our children; I promise to cherish and protect you and even, on occasions, to obey.'

She shook her head, tears of love pricking her eyes. 'And how do you know you can keep them all?'

'Because now I have something I've lacked all these years. Faith. You've given that to me, Jennifer. Faith in my own character—faith to know when the right woman finally comes along—faith in my love for my woman and hers for me—faith in the life and the future we can create together.'

She linked her arms around his neck, going on tiptoe to touch her mouth to his in loving homage and enjoying his heady response. 'Who would have thought when Sebastian arranged for me to have my baby that this would happen?' she sighed.

'Who indeed?' he murmured, so drily that she tilted her face up with a frown.

'What?' She saw the answer in his face and her jaw dropped. 'You think he *planned* for this to happen?'

'Well, I don't know about *this* exactly.' He nudged her with his hips, enjoying her sudden flush. 'But he certainly did his best to get us entangled in as many ways as he could after he was gone, didn't he? Maybe he hoped propinquity and nature would do the rest.'

Jennifer glanced over her shoulder at the mountain, smouldering quietly against a hazy blue sky. 'Well, nature certainly played its part.' She dimpled.

'But propinquity was the best bit,' he said, kissing her to prove it.

'What are we going to tell my mother?' she wondered ruefully when she surfaced.

He grinned. 'Nothing. She's happy we're husband and wife, so let's leave it that way—unless you want a big, flashy wedding?' He laughed when Jennifer shook her head frantically; she just wanted their lives together to start as quickly and smoothly and quietly as possible. 'Maybe after we give her a third grandchild we might start dropping hints about the secret of our romantic past,' he suggested.

'Romantic!' Jennifer rolled her eyes. 'You mean tormented and torrid!'

'That too. Speaking of which…' He scooped her up in his arms and began to carry her back to the house, looking down at her with the light of love and laughter in his eyes.

'Well, Mrs Jordan, I think that after we turn our pretend marriage into the real thing we'll have earned ourselves a *real* honeymoon. And I've got the perfect place for it…'

'Oh?' She heard the innocent note in his voice, and laughter was bubbling up from her throat even before he finished speaking.

'Yes—I know this fantastic little remote and isolated spot on the banks of the mighty Amazon…!'

Lucy Gordon cut her writing teeth on magazine journalism, interviewing many of the world's most interesting men, including Warren Beatty, Richard Chamberlain, Roger Moore, Sir Alec Guinness, and Sir John Gielgud. She also camped out with lions in Africa, and had many other unusual experiences which have often provided the background for her books. She is married to a Venetian, whom she met while on holiday in Venice. They got engaged within two days.

Two of her books have won the Romance Writers of America RITA® award, SONG OF THE LORELEI in 1990, and HIS BROTHER'S CHILD in 1998 in the Best Traditional Romance category. You can visit her website at www.lucy-gordon.com

Her next book is HIS PRETEND WIFE,
out next month in Tender Romance™!

Also, don't miss Lucy Gordon's brand-new
trilogy, *The Counts of Calvani*, which is coming
soon in Tender Romance™!

The Venetian Playboy's Bride – April 2003
The Italian Millionaire's Marriage – June 2003
The Tuscan Tycoon's Wife – August 2003

— These proud Italian aristocrats are about to propose!

RICO'S SECRET CHILD
by
Lucy Gordon

CHAPTER ONE

SHE'D longed to come to Italy, but not like this.

As Julie Hallam left the airport and got into the taxi that would take her to the centre of Rome, she suddenly knew that she'd made a terrible mistake.

On the face of it, she was to be envied—sophisticated, successful, arriving in the Eternal City with eight pieces of matching pigskin luggage filled with glamorous costumes and jewellery. Her clothes were expensive, her perfume musky, her grooming immaculate. She was a woman who'd made her way in the world and travelled to Rome on her own terms.

But long ago, she'd dreamed of coming here as the bride of Rico Forza.

She tried to put that thought out of her head. She'd survived the years since their parting by refusing to look back, but now it was as though all the memories she'd repressed had beaten down the doors at last, reminding her that here was something he'd described, and there was a place he'd promised to take her. And she would see them, but not with him.

'You are on vacation, *signorina*?' the taxi-driver called cheerfully over his shoulder.

'No, I'm here to work,' Julie called back, automatically putting on her bright, 'professional' face. 'I'm a nightclub singer. I have an engagement at La Dolce Notte.'

He gave a whistle of appreciation at the name of

Rome's most glamorous night spot. 'Then you must be very famous.'

'Not really,' she said, laughing.

'But La Dolce Notte hires only the best.'

'You've been there?'

'Not as a guest. One meal there would cost my earnings for a week. But many times I collect people in the early hours. Have you been to Rome before?'

'No,' she said quietly. She could have added, 'Only in my dreams.'

And what was a dream? Something that faded to nothing in the cold light of day and made you wish you'd never slept. In dreams, Rico took her in his arms, whispering, 'You're mine, *amore*, and nobody will ever part us.' But she always awoke to a cold, lonely bed and the knowledge that she would never see him again.

'Usually they employ only Italian singers,' the driver went on chattily.

She didn't want to talk, but anything was better than dwelling on her thoughts, so she said, 'I was singing in a London nightclub and this man was there at the front table. Afterwards, he came round and offered me this engagement. My agent said it was a big compliment. It's more money than I've ever earned before.'

The driver whistled respectfully. 'They must have been very anxious to secure you.'

It had seemed that way to her, too, and that puzzled her. Julie Hallam was a success and much in demand all over England, but she knew she hadn't reached the heights where foreign venues competed for her services.

Yet here she was, on her way to star at one of Rome's top nightspots. La Dolce Notte meant Sweet

Nights, and the club had a reputation for delightful decadence, liberally laced with money. Film stars and government ministers, the beautiful, the famous, the notorious, rubbed shoulders at its tables.

The manager had been so anxious to secure Julie's services that he'd provided free accommodation. It was close to the club, which would be useful for late hours.

The taxi had reached the Via Veneto, a broad, tree-lined avenue, full of expensive shops and open-air cafés. Halfway along, they turned into a side-road, stopping outside a large, ornate apartment block. The driver carried her bags inside, accepted her tip with a smile and departed.

The porter conducted her to an apartment on the second floor. 'Will you please call the club and inform them that you have arrived?' he requested with a small bow.

When she was alone, she looked about her in awe. She had a large living-room and a bedroom, both furnished in a palatial style. The huge bed was luxurious, as was everything else, including the bathroom. But the luxury made her uncomfortable. She was in Rome for three months, and it would have been nice to rent a cosy little flat. This place was more suited to an expensive kept woman.

She called the club and was put through to the manager's secretary. 'I'm afraid Signor Vanetti is out,' the woman said, 'but he would like you to be at the club tonight as his guest, and to meet some members of the press. A car will call for you at nine-thirty.'

Julie unpacked, then stripped off and showered, trying to dispel the unease that her surroundings had induced. She didn't belong in this opulent place.

Beneath the sophisticated façade, she still had much in common with the gauche girl who'd fallen in love with Rico Forza eight years ago. That girl had been called Patsy Brown, and her ambition was to be a singer. She'd taken a job at The Crown, a London pub, serving customers, collecting glasses. But every evening there was the music spot when she stood up and sang, accompanied by a pianist. The piano needed tuning and it was all very rough and amateur, but she could dream about being a *chanteuse*.

Then Rico had come to work there, and she'd discovered that life held more than singing.

He was twenty-three, an Italian visiting England to improve his English. He already spoke the language stiffly, but working at The Crown, he soon eased up and learned slang.

He was popular with the other bar staff and the customers. His comical mistakes endeared him to everyone. So did his ready laughter and the message that flashed from his dark eyes. He was tall and slim but strongly built, with a handsome face and a wide, sensual mouth. All the girls flirted madly with him, and he flirted madly back.

The only one he didn't flirt with was Patsy. When he spoke to her, it was always gravely, and sometimes his eyes rested on her with a burning, silent message that made her feel self-conscious. She began to realize that he watched her when she sang, standing stock-still as if entranced. And gradually she forgot everyone but him.

She stood there, her mass of fair hair framing her face like a halo, and sang the songs of youth and first love, of hopes and dreams that lasted for ever. And Rico never took his gaze from her.

Other men watched her, too, with slack mouths and drunken eyes, and one night, one of them was waiting as she left. His idea of a joke was to block her way, dancing about her in a way that made her feel sick.

'Please let me pass,' she begged in a shaking voice.

'All in good time. Why don't you stay and talk to me?' he said in a slurred voice.

'Because she doesn't want to,' said a voice from the darkness.

The lout whirled but wasn't in time to see the punch that connected with his chin. What happened then was too fast to follow, but suddenly her tormentor was running away, clutching his nose, and Rico was left there, blowing on his knuckles.

'Are you all right?' he asked gently.

'Yes, I—I'm fine.'

'You don't sound it. Come with me.' He drew her hand through his arm and walked for a few streets, saying nothing until they reached a fish and chip shop. 'Since I am in England, I am learning to like fish and chips,' he said. 'Cod? Plaice?'

'Cod, please,' she said.

'Sit down,' he commanded, pointing to a table for two by the window.

He brought plates of cod and chips, and large cups of tea, which he sugared liberally.

'I don't take sugar,' she protested faintly.

'You will take it now,' he said firmly. 'You've had a shock. You shouldn't be out alone at this hour. Why does your lover permit such a thing?'

'I don't have a lover,' she said shyly.

'That is an *infamia*. A beautiful girl should always have a lover. In my country, your solitude would be a reproach to every man.'

'And in my country,' she replied with spirit, ' a girl likes to be more than a trophy for the first man who can carry her off.'

'Not the first man,' he said softly. 'Only a man worthy of you.'

'And if I had a lover, I wouldn't ask his permission for anything I wanted to do.'

'If he was anything of a man, he wouldn't care whether you asked or not,' Rico retorted at once. 'If you were mine, I wouldn't let you walk alone in the dark.'

A silence fell between them. The conversation had opened up a minefield, and she wasn't sure she dared venture across. To cover her self-consciousness, she took a sip of tea. When she glanced up, she found him gazing at her with the look in his eyes that she'd seen before. But now it was more intense than ever, and something she found there made the colour flood her face, and her body burn as though a fire engulfed it.

'Why…are you looking at me like that?' she whispered.

'I'm thinking how much I want to make love to you,' he said simply.

She dropped her head so that he couldn't see her sudden shyness. No man had ever spoken to her with such frank intimacy before.

'You mustn't say that,' she said, blushing furiously.

'Why not?'

'Because—because we don't know each other. We've barely ever spoken before.'

'Words? What are they? I've watched you ever since the first day, and every time I've seen you, I've wanted to make love to you. I've thought how beautiful your lips are and what it would be like to kiss them.'

As soon as the words were said, she knew that there was nothing in the world she wanted as much as to kiss him. She was sure her desire must be obvious. She was completely vulnerable, with no defences against him. It alarmed her to realize that he could ask her anything and she couldn't refuse, wouldn't even want to try.

Before this, she'd been a well-organized person, her sights set on her ambition. Now everything was out of her control, and she was being rushed headlong to an unknown destination. She could run away, or she could put her hand into Rico's and let him lead her there.

She raised her head and gave him a glowing smile, full of trust.

He lived in a small backstreet boarding-house. They slipped in quietly and crept upstairs. He had one room that served as both bedroom and living-room, plus a kitchen no bigger than a cupboard, along with the use of a communal bathroom. Everything about it was shabby, but to her it was an enchanted place.

The bed was a bit cramped for two, but they didn't care. They had their passion and the beauty of its fulfilment.

She'd never made love with a man before, but with Rico everything seemed natural. He undressed her slowly, as though paying homage to her body, and when she was naked, his look of worship told her she was perfect.

'You are beautiful, *carissima*,' he murmured, his mouth against her smooth skin. 'Such beauty I've never seen before. I want to kiss you everywhere.'

He'd done just that, trailing his lips softly over her neck, her breasts, the inside of her thighs. Her shyness vanished under the sensations he was evoking. She had been made for this moment.

He loved her slowly, giving her time to overcome her shyness and relishing the beauty that she offered him as a perfect gift. Wherever his lips and hands touched her, he left a trail of delight.

'Rico,' she whispered, 'Rico—'

'Hush—trust me—say that you belong to me.'

'I belong to you,' she said, helpless against the rising tide of passion. 'Rico...Rico...oh, yes!'

She felt him seeking and claiming her. Nothing had ever felt so wonderful as the sensation of him inside her, loving her with passion and tenderness. She hadn't dreamed that there could be such joy.

His body was wonderful to her, young, strong and smooth, with the power to bring her own flesh to glorious fulfilment. She loved him for that, and for his gentleness. But most of all, she loved him because he was himself.

After their first loving, nothing was ever the same again. The world was bathed in new colours, each one bright and glowing. Now she knew what a man and a woman could be to each other, how passion could transform them into new selves and create another self that was neither one of them, but the love of them both together.

She moved in with him and found that he had many sides. There was the young man who'd arrogantly declared, 'If you were mine, I wouldn't let you walk alone in the dark.' But he could also be humble, treating her with reverence, passionately grateful for her love.

If he woke first, he would make tea and bring it to her in bed, watching anxiously until she'd sipped it and pronounced it perfect. Late at night, he would often cook for her, and when she protested that he did too much, he said simply, 'Nothing that I do for you is too much. You have given me everything.'

He said very little about his life in Italy beyond the fact that he came from Rome. She formed the impression that he'd grown up lonely and deprived of love. He was one of those rare men who knew how to appreciate what a woman had to give, not merely passion but affection. He loved her gentleness, her solicitude. When he started a feverish cold, she made him stay in bed and nursed him. He seemed overwhelmed by her care, as though nobody had ever looked after him before.

Then his mood would change and he would be merry, teaching her how to cook Italian food because, as he said, 'You're a disaster in the kitchen.'

Patsy had had nobody to teach her to cook since she was twelve and her mother had left home, unable to endure life with a husband who treated her as a slave.

The girl had been left to look after her father and brother, who expected to be waited on. Her father had been an idler, whose income came from cheating the social security system and the proceeds of petty crime, and he'd taught his son to do the same. She'd seldom had any money for herself because the two of them spent every penny in the pub.

She'd dreamed of escape, and her chance had come at seventeen when they'd both had to serve a short spell in prison. Patsy had slipped out of the house one night, made her way to the bus station and caught the next bus to London.

She'd told her story frankly to Rico. 'I'm going to make my own life,' she said fervently. 'I'll get engagements in the most glamorous places in the world and make lots of money and be my own woman.'

'Not mine?'

'Oh, Rico,' she said, instantly contrite, 'you know that's different. Of course I'm yours. It's just that...'

But there were no words to explain what drove her. With youthful confidence, she assumed that everything would work itself out, and she could have both her love and her career. For the moment, she simply enjoyed playing house, looking after her man, cherishing him in the little ways that seemed to mean so much to him.

'Who taught you to cook?' she asked one evening as he served her with spaghetti carbonara. 'Your mother?'

A strange look crossed his face. 'No,' he said after a moment. 'It was our—it was Nonna.'

'Your grandmother. That is—I believe that's what Nonna means.' She blushed in case he should suspect that she'd been studying Italian.

'Yes, it does. She wasn't actually my grandmother, but she was like one to me. When I was little, I used to spend time with her in the kitchen, telling her my troubles. She told me to make myself useful, so I chopped things and mixed things, and when I did it wrong, she yelled at me. And that's how I learned to cook.'

His manner was so droll that she laughed, then said, 'You told her your troubles? Not your mother?'

'Both my parents are dead,' he said, his humour fading. 'I'll get you some more tea.'

'No more, thank you. Tell me about your mother.'

'Another time.'

'Why not now? Darling, I want to know everything about you—'

'*Basta*!' he flashed. 'Enough!'

She stared. Rico had spoken softly but with an imperiousness that astounded her. For a moment, something flashed in his eyes that didn't fit with what she knew of him. How did a poor barman come to have that instinctive authority, that proud insistence on being obeyed?

Then, like lightning, he was his old self again, laughing, kissing her, making silly jokes. It might never have happened.

But that night, as she lay in his arms, feeling his body's warmth and the soft thunder of his heart close to her ear, the moment came back to her. Of course, Rico was Italian, and no doubt a touch of arrogance was normal in Italian men. Thus she tried to reassure herself and silence the little tremor of apprehension that warned her something ominous had happened.

When she awoke, the apprehension was gone in the blinding light of her happiness. She'd thought she knew what love was, but that seemed long ago in her ignorant girlhood, before she'd experienced the searing delight of the beloved man urgently claiming her. There were feelings that couldn't be described, like the hot pleasure as he entered her, whispering, '*Mio amore…sempre…per eternità…*'

Her emotion went too deep for speech, but her heart echoed his words: My love, always, for eternity. She couldn't see the change in herself or hear the new, deeper inflections in her voice, full of the memories of giving and taking, feeling his smooth brown skin next to hers, drinking in the intoxicating scent of male passion.

But these things were plain to everyone who heard her sing the songs of love. Her sensual awakening infused every word, every inflection, making her audience stop and listen with new attention and a sudden ache in their hearts.

Rico was a jealous lover, watching her with brooding eyes when she performed, angry with other men who saw her, although he knew she sang only for him. There was one song that she directed at Rico with special meaning.

Whatever happened to my heart?
I tried to keep it safe,
But you broke through
And stole it right away.
Take good care of it,
I'll never have another heart to give.

Once as they lay together, his head resting between her breasts, he whispered, 'You'll never leave me, will you, *carissima*?'

'Never,' she murmured.

'You must promise me,' he persisted urgently. 'Let me hear you say that you'll never leave me as long as you live.'

'I'll never leave you as long as I live,' she repeated, glorying in the words.

'And you'll never love another man.'

'I'll never love another man. Oh, Rico, how could I love anyone but you? You're all the world to me.'

She kissed him fiercely, and he responded with an abandon in which she thought she could detect a hint of desperation. As though he were afraid of something…

She didn't think of that at the time. Lying in his arms, her young body sated, she thought simply of pleasure. It was only later, when the world had collapsed and they were far apart, that she understood the strange note in his voice.

They'd had each other and the bliss of love fulfilled. And it had been enough, until the day they'd learned that someone else was about to enter their lives.

'A baby!' Rico had shouted with delight. He was an Italian. He'd been born with a father's heart. 'Our own baby. Our little *bambino*.'

He'd rushed out and bought her a locket with a picture of the Madonna and child. It was a cheap item, but to her it was pure gold, and she treasured it with her whole heart, especially when he took a coloured pencil to the Madonna's face and, with a few strokes, made it more like her own.

She'd been thrilled at his enthusiasm and the way his heart expanded at once to welcome their child. But her practical side wouldn't be silenced.

'Darling, we've no room for a baby and no money.'

'These things will sort themselves out. What matters is that we have a child of our own. And we will love it, and love each other, and love all the world because we are so happy.'

Had any young man ever been so recklessly full of joy? Where had it all gone?

With dreadful timing, her career had flared into life at that moment. The owner of The Ladybird, a small but elegant club, offered her an engagement. But Rico

had insisted that she refuse it, which led to their first
quarrel. He'd accused her of resenting their baby because it interfered with her career.

It wasn't true. She wanted his baby desperately, but
she also wanted to be a star. And she was still young
enough to think she could have it all. She'd learned
better.

They'd made up the quarrel in each other's arms,
and for a while all had been well. But the first crack
had appeared.

Julie came out of her unhappy reverie to realize that
she was staring into space. So much happiness
crammed into such a short time. So much grief to follow. So empty the years since.

She gave herself a little shake. This was her moment
of triumph, and she was going to give it all she'd got.
And that meant refusing to think about Rico Forza or
what might have been.

She slept for a couple of hours and rose in good
time to get ready. Tonight she would be professionally
'on display', so she chose an elegant dark blue dress
that shimmered as she moved and swept up her honey-
blonde hair into an elaborate confection on top of her
head. Her make-up was applied with great skill to look
glamorous but discreet. It helped her feel she was ban-
ishing little Patsy who'd loved and lost, while conjuring up Julie Hallam, *chanteuse*.

At nine o'clock, she answered a knock on her door.
A bellboy offered her a small package and vanished.
She opened it, then stopped dead.

Inside was the most magnificent set of diamonds she
had ever seen. Necklace, earrings, bracelet, even an
ornament for her hair—all were flawless and obviously real.

The card said only, 'With the compliments of La Dolce Notte.'

Slowly she put them on, feeling more puzzled and uneasy by the moment. The diamonds must be worth thousands of pounds. Surely they couldn't be a gift?

But of course, they were only for display, and she would return them at the end of the evening. That must be it.

Precisely at nine-thirty, the receptionist rang to say that her car was ready, and she swept out to the luxurious limousine. The chauffeur held open the rear door. A man was sitting in the back, but all she could see clearly was the hand that he stretched out to assist her. She took it and felt him draw her inside. The door was closed behind them, the chauffeur got behind the wheel, and they were away.

Julie turned to look at the man sitting beside her. And she froze.

'*Buon giorno, signorina,*' said Rico Forza.

CHAPTER TWO

'RICO,' she whispered.

She felt as though her heart had stopped from the shock. Then she pulled herself together. She'd been thinking of him so much that she'd started imagining things. It was dark in the car except for passing flashes of light, and she peered, trying to see the man better.

'I'm sorry,' she said. 'I thought for a moment…'

A sharp beam of light swung round the car and away again. For a split second, it fell on Rico, his face a mask of cold, jeering triumph. Then it was gone.

His voice spoke from the semi-darkness. 'It was kind of you to wear the diamonds I sent you. Their splendour is matched only by your own.'

He didn't know her. But how could he? Eight years had so changed her that she hardly knew herself. Patsy Brown was dead and buried under a mountain of grief. Long live Julie Hallam!

'I am Rico Forza, the owner of La Dolce Notte, also of the hotel where you're staying,' he said smoothly.

'I—I was expecting Signor Vanetti, the manager,' she stammered.

'And you find me instead. I hope you're not too disappointed. And your accommodation? Do you like it?'

She fought for something to say. At last she managed, 'Well…no, I would've preferred something smaller, less expensive. All that luxury oppresses me.'

'Excellent,' he said. 'The star who remains a simple

girl at heart. It's a good line. You should use it when
you talk to the press tonight.'

'Must I?' she asked desperately. 'Of course I'll meet
them, but perhaps not tonight.'

'I've already arranged it.'

The blunt assertion of power silenced her.
Frantically she cast around in her mind for a way to
end this. She must tell him the truth, but there was no
time now. The short ride to La Dolce Notte was almost
over. When they drew up to the kerb, he stepped out
and reached in to help her. The hand that had once
touched her with such reverent intimacy now held hers
in a steely, indifferent grip. He wasn't even looking at
her.

She drew on all her courage. This was going to be
a difficult evening, but it would have been worse if
he'd recognized her. Somehow she would find the
strength to get through the hours ahead.

The outside of the club bore posters advertising the
forthcoming appearance of 'Julie Hallam, glamorous
singing star'. Two life-size pictures of her framed the
door, and a small crowd on the pavement applauded
when she appeared. Rico held out his arm, she slipped
her hand through it, lifted her chin, and together they
walked through the door.

There was more applause inside. Many of the staff
were there as well as some photographers. Julie smiled
into the flash bulbs and carried her head high.

The tables were arranged around a dance floor,
where one or two couples were dancing smoochily to
a small, expert band. Rico handed her to a table at the
front with the ease of a practised host, then indicated
for her to take her seat.

Now she could see him better. It was Rico and yet

not Rico. He was as handsome as ever, in fact more so. The unformed boy had grown into a man whose lines were clear and firm. Something in his face that might have gone either way had settled for hardness. His dark eyes, whose depths had once held such tenderness, now seemed to swallow light and reflect back only some cold, alarming emotion.

Since she'd found him in the car, she'd felt numb with shock. Now her heart had returned to life and was thumping uncomfortably. Their last meeting had been when he left for Italy 'to tell my family about you, about our love, and our baby'.

The parting was to be a matter of only a few days, but they'd never seen each other again.

'Why can't I come with you?' she'd begged.

'Because...it's best this way.' Rico had spoken uneasily, and soon, in misery and despair, she'd found out why.

And what of his despair, when he'd returned to find her vanished, leaving behind a letter that would break his heart and the locket he'd given her with such love? Since then, she'd wept many tears for his pain, wondering what that betrayal would do to him. Looking at him now, she thought she knew.

She remembered his open-hearted relish for life and people, his desire to give more than he took. But something had drained all that from his face, leaving behind reserve, caution, mistrust. This handsome, wealthy man with the world at his feet had a withered heart.

And it was her fault. If only her courage hadn't failed her all those years ago...

On the table lay a small packet, elegantly wrapped in gold paper.

'Open it,' he said. 'It's yours.'

'But—but there's no need. I mean…these…' She touched the diamonds about her throat.

'Open it,' Rico repeated in a quiet, dead voice.

Inside was an emerald bracelet. He fastened it onto the same wrist where she'd placed the diamonds. Her hand felt strange and top-heavy.

'It's lovely, but it's not necessary for you to shower me with jewels,' she protested. She touched the necklace again. 'Of course, I understand that these aren't mine. You wish me to wear them for tonight, but they belong to the club.'

'Have I said so?' he asked with a shrug.

'No, but you can't really mean to give a fortune in jewels to a woman you don't know.'

'It's strange, but I have the feeling that I do know you. Why would that be, *signorina*?'

'I don't know,' she said softly.

'The jewels are yours, all of them. Such a beautiful woman should attract expensive tributes from men.'

The emphasis on 'expensive' was faint but unmistakable, and his ironic tone almost turned the words into an insult. Julie began to feel as if she were moving through a nightmare. For years, she'd imagined that she might meet Rico again. In dreams, she'd run into his open arms. He would hold her close, telling her how much he'd missed her, but at last they were together again for ever.

Instead, she found a bleak-eyed stranger, who radiated hostility even while he played the perfect host. There was no tenderness in his voice, only a kind of grating quality that made her uneasy.

His shoulders were broader than she recalled, and his whole frame seemed heavier. He was still lean, without an ounce of fat, but the slender lad had been replaced by a man whose every line proclaimed power, force, dominance. He was a man to fear.

'Champagne,' Rico said to the waiter.

They'd drunk champagne together once, a cheap half bottle bought at cost price from the pub. They'd sipped from tooth glasses, giggling like children, and it had been delicious. The champagne he offered her now was like liquid gold, three hundred pounds a bottle, chilled to perfection. She could barely get it down.

'I've taken the liberty of ordering for you,' Rico said. 'Lobster salad, followed by...'

Bread and cheese, spiced up with the remains of a jar of pickles, washed down with lemonade. And love.

'The press will be visiting our table,' he said. 'Your arrival has caused great interest.'

'I didn't know anyone over here had heard of me.'

'I have ensured that they do.'

'Why are you here with me tonight? Surely it's the manager's job?'

'True, but I like to involve myself with this club. I have many investments, but some give me more pleasure than others. It suited me to be your host tonight.'

Something in his tone made her say, 'And you always do what suits you?'

'I do now. It wasn't always possible, but I've taken steps to ensure that these days things happen according to my wishes.'

'And other people?'

'I persuade them to see things my way.'

I will do anything, make any sacrifice for you, heart of my heart. Nothing matters to me more than to make you happy.

Had those words really been spoken by this same man?

No, another one, younger and full of hope. Something caught in her throat with pity for him.

Ironically it was the kind of night she'd dreamed of long ago. The food and wine were of the best; her diamonds sparkled under the lights. The press crowded around, but respectfully, with apprehensive glances at Rico. They, too, were afraid of him, Julie realized.

They began by addressing her in hesitant English but applauded when she responded in Italian. She described the highlights of her career, her favourite songs. 'I've also developed a repertoire of Italian songs, in honour of my Italian audience.'

They murmured approval, and a man asked, 'Have you ever lived in Italy, *signorina*?'

'No, never.'

'You have Italian relatives, friends?'

'Neither.'

'I was only wondering how you come to speak such good Italian.'

'I…' Briefly she floundered, then her quick wits came to her rescue. 'I've always wanted to visit this beautiful country and I prepared myself.'

The dangerous moment passed. Someone else said, 'Tell us about yourself. You have a husband, children?'

She could feel Rico's eyes burning into her as she answered in a stifled voice, 'No—neither.'

The questions lasted for a few more minutes until Rico brought them to an end by saying decisively, 'La Dolce Notte values its stars. It gives me great pleasure to present Signorina Hallam with this gift, one that I know she will value as no other woman could.'

He slipped a small box across the table towards her. Like the other one, it was wrapped in gold paper, and she had a sense of ill omen. Too many gifts and none of them given with kindness. There was something monstrously wrong here.

'Open it,' Rico said with a smile like a knife.

Although it was hard, she returned the smile and opened the little packet. And when she saw the contents, she drew a sharp, horrified breath.

It was a gold locket, studded with diamonds and sapphires. Inside was a picture of a Madonna and child, the very same picture that he'd given her long ago. She could still see the marks where he'd altered the face to make it like hers.

She looked up sharply and saw Rico watching her with eyes like stones. He knew her. Of course he did. He'd known from the beginning.

She had an eerie sense of pieces fitting together. It was unbelievable, and yet somehow inevitable. The club's determination to hire her was now explained. Rico Forza had bided his time for eight years until finally he'd lured her into his power.

He offered her his hand. 'We dance.' It wasn't a request.

She put her hand into his and felt him draw her to her feet and onto the dance floor. The band was playing a waltz, and his hand in the small of her back pulled her close to him, holding her firmly.

'Look at me,' he said quietly.

Glancing up, she found his mouth close to hers. How often had she kissed it? How hard and unforgiving it looked now!

'Rico,' she whispered.

'Smile when you say my name. People are watching.'

Calling on all her strength, she forced herself to smile, but she felt giddy. 'You knew me from the first moment, didn't you?'

'From before then, *signorina*.'

'Don't call me that.'

'It's a respectful way for a man to address a woman who is a stranger.'

'A stranger? Me?'

'You always were. There was a time when I thought I knew you—' he drew a sharp breath '—but I was wrong.'

'Don't hold me so close.'

'That's not what you used to say. You whispered, "Closer, Rico, closer. Make me a part of yourself."'

She didn't need the words to remind her. She could feel his body fitting against hers, the movement of his legs, recalling the steely power of his thighs and hips, power that had once made her cry out with pleasure. *Make me a part of yourself.* And he'd done so, again and again, until they'd been one person, for ever.

No, not for ever.

His mouth was so near to hers that she could feel his breath. 'You've forgotten all that, haven't you?'

'No,' she murmured, 'I'll never forget.'

'Then you decided to throw it away, and that's worse than forgetting.'

'It wasn't like that. There's so much to explain—'

'There's nothing to explain. It was all very clear.'

'And you think the worst of me, but you're wrong, truly you are. I want to tell you everything, but not here. Let me go…for pity's sake, let me go.'

The strain of being held against him was becoming

too much for her. In another moment, she would faint. Luckily the music was coming to an end.

'The cabaret's about to start,' Rico said. 'We'll leave now.'

Their departure was as much a triumphant ceremony as their arrival had been. She didn't know how she endured the short journey back to the hotel. As soon as they reached her suite, she turned to face him.

'Why?' she demanded passionately. 'Why?'

'Why what?' He was leaning against the door regarding her satirically.

'Why did you pretend not to know me?'

'Because it suited me to choose my moment. I've waited a long time. I could afford to wait a little longer. Let me look at you.' She tried to back away, but he gripped her shoulders and held her still while his eyes raked her. 'You look very different from what I remember, but then, my vision of you was always a delusion, wasn't it?'

'No, never. I loved you. That's the truth.'

He gave a mirthless laugh and released her suddenly. 'You used to be a better liar than that. Perhaps too much practise has blunted your edge for the finer subtleties of deception.'

'It was no deception,' she cried wildly. 'I loved you, Rico.'

'You loved me. You loved me so much that you deserted me while I was away preparing my family. I can still see myself returning home, running up the stairs, calling your name, waiting for the moment when you would throw open the door and enfold me in your arms.

'But you weren't there. There was only emptiness—

and your letter to me.' He took a step closer and said softly, 'Shall I remind you what that letter said?'

'No!'

'It burned itself into my brain so cruelly that even now I could repeat it word for word.'

'Don't,' she pleaded desperately.

'"We had a good time together, but nothing lasts,"' he recited. '"I've been thinking while you were away and I know what I really want from life." Do you remember writing that?'

'Yes,' she choked.

'You astonish me. Why should something so trivial linger in your mind? And the locket I gave you, that I chose with such love, to honour you as the mother of my child? Tossed aside as nothing.'

'And you gave it back to me tonight on purpose,' she accused.

'Covered in diamonds, a currency I thought you'd appreciate. You didn't want what a poor man could offer you. You wanted money, success and admirers. I shouldn't have taken my eyes off you for a moment, but like a fool I trusted your love. And then you were gone. So was my child. But I don't have to ask what happened to my child, do I? You never really wanted a baby.'

'That's not true,' she cried.

'Don't lie to me. I have a long memory. I can remember what you said about the problems babies brought, money, space—'

'I was just trying to be practical.'

'Oh, you were practical, all right. To me you were sacred. Our baby was sacred. But to you it was just an inconvenience. How foolish of me to expect you to interrupt your career to look after a baby.'

'You blame me for a great deal, Rico, but were you fair to me? You never told me you came from a great family who wouldn't think I was good enough for you. You left me to face your lawyer unprepared.'

'What the devil are you talking about?'

'While you were away, your grandfather's lawyer came and forced me to give you up.'

'I don't believe you. My grandfather was delighted at my news. He wanted me to settle down.'

'That may be what he said to you, but he was actually scheming to separate us. He sent a man called Vanzani to say that if I didn't leave you, he'd arrange to have you locked up. I couldn't take the risk.'

'I've never heard of the name Vanzani. The family lawyer is called Piccere.'

'I only know what he told me. He forced me to write to you—'

'Did he force you to return my locket as well?' Rico demanded in a voice that was almost a sneer.

'Yes, he did.'

'Oh, please, you can do better than that. If any of this were true, you could have contacted me. I'd have protected you from anyone.'

'It wasn't me they were threatening. It was you. I did it for you.'

'That's very good,' he said sardonically. 'If I still had a heart, I'm sure it would be melted by such a line. As I haven't, I advise you not to waste your time.'

'No,' she said slowly, looking at him. 'You have no heart now, have you?'

'Not since you destroyed it. I should be grateful to you. Life is so much more convenient without a heart. There's no pain. I once felt things far too much...' He checked himself with a sharp breath. 'Well, you know about that.'

'Yes, I used to be afraid for you because you felt everything so much,' she said. 'It meant you were always in danger. I wanted to stand between you and the world's pain, but…I couldn't. I didn't want to leave you, but I had no choice. It's the truth, Rico. Please believe it.'

He regarded her, his mouth twisted in cruel irony. 'Believe you? I'm not that much of a fool any more. The discovery that the woman I loved had betrayed me sent me a little crazy. Perhaps I still am. Be very careful what lies you tell me now. I'm a dangerous man to cross.'

'Yes, I can see how different you are,' she said slowly. 'The Rico that I loved would never have behaved as you have tonight. What do you want? Why have you loaded me down with all these jewels?'

'Call them the symbol of your success. Only I know the price you paid for that success. Tell me, *signorina*, was it worth it?'

She wanted to cry out that nothing had been worth the pain of losing him. If she could have found the words, she would have told him of the long, lonely years, aching for his love, knowing that no other man could be to her what he had been. But looking into the eyes of this cruel stranger, she knew that she could say none of this. He wouldn't understand.

The jewellery he'd loaded onto her seemed to burn her skin. She began to strip it off. 'Take it,' she said with horror. 'Take it all.'

'Don't tell me you no longer appreciate the luxuries of life,' he said ironically, 'especially when you've worked so hard for them?'

'You know nothing about me now, Rico. We're strangers to each other, and the sooner I'm gone the better. We should both try to forget that we ever met again.'

'What makes you think you're going to leave?'

'Do you think I'll stay now? I'm out of here on the next plane.'

'If you try that, I'll come after you and fetch you back. And I'll make sure the world knows how Julie Hallam treats her contracts. You'll never work again.'

The ruthlessness in his eyes shocked her. He meant every word.

'But can't you see how impossible this is,' she cried.

'You have a contract. You keep it. What's impossible about that?'

'For you and me—to work together—feeling like this.'

'Like what?'

'With all the past between us—'

'You're wrong,' he said harshly. 'I feel nothing where you're concerned. Nothing at all. Except perhaps anger at a woman who's trying to get out of her promises. But you'd know all about that, wouldn't you? After all, what is a promise? Something to be tossed aside when it suits you. You did that to me once. I won't allow you to do it again.'

'I think you must be a monster. All this time, you've sat planning your revenge like a spider at the centre of a web. How long have you been watching me?'

'Long enough. You weren't easy to find. Patsy Brown vanished very completely. But I went on searching because I had an old, unforgiven wrong to avenge. For the next three months, you belong to me.'

'I belonged to you once,' she said, hardly able to breathe. 'But not any more.'

'You belong to me now,' he said, taking her shoulders and forcing her to face him. 'I've paid your price in advance. I thought you would appreciate that.'

'My price? Are you daring to suggest that I—'

'Know how to drive a hard bargain. I respect that, but so must you.' His voice became soft, deadly. 'You've been bought and paid for. Knowing the kind of woman you are, I'm sure you understand.'

CHAPTER THREE

BOUGHT and paid for.

The words echoed in her head, the cruelest kind of insult, but one he felt she deserved. And as though a flash of lightning had illuminated the world, she saw herself through his eyes, a woman whom any man could insult because she'd traded her heart for gold.

As if to confirm it, he added, 'I've paid in the currency you understand. Diamonds, champagne, luxury. I always pay my bills in full.'

'I won't make that kind of bargain with you,' she gasped, outraged.

'You've already made it. And you'll keep it.'

'No,' she cried, trying to wrench herself away. But his fingers were iron on her shoulders, drawing her closer until she was pressed hard against him. Then his mouth was on hers in a swift movement that left her no chance to struggle.

She raised a hand to fend him off, but he had twice her strength. One arm went behind her neck, the other around her waist, holding her helpless while his mouth moved over hers with hard, driving purpose that angered her even while she felt her loins responding to it.

She knew now that from the moment she saw him tonight, she'd been waiting for this, wondering if his lips would feel as good against hers as they always had. But they weren't his. They belonged to a cruel stranger, and after the first shock of pleasure, her head cleared and everything in her denied him.

'I…won't…let you do this,' she said desperately.

'No blushing violet act, please. Surely those diamonds entitle me to something better?'

He covered her mouth again before she could answer, and this time his tongue found its way to its old home, where once it had been so welcome. Her responses to the flickering tip were still there, still waiting for him after all this time. Fire. Passion. Eager desire. Wanting him. Only him. Forgetting all else.

'No…'

The denial came up from deep within her, but it was words only. Her quivering flesh consented despite all her resolutions. She had a terrifying sense of danger, not from him but from herself. After all this time, his touch could send her wild, making her want him as much as before, while his own heart remained cold. For him this was an exercise of will, and if she yielded now, she would earn only his contempt. And her own.

'No! Rico, stop this, please—'

'I've paid for you,' he said grimly. 'And what I've paid for, I will take.'

Once he'd kissed like a boy with his first love. Now he kissed like a man who'd kissed too often and for the wrong reasons. But she, too, had changed. She'd become what she once told him she would be. Her own woman. Pride and self-respect revolted, and she fought him in the only way she could—with stillness. It was difficult because the fire was raging in her, but she called up all the strength she'd learned in the hard years.

At last, the message of her silence got through to him. He drew back and looked at her, his eyes glittering. 'How you've changed! Once you knew how to give. Now you know how to withhold, but no matter, since I've learned to take. The years have made you more beautiful, and taking will be a pleasure.'

She couldn't speak for the thundering of her heart. She could only watch his eyes with their strange look, as though they were seeking the very depths of her.

'Kiss me,' he said quietly.

'No,' she said. 'Not like this.'

'Kiss me,' he breathed against her mouth. 'Kiss me with lies on your lips, as you did before. But this time, I shall know that they're lies and then I'll be cured of my memories.'

'You can't cure memories, Rico. I've tried hard enough.'

'Do you think I'll be a prey to them all my life?' he raged. 'Kiss me now, so that I can watch you being the cynical little schemer you are.'

Her courage came flooding back. 'Are you sure that's all I am, Rico? Is it so hard to convince yourself?'

Without giving him the chance to answer, she did what he'd demanded and kissed him. Her lips were soft and they lingered on his, purposely conjuring up memories that went back beyond his bitterness, memories of the boy and girl they had been.

'Is that how you mean, Rico?' she whispered.

She wasn't fighting him now but melting in his arms, challenging him to go on hating her while she worked sweet magic on his senses. She caught a glimpse of his face, filled with desperation, felt his arms tighten about her, and the next moment she was lying on the bed with him beside her. Her heart filled with hope, but his words destroyed it.

'You're more skilful than I thought.'

'Wh-what?'

'You knew just what to do, didn't you? Nice to know we're two of a kind. Now we can just enjoy ourselves.'

His lips traced the line of her jaw, teasing her lightly as they moved over her skin, down her long neck to the base of her throat. If only his heart was in this, it would be wonderful, but he'd set out the terms. Barter and exchange—a cold, bitter bargain between two people who neither loved nor trusted each other.

Whatever he said about being strangers, as lovers they knew each other as well as any man and woman ever had. Rico knew the sensitive spot beneath her ear where she loved to be kissed, knew the little pulse that throbbed at the base of her throat when she was aroused. These memories still lived in him, and he made skilful, pitiless use of them.

'You devil…' she whispered.

'Not a devil,' he murmured back. 'Just a man who knows your body well, if not your heart. And your body is all I want. It remembers me, too, doesn't it?'

'Yes,' she gasped.

'I wonder how many men have kissed you over the years. Did they know you as I did? Did they understand the little signals you give to show a man that he's pleased you—or tell him what you want him to do? Or do you keep a different set of signals for every man?'

The contemptuous words were like a flood of freezing water, shrivelling her passion. Julie's eyes flashed with anger and she mustered all her force to thrust him off. 'Get out,' she cried. 'Get out of here now.'

She'd taken him by surprise. He gave a sharp intake

of breath, then his mouth twisted ironically. 'Perhaps you're right. Some things are better postponed. The anticipation is a pleasure in itself.'

'Never,' she choked. 'That will never happen.'

'Don't be so sure, *amore*.'

'Don't call me that. It's over. Everything between you and me is over.'

'You're wrong. Love is over, but love isn't the only emotion, or even the most enjoyable. It will be over when I say so. Not before.'

'You've turned into a monster,' she breathed.

'Maybe I have. And maybe you know why. Remember, you owe me a debt, and while it's outstanding, you belong to me.'

Driven beyond endurance, she seized the diamond necklace and hurled it at him. 'Take it!' she screamed. 'I want nothing from you.'

He caught it and tossed it aside like cheap glass. 'This isn't the debt I meant,' he grated. 'You can return jewels, but how will you ever restore the things you stole from me? My child…my heart…my life—'

He stopped abruptly and the silence seemed to echo with his anguish. His face was white and shocked, as though he'd revealed too much and despised himself for it.

'Rico,' she pleaded, 'it wasn't like that. If only I could make you understand—'

'For pity's sake, shut up! Do you think I care what you have to say? Will explaining change the past?'

'It might help you understand it.'

'And will understanding give me back my child?'

'Rico, I—about our baby…' It was on the tip of her tongue to tell him everything, but a thousand fears screamed in her mind.

'Yes?' he asked harshly.

'Nothing.'

He seemed to withdraw into himself. The fierce bitterness that had possessed him fell away, to be replaced by bleak formality. 'It's late. You should get some sleep to prepare for your first rehearsal tomorrow morning.'

'Don't worry. I'll be there.'

'Then I'll bid you good-night and offer you my best wishes for a successful engagement at La Dolce Notte.'

'Rico,' she whispered.

'Welcome to Rome, *signorina*.'

He gave her a small bow that was like a slap in the face. Then he was gone.

She stood staring at the door, unable to move. She didn't cry because she'd cried herself dry long ago. But she was possessed by pain such as she'd thought she would never know again.

How could he have accused her of such things? How could he believe that she would betray their love by giving away his child? The truth was so different. So very, very different.

She'd known that something was badly wrong when she opened the door and found the sharply dressed man standing there. He was terrifyingly neat and tidy, with short hair slicked into place, and she'd become awkwardly aware of her shabby dress.

'I'm looking for Signorina Brown.'

'I'm Patsy Brown.'

She stood back to let him pass. He gave the room the same appraising look that he'd given her. His smile was half a sneer.

'I dare say you've been expecting me, *signorina*.'

'No. Why should I? I don't know who you are.'

'My name is Ettore Vanzani. I am a lawyer and I represent the Forza family in this matter.'

'What matter?'

'The matter of your attempted entrapment of Rico Forza.'

'My what?' she asked, aghast. 'What are you talking about?'

'Please, *signorina*, no denials. We both know how things stand. You've played your cards very cleverly. Rico himself thinks you're pregnant—'

'It's true. I'm carrying Rico's child. I love him. We're going to be married—'

'Yes, yes, you have a very strong hand. The young man is besotted with you, and you can ask a high price from his family.'

'That's nonsense! Rico's family is as poor as I am.'

'His people, as you know, are wealthy bankers who would pay a good deal to free him from this entanglement.'

'Nonsense. If Rico comes from a rich family, why is he living like this?'

Vanzani shrugged. 'Youthful rebellion takes many forms. A young man who has had every luxury since birth probably finds these surroundings romantic.'

His cool assurance was frightening. It was impossible that what he was saying was true. And yet…

'I don't believe you,' she said weakly. But she was trying to silence the fears that shouted in her mind. 'Rico loves me. He went home to tell his family that we were to be married—'

'He certainly told them that. His grandfather immediately contacted my firm to have you investigated.

The Forza family is choosy about who marries into it. Your own family doesn't stand up to scrutiny. Your father and your brother are petty criminals, constantly in and out of prison.'

'That's not my fault.'

'In my country, family connections matter. Signor Forza will do anything to stop his grandson from marrying you. And I assure you, anything means anything.'

'Are you daring to threaten me, my baby—'

'The threat,' Vanzani said silkily, 'is rather to Rico himself. His grandfather will have him locked up, if necessary, until he comes to his senses.'

Suddenly courage came to her. 'I don't believe a word of it,' she said flatly.

'Then tell me this. If Rico is poor, why am I here? Who pays my fee? Who would care whom he married?' While she struggled to find an answer, Vanzani opened his briefcase and took out an envelope. 'You may find these of interest,' he said coolly.

The envelope contained photographs. The centre of each one was a young man, clearly recognizable as Rico when he was younger. This was Rico as she'd never seen him, dressed in expensive clothes, standing against backgrounds of palatial luxury. In one picture, he was mounted on a horse that looked like a thoroughbred. In another, he was with an old man with a hard, lined face.

'That is Arturo Forza, the head of the family and Rico's grandfather,' Vanzani said.

'Why did you bring these?' Julie asked, and to her own ears her voice sounded thin and unnatural, the voice of someone fighting off hysteria.

'In case you needed convincing.'

'But you said I'd always known about Rico's background. If that were true, why should I need convincing?'

Vanzani acknowledged a hit. 'You're intelligent, *signorina*. Very well, I acknowledge that I wasn't quite sure. Perhaps you're truly the innocent you claim. In that case, I pity you, but it makes no difference. The old man won't tolerate you in the family, and he'll smash Rico rather than let it happen.'

'But if he understood that I really love Rico, that I could make him happy…' The words withered and died under Vanzani's sneer. This man, and those who employed him, weren't concerned with feelings. She made one last try. 'You're bluffing. I don't care how powerful his grandfather is. People can't get away with that kind of behaviour these days.'

Vanzani didn't answer this in words. He merely pointed to the wicked old face in the picture. She believed him then. A man with such a face was capable of anything.

To her horror, she was suddenly swept with nausea. She clapped a hand to her mouth and fled the room, running along the corridor to the little bathroom. When she returned, she was white and shaking.

'I suppose your pregnancy is real,' Vanzani said with a shrug. 'That's a pity, but the marriage is still impossible. I'm not bluffing. My employer has friends in government and in the police. Rico can be arrested on trumped-up charges and held behind bars as long as necessary.'

It was fear for Rico that made the decision for her. Vanzani saw the moment of defeat in her face and went into action.

'My employer is not unreasonable,' he purred. 'I

have here a banker's draft for ten thousand pounds. This will compensate you for any distress. You will write to Rico breaking off your relationship and you will make no further attempt to contact him. If you disobey, the consequences will be dire—for him.'

He insisted on having the letter immediately. Feeling as though she were dying inside, she wrote it, but he pushed it back to her.

'That won't do. It has to be convincing. You should put in some little detail from the life you shared with him. Something about your singing career, perhaps.'

'How do you know about that?'

'Rico told his grandfather all about you. It was very touching. Get on with it.'

Somehow she managed to get the dreadful letter written.

'He'll see through it,' she whispered, choking with grief. 'When you give him this, he'll know you made me write it.'

'You're going to leave it here when you go. He'll find it when he returns. But he won't find you unless you want very bad things to happen to him. This place, and the pub where you work, will be watched and the mail checked. I'm warning you not to write and to stay well clear.'

He read the letter through and grunted. 'It'll do, but there should be something else.' His eyes raked her, taking in the locket about her neck which she'd instinctively clutched. 'Did he give you that?'

'No,' she said hastily. 'No, he didn't.'

'You're lying. Let me see.'

She tried to back away, but he seized the chain and yanked the locket from her neck with one ruthless jerk.

She screamed, but he shrugged and turned away, clicking the locket open.

'A Madonna and child,' he sneered. 'How touching.'

'Give it to me!' she screamed. 'Give it to me, *please*.'

'You have no further use for it. Get your things together now.'

But she couldn't move. This last cruel detail had sapped her courage, and she collapsed with her head on her arms, sobbing frantically. Vanzani hauled her to her feet and shook her.

'Shut up!' he snapped. 'This won't do you any good, do you hear? Do you hear?'

He shook her again, and it had the effect of clearing her head. This was a brutal man, and if she stood up to him, he might do something that would harm her child. She forced herself to calm down and nodded obediently.

'Good.' He released her. 'Now get your things. I won't tell you again.'

No detail was left to chance. He'd taken her to an hotel that night and kept her there for a week. Then, suddenly, it was over.

'Rico has returned and found your letter,' Vanzani told her. 'He spent some time searching for you, but now he has accepted your decision and returned home to Italy. You are free to go. Anywhere you like, except that room and the bar where you used to work.'

He had one final thing to say. 'Rico Forza must not be named as the father of your child. This can be checked. Do not disobey.'

She found a room to live, shut the door and cried without stopping for two days. She cried until there was nothing left inside her heart but emptiness. It was the thought of her baby that brought her back to life. She forced herself to eat and grow strong, but she tasted nothing.

Vanzani had vanished, but even so he seemed to control her. Briefly she thought of asking a mutual friend to call Rico, but they had none. They'd been everything to each other, with no need for anyone else. She dreamed of a thousand ways of contacting him but abandoned them all. The fear of causing Rico harm paralysed her.

At last, she left London, settled in a small midland town where nobody knew her and began wiping out all traces of her past identity. Her new name, Julie Hallam, was an invention that couldn't possibly be traced back to Patsy Brown.

She lived frugally, making the money last as long as possible. She would have loved to hurl it back at the cruel Forzas, but she needed it for her baby. She could never destroy her last link with her beloved.

Her little son had his father's dark eyes and hair, and she longed to name him Richard. But it was too much like Rico, and she was frightened even to venture that tiny step. In the end, she called him Gary. As he grew, she also found in him Rico's warmth and intensity, plus his mercurial nature. Sometimes he was so like his father that her heart ached, but he brought joy to her life and made everything worthwhile.

It was hard to pursue a career and raise a child, but a stroke of luck put her in touch with a distant cousin in her fifties. Aunt Cassie, as Julie and Gary called her, was lonely and only too glad to take them in as lodgers. If Julie had to be away, she cared for Gary like a second mother.

Gradually Julie Hallam worked her way up the bill-boards until she reached the top. The slight chubbiness that had blurred her features at seventeen fell away, leaving her face fine with hollows under the cheek-bones. As her success increased, so did her elegance and sophistication. She could project a song with a subtle sensuality that made club managers clamour for her services.

It was the career she'd dreamed of, but now it came second to the precious moments when she could close the front door behind her, open her arms to her darling son and leave the world behind.

She raised him to speak Italian as well as English, learning it herself so that they could converse in his father's language.

Many times during those years, she thought of Rico with pity for the joy he couldn't share. Perhaps one day, she reflected, they would meet again, then she could show him his son and see the pride in his eyes.

But now the meeting had come, and it was a disaster. Rico had planned this for a reason. After eight years, he wanted his revenge.

She slept badly. Her dreams were filled with Rico as he had been long ago. His hands touching her gently, then with eager purpose, his voice murmuring, 'My love—for ever.' Then the feel of him inside her, filling her with pleasure and satisfaction, filling all the world with love. And the fierce, joyful heat of two melting into one.

Every image was one of warmth, and now she saw clearly how that warmth had infused their whole re-lationship night and day. His hands had been warm as had his heart. When he smiled at her, the warmth in his eyes had seemed to reach out and enfold her, protecting her from the world.

But the world had broken through. All their love hadn't been enough to save him from having his heart broken, and now everything in Rico seemed to have turned round to its opposite. Love had become hate, and joy had turned to bitter, icy vengeance. Once he'd treated her with reverence. Now he regarded her with contempt.

She looked back over the terrible scene between them, wondering why she hadn't told him that she'd kept his son with her, treasuring the child as her last link with the man she loved. But she'd been too frightened of him. He was a man without a heart. He'd boasted of it. A man who used authority and self-will to fill the void where feeling had once been.

And this dreadful change in Rico had been the work of years. It couldn't be reversed by one disclosure, however welcome. Now he cared only for *vendetta*, and what better revenge than to punish her by snatching her son?

And so he must never know that Gary lived with his mother. She must get through these next few weeks and then escape him, without letting him suspect her secret. It would be a test of endurance, but she had already proved herself a survivor.

CHAPTER FOUR

HER first rehearsal was next morning. She dressed for it plainly, in russet slacks and a fawn silk shirt, with the barest minimum of make-up. As she was about to leave, the phone rang, and a man's voice spoke from the desk downstairs.

'Your car is here, *signorina*.'

'I'm not expecting a car.'

'The club has sent one to collect you.'

She thanked him and went down to where Rico's driver was waiting. 'I'm sorry you've had a wasted journey,' she said, smiling at him. 'I prefer to walk.'

He paled. 'But the boss—'

'He'll understand.'

The driver's face showed that he doubted this, but Julie walked out of the hotel quickly. It was vital to her to keep these small signs of her independence.

But there was another reason. Yesterday she'd called home from the airport rather than waiting until she reached the hotel, for which she was now profoundly thankful. If she'd used the hotel phone, Rico would have a record of her home number.

All the negotiations for this engagement had gone through her agent, and it was clear that Rico didn't know where she lived or he would have known that Gary lived there, too. She must keep it that way.

She found a side-street and took out her mobile phone, thankful that she had one that could make calls abroad. In a few moments, she could hear her son's voice, feeling the little tremor of pleasure that it always gave her.

'Hallo, darling,' she said tenderly.

'Hallo, Mommy!'

'What were you doing when I called?' she asked as she always did.

'Aunt Cassie and me were washing up breakfast,' he said. He was still at the stage where washing-up was a game. 'But I broke a plate.'

She laughed fondly. 'Never mind, darling. I wouldn't care if you broke a hundred plates.'

He giggled, and a surge of happiness went through her. For him, anything was worth it.

They talked some more, and then he gave the phone to Aunt Cassie.

'Cassie, have you seen anybody hanging round the house?' Julie asked urgently. 'Any strange men, anyone come to the door?'

But she had seen nothing and nobody. Julie began to relax. But she wasn't taking chances.

'Remember when we went to the Lake District last year?' she said. 'I want you to go there again, today, this minute. Just put Gary in the car and drive. And don't tell anybody where you're going.'

'Julie, whatever's wrong?'

'I'll explain next time. But get Gary away today.'

'Can't we come over there and be with you?'

'No,' she said frantically. 'Please, Cassie, just do as I ask. Call me when you get there.'

She hurried the rest of the way to the nightclub and caused a sensation when she walked in off the street. The doorman, who'd seen her approach, was pale.

'The boss sent the car for you,' he muttered uneasily.

'I know. I simply preferred to walk.'

'But—' he looked nervously up and down the street '—the boss said, well, he wanted you to take the car.'

She recognized the same frisson of fear that she'd sensed in the driver. 'The boss' had to be obeyed. How could this man be the Rico she'd known and loved?

But he was no longer that Rico. He was a different man. She would be wise to remember that.

She hurried on into the club. A piano had been set up on the stage, and a bald, middle-aged man was seated at it, softly strumming. He rose and advanced towards her with outstretched hands.

'I am Carlo Peroni, the musical director. I am so pleased to see you.'

She liked him at once. There was a genial, no-nonsense air about him that she knew she could work with.

The club looked very different by day. The tables were bare, the lighting harsh. The carefully constructed illusions of the night had been packed away until needed. But Julie was content in this atmosphere. This was where she worked, doing what she was good at, preparing an act that would please her audience. It was also how she managed to survive, by pushing painful feelings aside and submerging herself in her music.

They ran through a couple of songs while he listened closely to the timbre of her voice. Mildly he suggested a couple of key changes. She tried them and was pleased with the result. She began to relax. But her peace was shattered by the sound of a door closing sharply as someone entered the club.

Rico strode down the tiered rows of tables to stand watching her at the front. He was angry.

'Good morning,' he said to her coldly.

He was casually dressed in white shirt and slacks and, despite the informality, was perfectly groomed. The shirt was crisp and snowy. Had she really once seen him living in jeans?

'I sent the car for you,' he snapped.

'I preferred to walk.'

'And I prefer that you follow my wishes.'

It took courage to stand up to the man he had become, but she forced herself to do it.

'Don't try to control my every movement, Rico,' she said softly. 'I'm here and I'll fulfil my engagement, but that's all. You don't own me.'

'I thought I'd made it plain that I do.'

'You think you do, but I won't let you. You're such a different person that I don't know you any more—'

'We'll discuss that sometime—'

'But I'm a different person, too. I'll stay here, but I'll fight you if I have to.'

His face became hard with anger. Then his mouth twisted, and he shrugged. 'Very well. War it is.'

He stepped back and swung out a chair, seating himself on it and leaning back with an expectant air.

'Are you going to stay here?' she asked in dismay.

'Why not? I've made a heavy investment in you. Naturally I want to study your progress. You object?'

It was useless to protest. She shrugged and returned to the piano, where Carlo was quietly fingering the keys. He gave Rico an abstracted greeting. He was one of the few people who weren't afraid of him, Julie came to realize.

They resumed. Carlo already knew most of her material, and they were soon working together easily, stopping here and there to try out a phrase in a new way. It would have been a good rehearsal but for her awareness of Rico, watching her, a prey to thoughts she could only imagine.

When they took a break, Julie found coffee waiting for her at Rico's table. She could stand it no longer. 'Please go,' she said as firmly as she could manage. 'You're distracting me from my work.'

'I'm sure that such an experienced professional isn't that easily distracted,' he said smoothly. 'Besides, I can't resist the chance to watch you exercise your charms again.'

'What I do on stage is an act,' she insisted. 'It has nothing to do with what I feel in my private life.'

'Nonsense. Who knows better than I do that your private life, too, is an act?'

'You really do hate me, don't you?' she said softly.

'I'm glad you understood.'

'But how long can hatred last, Rico?'

'Longer than love,' he murmured. 'Years longer.' He raised his voice so that Carlo could hear. 'I've asked Julie, as a favour to me, to sing a special English song called ''Whatever Happened to My Heart?'''

'No,' she said quickly. 'Not that one. I—I don't know it any more, and Carlo won't have the music.'

'But he has,' Rico said. 'I arranged for a copy to be sent to him. He's been practising it, haven't you, Carlo?'

'Night and day,' the plump little man replied cheerfully. 'Ever since the boss said this was an important song for him.'

And the boss's word was law. Julie felt a frisson of unease at how carefully Rico had planned everything. And yet try as she might, she couldn't help a brief, aching pleasure that the song still had some significance for him.

Carlo struck the first chord, and she began to sing in a soft, husky voice.

'Whatever happened to my heart?'

She refused to look at Rico. She didn't want to see him now. She preferred to remember the other Rico, who'd watched her with such adoration long ago in another life.

'I tried to keep it safe,
But you broke through
And stole it right away.'

She'd been right not to want to sing this. The past was too close, too painful still. He'd stolen her heart, leaving her in a wilderness.

'Take good care of it,
I'll never have another heart to give.'

At the end, she could hardly manage to sing. Her voice thickened as memory overcame her, and she faltered to a halt. Her eyes were blurred with tears. She brushed them away and sought Rico. Surely he, too, had remembered and been moved?

He was leaning back, applauding her ironically. 'The tears are good,' he said. 'Keep them. It looks convincing.'

She stared at him in disbelief, feeling herself die a little inside.

She forced herself to keep on, trying not to let her

growing agitation affect her voice. Rico didn't inter-
vene again, but she was aware of his eyes, cold, vengeful, not leaving her for a moment.

'That's enough,' he said at last. 'It's time for lunch.'

'Of course,' Carlo said easily. 'We'll share a glass
of wine.'

'Not today,' Rico said. 'Julie will have lunch with
me.'

He wound her fingers in his as he spoke. It looked
like a gesture of romantic possessiveness. Only Julie
was aware of the power of his grip and the steely
determination within him.

He took her to his office, which was two floors up,
with a view overlooking the Via Veneto. It was spacious and airy, with huge windows that flooded it with
light. There was a large desk on which stood a few
items, neatly arranged.

Everything was clean, sparse, austere. The sense of
emptiness was like a terrible echo sounding through
her. How untidy he had once been! In those days,
everything about him had overflowed: his clothes, his
books, his heart, his joyous love of life. Now everything was neatly buttoned down. And dead.

A table was laid for two. The cloth was snowy, the
crystal gleaming. There was a bottle of sparkling mineral water and one of white wine.

'I ordered a light lunch for you,' Rico said, gesturing. 'I remember how little you ate when you were
singing. Wine?'

'Just mineral water, please.' Julie sat and waited
while he poured the glittering liquid.

In the bright light from the windows, she could see
his face better. He looked very pale and drawn, as

though he'd had a bad night. She wondered if it had been as bad as her own.

'I thought you'd like to know that I've done some investigating,' he said. 'And I discovered that Vanzani exists. He calls himself a lawyer, but he's more of a small-time enforcer.

'But at least you know that I was telling you the truth,' she said eagerly.

'He remembers going to see you on my grandfather's orders,' Rico agreed.

'Well, then…'

There was no softening in his face. 'He also recalls something that you "forgot" to tell me—that you accepted a pay-off of ten thousand pounds.' He watched her face. 'Well? Aren't you going to deny it?'

'No, it's—it's true,' she stammered, 'but—'

'But what?'

'I was going to tell you about it,' she said truthfully, 'but last night everything was so confused…' She gave up in despair. Without telling him everything about Gary, there was no explanation she could make.

'No answer?' he mocked. 'Well, perhaps you're wise.'

'Yes,' she agreed. 'Too wise to waste my words on a man who's made up his mind in advance. Let it be, Rico. We have nothing more to say to each other.'

'Can you say that so easily?'

'Not easily. But let's face the truth. We've both changed beyond recognition. We can't go back to what might have been.'

'*Tell me about my son.*'

The abrupt demand, coming out of nowhere, made her stiffen. Rico's face was tense, unyielding, but revealed a terrible anxiety as he met her eyes.

'Tell me about my son,' he repeated softly. 'Or can't you tell me? Did you give him away without even seeing him?' His voice flicked like a lash.

'No, I—I saw him.'

'What was he like?'

'He was a big baby. He weighed eight pounds nine ounces. And he had lovely dark eyes.'

'I thought all babies had blue eyes for the first few weeks,' he said sharply.

'They were dark blue,' she amended quickly.

And they'd soon turned deep brown, matching his father's. But she couldn't tell him that.

'Did you ever hold him?'

In the first hour, she'd held him against her breast in a passion of love. She'd rained tears of joy and pain over the tiny form that lay in her arms, exhausted by his perilous journey. He'd been oblivious of the storms that raged about his head, while she wept and whispered, 'My love, my darling.'

Whom had she really been talking to?

'Yes, I held him,' she said.

'And then you gave him away,' Rico said bitterly. 'All these years he's lived with strangers, where I can't see him. My son. Mine!'

If she'd doubted her decision to keep Gary hidden, those doubts were silenced now. The look of brutal possessiveness on Rico's face as he said 'Mine!' confirmed her worst fears about the man he'd become. Arturo Forza had sent his emissary to crush her. And this was his heir.

'Tell me where he is,' Rico said harshly. 'Tell me where my son is. Tell me.'

'Forget him, Rico. You have no son.'

'Damn you!' he said softly.

'Do you think I'd want him growing up here, learning to be like you and him?'

'Him?'

'Your grandfather. A man who terrifies everyone into submission. I'll never let him near my child.'

'My grandfather died two years ago.'

'But he lived long enough to damage you, perhaps to make you like him. Don't forget, I've been on the receiving end of his ruthlessness. He threatened to have you locked up if I didn't give in. How could he do that if he loved you? But he didn't love you, did he? His own grandson!'

He looked uneasy. She'd got through to him.

'My grandfather loved people in his own way,' he said at last. 'That doesn't mean his feelings weren't real.'

'But his feelings were more pride than affection, weren't they?' she insisted.

'What do you think you know about him?' Rico demanded with swift anger.

'After the way he treated me, I know a great deal. "Loved people in his own way" means he loved them as long as they did what he wanted. Heaven help them if they didn't! What would have happened to you if I hadn't given in?'

'You really expect me to believe that he'd have had me locked up?'

'That was what Vanzani said.'

'Then why didn't Vanzani tell me that himself?'

'How can I know? Maybe he was too scared to tell you everything about Arturo's behaviour. He might have thought you wouldn't like it.'

Rico thought of his meeting with Vanzani in the early hours of that morning. The man had been shaking with nerves, had repeated himself, contradicted himself. He certainly hadn't been in a hurry to lay blame on Arturo Forza. Not to Arturo's grandson.

Certain vague memories of his childhood whispered past Rico: things half-seen, things fully seen but only half-understood, disjointed words that trailed into silence, glances quickly averted. Fear on people's faces. Fear in their voices. For a moment, the miasma of mistrust that had surrounded his grandfather seemed to choke him again.

'He said you would be locked up if I didn't cooperate,' Julie repeated. 'Maybe it was an idle threat. Should I have taken that chance with your safety?'

She saw the uncertainty in his face. He couldn't be quite sure. But that didn't mean he believed her.

'I know he was a hard man,' Rico said slowly.

'What did he say when you told him about us?'

'He was delighted. He said it was time I settled down and he looked forward to meeting you. He even asked me your favourite flowers so that he could fill the house to welcome you.'

'And you weren't suspicious?'

'I was surprised at his welcome. We'd parted on bad terms when I insisted on coming to England. But he greeted me with smiles...'

He stared at her.

'While he was smiling at you, he was sending Vanzani to bully me,' Julie told him. 'Vanzani walked in and took me by surprise. He made me write that letter, then he forced me to leave with him at once. He kept me in an hotel for a week, watching my every move in case I tried to contact you. He must have had someone watching our rooms to see when you returned.'

'I looked for you like a madman, but nobody knew where you'd gone,' Rico said sombrely. 'When I despaired of finding you, I came home to Italy. My grandfather was all sympathy—'

'Of course. He'd got what he wanted. Rico, didn't you know what he was like?'

'I knew he was ruthless, but this—my God! No, I don't believe it. This is a tale to justify yourself.'

'Vanzani snatched your locket from my neck. It left a mark that's still there. Look.'

She pulled aside the fawn silk of her shirt, revealing a faint line on the side of her neck where the chain had cut her. Frowning, Rico came close. He raised his hand and she felt the faint touch of one finger.

Light as it was, it caused a tremor deep within her. He was dreadfully near. For a moment, their faces almost touched. Then he drew back sharply.

'How do I know when that mark was made?' he demanded. 'You would say whatever suited you.'

'And of course you can't take my word for anything, can you?' she asked quietly.

'Do you expect me to?'

'Yes. At first you didn't believe your grandfather sent Vanzani to me, but now you know that's true.'

'He sent him to buy you off, that's all I know. You named a high price and took it. You gave my son to strangers and lived on blood money while you established your career.'

'No!'

'Don't lie to me. I know too much.'

'You know nothing,' she said desperately.

'Years ago, I set a team of inquiry agents onto the case. It took them time to track down Patsy Brown because the name was so common. Eventually they discovered that a Patsy Brown had given birth to a son at a hospital in a northern city, seven months after I last saw you. But then she vanished into thin air. Now I know it was because you'd changed your name.

'It took them years to pinpoint Julie Hallam as the same person. She lived in London, in Mayfair—the fashionable area, very expensive. And she lived alone. No sign of a child. But then she changed address and they lost her again. That was why I had to proceed through your agent.'

Julie turned away to hide her relief that Rico's spies hadn't been more efficient. She didn't live in Mayfair. Her home was Aunt Cassie's cottage in a modest London suburb. But she'd once stayed in Mayfair for two months, in a friend's borrowed flat, to be near a demanding engagement.

Aunt Cassie had taken Gary to visit friends in Scotland, too far for Julie to visit. If they'd watched her for those two months, they could easily have thought she was childless and lived alone.

Her press cuttings wouldn't have helped them, either. She'd refused several requests for interviews at home. Journalists were allowed to meet her at work or not at all, and she'd always kept Gary's existence a secret.

'I was determined to get you here and make you tell me what became of my son,' Rico continued. 'If you don't know his whereabouts, tell me the names of the authorities who acted in the matter. I'll contact them myself. He was adopted without my consent. I'll go to law—'

'Rico, it wasn't like that—'

'How old was he when you gave him away? Or didn't you give him? Did more money change hands?'

'How dare you!' she breathed.

'I dare say anything because I don't know you. You could be capable of any depravity.'

'Could be,' she echoed, facing him steadily. 'But do you really think I am?'

He looked at her desperately for a long moment. 'How do I know?' he asked hoarsely. 'Where is my son?'

'Leave him, Rico. There'll be other sons for you.'

'Are you mad? He's my first-born. Can't you understand what that means?'

'He was my first-born, too, and I want what's best for him. I want him to be happy. Could he be happy here, growing up to be another Forza, thinking of nothing but power and money? I want better for him than that.'

Rico's eyes narrowed. 'You have great courage to defy me.'

'I learned courage at the hands of your family. There's only one way with bullies. Stand up to them.'

His face was very pale. 'Does that include me?'

'If necessary.'

'You talk of power, but you have no idea how truly powerful I am. I wonder how long you think you can hold out against me.'

'What will you do, Rico? Threaten to have me locked up? And when that fails—what then?'

'I don't fail,' he said, his eyes kindling. 'As you will discover.'

'I'm not afraid of you.'

'Then you are very foolish,' he said in a voice that was deadly quiet.

'I don't want a battle, but if you force me to fight, I will.'

'And how many weapons have you? Only one. Your stubbornness. And that can be overcome. I have more weapons than you can dream of. Come, it'll be better for you to simply do what I want. You won't regret it. I know how to be generous when I'm pleased.'

His voice had grown softer. His dark eyes were hypnotic, forcing her to look only at him and forget the world. Now she knew how he ruled, by silently taking control of an opponent. He wanted her to think that she had no will but his, and she could almost believe it.

'Patsy…' he murmured.

'Don't call me Patsy,' she said unsteadily. 'I'm not Patsy any more.'

'Are you so sure of that? I'm not. I, too, thought Patsy was dead until I held you in my arms yesterday.'

'That—that shouldn't have happened,' she whispered.

'It was always meant to happen. From the moment you vanished from my life, it was inevitable that we would find each other again. You know that's true.'

'I—'

'Did you think you would go through the world and never meet me again, never kiss me again, never feel me kiss you? Some things are meant to be.'

As soon as he said it, she knew he was right. Some things were meant to be, and it was as inevitable as the moon and stars that one day she would be in his arms again.

She didn't know when he moved or when his hands first touched her shoulders, drawing her to him. It wasn't wise to melt against him as though the years had never been, but nothing could have stopped her.

She'd armoured her heart against her memories, but no armour could protect her from the real man, so close, so warm.

Yesterday he'd kissed her as a cruel assertion of power, but today he was as uncertain as herself. Patsy or Julie? He wasn't sure which woman he held in his arms. Or both?

She moved her lips against his, softly. She knew what happened next. His arms would go right around her in a gesture that enfolded and protected her. He would hold her against his heart, telling her that there, and there only, she belonged.

But not now. He kept his hands on her shoulders from where he could either draw her close or fend her off. He, too, had crafted armour to protect his heart. He was afraid. She sensed it. Afraid because his life was built around control, and it was slipping away.

But she, too, was afraid. An uprush of caution made her tense against him, pulling back to study his face. A stranger looked back at her; he had Rico's face and Rico's passion, but he was a stranger.

'No,' she protested, pulling away. 'Rico, stop this, please. We can't be at daggers drawn one minute and in each other's arms the next.'

'It seems that we can. But you're right. It shouldn't happen. We must…' He stepped back sharply and ran a hand distractedly through his hair. 'Many times, I imagined what it would be like meeting you again,' he said at last. 'But things don't always work out the way you plan.'

'I dreamed of our meeting, too,' she confessed. 'But I never thought of this. You've lived in my mind as you were then. I forgot that people move on.'

'And you've lived in my mind as a cruel betrayer.
Now I find that partly untrue. But only partly...'

Suddenly Julie couldn't face talking any more.
Since she arrived, she'd been in a state of continuous
strain, and it was catching up with her now.

'I'm tired,' she said. 'I need to rest before this afternoon. I'd like to go to my dressing-room.'

'It isn't quite ready. You can rest here.' Rico indicated a leather couch.

He began to go round the huge windows, closing
the shutters one by one, until the room was sunk in a
soft, shadowy light. Outside, the fierce heat of Rome
was at its height, but inside, all was peace and quiet.

'You won't be disturbed,' he said, then walked out
before she could say anything.

Julie felt totally drained. All she wanted to do was
lie down and let the tensions fall away. The leather
couch was surprisingly comfortable and she stretched
out on it, her hand over her eyes. In a few moments,
she was dozing.

Her dreams were confused. Again she was in the
plane that had brought her here, but the plane was
attached to a thread. And on the other end was Rico,
drawing her in, the catch he'd planned and schemed
for.

His lips were on hers, kissing her ruthlessly, but
then the years fell away and he was a boy, kissing her
with reverence, whispering, 'I am yours, always.'
They couldn't be the same man, but they were.

Then the dream grew very strange, for she dreamed
that she half opened her eyes, and through her eye-
lashes thought she could see Rico sitting beside her,
watching her closely. He looked vulnerable, baffled.

He leaned towards her. 'Julie,' he said softly. 'Julie.'

'I've missed you so much,' she whispered. 'So many long years without you. So many nights I cried, but you weren't there.'

'Hush.' He laid a finger over her lips as though what she was saying hurt him too much to bear. 'The nights were long for me, too.'

She thought his lips brushed lightly against hers, but then the dream faded into darkness.

CHAPTER FIVE

WHEN she awoke, she lay for a while, thinking, wondering what was true and what fantasy. She could almost feel Rico's lips brushing against hers, no stronger than a whisper. But that was the power of dreams. They could seem so real even when it was only your own lonely heart producing the illusion.

But when she saw him again, she would know.

She yawned and stretched, feeling better. A woman in her fifties, with a kind of austere beauty, looked in.

'I am Galena, Signor Forza's secretary,' she said. 'I have brought you some coffee.'

Her calm maturity made her seem strangely out of place in these glitzy surroundings, and Julie asked, 'Have you worked for Signor Forza very long?'

'Only two years. Before that, I worked for his grandfather.'

'You knew Arturo Forza?' Julie asked quickly.

'Sì. Many years,' Galena said fervently. 'He was a great man.'

Julie knew that some people were fascinated by authority, however cruel. Obviously Galena was one of them.

'Tell me about him,' she invited. She sensed that Arturo was one of the keys to understand Rico.

The secretary left the room and returned with a large book. 'This is mine,' she said. 'I collected every word ever written about him.'

It was a scrapbook full of press cuttings. Curiously

Julie leafed through it. Nothing she found changed her
opinion of Arturo Forza as a man who was coldly
ruthless, sly, scheming and brutal.

At the end, she found a magazine feature, written
when he died. It described the passing of 'a man cast
in the mould of the ancient Roman emperors: a man
of stern will and all-embracing vision'.

He came from a people that once ruled the known
world, and the pride of that conquest still lived in
him. In its own way, his financial empire was as
mighty as the land empire that the Romans won by
force centuries ago. His power stretched into many
countries and affected millions of lives.

The writer then turned to Rico, Arturo's only relative, calling him 'the rebel', heir to banking millions
but with no interest in banking. He owned shares in a
film company, and starlets flocked to be seen on his
arm. Women came and went. None seemed able to
hold his volatile interest. He travelled, investing in different enterprises, always making money, then shrug-
ging and moving on.

There emerged a picture of a restless man, not at
ease with the world or himself. An unhappy man,
seeking something he couldn't find, mourning a loss
for which there were no words.

It struck Julie that she was the only person who
understood that loss. Rico had had no child to put baby
arms about his neck and fall asleep sweetly against
him. She'd known a joy to compensate for her own
grief, but for him, nothing. Could she blame him for
what he'd become?

Suddenly her fears seemed exaggerated. She would

tell Rico about Gary and get Cassie to bring the boy
out to Italy. As he got to know his son, his heart would
soften and perhaps…perhaps…

The past was over, but surely the future might yet
be sweet?

To her disappointment, there was no sign of Rico
at the afternoon rehearsal. But when she'd finished, a
messenger slipped a note into her hands. It said simply, 'Nine-thirty this evening. We're going out on the
town. Rico.'

By now she was used to his abrupt commands, but
this time she wasn't offended. The feel of his kiss had
lingered with her all afternoon. She longed to see him
again. And there was in this note some hint of the boy
he'd once been, who loved to tease her with surprises.

That evening, she took loving care over her appearance, choosing a dress of white silk chiffon that
swept her ankles, and dainty silver jewellery. She was
sufficiently dressed up to be elegant, but this wasn't
the full professional gloss that she would have applied
for a singing engagement. Tonight she would be only
a woman enjoying the company of a man who could
still touch her heart. It was absurd that her pulse still
raced at the thought of meeting him, but she couldn't
help herself.

He was waiting for her in the foyer, wearing a dinner jacket and bow-tie. He smiled and kissed her hand,
and she thought she saw something warm and ardent
in his eyes.

He led her out of the hotel, gesturing towards something that stood by the kerb. Julie gave a little cry of
delight at the sight of a *carrozza*, one of the horse-
drawn carriages that plied their trade on the streets
of Rome.

'Ours for the evening,' Rico said, smiling.

'Oh, it's just as you…' She bit back the rest of the words. In their blissful youth, he'd promised to take her around Rome in a *carrozza*. Perhaps it wasn't tactful to remind him of that now.

But his eyes said he remembered.

He handed her in and she settled back happily against the leather upholstery. It was a light vehicle, with two large wheels and one shaggy black horse between the shafts. When they were seated, the driver started up. In a few moments, they were heading down the Via Veneto, the horse trotting steadily, unfazed by the clamorous traffic.

'You thought I'd forgotten, didn't you?' Rico asked her. 'I promised you this long ago.'

'I thought you might have chosen not to remember,' Julie said, picking her words with care.

'Tonight we cease hostilities,' he said. 'We think only that we are friends who have met again after too long apart.'

'That would be nice,' she agreed.

But was it really possible to be friends with a man of such vibrant sexual magnetism when her heart and body had come totally alive to him again? She had never seen him look more handsome than he did sitting beside her now.

'One may choose not to remember,' he said, taking up her words, 'but it isn't always a matter of choice.'

'No,' she agreed, 'it isn't.'

Darkness had fallen, and the city was coming to life in a different way from daytime. Brilliant light streamed out from windows and doors while strings of coloured lamps illuminated pavement cafés, winking off crystal and silver. And every building of note was bathed in floodlight.

Now was her chance to see some of the great monuments of Rome. The Castel Sant' Angelo, the huge old fortress prison on the banks of the River Tiber, came looming up, sinister and beautiful in floodlight, as they crossed the river. And there was St. Peter's, magical down the long vista of the Via della Conciliazione. Julie watched it in breathless silence, feeling her heart begin to grow content again in the warm night air.

Enraptured though she was, she never stopped being conscious of Rico or the fact that he was watching her intently.

Then they were moving out of the centre of the city and rising gradually until they reached a small inn, with tables set out under the stars. The landlord was expecting them and ushered them to a table by a wooden railing, with a view over the whole of the city.

The table was laid for two, with wine already uncorked. Rico had gone to a great deal of trouble, Julie realized.

'I promised you this, too,' he said, holding out her chair.

'"We will sup nectar and dine with the gods,"' she quoted wistfully. '"And Rome will be ours."'

'I was thinking of this very spot when I said that,' he said, seating himself opposite her. 'When I was a boy, I used to run away up here. I would look at the view and feel like an emperor. What is it?' he added, frowning for a shadow had crossed her face.

'Nothing,' Julie said quickly.

'Yes, tell me.'

'It's just that…it gives me a strange feeling when

you talk about your boyhood. It reminds me that everything you told me before was a—left a good deal out.'

'Was a lie.' He supplied the word she hadn't wanted to use.

'I didn't mean it like that,' she hastened to respond. 'But it was a shock to discover that what I believed about you simply wasn't true. It was like discovering that you'd been nothing but a ghost all the time.'

'I was so immature then,' he said thoughtfully. 'It never occurred to me that my harmless pretence—as I thought of it—was a kind of dishonesty.'

'What made you come to England and live as you did?'

Rico gave a wry grin, whose mockery was directed at himself. 'I'd been raised in luxury, so naturally I rebelled against it. I thought I was a big, independent man, rejecting the comfort I'd always known and living by my own efforts. I believed there was something noble in working for a pittance. Of course, I was only playing. If I hadn't been so young, I'd have seen that.

'But I was defying the powerful Arturo Forza and I was very proud of that. He was so angry that he even cut me off without a penny, which I thought was very adventurous.'

'So you knew what he was like?'

'I suppose I did,' he answered thoughtfully. 'Talking to you has brought back so many things I'd forgotten. He could smile and seem all benevolence, but behind the scenes he was always pulling strings. He used to tell me, "Once Romans ruled the world by military might. Now there are other ways to rule."

'If I wanted affection, I sought it from our cook. I

told you about her. I called her Nonna—Grand-mother—because I loved her. I used to pretend that she was my real nonna.'

'So all that was true?'

'About her teaching me to cook? Yes, that was true. I was never so happy as when I was in the kitchen, telling her all my childish troubles. To this day, there are certain kitchen smells—garlic, paprika—that make me feel good.'

His eyes were glowing with reminiscence. For the first time, she saw him relaxed and at ease, as he had once been all the time.

'Of course,' he added drily, 'Grandfather disap-proved of my spending so much time with a "ser-vant". I wanted to get away from his kind of thinking. Now I remember. That was Nonna's idea. "Go some-place where the air is cleaner", she told me. So I came to London, took any unskilled job I could find and felt free and happy for the first time in my life. And then—'

'Stop,' Julie said suddenly. 'Don't say any more.'

Looking into her face, he understood. Any mention of their happiness led remorselessly to their grief, and she didn't want to remember that now. Neither did he. He wanted to enjoy the flickering candlelight on her face.

When he first saw her the other night, he'd thought how changed she was. But now, in the soft lighting, watching the pleading look she'd turned on him as she begged him not to tread on dangerous ground, he thought her miraculously unaltered. How young and vulnerable she looked—as she had always looked.

The landlord appeared and served them with *strac-ciatella*, a soup made with chicken, eggs, Parmesan cheese and a little magic. Julie tasted it and gasped. 'But this—'

'Is the first thing I ever cooked for you,' he said with a grin. 'You said you'd died and gone to heaven. Wait till you see the next course.'

'Don't tell me,' she said eagerly. 'Let me guess. That thing you made after our first quarrel—'

'We never quarrelled,' he said at once. 'We had small unimportant tiffs, which were all my fault. But after the first one, I made something special to show you how sorry I was.'

'Macaroni with ham and eggs.'

'That's right.'

'But, Rico, you haven't—'

'I ordered a special menu tonight, hoping it would please you.'

She was awed by the trouble he'd taken, and the delicious food cast the spell that he'd obviously intended. She was whisked back to their attic as though on a magic carpet. But this time there was no sadness in the memories. Macaroni to make up their tiff, followed by Roman beef stew, 'because I love you more than my life, *carissima*.'

He'd made love to her with his hands and his loins, but he'd also seduced her with his cooking. It all came back now in a blaze of delight.

'You eat ice cream like a little girl,' he said when she was on the sweet course. 'As though it was a big treat and you were afraid someone was coming to snatch it away.'

'Someone always did when I was a child. My brother grabbed everything he wanted. Being able to eat ice cream without looking over my shoulder was really a treat.'

There in her mind was the ice-cream parlour, just around the corner from their little home, where he'd taken her one evening. She'd been dazed at the variety of flavours on offer, but Rico had been loftily dismissive.

'One day I'll take you to Italy, where we really know how to make ice cream,' he'd boasted. 'This is nothing. But it will do for now.'

How tenderly he'd laughed as she tried to decide between the merits of pineapple and pistachio, mint and chocolate, strawberry, banana—the list went on for ever. His wallet had been full of a hard-earned bonus.

'Rico, that's all the money from your overtime.'

'How better could I spend it than on you, piccina?'

Now she looked up and saw the same memory in his eye. Neither of them spoke. They didn't have to.

'My plate's empty,' she said with meaning.

'Let's see what else they've got.' He looked around for a waiter, but there were none in sight. 'I'll find someone.'

While she waited, Julie glanced over to a nearby patch of grass, where the *carrozza* stood. The horse had his nose in a water trough, and the elderly driver was leaning back, looking up at the stars. Impulsively Julie took a clean glass, filled it with wine and went over to them.

'*Grazie*,' the old man said, accepting the glass. He held it up.

'*Salute!*'

'*Salute!*' She raised her own glass to meet his.

The horse finished drinking and snorted noisily.

'He looks quite old,' she said. 'What's his name?'

'Miko,' the driver said. 'He's nearly twenty. He's

earned a rest but…' He shrugged, and Julie guessed he couldn't afford to retire the old horse. She stroked its long nose.

'I usually only work him during the day,' the driver went on. 'My cousin was supposed to do this job, but his horse went lame. It's good money. We can't afford to lose it.'

'You mean Miko has already done a day's work?' Julie asked in dismay. He nodded. 'Poor old thing,' she murmured. 'I thought he was making heavy weather of that hill.'

She saw Rico searching for her, holding a plate piled high with ice cream. Smiling, she joined him.

'You were right,' she said when she'd scraped the plate. 'Italy does make the best ice cream in the world.'

'If you've finished, we can go now. I have still much to show you.'

Miko stood patiently as they climbed into the *carrozza*, but Julie was glad for his sake that this time the way was downhill. Soon they found themselves trotting through narrow backstreets, where yellow lamps glowed on the cobblestones.

'Where are we going now?' she asked.

'To the Trevi Fountain. That's another place I promised to show you.'

But it seemed that Miko had other ideas. Without warning, he tried to swerve left, and it took all the driver's efforts to keep him going straight.

'*Scusi*,' he apologized when they had come to a halt. 'That's the way home.'

Julie jumped down, ran to Miko's head and patted his nose soothingly. The old horse stood docilely, watching her out of beautiful brown eyes. 'You poor old thing,' she said. 'You've had such a long day.' She spoke to Rico, who'd followed her. 'We don't need them any more, do we?'

'I'm being paid for the whole evening, *signorina*,' the driver said nervously. 'There are another two hours—'

'Rico, can't we take a taxi and let them go home?'

'Of course,' Rico said at once. He handed some money to the driver. 'Thank you. You can go now.'

The old man's eyes widened as he saw the amount. He peeled off some notes and tried to return them to Rico, who waved them away.

'It was the agreed fee,' he said. '*Buona notte*.'

'*Grazie, signorina*,' the driver said fervently to Julie. 'Eh, Miko! Home to bed.' He slapped the reins, and they were gone.

'Why are you looking at me like that?' Julie asked, for Rico was regarding her with a tender half smile.

'The landlord of The Crown had a dog that liked to drink beer,' he said. 'The regulars thought it was a great joke to get the poor creature drunk, until you hit the roof. You called them a bunch of no-good louts, and you told the landlord that he should be ashamed of himself.

'I thought he was going to fire you on the spot, but you didn't care. You just waded in, and nobody ever saw that dog in the bar again.'

'What's that got to do with tonight?'

'Everything,' he said, slipping an arm about her shoulder and beginning to walk. 'Everything.'

They were closer to the centre of Rome than she'd realized, and after they'd strolled through a few streets, she heard the sound of cascading water. The next moment, they turned a corner and the glory of the Trevi Fountain burst upon her.

It was huge. At its apex towered the god of the ocean, his chariot borne by marine horses, plunging and swooping in and out of the water. At every point, water gushed out into the great basin, its droplets shining, the noise so loud that Rico had to raise his voice to talk.

'Here,' he gave her a coin and turned her so that her back was to the fountain. 'You must toss it over your shoulder and make a wish to return to Rome.'

But how could she make such a wish? She'd sworn that when she left here, she would never come back, never risk seeing Rico Forza again. How could she return, unless…?

Taking a deep breath, she closed her eyes, tossed the coin over her shoulder and wished.

'Did you make the wish?' he asked.

'Maybe.'

'Did you wish anything else? Most people do.'

'That would be telling,' she teased.

She felt light-headed with happiness. The journey from sadness to joy had been so swift that it left her giddy. It seemed too good to be true that Rico's heart should have melted towards her so suddenly.

Too good to be true.

She pushed the uneasy thought aside, telling herself not to be suspicious.

From somewhere nearby, Julie could hear the sound of an accordion. They followed the music and found a little café in a cul-de-sac. Couples were dancing in the street, and Rico took her into his arms.

'Do you remember that tune?' he asked as they moved dreamily in time to the music. 'It was an Italian

song, and I taught it to you. At least, I tried. You were
very uncomplimentary about my voice.'

She laughed. 'I said you sounded like a corncrake.'

'And you wrote your own words to the song and
sang it in the pub that night.'

'So I did.' It was coming back to her. The tune was
fragile, almost nothing, the kind of thing that belonged
in a music box, with a little revolving figure. She'd
picked up that echo at once and built a pretty fantasy
around it.

She began to sing in a soft, murmuring voice.

'The world is turning again and again,
Everything comes around.
Sleeping or waking, loving or sighing,
Never ending, never beginning,
Round and round it goes.
Still I keep turning again and again,
Never know when to stop.
Loving you, missing you, hoping and hurting,
Never remembering, never forgetting,
Round and round I go.
My heart is turning again and again,
You never let it go.
Holding me, leaving me, calling me, grieving me,
Never beginning, never ending,
Round and round we go,'

'Fancy you remembering the words after all this
time,' he said.

'I remember everything. I've tried not to, but—
you're right. It isn't a matter of choice.'

Suddenly she was crying. She didn't know where
the tears had come from, but they were pouring down

her cheeks as though the grief of years had distilled into this one moment.

'Julie!' he said, horrified.

'We were children,' she wept. 'We thought because we were in love the world had to be ours.'

'We made our own world,' he whispered against her hair.

'Yes, and we fooled ourselves that it was the real world. But it wasn't like that. It couldn't be.'

'Don't cry,' he pleaded. 'Look up at me.'

She did, and found his lips caressing hers tenderly. His hand was gentle beneath her head. She felt herself melting. All her hard-won caution couldn't win out against the emotions that lived in her, only for him.

His mouth was as she remembered—full, sensuous, ardent. But above all, hers. The first night he'd kissed her cruelly, coldly, asserting possession and authority. But now, miraculously, after all that had passed, he kissed like a boy, breathless with first love. She gave him a heartfelt answer and felt his response in the tightening of his arms, the increasing intensity of his breathing.

'*Mia piccina*,' he murmured. 'Do you remember when I used to call you that?'

'I remember everything,' she said fervently.

'And so do I. I've tried to forget, but you were always there. There was always this.'

On the last word, he smothered her mouth again. Now all uncertainty was gone and he was the passionately possessive lover, reclaiming what he had never truly relinquished.

Here in the public street, they could kiss without fear of being noticed because many other couples were doing the same. It was a place for lovers and a night for lovers. And they were lovers again, as they had always been.

'Let me come back with you,' he whispered. 'I want to stay with you tonight. Please.'

'Rico…' She looked at him in wonder.

'We've been apart too long, *mio amore*. Don't you feel that, too?'

'I've never wanted to be apart from you and I've thought about you every moment of the past eight years.'

He took her hand. 'Come with me. Now the parting is over and the love can begin again.'

CHAPTER SIX

RICO led her out of the side-street and close to the Trevi Fountain.

'There's a *carrozza* rank just around the corner,' he said. 'We can take one back to the hotel. What is it?' For Julie had freed her hand.

'You go on and get the *carrozza*,' she said. 'There's something I want to do first.'

She watched him go, feeling as though she might burst with happiness. What she'd longed for had happened. Rico's heart was open to her again in trust. She could tell him everything about their son, bring the boy out to meet him. She drew in her breath at the thought of that meeting and what might result from it.

It was still a risk. He might be angry at the way she'd kept Gary hidden. But the prize was a happy future for the three of them together, and it dazzled her. And she would protect herself against the risk by a tiny superstition.

She turned back to the Trevi Fountain. Rico had said that most people uttered a second wish, and this would be hers: that Rico would receive her revelations in the right way.

She took out a coin, kissed it, closed her eyes and tossed it over her shoulder, wishing with all her heart.

And then something very strange happened. Opening her eyes again, she found herself looking straight at a man whose face was familiar. He turned away so quickly that she was puzzled. It was almost as if he'd been watching her but didn't want to be noticed himself.

She looked around, and there was another familiar face on one side and yet a third on the other. They, too, stepped back into the shadows to avoid her glance.

Oh, no! she thought. I'm imagining things. He wouldn't do that. But a prickle went up her spine as she recognized the dreadful truth. She'd seen these men at La Dolce Notte. They all worked for Rico.

Suddenly the monstrous situation was clear to her. While her heart had been melting to him, he'd had her watched by his hired heavies. Spied on like an enemy because, to him, that's what she was.

Nothing about tonight was real. The whole evening, so beautiful until this moment, had been a set-up. Rico had sweet-talked her, making love with his eyes, his choice of food and a certain note in his voice, recalling the past in order to seduce her into a compliant mood.

He'd succeeded frighteningly well. And now the stage was set for the last act of the comedy. Then, lying in bed in his arms, overwhelmed by passion, she would tell him what he wanted to know. That was how he'd planned it.

Too good to be true! Some corner of her mind where reason still lived had called out the warning that her heart had refused to heed. Believing him because she longed to do so, she'd come within a hair's breadth of falling for his cruel scheme.

She'd thought she knew bitterness before, but now she realized she'd barely tasted it. The sense of betrayal made her giddy.

Rico was approaching, the *carrozza* just behind

him. He held out his hands to her, smiling. 'Let's go now,' he said. 'This is a wonderful night.'

'Yes, it is,' she said steadily. 'And I'll tell you what's wonderful about it. This is the night when my eyes were finally opened.'

'What do you mean by that?' he asked.

'I fooled myself that part of you was still the man I loved. But that man would never have hired guards to keep me in view while he was acting as though…' She was unable to go on. She couldn't put into words what the evening had meant to her.

Rico's face darkened, and he swore under his breath. 'Please, this wasn't meant to happen—'

'No, I wasn't supposed to notice them, was I?'

'I meant—I was going to call them off.'

'Am I watched everywhere I go?'

'Before this—yes. But if you'd only—'

'I wonder what exactly their job is, Rico? Make sure I don't escape or just report if I make any phone calls? After all, whoever runs the hotel switchboard must have told you by now that I never use the phone in my room.'

He stood silent under her accusations. He had no answer for them.

'How could you do it?' she breathed. 'No, don't try to tell me. I don't want to know.'

'Julie, please, I'm sorry you found out this way—'

'Yes, it shuts off one of your options, doesn't it?' she demanded angrily. 'After this, I won't fall for the "You've always lived in my heart" line.'

Even in this poor light, she could see that he was as white as a sheet. Whatever he'd meant to happen, this was distressing him. She didn't care. She wanted to hurt him as dreadfully as he had hurt her.

'How far were they meant to follow us, Rico? Into my hotel suite? Perhaps they'd have hidden behind the sofa while we—'

'Stop it!' he said harshly. 'It wasn't what you—well, we'll talk about that later.'

'We'll never talk about it. After this, please stay out of my way. Good night.'

Before he knew what she meant to do, she turned and darted away down a side-street. In a moment, she was lost in the darkness.

The three men who'd been watching made a move to go after her but were halted by a look from Rico. He stood there scowling while the *carrozza* driver jumped down and came to the horse's head, looking questioningly at Rico.

'Take it away.'

'The *signorina*…?'

'I said take it away,' Rico snapped, tossing him some money.

The driver allowed himself a small grin. A man whose woman had walked out on him in public was an object of derision. Then he saw the dangerous little pulse that beat at the corner of Rico's mouth and his grin faded. He grabbed the money, jumped aboard and fled.

Rico knew what kind of a figure he cut. His own henchmen had witnessed his being made to look a fool, but they were too wise to get near him. They understood very well the cold menace in his eyes.

He dismissed them with a curt nod and returned to the hotel on foot. He needed the walk to calm his fury: fury at Julie for treating him with contempt, fury with himself for having handled matters badly.

The receptionist confirmed that she was upstairs. He

went up and rapped on her door. When there was no reply, he rapped again.

'Please go away,' came her voice. 'I've gone to bed.'

'Then you can get up again and talk to me,' he said grimly.

'I have no wish to talk to you, now or ever.'

'Open this door!'

'No.'

He controlled himself.

'What happened tonight was unfortunate—'

'Is that your word for it?'

'I'm sorry you found out this way, but I must find my son, and you're the only person who can give me a lead. You have to. I'm in deadly earnest.'

'And I'm in earnest when I say that a man who acts like this is no fit father for my son. I won't help you find him, and if I have my way, he'll never so much as know you exist.'

'I'll tell you one more time. Open this door!'

'And I'm telling you for the last time. No!'

Rico drew a sharp breath. Nobody had defied him for years.

Then he heard a terrible sound. The faint unmistakable sound of a smothered laugh.

He whirled and saw a waiter moving away down the corridor. The man had undoubtedly heard more than enough. And he'd laughed. That made twice in one night that Julie had exposed him to derision.

'Damn you!' he said under his breath. 'Damn you for making a fool of me!'

Julie waited until Rico's footsteps had faded before she allowed herself to relax. She'd been standing

against the door, so tense that her body ached, but
even though her tension now drained away, she found
she was still aching all over.

But her muscles could never ache as painfully as
her heart.

She'd lied when she told Rico that she'd gone to
bed. When she reached her room, she'd been unable
to do anything but sit on her bed, shivering. She was
still sitting there when he knocked. She'd forced herself to rise, and it had been almost a surprise to find
that she could still walk.

When Rico had gone, she stayed leaning against the
door without the strength to move. It was safe to cry
now. She'd suppressed tears as long as there was a
chance he might hear, but at this moment she felt as
though she would weep forever.

She stripped off the lovely dress that she had
donned so happily such a short time before. Her emotions raw, she looked back at that earlier self and realized how much senseless hope had been in her heart.
She got under the shower, letting the water lave her.
Here she could weep unrestrainedly and the cascading
water would hide the sound.

All the carefully constructed defences of the years
had been destroyed in one evening by his cynical ma-
nipulation. She'd sworn not to love Rico Forza because, if she wanted to keep sane and functioning, she
couldn't afford to. But with a few soft words and false
kisses, he'd returned her to the past when she was a
vulnerable girl, adoring him with all the passion of
first love.

And the feelings, once reawakened, wouldn't die.
She couldn't kill her love with the knowledge of his
betrayal.

She'd heard that love and hate were two sides of the same coin. Now she knew it was true.

To her relief, there was no sign of Rico at rehearsal next morning. After her disillusionment of the night before, she never wanted to see him again.

Carlo was ready for her, and they plunged into a lively session in which everything seemed to go right. Julie felt a little comforted. There had always been music to turn to when her life went wrong.

'I can't wait for your opening night,' Carlo said after finishing on a triumphant chord. 'You're going to knock them dead.'

'Well, if I do, the credit's yours,' she insisted. 'You keep pushing me to take risks.'

'And you bring them all off.'

They smiled together like conspirators. Julie's spirits rose and she thought she could even cope with Rico.

Then she saw him.

He'd appeared at the back of the club, accompanied by a young and very attractive woman. She had a dainty, curvaceous figure and a generous bosom, as an extremely low-cut sweater revealed. Her hair was piled high and elaborately on her head, and her exotic looks were emphasized by flamboyant make-up.

A chill wind seemed to shiver through Julie as the words of the magazine feature came back to her. Seldom seen without a starlet on his arm…the most beautiful women, his for the taking…

His for the taking. When she arrived, Rico had made it clear he considered that Julie was his for the taking. But last night, she'd struck back, forcing him to see her as a woman to be reckoned with. This was his retaliation.

Rico escorted his beautiful companion down to the stage and brought her over to Julie.

'Mariella, *cara*,' he said, 'I want you to meet Julie Hallam, the new star that everyone is talking about.'

Mariella made a sound between a simper and a giggle, then enveloped Julie in a scented embrace.

'I've been so longing to meet you,' she said. 'Rico has talked about nothing but Julie Hallam ever since he booked you. It's been Julie Hallam this and Julie Hallam that until I've almost been jealous.' She performed the simpering giggle again. 'Not really jealous, of course.'

'I'm sure you have no need,' Julie said politely. Inside her, a storm of dismay had seized her without warning and was whirling her about. She forced herself to smile and look composed.

'Well, that's what my Rico says,' Mariella tittered. 'He says, "*Carissima*, how could there be anyone for me but you?" And then he gives me something beautiful to show how much he loves me.'

'I'm sure he's very generous,' Julie murmured, hardly knowing what she was saying.

'Oh, all the time. Look at my new present.' She stretched out her wrist to display a gleaming emerald bracelet. 'He called me up last night and told me to meet him at our favourite jewellers in the Via Condotti. The shop was closed, but for him they opened up. And then he just swept me inside and told them to bring out their very best.' Her voice dropped. 'Do you know Rome?'

'I—no.'

'Then you don't know the Via Condotti. It's the

most expensive street in the city. The most luxurious jewellers and dressmakers are there, and my darling Rico has accounts with all of them. I simply order what I want. But it's best when the man takes you himself, don't you think?'

By now, Julie had herself in hand and was able to smile and say, 'I'm sure it is.'

She hadn't missed the significance of 'last night'. It could only mean that Rico had gone straight from her to Mariella; from one woman who gave him an uncomfortable glimpse of himself to another who would soothe his pride with flattery that he'd paid for. And after they'd left the jeweller? What then?

'Have you asked her?' Rico asked, coming over from where he'd been talking to Carlo.

Mariella shrieked with affected laughter. 'We've been so busy talking that I forgot. Julie, Rico and I are having a house-warming party the day after tomorrow. Simply everybody will be there. And to make it perfect, you must come and sing for us.'

Rico and I. A house-warming party. They lived together.

'You're very kind,' she said, 'but I'm saving my voice for the opening night. I'm sure you understand.'

Mariella's pout showed that she didn't understand anyone who said no. 'But you must,' she insisted. 'You must.'

'It's kind of you to ask me, but I'm afraid it's impossible,' Julie said firmly.

A faint noise came from the back. Somebody had arrived and attracted Mariella's butterfly attention. She gave a shriek and launched herself toward the newcomer in a cloud of frothy endearments.

'It's impossible,' Julie repeated.

'Surely not,' Rico said. 'I'm looking forward to hearing you sing in my house. I'm sure you won't disappoint me.'

'As I did last night, you mean?'

'The less said about last night the better. You chose to think the worst of me—'

'It wasn't very hard.'

'Now you can think whatever you like. Just do as I say.'

'Arturo Forza has spoken,' she flung at him.

'Do you think you insult me by likening me to him? You're mistaken. It makes me proud.'

'At one time, you'd have known it was an insult. You were a better man then, Rico.'

He took a step closer and spoke in an undertone. 'You dare say that? Who knows more than you what made me the man I am?'

'A man who'd lie to a woman who used to love him and thanks heaven that she doesn't any more. A man who'd use every trick and laugh up his sleeve while he fooled her.'

'I didn't—'

'Arturo would have been proud of you last night. What a pity it didn't work.'

'Yes, I was clumsy, wasn't I?' he said harshly.

'Don't worry. It didn't make any real difference. I wasn't going to give in even before I spotted your hired heavies. I've changed, too, you see. I've learned caution and suspicion. It would take a lot more than an evening's glib talk and a few false kisses to win me over.'

Pride and desperation drove her to utter what she said. 'Don't fool yourself that you were the only one playing games. I was very curious to know how far you'd go.'

A withered look crossed his face. 'You're lying.'

'Am I? Of course, you'd know about lying, wouldn't you.'

'What does that mean?'

'There are lies of omission. You never mentioned that you were living with Mariella.'

'Mariella has nothing to do with you and me.'

'There is no "you and me".'

He drew a sharp breath. 'It is pointless to discuss this. I wish you to sing at my house the day after tomorrow.'

She looked at him angrily. This was another demonstration of power, and it was cruel, vengeful.

'Rico, what are you playing at?' she said tightly.

'I don't play games. I'm giving an important function. People who matter to me commercially will be there, and I want the best. You will please attend to my wishes.'

'This wasn't in my contract. I sing at the club. I'm not yours to move around like a pawn.'

'I thought we'd already settled that you were. You owe me, Julie. Never forget that you owe me a huge debt. Let's just say that I'm claiming payment in my own way.'

'I don't want to do this,' she said desperately.

His smile was like ice. 'I'm sure you don't. But you'll do it.' He called to Mariella. 'It's all right, *carissima*. Julie has agreed to grace our party.'

'My God, I hate you,' she whispered.

'Then we're agreed about something. I've already given Carlo a list of what you will sing.'

He turned away, calling to Mariella. She came tittuping towards him, embraced him in a theatrical gesture, and they went out together.

On the day of the party, Carlo drove Julie to Rico's house on the Appian Way. They went in the early afternoon to allow time for a brief rehearsal and sound check, and Julie had leisure to observe the old tree-lined avenue.

'What are those buildings every few yards?' she asked Carlo. 'They're too small to be houses.'

'They're mausoleums,' Carlo replied. 'This road is over two thousand years old. The old aristocratic families built their tombs along here. And farther along are the catacombs where the early Christians used to hide.'

'Two thousand years,' Julie mused.

'Rome isn't called the Eternal City for nothing. The past is still here. When I get depressed, I think of all the people who have come and gone. In another thousand years, that's what we'll be—people who came and went.'

After a moment, Julie said, 'Do you mean anything special by that?'

'Rico's been on hot coals since he knew you were coming. Normally he's very cool about women. He can have all he wants, and none of them matter. But you've got him strung out.'

'What about Mariella?'

Carlo gave a snort. 'Mariella, Ginetta, Santuzza—they're all the same.'

'But isn't he living with her?'

'She'd like to think so. But she has her own apartment in the city. She goes to Rico's house when he snaps his fingers, then leaves when he tells her to.'

'Everybody does everything when he tells them to,' Julie said with a faint touch of bitterness. 'Arturo Forza's grandson.'

'Did you know the old man?' Carlo asked in surprise.

'No, but I—I've heard of him.'

'He was a real—' Carlo used a very expressive word. 'Rico is frighteningly like him. There was a time when I thought he might break out of Arturo's shadow, live his own life with human values, not commercial ones. But—I don't know—perhaps he still can.'

He waited to see if she would answer this. When she didn't, he began telling her who lived in the luxurious houses they were passing, and in this way they completed the journey.

Rico lived in a palatial villa set in extensive grounds. The building was three storeys high with a row of stone columns at the front. It was less a home than a palace for a prince, and Carlo confirmed that it had once belonged to an old aristocratic family.

'Arturo set his heart on it and got the family in a financial stranglehold. Then he tightened it until they sold at his price.'

'I can believe it,' Julie said.

At every turn, the evil old man had left his mark. He might be dead, but he was still a malign presence in her life.

'Why did Mariella call this a house-warming party if Rico inherited it from his grandfather?' she asked.

'He's renovated the picture gallery. There are some valuable paintings in the collection, and its reopening is an occasion.'

They climbed the broad stone steps to the entrance.

As soon as they were inside, Julie saw Rico and
Mariella.

Although it was afternoon, the starlet was dressed
to kill in a tight, low-cut dress and adorned with a
mass of jewellery that would have been more suitable
for evening. She was giving directions to servants in
a sharp voice that contrasted dramatically with her
usual breathless tones. One by one they scurried nervously away.

Mariella turned and spotted them, then immediately
switched on her smile and flowed across the mosaic
floor, hands outstretched in a parody of welcome.

'I'm so glad you managed to get here,' she cooed.
'We're all looking forward to your performance. Of
course, you should really have used the rear door, but
never mind.'

'Sorry,' Julie said, understanding this perfectly.
'Nobody told us where the tradesmen's entrance was.'

Mariella's smile wavered a fraction.

'Why should they?' Rico said, coming up behind
her. 'You're not tradesmen.'

'We're the hired performers,' Julie reminded him.
She could see that he was discomfited by Mariella's
rudeness.

'You are my honoured guests,' he said firmly. 'Mariella, which room have you allocated to Julie?'

'Room? But why—'

'She will need somewhere to prepare for her performance.'

'But of course. She can use my room. I'll take her
myself.'

As they went through the house, Mariella showed
off its glories with a proprietary air. Her own bedroom
was a lavish show-place, furnished in palatial style. It

was dominated by a huge four-poster bed, which Mariella assured her was 'the most comfortable in the world'.

'The old mattress was rather lumpy,' she confided, 'and I told my Rico that I simply must have a new one. He said I should order anything I liked, so I called the store and told them I wanted "a bed for lovers". I think everything should be perfect for love. Don't you?'

Julie looked her in the eye. 'I think it takes a great deal more than a mattress to make love perfect. Thank you for your hospitality.'

Mariella flounced out without another word. Julie watched her go with a wry smile, but the smile faded when she was alone. It was easy to be amused by the starlet's stupidity and greed, but it didn't change the fact that she was here with Rico, flaunting her position as mistress of his house.

And it hurt, she realized. After all her brave thoughts about being finished with him, it still hurt to see him with another woman, hearing Mariella talk about 'My Rico' and boast about a lovers' bed.

Julie could have told her that if you were in the arms of the man you loved, it didn't matter if you were in an old iron bedstead with a mattress that was too narrow and full of lumps. She put a hand over her eyes, and for a moment her lips trembled.

After a while, she went down to find the picture gallery, her footsteps echoing on the mosaic floors. She felt dwarfed by the high ceilings and huge rooms with their lush frescoes, and suddenly she desperately needed some fresh air.

When she arrived on the ground floor, a faint breeze reached her, and she saw that a door to the garden stood open. She hurried through it with relief, then stopped, feeling as though she'd stepped back in time.

It was impossible but true.

She'd been here before.

CHAPTER SEVEN

SHE looked around wildly, trying to understand the shattering thing that had happened. How did she recognize the curve of that path? How could she know the shape of the fountain even before she saw it?

And then she caught her breath as the truth dawned.

Long ago, a man with the power of a Roman emperor had been photographed here with his grandson, a boy he was rearing to be like himself. And those pictures had been used to break the heart of the boy and the girl who loved him.

Everything that Vanzani had shown her lived in Julie's mind, engraved there by grief. Now she saw place after place that she remembered from the pictures, and a kind of horror rose in her.

She pulled herself together, refusing to give in to the feeling. She hadn't yet called Gary, and the privacy of this garden was her chance. Her mobile was in her bag, and after a quick look round to make sure she was alone, she dialled. In a few moments, she was talking to her son.

Thrilled to hear from her, he chatted eagerly about a boat trip he'd taken, the sights he'd seen and the present he'd bought her. Julie listened, a happy smile spreading over her face as tension was replaced by delight.

'Gary, listen,' she laughed, trying to break into his babbling talk. 'Gary—' When she could get a word in

edgeways, she whispered the endearments that she
knew he loved.

'I love you, Mommy,' he said.

'I…' She was about to say she loved him when an
awareness of danger made her look up and stiffen.

Rico was standing nearby, watching her.

'Me, too,' she said quickly. 'I must go now. Bye.'
She hung up.

'I hope you didn't shorten your conversation because of me,' he said. 'I'm sure "Gary" was desolate.'

'I said all that was necessary,' she replied stiffly.

'Of course, if he's madly in love with you, the clev-
erest thing you could do is hang up,' Rico observed
ironically. 'Keep him wondering.'

'I should go inside. They'll be waiting for me.'

'Don't rush. I've looked forward to showing you
my home.'

'Your lady friend has shown it to me, and I congratulate you on its magnificence,' Julie said, trying to
leave.

He detained her with a hand. 'You don't sound very
enthusiastic.'

'Maybe I just don't care for magnificence. It's a
show-place, not a home.'

'Have you thought that it might have been yours?'

'Never,' she said at once. 'This place is poisoned. I
couldn't have lived in it.'

'It was the home of my childhood.'

'And it poisoned you, too. How much, I wonder?
How badly harmed had you been already when you
came to live in London?'

Then he said something unexpected. 'Badly, perhaps. But you could have made me better. Happiness
brings out the best in a man, and misery the worst.

Now we'll never know what might have happened.'
He turned accusing eyes on her. 'Don't ask me such
questions. Do you want me to hate you more?'

'Could you hate me more?'

'I thought I couldn't. I've thought that many times,
but I always found new depths. Hatred is unending
and bottomless. You taught me that lesson, not my
grandfather, whom you try to blame for so much.'

She had nothing to say to that.

'Shall I show you the garden?' he asked politely.

'No need. I already know it very well. That fountain
used to have two winged horses. One of them has been
removed in the past few years. And you had a piebald
pony that would put his front hoofs on the fountain
edge. You loved that little horse. You used to put your
arms right round him and press your face against his
neck.'

'How the devil did you know that?' he asked, going
pale.

'It was in the photographs Vanzani showed me.
He'd brought them to demonstrate how far above me
you were. So coming here now is like meeting ghosts.
Maybe I'll meet your ghost round the next corner.'

'But I'm not dead.'

'Mariella keeps calling you "my Rico". She's welcome to you. My Rico died a long time ago.'

'Yes,' he said quietly. 'A long time ago. On the
same day as Patsy Brown.'

'Rico, *caro*.'

Like people waking up from a dream, they turned
to see Mariella waving and hurrying along the path
towards them, her face hard with suspicion.

'Why do you waste your time with women like
that?' Julie demanded in disgust.

'They make the best companions,' Rico said wryly. 'You always know where you are with them.'

He walked away to meet Mariella. Julie waited till they were gone before she returned to the house and found the picture gallery, which, luckily, was on a more human scale than the rest of the house. She and Carlo ran through a couple of songs, and Julie found the acoustics excellent.

'You'll meet Beppe in a minute,' Carlo told her. 'He's going to be second on the bill at La Dolce Notte, and he'll also be doing a song tonight.'

'I think I've heard of him.'

'He used to be a big star in Italy, but the fashion has rather passed him by. You'll like him.'

Julie did like him. Beppe was a roly-poly charmer. He had neither looks nor youth, but he did have a roguish twinkle in his eye that instantly captivated her. He greeted her with a wildly dramatic flourish, kissing her hand and presenting her with a red rose. She couldn't help laughing, which seemed to please him.

Carlo took Beppe through his song, but then the elderly singer had a surprise.

'Listen,' he said sitting at the piano. He sang 'Whatever Happened to My Heart?' His eyes invited her and she joined in. They sounded well together. 'We sing it tonight?' he asked.

'Why not?'

They tried it again, this time with Carlo at the piano. Beppe stood next to her, looking tenderly up into her eyes, for she was three inches taller. If he'd been a younger man, she couldn't have sung this song with him, but he was funny and irresistible.

When they finished, he embraced her, and Julie

hugged him back, laughing. But then she looked up
and her laughter died.

Rico was standing there, his face as pale as death.
For a moment, she thought he would speak to her, but
instead he walked away.

Soon the important guests began to arrive for a ban-
quet, followed by the entertainment. Julie declined to
join the party. She didn't want to see him and Mariella
together. Not that she cared what they did. She just
didn't want to see it.

She showered in Mariella's ornate bathroom, then
put on a towelling robe and prepared to take forty
winks, as she usually did before a performance.
Nothing would have persuaded her to lie down on the
bed, but luckily there was a couch, long enough to
stretch out on. She took a spare blanket from the
closet, set her small travelling alarm to wake her in an
hour and lay back, taking deep breaths.

But she couldn't sleep. She was haunted by Rico's
voice saying, 'You could have made me better.'

She'd been little more than a child, struggling
against monstrous forces that were too strong for her.
She'd paid the price and lived with it. But the price
that Rico had paid almost made her believe that she'd
given in too easily. And betrayed him.

She covered her face with her hands, refusing to
think such thoughts in case she went mad.

There was a sharp rap on her door. Rubbing her
eyes, she went to open it. Rico stood outside, handsome and severe in a dinner jacket.

'I shan't keep you long,' he said, walking in and
turning to confront her. His face was austere. 'I told
you the other day what you were to sing. Beppe also

has his instructions. I wish you to keep to that programme with no alterations. None at all.'

'Whatever...?' she began to say.

Then she remembered Rico watching her with Beppe. And listening to the song they'd sung together.

'On my first day, you virtually ordered me to sing that song,' she objected.

'Alone,' he said in an iron voice. 'I do not consider it suitable for a duet.'

Except when sung by a boy and girl, brilliant with the joy of youthful passion, her caressing tones struggling with his tuneless grating so that they both laughed. And laughter melted into love.

'You're right,' she said after a moment. 'It never was suitable for a duet. I'll tell Carlo and Beppe.'

'I've already done so.'

He inclined his head curtly and was about to leave when his gaze fell on the couch with its rumpled blanket.

'I'm sure Mariella wouldn't have minded your using her bed,' he observed.

She didn't answer except with her eyes. He understood. After a moment, he left the room.

That night, she sang with a hundred priceless paintings looking down on her from the walls, and her performance was a tremendous success. She had a perfect view of Rico and Mariella sitting together in the front row, but after the first glance she didn't look at them again. The members of the audience were well fed, content with their money and status, and ready to enjoy themselves. The room resounded with their cheers.

Afterwards she refused Rico's invitation to remain and join the party, although Carlo and Beppe accepted. 'I'd rather have an early night,' she said.

'In that case, my chauffeur will take you home.'

She collected her things, and by the time she was downstairs, the car was waiting. Rico handed her in, thanked her again and said good-night. His manner was cool. They might have been no more than distant acquaintances. But he stood on the step, watching until the tail-lights had vanished, and Mariella had to say his name twice before he answered.

Singing at the villa had been a strain, but Julie was glad to have done it. It made a useful dress rehearsal for the club. Now she knew that she could stand up in front of Rico and sing songs of love and longing without breaking down.

On opening night, she sat in her dressing-room, applying her make-up. Gina, the elderly dresser, had told her that La Dolce Notte was filled to overflowing.

'You are so beautiful,' she said, standing back to admire. 'Not many women can wear such a dress.'

It was black satin with rows of sparkling beads around the hem. The cut was very tight, but Julie had the perfect figure to get away with its daring lines.

Gina excitedly ran through the names she'd spotted at the best tables. There were some show business celebrities and several prominent politicians.

'Guess who's sitting at Signor Rico's table? Salvatore Barono.'

Julie was startled at the name of the internationally famous Italian film star. He'd enjoyed a lucrative career in Hollywood, playing smooth Italian lovers, but he made occasional trips to his villa just outside Rome. These were always followed by press interviews about his need to return to 'the simple country pleasures'.

Rumour had it that behind the villa walls his pleasures were more scandalous than simple.

'What about Mariella?' Julie asked.

'She's here. She made sure she sat next to Signor Barono. Oh, *scusi, signore.*'

Rico had entered silently. He gave Gina a brief nod and she scuttled away. He didn't speak, but his eyes met Julie's in the mirror. She was startled. She hadn't seen him since the evening at the villa, and the sight came as a shock.

He was full of tension. His face was pale except for the dark shadows under his eyes, and there was a curious withered look about his mouth, as though he'd finally resigned himself to something unbearable.

'Are you all right?' he asked, and she heard in his voice the faint huskiness that meant he was sleeping badly.

'I'm fine. Did you come to see if I was wearing your diamonds? Don't worry. I know my duty.' She indicated the box on the dressing-table.

'Allow me.' She sat still while he draped the heavy jewels about her neck. 'They look splendid on you,' he said. 'In fact, your whole appearance is perfect.'

Once she'd sung in jeans and sweater and he'd whispered, 'I am jealous of every man who looks at you. You must be beautiful only for me.'

And she had answered, 'I don't see the others. Only you exist.'

But that was then. 'I'm glad I meet with your approval,' she said now.

'Are you nervous?'

'A little. That's good, though. It makes me perform better.'

'Anything for the performance,' he said wryly.

'Well, that's what I am. A performer. But after all, Rico, so are you. We just have to play the comedy out to the end.'

'I wonder what the end will be?'

'I'll complete my engagement, we'll shake hands and never see each other again. You'll probably marry Mariella. I wish you every happiness.'

'Shut up!' he said with soft violence. 'Do you think it helps to talk like that?'

She rose and faced him. 'What would help, Rico? I wish I knew, because somehow we have to get through the next three months. Ever since I came to Rome, we've done nothing but hurt each other. Let's keep well apart from now on.'

'It didn't have to be like that.'

'Perhaps it did. I don't think you could have stopped yourself from setting spies on me. It comes naturally to you to mistrust people. You can't stop now.' She saw him flinch as though her words were knives. In a gentler voice, she added, 'We had so much happiness once that I think we used it all up. Now we're getting all the pain in one go.'

'In one go?' he echoed bitterly. 'What about the past eight—' He stopped sharply.

So he, too, had lain awake in anguish, cursing the darkness but cursing the dawn still more because there was another day to be struggled through. And no baby caresses to sweeten his life.

Rico ran his hand through his hair in a gesture that was almost despairing. 'I wish I could say how I feel.'

'I think I know,' she said with a sigh. 'A little love, a lot of hate. And the hate is too strong for anything else to live in its shadow.'

His face hardened. 'Do you realize that you've just described your own feelings?'

She was about to say that she could never hate him. If her love didn't still burn brightly, he couldn't hurt her as he did. But she stopped herself. Rico was too dangerously strong. She must stay on her guard.

'Well, maybe you're right,' she said at last.

A light went out of his eyes. 'As long as we both know.' Then his manner became formal. 'Please accept my best wishes for your opening night. La Dolce Notte is very proud to have you as its star.' He gave her a curt, formal bow and departed.

She sat listening over the intercom as the orchestra struck up and the cabaret began. First a troop of dancers, then Beppe, singing the old songs, followed by a comedian. And finally...

'Ladies and gentlemen, we are proud to present that international singing sensation, Julie Hallam!'

She'd moved to the side of the stage, breathing slowly as she waited, concentrating every fibre of her being on the forthcoming performance. When she heard her name announced on a note of triumph, she burst onto the stage, smiling into the dazzling lights, acknowledging the applause with a wave, then storming into the first song before the applause had died.

She'd picked a razzle-dazzle opener that showed off her wide vocal range. It had no emotional depth, but the pyrotechnics grabbed her audience's attention and served notice that she had some surprises to spring. When she finished, the applause was loud and had the 'edge' that she always listened for. That edge was the first sign things were going well.

Having captured their attention, she segued into a dreamy ballad, and they listened eagerly, falling will-

ingly under the spell she cast. She followed this with
a song that was smoochy but with a hint of humour.
Her eyes glinted with fun while her voice caressed the
notes, offering her audience an experience that was
both erotic and light-hearted. They responded with
delight, and this time the applause had the full body
that meant they were settling back to enjoy themselves.

After the third song, the lights came up for a few
minutes to allow latecomers to get to their tables. Julie
used this time chatting to the audience in the Italian
she'd perfected. She enjoyed doing this as it gave her
a chance to see their faces and establish a closer rap-
port. Tonight someone cried, '*Bellissima*!'

Laughing, Julie acknowledged the tribute with a little wave. '*Grazie, signore.*'

Once, little Patsy Brown had dreamed of commanding an audience in just this way. Now it was all coming true. Power streamed from her, the power of an
artist at her peak, and she gloried in it.

She didn't need to look at Rico to be aware of him.
She knew that he was sitting quite still, with an arrested quality to the angle of his head. And as if she'd
gained second sight, she knew that she'd taken him
by surprise.

He'd last seen her singing in the pub, little more
than a raw amateur. Now she was a poised *chanteuse*
who could hold an audience in the palm of her hand
and do what she liked with it. He was watching her
with eyes that feared to lose a moment, while Mariella,
forgotten, sat beside him.

The starlet regarded him with narrowed eyes before
turning a megawatt smile onto Salvatore Barono be-

side her. He returned it with some wattage to spare. They were two of a kind.

The lights dimmed again and Julie got seriously to work on her audience, teasing them, surprising them whenever they thought they had her measure, beguiling them with enchantment.

Then she grew very still, waiting for perfect silence. In a slow, husky voice, she began to sing the song that held a special meaning for one man.

'Whatever happened to my heart?
I tried to keep it safe,
But you broke through
And stole it right away.
Take good care of it,
I'll never have another heart to give.'

Tonight her voice had a passionate, edgy intensity that had never been there before. And he had done this, reviving turbulent emotions, giving her new depth as a singer and as a woman. Suddenly the sophisticated club was alive with raw emotion. The fleeting joys of first love, the aching knowledge of 'might have been' and 'too late'. These worldly people had forgotten such feelings, but she made them remember and fall silent.

Rico was shattered. She seemed to play with him at will, haunting him with the past while showing him how irrevocably the past was gone. It was like a physical pain, and he clenched his hands. He was shocked at his own weakness. She was his enemy, yet she could make him forget everything except how badly he still wanted to possess her. Anger burned in him, directed at himself as much as at her.

Julie had worked on her voice, extending her range so that she could stream up to an impossibly high and thrilling note. She saved it for the last song and gave it everything she had. Her performance brought the audience to their feet, clapping and cheering for so long that it seemed they would never let her go.

Before she could leave the stage, Rico rose and stretched out his hand, silently commanding her to take it. She did so.

'I promised you all the best,' Rico declared to everyone as the lights came up. 'And I delivered.' He kissed Julie's hand theatrically. 'You were wonderful!'

He snapped his fingers and a waiter handed him a single rose. It was dark crimson, velvety and perfect. Before the cheering crowd, he kissed it and presented it to Julie. She took it with a smile that matched his own, but she could see his eyes, and they were bleak.

He led her to his table and gestured for her to sit beside him. At once, Salvatore Barono leaned over and blasted her with brandy fumes.

'Eh, Rico! Introduce me to your little friend.'

He was older than he seemed on screen and had an unhealthy, raddled appearance. Julie greeted him politely but refused his invitation to sit beside him. And she had to fight not to back away from his drink-sodden breath.

The orchestra struck up for dancing, and the lights dimmed again, just enough for couples to be intimate in privacy. Barono flung out a hand towards Julie. 'We dance!' he announced, so melodramatically that she had to suppress a giggle.

'Please excuse me,' she said quietly but firmly. 'I'm a little tired after the performance.'

'A magnificent performance,' he declared. 'I wait

until the goddess is rested.' Turning to Mariella, he flung out his hand again and cried, 'We dance!' in exactly the same tone.

Concealing her chagrin at being so obviously second-best, Mariella took his hand. Together they smooched around the floor, each giving an exaggerated impression of being absorbed in the other. Julie placed her fingers tactfully over her mouth.

'He paid you a great compliment,' Rico observed. 'How unkind of you to laugh at him.'

'I can't help it. He's such a ham. And so is she.'

'You were superb tonight,' he said. 'Beyond my wildest dreams.'

'But you took a risk,' she reminded him. 'It wasn't my talent that made you bring me here. I might have disappointed you.'

'I knew your *singing* wouldn't disappoint me,' he said, emphasizing the word slightly. 'As for the rest, yes, I'd forgotten your stubbornness.'

'Eh, Rico, you did it again!'

A big man with a red face sat down at the table, bawling his appreciation. Rico winced and introduced him to Julie. She smiled and said the right things, and after a while he departed. His place was immediately taken by another man out of the same mould. He paid her fulsome compliments that she accepted with practised charm. Neither man could have guessed how she longed to be rid of them.

'Are you still angry with me?' Rico asked when they were alone again.

'No, only with myself. You warned me you'd try any trick to get the better of me. I should have listened. But I know now.'

'What do you think you know?'

'Everything about you that I'd rather not have known. You belong in this place. It's cold and obsessed with money and power, and you fit perfectly. I wish I'd never met you again.'

'Shut up!' he said with repressed fury. 'You don't know what you're talking about. You know nothing about me. And this place is your setting, too, don't forget. This is where you always wanted to be.'

'For my work, not my life,' she replied defiantly.

She gave a small gasp as his hand tightened. He'd been clasping her fingers ever more tightly as they spoke, and her last words made him so tense that his grip became unbearable.

'I'm sorry,' he said, releasing her at once. 'I didn't realize—I hope I didn't hurt you.'

'My fingers will recover. And perhaps in the end my heart will recover, too.'

'Then you are fortunate,' he flung at her. 'Damn you for sitting there so coolly while you wreak havoc everywhere! And damn my own stupidity for seeing in you anything but a heartless schemer. The sooner this farce is over, the better.'

'Rico!' A hot, damp hand grasped Julie's arm. Salvatore Barono had returned, his voice booming at them over the music. 'Wonderful evening! Wonderful singer! What a star!' His hand was inching its way round her waist.

'Thank you, you're too kind,' Julie murmured, trying to free herself from him.

'Don't be a dog in the manger, Rico,' the film star shouted, refusing to be dislodged. 'It's my turn to dance with the lady.'

'But you already have a partner,' Julie reminded him, indicating Mariella, who was looking furious.

'Oh, she'd rather dance with Rico,' Barono said
blithely. 'And I'd rather dance with you. Come on,
Rico, don't be greedy. It's time to share your toys.'

Julie's temper rose at this way of referring to her.
She waited for Rico to drive the man away, but to her
horror he made a gesture for her to accede.

'Rico,' she said urgently.

'You don't object to dancing with my friend,
surely?' he asked her.

'But—'

'We're all friends together on these occasions.'

Rico silenced further argument by rising and taking
Mariella into his arms. Reluctantly Julie let herself be
claimed by Barono. He danced smoochily, holding her
close and looking deep into her eyes. Julie wasn't
fooled by this. It was for the public. And sure enough,
there were photographers in place to record the moment.

'*Signorina*, you are very beautiful,' the actor said
throatily.

'Really, you shouldn't—'

'But no, I speak only the truth. You are a radiant
star in the firmament. What a couple we will make—'

'We aren't a couple,' she protested, trying to put
some space between them.

He tightened his hand against the small of her back,
drawing her close again. 'But we will be, we must...'

She turned her head, trying to avoid the booze
fumes. But nothing could stop him. How could Rico
subject her to this? she thought angrily. However
much he hated her.

'We will go everywhere, and together we will make
beautiful music.'

She couldn't believe he'd actually said that. Surely

nobody talked that way any more? Despite her annoyance, her lips twitched.

'You're teasing me,' he said. 'That means you secretly want me to make love to you—'

'It means no such thing,' she insisted, beginning to struggle in earnest. 'Let me go at once.'

'When we make love, you'll never want me to let you go.'

'We aren't going to make love—'

'I'm on fire for you. I can't wait.'

He tried to fix his mouth on hers, but she twisted aside. Instead he kissed her neck, sliding his lips down its length to the base of her throat. Julie wrenched her hands free and tried to thrust him away, but he was like a snake, insinuating himself everywhere. She felt as though she were struggling in a nightmare.

Then, suddenly, there was no need to struggle. Flashbulbs blinded her. Somewhere in the background, a woman screamed. There was a loud commotion. Barono slithered out of sight.

Rico had knocked him to the ground.

CHAPTER EIGHT

IN THAT second, something snapped inside Julie. As she saw Barono land on the floor with Rico standing over him, looking murderous, she fled blindly, not caring where she was going but plunging out through the audience.

She heard Rico call her name, but she didn't look back. She had to get away from here, away from him. For ever.

In a few moments, she was up the stairs and at the club entrance. Startled, people stared at her tear-stained face and distraught eyes, but nobody dared to stop her.

Then she was out in the street, running down the Via Veneto as fast as the tight dress would allow her. All about her were curious glances, but she ignored them and kept on. Safety was only a short distance away. The next side-street. She stumbled round the corner.

But everywhere was strange. It wasn't the right street. She looked frantically hither and thither, realizing that she was lost.

She turned back into the Via Veneto. She thought of the picture she presented, wearing a glamorous evening dress with no bag, no escort. The glances became leers and, horrified, she guessed what people must be thinking about her.

She tried to pull herself together. She must have turned the wrong way. It was just a question of retracing her steps. But that meant going past the club, and she wasn't sure she could do it.

Then a car screeched to a halt beside her. The driver uttered an oath as he saw her state, then leaped out. 'Get in,' Rico said.

'*I'm not going back there.*'

'No, I'll take you to the hotel. Get in.'

She looked at him wild-eyed, but she was too drained to resist. Gently but firmly he urged her into the car and drove in silence for the short distance. To her relief, he didn't go to the entrance but swung the car round the back and into an underground car park. From here the elevator ensured that they reached her suite undetected.

'My key,' she groaned. 'It's downstairs.'

Rico lifted a house phone on the wall and barked something into it. A moment later, someone came up in the main elevator with the key. Rico took it and opened her door. She slipped inside and tried to shut it in his face, but he wouldn't be refused.

Julie didn't even bother to switch on a lamp. The shutters were open and some of the glittering, multi-coloured lights from the street lit up the room in some places, throwing strange shadows in others. Julie began to strip off the jewellery, tossing it down without even looking where it fell.

'Have every last piece back.' she told him desperately. 'I can't stand any more. I'm getting the next plane out of here.'

'Julie, stop this, please. Listen—'

'No, you listen. I'm finished. And don't tell me I have a contract because the contract wasn't for any of the things you've made happen. You can sue me. I don't care if I ever work again. I don't need bright lights and fame. I just need…' She only needed Gary, but she checked herself on the brink of a dangerous revelation. 'I just need a quiet life,' she finished hurriedly.

As she spoke, she was tearing at a bracelet, but her shaking fingers couldn't undo the intricate clasp. At last she gave up and turned away from him, leaning against the wall and trembling with shock.

'Don't come near me,' she warned him in a fierce voice.

'Please, I only want to comfort you.'

'There's no comfort to be found in you, only tricks and heartless pretences.'

'You call *me* heartless?'

'What else should I call you? Everything about you is cold, heartless and merciless. There's nothing inside you any more, Rico, and that's what you can't bear, isn't it? Emptiness. A hollow where your heart should be. I'm sorry for you, and I'm sorry if it's my fault. Perhaps it is. Perhaps I did everything wrong all those years ago, but I was only seventeen. What did I know about anything?'

'Julie—'

'*Don't touch me*! Don't ever try to touch me again. Go back to Mariella and the others. They're all you're good for.'

His face darkened. 'Would you condemn me to that?'

'You condemned yourself a long time ago. Stick to them. Use them as they use you. Sleep with them. Tell them all the lies they want to hear, then pay them off. That's the language they understand. But don't confuse me with them. How—how could you make such an exhibition of me?'

'Of myself, surely,' he said harshly. 'Now the world knows that I can't endure you to be touched by another man. Do you think I wanted that?'

'You forced me to dance with him.'

'Because I was mad with rage and pride. How else could I be when you—'

'Stop it! I don't want to know. I'm taking the first plane out. Don't try to stop me. Don't follow me. For pity's sake, Rico, let this be the end!'

Now he would vow to watch her for ever until he found their son. But instead of threats, he spoke the very last words she had expected in a quiet, melancholy voice. 'You mean to abandon me yet again?'

'You manage very well without me,' she said huskily. 'Go back to your money and your mistresses.'

'Only one woman has ever been mistress of my heart,' he said in the same quiet voice, as though he was discovering the truth only as he spoke it. 'Once, I needed you very much. You'll never know how much. You left me stranded in a frozen nothingness and now you can't bear what I've become, so you're going to desert me again. You've called me many names tonight, Julie. I wonder how you'll like the one I call you. Coward.'

She stared at him, shocked by the accusation.

'Maybe I'm all that you say,' he went on. 'Cruel, treacherous, untrustworthy, and many more things you don't dream of. I seek bad company because that's where I'm most at ease. But you, more than anyone in the world, know that I once was a better man.

'Perhaps you're right to go. Nobody will try to follow you. My word on it. As soon as you've gone from here, you'll also be gone from my life, and I will wipe you out of my heart.'

It was the worst threat he could have uttered. To exist for him no more!

'I'll make sure you're left in peace,' he said. Then he gave a short, mirthless laugh. 'Peace. For us. Is there such a thing?'

'Rico…'

He stopped at something new in her voice. He didn't look at her, but he grew very still as though trying to believe what he'd heard.

'*Rico*…'

He moved fast, and the next moment he'd seized her up into his arms. She reached out, clinging to him desperately, crying his name in a choking voice.

'Don't leave me,' he said. 'I won't let you.'

'How can I stay? How can I go?'

'I didn't mean it to happen like that tonight. I went mad watching you—I thought I could stand it but— kiss me, *kiss me*—'

He smothered her mouth like a man at the limit of endurance. His lips were hard and purposeful, just as she'd always loved them. Before she knew it, her arms were about his neck, and she was obeying his order to kiss him—obeying it again and again. She'd never loved him as much as now when his need and desolation were spread before her.

'I could have killed him,' he grated. 'How dare he touch you!'

'You wanted him to—'

'*Like hell I did*!'

Her head was spinning. She was sure there were things they ought to say first, but she couldn't remember them. The terrible words they'd hurled at each other vanished into the past. The passion of his kisses blotted out all memory of his actions.

'Rico—'

'No,' he said firmly. 'No more words. It's with words that we hurt each other.'

He kissed her again before she could answer. She sensed that he was quickly losing control, and the knowledge thrilled her. Her own control was slipping fast. Over the years, she'd suppressed all desire until she'd almost forgotten how it felt. But with Rico the years vanished. Desire still burned with a steady flame, ready to leap up to new heights, as it was doing now.

But even as it flared, she felt Rico put a brake on himself. He fixed his hands on her shoulders and drew back, gasping.

'What's wrong?' she asked, bewildered.

'Tell me that you're sure,' he said urgently.

'I'm sure. Truly.'

'We've made so many mistakes. If this isn't what you really want—'

'There's nothing I want more than this. Don't say any more. You said it yourself. We don't need words.'

Nothing could have held him after that. Quickly he removed her dress, pulling the long zip down her back so that the satin slid down with a whisper. It seemed as though her sophisticated persona fell away with it, and she again became a trusting girl, blindly following her heart into the arms of the boy she adored.

'Tell me that you want me,' he murmured. 'Promise me that it's true.'

He was kissing her between words, enticing her with his lips, sending flickers of feeling along her ragged nerves. She tried to think, but he was purposely denying her the chance, invoking her desire. Julie clung to him, longing for the strength to break away and longing, too, to stay in his arms for ever.

'I want you,' she whispered in answer as he drew her to the bed and lay down with her. 'I've always wanted you…all these years—'

'Hush,' he said against her mouth. 'The years have never been. We met today, and there is no tomorrow.…'

He smelled of spice and earth, of sun and wind and desire. His skin was hot with passion yet smooth as marble, his frame lean, muscular and powerful. He was the man who had brought her flesh to life long ago, in another life. It had vibrated to him alone. Now it lived again under his touch.

There was skill in his fingers. They knew how to give feather-light caresses that she barely felt, except that they increased the fires raging inside her. He traced the length of her, the beautiful swell of her breasts, her tiny waist and the womanly curve of her hips, and with every touch, he reclaimed her.

Julie gave herself up to him as simply as she had done the first time, without fear or reservation. And he was everything she'd hoped—passionate but tender, loving her with care. He evoked her desire slowly, seeking to please her, savouring the miracle that had been given back to them. When their moment came, he asked again, 'Do you really want me?' as though he were afraid of the answer. She gave him the answer he wanted with her mouth, with her body and with her whole soul.

After so long apart, they were like strangers, yet strangers who knew each other mysteriously well. Over the years, he'd gained in skill and control, but his ardour was the same, as was the reverence with which he touched her body.

Their union was heart-stopping in its beauty. She

had forgotten that such pleasure existed, but great as it was, it was still less than the flowering of love. How had she lived so long without him? How could she bear to be without him ever again?

'*My love,*' she whispered. '*My love…*'

'Tell me that you forgive me,' he said as they lay quietly together, wrapped in each other's arms. 'Say it, for I need to hear it very much.'

'I forgive you,' she murmured against his skin.

She regarded him with wonder, awed by what had just happened. The lights from the street that never slept flickered over his body in a myriad of colours. In the shadows, there were no details, only the magnificent outline of a male body in its prime. She had left a boy. She found a man.

'What are you thinking?' he murmured.

'I'm not thinking,' she said with a little smile. 'Who wants to think when they can feel like this? Are you thinking?'

He shook his head and gave the laugh of a man who had just conquered the world and found it lovely. It did her heart good to hear him.

'Yet perhaps I should be thinking,' he mused. 'I've done so many clumsy things to offend you.' He saw a shadow cross her face. 'About the other night—I'm not as guilty as you think me. It's true that I had you watched as soon as you arrived in Rome—'

'And that evening?'

'Yes, that evening. It began as you thought, a way of persuading you. But that's not how it ended. You sent that old horse home, and I remembered the dog and how you could never bear any creature to be hurt. Then I knew that you were still Patsy.'

'No,' she said quickly.

'Why won't you let me call you Patsy?'

'Because she belongs to the past, and the past is over. The love we had then was beautiful, but we can't have it back. We can only build on the present and make a new love from the people we are now.'

'Can we do that?'

'I don't know. We can try.'

'How wise you are. Then are you wise enough to understand that that night I forgot everything except the happiness of being with you? I even forgot the men who were watching us or I'd have called them off. I swear I would.'

He made a grimace of self-mockery. 'If you wanted to punish me, you succeeded. I was a laughing-stock, both at the fountain and in the hotel. Rico Forza, stood up like a ninny, hammering uselessly at a woman's door.'

'I was just too unhappy to think straight. I wasn't trying to punish you, Rico.'

'I know that now.' He smiled wryly. 'I just thought you might enjoy the joke.'

'And Mariella? Is she a joke?'

'Mariella and I have what is practically a business relationship. We show each other off for the paparazzi. But after tonight she won't waste her time with me. Barono will suit her better, and he's welcome. I've been lashing out, hurting you and myself, not knowing why I did so. But I know now, *mio amore*. It's because I—'

'Hush,' she said urgently. 'Don't say it unless you're sure.'

'You think I'm not sure? Why have I been unable to love any woman but you, years after I should have forgotten you? And you? Whom have you loved? No, don't tell me.' His finger was quickly across her mouth. 'I don't want to know. It's enough that you are in my arms now.'

She understood. The shoals that threatened them still lay underneath. There was so much they didn't dare talk about. But like him, she wanted to forget the problems and think only of the beauty. And there was so much beauty.

He enfolded her in his arms again and they loved away the night. She was dazed with delight and a touch of disbelief that everything had been given back to her so completely.

Too good to be true.

That phrase had rung in her head before, and she'd found it disastrously true. But not now. This time, she had to believe in him because the lover who adored her so reverently could only be true to her. On that thought she fell into a peaceful sleep.

Rico found that if he only opened his eyes halfway, he could see the dawn but not the details of the room. In that way, it was possible to believe that time had moved back eight years, and he was once again in a shabby room in London. The girl he loved was nestled against him, softly breathing in the satiety of love. His arms curved about her protectively as well as possessively. They were young and in love, and the world belonged to them.

Then he opened his eyes fully. The room came jarring back into place, and he groaned at how easily he'd been seduced by a memory. He'd sworn never to forget the injury this woman had done him, yet he'd forgotten it with the first kiss. How willingly he'd let her take him back to their golden days, days that could never be recovered except in dreams.

He recalled his own passionate, loving words—words he'd used to no other woman but her. What a fool he'd been! A blind, besotted, sentimental fool, to let her know how easily she could conquer him! His pride revolted at the thought of how she would laugh.

He moved slightly, and it disturbed her. She rolled onto her back so that her head was turned towards him and he could see her face. It was pale in the morning light and oddly defenceless. He could see shadows beneath her eyes, and even in sleep there was a look of strain about her mouth, as though she knew of some burden that would weigh her down the moment she awoke.

Despite his angry thoughts, he could feel himself softening towards her. Her tousled hair made her look younger, vulnerable, and the old tenderness began to warm him again. How often had he longed to gather her up in his arms, hide her away where the world could never find her and take her to a place where they could live only for each other?

But no such place existed. There was only the harsh world of buying and selling, cheating and lying, winning and losing. Who knew that better than he did? And who but she had taught him?

He thought of the damage he'd done to himself last night, the film deal with Barono that would fall through now, the lawsuit that would cost him a fortune. And all because the sight of her being pawed by that slimy lecher had been too much to swallow. He'd forced her into Barono's arms as a gesture of power, and that action had rebounded on him, as everything about this woman did.

He eased himself quietly out of bed, then dressed quickly. Shame scalded him at how easily he'd become her dupe again. She mustn't suspect. He could better live with his weakness if it were known only to himself.

He let himself quietly out into the corridor. His last view was of Julie sleeping like a baby, her arm flung out to the place where he ought to have been. It made him feel like a murderer, but he didn't stop. He was like a man escaping with his life.

It was dawn and the streets were almost empty as he drove, not to his villa, but to a small room in the unfashionable part of the city, which he used when he needed to shake off the shiny trappings of his life and be himself alone. He kept his mind deliberately empty to avoid brooding on the way he'd abandoned her within hours of the most tender loving they'd ever known. If he didn't think about it, he might feel less of a murderer.

But he'd chosen the wrong place for shutting her out. This was where he kept his mementoes of her. There weren't many, just the things he'd taken with him on his trip to Italy. A scarf he'd bought her, which had still borne the fresh, flowery perfume she used; a picture to show his grandfather.

'Look, Grandfather, how pretty she is!'

'You're very lucky, my boy.'

The old man's smiling face. And all the time, *smash, smash* behind his back. Until there was nothing left of love, or hope, or youth.

She'd trusted him totally. Her face, as she saw him off, had been without fear.

And how had he repaid her trust?

The scarf and the photograph were in his hands

now. He'd thrust them into the back of a drawer, telling himself that one day soon he would destroy them. But one day had never come.

Her face was heartbreakingly young, looking back at him from the picture. '*I was only seventeen. What did I know about anything*?'

He threw off his clothes and showered, trying to find peace and a feeling of cleanliness. But both had deserted him. He recalled his anger, hoping it would justify his behaviour to himself. But all that would come into his mind was the memory of Julie lying in his arms, her face aglow with joy, whispering, 'My love...my love...'

He could see her now, waking up, smiling and reaching for him, finding him gone.

The thought of her face when she discovered his desertion almost made him weaken. There was still time to put it right. A bouquet of red roses with a note making some excuse for his early departure, asking to see her this morning...

He found he was forming the words in his head. He reached out a hand to call the florist.

Then he froze.

This woman could make him weak as no other woman could, and weakness was a sin that he'd abjured years ago. He must fight her even if it meant fighting his own softer nature. To do that, he needed to get away. He wasn't safe in the same city, the same country. He should call, not the florist, but the airport.

But never to hold her in his arms again, never to hear her voice whispering his name out of the depths of passion, never to see her eyes shining with love.

For a long moment, he stayed as he was, tortured by indecision.

Then he lifted the receiver...

CHAPTER NINE

WHEN she opened her eyes, Julie knew she would find Rico looking down at her tenderly, as so often in the past. She was so convinced of this that she delayed the pleasure, lying still and listening for the sound of his breathing. When she couldn't hear it, she gave a puzzled little frown and opened her eyes.

She was alone in the bed. Only the rumpled sheets on the other side showed that Rico had ever been there. There was no sign of him.

Perhaps he was having a shower. But the bathroom was empty. Rico was nowhere to be seen. His clothes, too, had vanished.

It was seven in the morning. He had risen at the crack of dawn, dressed quietly and slipped away without a word, without leaving behind him even so much as a short note.

Julie stood in the centre of the floor, looking slowly about her, trying to take in the fact that she had been abandoned. A chill seemed to start deep down and rise until it enclosed her heart.

The memory of his love was still in her flesh. Last night she'd lain in his arms, listening to his impassioned words. And this morning he was gone. Surely he would call at any moment to say he'd had to rush home because he was expecting a vital phone call.

She breakfasted in her room, waiting. But there was no call.

Finally she could deny the truth no longer. His disappearance was a cold snub. He'd gained what he wanted, then vanished without a backward glance.

On the first evening, he'd said, 'I've paid for you. And what I've paid for, I will take.'

And now he'd taken it. Or rather, he'd beguiled her into offering it freely. This was his revenge for her refusal to tell him about their son.

She lifted her head and told herself that she didn't care. To give herself something to do, she went sight-seeing around Rome, trying to believe that she was interested in the ancient monuments. Afterwards she couldn't remember where she'd been.

She returned to the hotel to find that there were no messages for her. She walked to the club, wondering if Rico would be there, what he would say to her, how he would look.

But instead she met Galena, his secretary, about to leave, looking ruffled.

'Why does he dump these last-minute decisions onto me?' she demanded. 'He never said anything about New York before, but all of a sudden he has to be there today. First flight out. Everything done in a rush.'

'New York?' Julie echoed, stunned. 'He's gone?'

'This morning. Just like that. I don't know what the crisis is, and he didn't tell me. I've been on the phone all day changing his appointments.'

'You mean…rescheduling them for when he returns?' Julie said, trying not to sound as though her heart was hammering.

'I don't know when he's coming back,' Galena said bitterly.

'But…surely he won't be away for long?'

Galena looked at her shrewdly, and Julie suddenly

saw herself through the secretary's eyes: another of
Rico Forza's women who'd served her purpose and
been shrugged aside. There was even a hint of sympathy in the older woman's eyes that made Julie's
cheeks flame.

'Maybe he isn't coming back,' Galena said. 'He has
an apartment over there, and the last time he went, he
stayed for over three months.'

Three months. By that time, she would have left
Rome. It was a slap in the face.

She seemed to perform on automatic that night, but
the audience noticed nothing wrong. They cheered her
enthusiastically. She was still in a state of shock when
she returned to the hotel.

She went out early next morning. She didn't know
where she was going, but she had to get away. She
found a small car-hire firm just opening, asked for a
convertible and drove off.

Her driving was steady, but her mind seethed. Rico
had snubbed her cruelly, and he'd done it after a night
when their souls had seemed as close as their bodies.
She could almost feel her heart breaking in her breast,
but she refused to feel it. Nor would she let herself
cry. She'd wept enough tears for Rico. The time for
weeping was over.

Soon she began to smell salty air. She'd travelled
barely fifteen miles when the glittering sea came into
view, and she slowed down to look at the most beautiful shoreline she had ever seen.

It had a long stretch of fine golden sand, edged by
a small forest of sea pines. Villas and bungalows were
dotted about under the trees, and from them issued
bathers, clutching towels, which they spread out on
the sand.

What a delightful spot this would be for a vacation, she thought. The beach was clean and well equipped, but not crowded. How Gary would have loved it here!

She kicked off her shoes and began to stroll along the water's edge. This magic place made such a blessed contrast to the world she'd escaped, a world of jagged nerves, tortured feelings and betrayal.

She had the strangest sensation, as though a tunnel had opened up in her mind. Looking back through it, she could see that the signs had been there all along. Rico had never quite been convincing as a poor boy. That touch of imperiousness had always been there, ready to flash out without warning. The arrogance of the Caesars had been born in him, and only her ignorance had prevented her seeing it.

He'd been a stranger in her country. She'd had all the advantages, but despite this, he'd led, she'd followed. It seemed natural. She remembered how he sometimes instinctively gave orders. She would make fun of him, saying demurely, '*Sì, signore.*' And he would redden and quickly add, 'Please.'

She tried not to let her mind dwell on the night they'd shared, which already seemed a million years ago. His tenderness and ardour had moved her to tears, and she'd dared to hope that she'd touched his heart again. And all the time his cold pride had been rejecting her.

Some part of her life had ended. She wept for him more than for herself. Over the years, everything had been taken from him, his young passion, his child, the generous nature that had made him so lovable. Now he'd lost the last thing of all—her love. And he'd lost it because it no longer meant anything to him.

Standing by the water, looking out over the sea, she made the saddest resolution of her life.

I will love him no more.

It would be hard and terrible, for loving him had been her pride and joy. But she couldn't afford to love the man he had become. She'd fought Arturo Forza for Rico's soul. And she'd lost.

She found a coffee-shop on the edge of the beach. It was already busy and she had to share a table with a cheerful family. They were happy to tell their business to the whole world, and soon she knew how long they'd been in this little resort, which was called Fregene, when they were going home and how much they'd paid for their villa.

'Lovely place for kids,' the father said. 'Right on the beach, smashing weather. Plenty to do. You got kids?'

She told them about Gary, and as she talked, her longing for him grew. It seemed an age since she'd seen him. As soon as she could, she escaped and put through a call to Aunt Cassie.

'Thank goodness I caught you,' she said. 'I was afraid you might have gone out.'

'No chance of that,' Cassie said. 'It's raining cats and dogs for the past four days. Gary's being very good, but the poor little soul is bored stiff. Here he is.'

The sound of her son's voice brought an ache to Julie's heart.

'Hallo, Mommy. Are you having a nice time?'

'It's not a holiday, precious. I'm working.'

'I know. But I wish you didn't have to go away to work.'

'I'll never go away from you again,' she vowed. 'After this, we're going to stick together.'

'I miss you, Mommy.'

'I miss you, too, darling.'

'When are you coming home?'

'It'll be a while yet. I—oh, darling, please don't cry.'

'I'm not crying, Mommy,' he said, trying to sound firm, although she could hear his voice wobble.

Julie made a sudden decision. 'Would you like to come out here and see me?'

'Yes, please.' His eagerness thrilled her and demonstrated how badly he'd missed her more than his words ever could.

She talked to Cassie again and briefly outlined the inspiration that had just come to her. 'This place is only about fifteen miles from Rome. I can rent a villa on the beach for you and visit as often as possible.'

I'm crazy, she thought as she hung up. There might not even be any villas free. I don't even know how to hire one.

But luck was with her. Fregene was a small place and she found the agency hiring the villas without difficulty. There was one vacancy, a tiny bungalow, just big enough. Julie snapped it up with a sense of exultancy.

It seemed like fate to have all the pieces falling into place so easily. Only a little while earlier, she would never have dared bring Gary to Italy, so close to Rico, but her resolution to fight back had given her a feeling of power. Suddenly there was no problem she couldn't solve.

She called Cassie again, gave her the details and told her to take the next plane out. She was smiling as she went back to the car. In a day or two, she would embrace her darling little son again. She could hardly contain her excitement.

She took possession of the empty bungalow at once, then spent a rapturous day buying gifts for Gary to find there when he arrived. By that afternoon, she had several new sets of clothes, a bucket and spade, a beach ball and some colouring books. For Cassie, she bought a pure silk scarf and blouse.

Rico hadn't returned and there was no word from him. It looked as though his absence was going to be prolonged. Julie summoned up all her strength and behaved as normal, showing no reaction. She even booked Carlo for a rehearsal next morning as she wanted to make some changes in the act.

She removed some of the livelier numbers, replacing them with sad songs, which made Carlo's eyebrows rise. He said nothing directly, but when they'd finished and were having a drink in the bar, he observed casually, 'I gather there's no sign of Rico coming back yet.'

Julie shrugged.

'Don't,' Carlo said gently. 'Don't pretend you don't care. It doesn't suit you.'

'You've got it all wrong, Carlo. There's nothing between Rico and me.'

'Julie, *cara*, you're talking to a man who had a front-row view of Rico's face when he knocked Barono down. He was ready to do murder. Whatever there is or isn't on your side, there's plenty on his.'

'Then where is he?' Julie asked wretchedly. 'How could he just walk out on me after—'

'I know Rico. When there's something he can't cope with, he simply withdraws deep into himself. For years now, he's lived by only allowing himself superficial emotions. It's his defence. If something has pierced it, then that's what he's most afraid of.

'It's lucky he didn't become a banker. He's got a way of acting impulsively, then regretting it when it's too late. But in the past, it's always been about things that didn't matter too much. If he's found something that matters…there's no knowing what he may do.'

Julie was at the airport with an hour to spare, agitated in case the plane was delayed. But it was on time, and there was Cassie and Gary waving at her. Gary came flying into her arms, almost suffocating her with his hug.

'Oh, darling,' she said passionately. 'How I've missed you! Mmmm! Come here and let me squeeze you again.'

They made a merry journey to Fregene. She showed them over the villa, watched with delight as they opened their presents, then let Gary drag her down the beach to the sea. Cassie chose to stay behind and put her feet up.

Gary was thrilled with the golden sands, the sea, the delicious ice creams. They frolicked in the water, splashing it over each other and screaming with laughter.

Seeing Gary in this setting, she could appreciate how truly Rico's son he was, not merely because he resembled his father, but because he looked Italian. His black hair and large dark eyes belonged here. And although he was only seven, there was already something in his proud carriage that proclaimed his heritage. How delighted with him Rico would be! If only that day might come soon!

She stayed as late as she dared, aching to remain with him. Luckily the day's excitement caught up with him all at once, and he fell asleep as soon as his head touched the pillow.

Julie sat beside him, stroking his hair. 'I'll be back soon,' she whispered.

In fact, she was able to return the next day and the one after. The time they spent together on the beach would have been blissful but for the aching of her heart. She wondered if she would ever see Rico again.

He arrived one night when she was in the middle of her act, and stood, unnoticed, at the back of the club.

Julie had discarded the glitzy dress she'd worn for the opening and chosen something floaty in grey silk chiffon, with pearls the only adornment. She'd varied her programme, too. Some of the dazzling numbers had gone to make room for the songs of loss and desolation. She sang these as she'd never sung before, with an aching intensity that hushed the room. Rico dropped his head, listening with a hand covering his eyes.

Afterwards he vanished without a word, and Julie might never have known he'd been there but for Carlo's murmuring, 'Rico was in tonight.'

Late as it was, she arrived home to find his bouquet of red roses with a card that said simply, 'R.' She wondered whom he hauled out of bed at this hour to provide them.

She heard a soft tap at her door. Julie drew in her breath sharply at the sight of the man who stood outside. Rico looked as if he hadn't slept for a week. His face was ravaged and his eyes burned. He didn't speak but stood looking at her in silence until at last she stood back to let him in.

'You were wonderful tonight,' he said jerkily. 'As always.'

'Did you come here to discuss my performance?'

'No, I came to apologize. I know what you must think of me—going away like that. It wasn't…what you thought.'

'How do you know what I thought?' she asked quietly.

'I didn't just walk out on you—'

'But you did.'

'I didn't mean it like that,' he said roughly. 'I always meant to come back—no, that's not true. At first I never meant to come back. Do you mind if I sit down?'

The question burst out abruptly, and she realized that he was on the verge of collapse. When she nodded, he sat down heavily on the bed and buried his face in his hands.

'You look as if you've only just got off the plane,' she said.

'No, I—' he checked his watch '—I flew back last night. I was going to come and see you today, but I walked about instead. At least, I think so. I can't really remember. I can't sleep on planes and my body clock is still several hours behind. I'm not making much sense, am I?'

'Enough to tell me that you're half-dead from jet lag. You shouldn't have come here tonight, Rico. Go home and get some sleep.'

'I couldn't go home without seeing you first. I don't seem to have much courage left, but I have just enough for that. Perhaps it was a mistake, though.'

She was about to tell him angrily that it was the biggest mistake he'd ever made, thinking he could simply walk back into her life after delivering such a blunt snub. But the words died in the face of his exhaustion and the despair written plainly on his face. If she'd had a bad time, so had he.

Instead she said, 'Thank you for the flowers.'

'I wanted to say something on the card, but I couldn't think of anything to say. I spent five days in New York wondering where I was going. In the end, I knew the only right way was back to you.'

'Don't say things like that,' Julie told him quickly.

'No, I don't suppose you're ready to hear them, are you?'

'No,' she said quietly. 'We have a long way to go, Rico, and perhaps we'll never get there. I've been able to do a lot of thinking while you were away. It would have been better if we'd never met again. Perhaps it would have been better if we'd never met in the first place.'

'Do you really mean that?' he asked, looking at her out of distraught eyes.

Never to have known his love, no matter how much pain followed? Even if she hadn't been blessed with her son, would she really have wanted that? Dumbly she shook her head.

'When did you have something to eat?' she asked.

He shrugged. 'I had a few drinks in the club.'

'That won't do you any good,' she said like a mother. 'You need some proper food inside you and something to drink that isn't alcohol.'

She called room service and ordered omelettes and tea. Rico didn't move, but his eyes never left her.

'Go over to the other side of the bed,' she said. 'Then the waiter won't see you from the door.'

He obeyed her like a child. A few minutes later, she answered the knock on the door. The waiter had a small table that he wheeled just inside, but Julie prevented him from coming any farther in and setting it up. She signed the bill, gave him a tip and closed the door behind him.

'You'll feel better when you've had some of this,' she said, wheeling the table directly into the room. 'I ordered mushroom omelettes because I remember you like them. Rico?'

There was no answer. Rico was stretched out on the bed, dead to the world.

She sat beside him and laid her hand against his face, feeling all bitterness and anger drain away. She didn't know what would happen between them now. She'd learned caution in a hard school and was far from sure that they could ever find a future together. But she couldn't maintain her hostility to this vulnerable man.

She'd told herself that the battle for his soul was over. She'd conceded defeat. Now she knew it wasn't over at all because Rico himself was still fighting to reclaim his better self. How could she abandon him to fight alone?

She left him to sleep and turned the lights down, leaving herself only enough to eat by. Then she undressed quietly and went to sleep on the sofa.

After a while, Rico began to toss and turn restlessly, muttering in his sleep. Julie lay down on the bed beside him, putting her arm over him protectively. After that, he was able to rest.

*   *   *

Julie awoke first and was having breakfast when Rico opened his eyes. After he stumbled into the bathroom, she heard the sound of a shower, followed by the electric shaver attached to the wall. When he emerged, he'd dressed again in the ruffled shirt and black trousers he'd worn to the club last night.

She poured him a coffee. He was nervous. His arrogance had fallen away from him and he was watching her closely, trying to determine her mood. She wondered how much he recalled about last night.

'I'm sorry for passing out like that,' he said.

'You were just about ready for it.'

'I always seem to be making apologies to you.'

'It's not important, Rico.'

'No, I suppose not,' he said, sounding disconcerted.

He drank his coffee while wandering about the room. By the window, he discovered a pile of newspapers several days old.

'We made the front pages,' Julie said calmly. She was keeping her voice light and neutral, partly because she was feeling her way inch by inch, and partly because she didn't want to put any emotional pressure on him.

She had the strangest feeling that all the cards were now in her hands. She wasn't used to feeling this way with Rico, and it was taking her a while to come to terms with it. So she was playing her hand with great care, frightened of playing the wrong card or the right one at the wrong moment. Perhaps they had a chance. But only perhaps.

He seated himself and began studying the papers.

The headlines were stark.

Nightclub Owner Assaults Film Star.

Rico Forza Socks Barono In Jealousy Brawl.

There were several pictures, but the best one showed Rico standing over the supine Barono, who was rubbing his jaw and looking undignified. Julie stood there, looking horrified, while Mariella seemed at swooning point.

'I picked up a couple of papers yesterday,' Rico observed. 'Mariella has been giving interviews claiming that I assaulted Barono because I was jealous of the attentions he was paying her.'

'But he was dancing with me!'

'He'd been dancing with her a few minutes earlier. Apparently I'd been watching them, seething with rage and jealousy. I urged you to dance with him as a way of separating him from Mariella, but she used our dance to inform me that she'd transferred her affections, at which it seems that I was overcome by the strength of my feelings.'

'So why didn't you stay with her instead of rushing out after me?'

He shrugged. 'Anything for a good story. It doesn't have to make sense. I'm sorry to have exposed you to all this.'

'Don't worry. I got some lovely reviews. Look at page thirty-seven.'

It was a review any singer would die for. The critic had waxed lyrical about her technical skill and her deep emotional impact. Rico read it and grunted his satisfaction.

A terrible thought occurred to Julie. 'You didn't order them to write that, did you? You did. You've got shares in that paper.'

'No, I swear it. You earned this on your own merit. I'm glad for you, Julie. It's no more than you deserve.' He stirred his coffee. 'Where do we go from here?'

'I honestly don't know.'

'I wouldn't blame you for hating me.'

'I don't hate you, Rico,' she said earnestly. 'But loving you is too dangerous.'

'I suppose I asked for that.'

'I didn't mean—oh, dear.'

'We need time for a long talk. We'll spend the day together and—'

'Oh, Rico, I can't. I'm sorry.'

'I mean, will you please spend the day with me?' he corrected himself hastily.

'It's not that. It's just that I've made other plans.'

'Can't you break them?'

'No,' she said, thinking of Gary's face if she broke her word to come next day.

'What can you have planned that's more important than…? I'm sorry,' he quickly apologized.

'I could make it tomorrow,' she offered.

'Tomorrow it is, then.'

CHAPTER TEN

SHE knew she'd made the right decision as soon as she saw Gary next morning. They'd planned exactly how they would spend the day, and the little boy remembered every detail of every promise. It would have been terrible to let him down.

Both Gary and Cassie were crazy about boats, while Julie wasn't keen on sailing. So they set up a boat trip for the two of them the day after, and Julie was free to stay in Rome with Rico.

He came to her dressing-room that night as she was getting ready. She wasn't feeling very well, having spent too long in the sun. Now her head was aching, and she would have been glad of an early night. But her audience was waiting, expecting the best.

'Will you be all right?' Rico asked. 'You look tired.'

'I am,' she said, passing a hand over her eyes. 'But it makes no odds. I perform when I'm tired, when I'm sad, even—' her voice shook '—even when there seems nothing to hope for.'

'It's a sin to give up hope. Remember that.'

'Is it?' she asked with a little sigh. 'Then I must be a great sinner, for sometimes I—I don't think there's any point.'

'Julie, please…'

He made a movement towards her. She didn't know how she might have received it if they hadn't heard

Gina approaching in the corridor. Rico drew back as though stung, then hurried out of the room.

As she had hoped, as soon as she was in the spotlight, the adrenalin took over, and she sang her heart out. She couldn't see Rico, but she knew he was out there somewhere, listening to every word, every inflection of sadness and loss.

He didn't appear in her dressing-room afterwards, but she found him waiting outside, his back against the wall, staring at the floor, lost in thought. When she touched his arm, he looked up before his defences were in place. In his eyes she saw not just apprehension but the dreadful, sickening fear of a man who'd understood too late, when he'd already thrown the prize away.

He spoke as though roused from a dream. 'I'll drive you home.'

'I prefer to walk.'

'You can't walk home alone at this hour,' he said at once.

Was it an accident that he'd used words so close to the ones he'd spoken on that night long ago, the night when they'd found each other? His dark face made it hard to tell. But his next words settled it.

'Why does your lover permit such a thing?' he whispered.

She looked him in the eye. 'I don't have a lover. Only men who admire me, who want to own me or show me off. A lover is something different.'

He remembered. 'And you said that you wanted to be more than a trophy,' he reminded her.

'Yes, I said that. But a trophy is what I seem to have ended up.'

'Not to me,' he said quietly. He added with meaning, 'If you were mine, I wouldn't let you walk alone in the dark.'

'I'm not yours,' she told him. 'But you may walk me home.'

Together they strolled the three blocks along the Via Veneto, but at the corner of the street that led to her hotel, she stopped.

'We'll say good-night here.'

'I'll call you tomorrow?'

'Yes, but not too soon. I'd like to sleep late.'

'*Buona notte, signorina.*'

'*Buona notte*, Signor Forza.'

Next morning's papers were full of Barono and Mariella, who'd managed to get themselves featured every day since the incident in the nightclub. This time, they'd descended on the Via Condotti and raided every shop. Barono had loaded his new love with the costliest of everything, while ensuring that the camera didn't see too much of his black eye.

Julie read all this while eating a leisurely breakfast of rolls and coffee in bed.

The phone rang.

'I hope I didn't wake you,' Rico said.

'No, I was reading the papers. They've done it again, particularly in—' She named a Roman scandal sheet.

'I've been reading that, too. Perhaps we should give the press some pictures of our own, to make the true position clear. When may I call for you?'

'I'll be ready in an hour. And by the way, dress casually.'

'Where are we going?'

'I'll tell you when I see you.'

She was waiting for him downstairs, wearing designer jeans and a blue silk shirt, roped in at the waist by a multicoloured silk sash. A matching scarf kept her hair back. Rico had obeyed her injunction and was in shirtsleeves, with a fawn linen jacket slung over his shoulder.

'Where to?' he asked.

'The zoo.'

'The zoo?'

'You promised me long ago.'

'The zoo it is, then.'

'Is it far?' she asked as they began to walk.

He pointed along the Via Veneto. 'No distance. At the end of this street are the Borghese Gardens, and the zoo is on the far side. We could take a *carrozza* if we can find one.'

He looked around as he spoke, but it was Julie who saw something that made her give a delighted squeal.

'Over there!' she said, clutching his arm and pointing to an elderly horse clip-clopping placidly down the far side of the street. Behind him, the driver sat with his head sunk on his chest. 'That's Miko, I'm sure of it. Come on!'

'Julie, wait!' Rico roared, making a frantic grab for her, just too late to stop her from darting out into traffic. An oncoming car braked just in time. The driver, finding his engine stalled, stuck his head out and shrieked Roman curses. Horns tooted, drivers bawled. Rico raced across the wide road to where Julie had halted Miko in his tracks by the simple expedient of planting herself in front of him and seizing his bridle. Miko's driver seemed to wake up.

'*Buon giorno, signorina*,' he called cheerfully. 'Miko is very happy to see you again. And so am I.'

'Get in,' Rico said, grabbing her arm and shoving her unceremoniously into the *carrozza*.

'Hey—'

'Get in before you cause a riot, you madwoman. The Borghese Gardens,' he yelled to the driver.

'Is that man over there angry with me?' Julie asked, pointing back the way they'd come.

'Oh, no, he's not angry,' Rico said sarcastically. 'He's only saying that your mother was a cow and your father an imp from hell, and he's hoping that your children are all born cross-eyed and with one leg.'

'He doesn't like me much, does he?' Julie asked sunnily.

'What the devil were you thinking of, dashing out into traffic like that?' Rico spoke roughly because he'd had the fright of his life. 'Don't you know about Roman traffic? It doesn't stop for you.'

'That man stopped.'

'And now he can't start again. You'll live under his curse for the rest of your life. And mine, for giving me a heart attack. And what's so damned funny!'

'I'm sorry,' she said, controlling herself and speaking penitently. 'I don't know what's come over me today. I'm just in a holiday mood.'

Rico felt his heart turn over at the sight of her mischievous face. Since she'd arrived in Rome, it was the first time he'd seen her look so merry. Once, happiness had come to her naturally.

He took her hand firmly in his. 'From now on, you stay with me and you don't move,' he commanded.

'*Sì, signore*,' she answered meekly.

Finding the same *carrozza* had been like an omen. What had gone wrong before could be put right this time. The notion was irrational, but who cared about that?

As they clip-clopped along the Via Veneto, Julie became gloriously aware how bright the sun was, how brilliant the colours around her were, how fresh the air, how gentle and attentive her lover was being. She turned on him a smile of such happiness that his own heart was eased, and he managed a smile in return.

She had just terrified him and he was still shaking, but suddenly he, too, saw the sun.

The Borghese Gardens were a paradise of flowers and mysterious paths leading to small temples. As they drove through it, he pointed out its delights to her, venturing to take her hand. But almost at once he had to relinquish it because they had reached the *Giardino Zoologico*.

It was a small, charming zoo. The larger animals were separated from spectators by deep moats rather than cages and given a good deal of carefully designed freedom. Julie eyed the lions, who eyed her scornfully back. She set herself to outstare them and became so preoccupied that she missed the moment Rico slipped away.

He was back in a few minutes, loaded down with ice-cream cones. 'Chocolate,' he said, handing her one, 'because it's your favourite. Mint because it's your second favourite. And pistachio because you haven't tried it before.'

'How do you know I haven't?' she asked, tucking in.

'Whatever you've been doing the past few years, you haven't been in a place where they've made ice cream like this.'

'That's true.'

Keeping the fourth cone for himself, he twined his fingers in hers, and they strolled along together.

'What have you been doing all these years?' he asked casually. 'I know you've become a star, but what else?'

'Very little else,' she said, speaking carefully. Every word had to be examined in case she revealed her secret.

She didn't know that her sudden wariness had sent a shadow flickering across her face. It was gone in an instant, but not before Rico noticed it and wondered.

'You're surely not without friends,' he said a mite too casually. 'There must be someone at home who waits to hear from you. You can't always be calling your friend—what was his name?—Gary?'

'I call lots of people,' she said with a shrug. 'This is really delicious. What's yours like?'

'Delicious,' he said, accepting her change of subject.

It was disconcerting to find that he had to follow her lead. In the days of their first love, she had fallen easily into his arms, never giving him a moment's doubt, never forcing him to court her.

In fact, he'd never courted any woman. In Italy, women queued up to spend an hour on his arm and in his bed. He'd accepted them for what they were, treated them generously and forgotten them.

But now he was being forced to do what other men did—tread softly for fear of driving the beloved woman away. And he found himself in a new country without signposts.

'Why did it have to be that *carrozza*?' he asked.

'It was an omen. Like a second chance.'

He nodded, understanding at once what he would have struggled with before.

They strolled for a couple of hours, hand in hand like children, saying little but enjoying peace and contentment. Then somebody recognized them and a murmur went round. Soon they were being watched everywhere.

Near the elephant house, they found a café and settled outside on wooden chairs to eat snacks. A posse of paparazzi had caught up with them and were clicking determinedly away, rejoicing in the kind of shots nobody had ever thought to see: Rico Forza in casuals, eating burgers and exchanging silly jokes with a woman who made his eyes shine.

'Haven't they got enough by now?' he grunted.

'Oh, let them.' Julie said easily. 'Think how good this is for my career.' She chuckled to herself. 'And think how mad it'll make Mariella.'

'You've really got your knife into her, haven't you?'

'Yes,' Julie said simply.

He grinned. She'd made his day.

When they left the café the press followed them for a while, varying the shots as much as possible, but finally they gave up.

Julie never wanted the day to end. It was a perfect holiday from all the troubles that would still be waiting for her when it was over. But somehow the light was changing, and the troubles would never look quite as bad again. She might even find a way round them.

They chatted about this and that, keeping off dangerous subjects, but growing more at ease with each other until at last no subject seemed impossibly dangerous. Rico ventured to say, 'You once told me that singing made you more alive than anything else—except love.'

'No, that was someone else. That was Patsy Brown.'

'What became of her, Julie?'

'She found it too hard to exist. So now she doesn't. That's all.'

'That's all,' he echoed thoughtfully. 'Who would have thought so much could be contained in just two words?'

'In another time, you told me that you loved me,' she said wistfully. 'Only three words, but the whole world was there. All the world I wanted anyway.'

'Not quite all,' he reminded her. 'You wanted fame, as well.'

'Yes, but not…' She hesitated.

'What?'

'Not at such a price.'

They regarded each other and the truth that lay between them.

'Perhaps the past is too powerful,' she said.

'It doesn't have to be. We can make our own fate.'

She smiled ruefully. 'Spoken like a true Forza. But we can't all be ''rulers of the world''.'

'I don't feel like a ruler of the world,' he confessed. 'I feel like the boy who made you cry and tore his hair because he'd ruined everything.'

'You never made me cry in those days.'

'But I did, once. I was in a bad mood and it made me unkind to you.'

'I can't remember,' she said in a wondering voice.

'I can't forget. I was careful never to be unkind again. It destroyed me to hurt you.'

Silence. What was there to say?

'Mama! Mama!'

They both turned to where a little boy was dancing about in front of the chimpanzees, clutching his father's hand and trying to attract his mother's attention. A short distance away, a young woman was buying ice creams, but she hurried back to her family and let the child point out the animals to her. The father watched them both with a grin of possessive delight.

The boy must have been about the same age as their own son. Julie guessed what Rico was thinking and waited for him to remind her of what they'd lost. She saw his face take on a look of inexpressible sadness, as though a great burden weighed him down. But he said nothing.

After a moment, he gave her hand a squeeze and drew her away. 'Where shall we go now?' he asked.

'I must go back and get ready for tonight's performance.'

He seemed to come out of a dream. 'I'd forgotten about that. I'd forgotten everything.'

'It's been a lovely day, Rico, but the real world is still there.'

'Tomorrow—'

'I can't see you tomorrow,' she said. She'd promised Gary that she wouldn't miss another day.

He frowned. 'Do your plans matter more than being with me?'

She thought of seeing her child again and instinctively smiled. That smile troubled him. It was like the one she'd worn when he'd found her telephoning somebody in the garden of his villa.

'I'm busy tomorrow,' she said lightly but firmly.

'And you won't tell me what?'

'There's a way you could always find out.'

'No,' he said immediately. 'I promised never to have you watched again, and I'm a man of my word.'

'I know you are, Rico. Your word means I'm quite safe.'

'That's a strange thing to say.'

She took his hand. 'Come on. Let's start drifting back.'

They walked slowly for neither really wanted the day to end. By the elephant house, they stood and regarded two huge beasts who were nudging each other fondly with their heads and twining their trunks. Suddenly she laughed softly and pulled him into the shadows.

'If I were an elephant, would you curl your trunk around mine?' she teased.

'Anything that made you happy,' he promised.

That struck her as irresistibly funny and she laughed until she choked. He held on to her, feeling her laughter vibrate through him until he joined in helplessly.

All round, people were heading for the exit as the zoo prepared to close. The eager child was still chattering about everything he saw. Drinks sellers packed up, monkeys scratched and yawned.

In the shadow of the elephant house, a boy and girl kissed.

She found her dressing-room filled with roses, deep red ones from Rico and pink from Beppe. Just as the performance was about to start, the little man put his head round her door.

'We do duets, *sì*?' he asked cheekily.

'We do duets, *sì*,' Julie said.

The little man blew her a kiss and departed, almost colliding with Rico in the doorway. Beppe backed away, kissed both hands at her in a parody of adoration that made Rico pull a face.

'Do women really like that?' he demanded.

'He's fun,' Julie said. 'I like him. We're going to sing together.'

'I'd rather you—that is, is it a good idea?'

'It's a wonderful idea. I like to vary my act.'

'Did you have a pleasant day?' he asked with an effort.

'Yes, I had a lovely time.' She glowed as the memories came rushing back to her.'

'I'm glad.' His smile was a little forced.

He didn't see the smile on Julie's face as he left. It was full of tenderness. She knew what that concession had cost him. What was happening was too wonderful for words. If only it could last.

She spent the next morning rehearsing duets with Beppe. They went well together, and Carlo was thrilled with the result.

Afterwards, as she went to her dressing-room, she heard Rico's voice coming from behind the door of his office, which was slightly open. She hurried past, not wanting to eavesdrop. Even so, she couldn't help hearing, '*Carissima.*'

Darling! Rico was calling somebody 'darling'.

And then he laughed.

That laugh made her feet slow until they stopped altogether. It was tender and affectionate. He'd laughed like that with her at the zoo. And for who else? He laughed again, and the gentle intimacy told her, beyond doubt, that he was talking to a woman.

She gasped and steadied herself against the wall. It couldn't be happening. After yesterday, after the magic time they'd spent together...

She couldn't stop shaking.

It wasn't Mariella on the other end of that phone. Instinct told her that he didn't laugh with the glossy starlet in that fond way. It was a woman who was very dear to him. A woman he'd told her nothing about.

She clenched her hands, taking deep breaths to steady herself.

Then she heard Rico again, speaking softly and with love. 'Anna, *carissima…*'

Now she knew. His beloved was called Anna. Not Julie.

'I have to be going, Anna. I'll come to see you as soon as I can. I'd like to be there for the festival, and we can dance together in the street as we've always done. Goodbye. Take care of yourself.'

Julie moved quickly, closing the door of her dressing-room just as Rico emerged into the corridor. She heard his footsteps growing fainter.

How could this be happening? Rico had turned back to her with love in his eyes, and all the time his real love was elsewhere. It had been another of his tricks.

Something snapped within her. Whatever happened, she had to find Anna, see her, talk to her. There was a simple way of doing that, but strictly speaking, she ought not. Torn by temptation, Julie stayed motionless until she couldn't stand it any longer.

The corridor was empty. It took a moment to slip into Rico's office, lift the phone and touch the redial button.

After two rings, a voice answered, 'Ristorante Tornese.'

She made a hurried excuse and hung up.

She slipped away before Rico could return, then hurried back to the hotel. In her room, she leafed through the telephone directory until she found the Ristorante Tornese in the Piazza Santa Maria in Trastevere.

Now she remembered Rico telling her about Trastevere, the cheerful bohemian quarter that was to Rome what Soho was to London and Greenwich Village to New York. He'd made it sound like a place of colourful life and joy.

And now that was where his heart was.

The next day, she drove out to Fregene to spend another day with Gary. She stayed until he was asleep, then returned to Rome, thoughtful all the way.

It was the policy of La Dolce Notte to feature its star for only six nights of the week. Tuesdays were given over to rising young performers. Today was Tuesday, and Julie was free.

All the way to Rome, she told herself that she wasn't sure what she was going to do tonight. She even returned the car and went back to the hotel thinking that perhaps Rico had left a message for her. He knew it was her free night and would want her to spend it with him.

But there was no message from him, and after sitting in her room for an hour, she called a taxi.

The way to Trastevere lay past the Trevi Fountain and across the River Tiber. Almost as soon as she was on the other side, Julie became aware of a difference in the atmosphere. From somewhere up ahead, she could hear music interspersed by laughing and cheering.

'Here we are,' the driver called cheerfully over his shoulder. 'Just down there is the Piazza Santa Maria in Trastevere. I can't take you any closer because no traffic is allowed.'

The people here seemed to live their lives out on the cobbled streets. High overhead, washing stretched from window to window. Here and there were bars, cafés, their tables spilling out of cramped interiors, sprawling over the pavement. Light poured from every door and window, and from every direction came the sounds of merrymaking.

'My goodness!' she murmured.

The driver grinned. 'It's the festival tonight. Usually it's a little bit quieter. Not much, though.'

She paid him and began to make her way through the crowds. A group of tumblers came streaming along the street. One of them caught her in his arms, swung her round and was gone before she could catch her breath.

In the distance, she could see a hugely tall man walking on stilts. Behind his long legs bounded fire-eaters and dancers in old-fashioned costumes. They might be characters escaped from some Victorian circus, but in these old streets they looked just right.

She found the Ristorante Tornese on a corner. It was a small place but bright and cheerful. All the outside tables were taken and only one remained empty inside. Julie slipped in and took it.

She studied the waitresses and immediately saw the one who must be Anna. She was young and beautiful, with a fresh, angelic quality that made Julie's heart sink.

'What can I get you?' The girl stopped beside her.

'A—a glass of wine, please,' Julie stammered.

'You are ill, *signorina*?' the girl asked anxiously.

Julie pulled herself together. 'No, I'm fine. Just a glass of wine.'

The girl went to fetch it. Julie was close to the kitchen door, which swung back and forth constantly as busy serving staff barged in and out. A large, elderly woman was at the stove, cooking vigorously, surrounded by clouds of steam. She was shabbily dressed in black, with a black kerchief tied about her grey hair.

The door swung to, hiding her from sight, but she appeared a moment later with Julie's wine. 'You all right?' she demanded. 'Sara was worried.'

'Sara? That girl is called Sara? Not Anna?'

'Anna? No.' The old woman gave a bawling laugh. It was rich and earthy, and it shook her huge frame. She laughed and laughed, then wiped her glistening forehead with her black apron. 'I am Anna,' she said.

CHAPTER ELEVEN

'YOU are Anna?' Julie echoed, hardly daring to believe it. 'But you—'

Suddenly Anna let out a yelp of triumph. 'I know you,' she cried. 'You sing at my Rico's place. I see your picture.'

'Yes, I sing at La Dolce Notte. I'm Julie Hallam. And you—you are Rico's Anna?'

The old woman's eyes glowed. 'Rico has told you about me, *si*?'

'I…well…' She could hardly say that she'd overheard his conversation.

Luckily Anna ploughed on without waiting for an answer. 'Sometimes he calls me Anna. Sometimes Nonna.'

'You are Nonna?' Julie gasped as it all fell into place. 'Yes…I understand now. He told me that he calls you Nonna because you gave him all the love he ever knew.'

'That's my Rico.'

'Anna!' A heavy, middle-aged man had put his head round the kitchen door and bawled at her.

'I return. *Scusi.*' Anna fled into the kitchen.

Through the swinging door, Julie could see the old woman mopping her brow. Another man, out of sight, shouted, 'Anna!' She turned to him and the door swung to, hiding her.

A waiter near Julie hurriedly finished serving and hurtled back into the kitchen, yelling, 'Anna!'

Julie's relief at discovering Anna's identity was replaced by horror. So that weary, overworked woman was the person he claimed to love like a grandmother. He spoke lyrically about what she had done for him, yet here she was, so poor that she had to work like a slave at an age when she ought to be comfortably retired.

She'd loved Rico once for his warm heart. She realized that he'd changed, but had he really changed that much?

The door swung again. This time it was Anna, bearing dishes. As well as cooking, it seemed that she also waited at table. She served some customers near Julie, exchanged backchat with them and returned to Julie, sinking her vast bulk into the chair with a sigh of relief.

'So, my Rico tells you about me,' she continued. 'Always he says nice things about me.'

But he doesn't do nice things for you, Julie thought crossly. Anna's heartfelt joy at the sound of his name was making her angrier with Rico with every passing minute.

'What are you doing in here?' Anna demanded. 'Rico's friend has the best table.'

'It was the only one free—'

'You sit outside where it's nicer.'

She gabbled something in Romagnolo to a boy who looked about sixteen. He scuttled away and returned with a small table that he set up outside with two chairs. Anna whisked a cloth onto it, produced a bottle and two glasses, then indicated for Julie to sit.

'You drink this,' she said, pouring the Chianti. 'Best there is.' She seated herself in the other chair.

'I don't want to get you into any trouble,' Julie said

with a nervous glance at the big man with a moustache who was scowling at Anna.

'Trouble? Hah!' Anna's booming laugh echoed off the walls. 'I been working hard. I wanna sit down, I sit down. What you have to eat?'

'Well—'

'There's some spaghetti carbonara—very nice,' Anna said without letting her speak. 'I get it for you myself.'

She hauled herself to her feet and stomped away. Julie was left feeling as if she'd been flattened by an amiable steamroller.

In no time at all, Anna was back with the spaghetti. She set it down before her, then presented her with a snowy napkin. 'Eat,' she commanded.

'It's delicious,' Julie said after the first mouthful. 'Did you make it?'

'*Sì*. I make everything that is eaten here.'

'Everything?' Julie echoed, aghast. 'But the work must be enormous.'

Anna shrugged. 'I got a boy to help me, but he's an idiot. I tell him get outta my way.'

'You taught Rico to cook, didn't you?'

Anna beamed. 'He tell you that? When?'

Too late, Julie realized that she couldn't answer this without saying more than she wanted. 'Well…' she faltered, 'he's told me a lot about you, how the kitchen was his favourite place because you were there.'

To her relief, Anna allowed herself to be distracted. 'First thing when he gets home from school, always he comes to see me. Who else can he talk to?'

'What about his parents?'

'They are dead before he is ten years old. He lives with his grandfather. I tell you, that old man was a devil. Rico's father, Santo, was his only son. He plans a great marriage for him, but Santo runs away and marries the girl he loves. Maria is a nice, decent girl, but not important enough for Arturo.

'He is very cross, but what can he do? Nothing. The marriage is made and she is pregnant. Then soon after Rico is born, Santo dies. Arturo goes to Maria, and he acts so nice, so gentle, and he says, ''Come and live with me.'''

'She thinks he is being kind, but that devil only does things for himself. When they are in his house, he pushes her away. He hires a nanny for the baby. Maria hardly ever sees him. Once I hear him tell her, ''You are not good enough to be the mother of my grandson.'' Can you imagine such wickedness?'

'Yes,' Julie said thoughtfully, 'I can.'

In the light of her own experience, the whole story was horribly believable.

'Didn't she fight for her son?' she asked.

'Nobody could fight him,' Anna said sadly. 'Rico grew up hardly knowing his mother, and at last she gave up fighting. She began to drink too much, and Arturo made sure that there was always drink around. And she loved skiing, so he sent her on long skiing holidays.

'She died in a skiing accident. Perhaps she'd had too much to drink, I don't know. I say Arturo killed her.'

Shocked, Julie was silent. How could the old man have so brutally ignored the needs of the little boy in his obsession to have his own way? And now, of course, his behaviour to her was explained. His son had slipped through his fingers, and it must have

seemed that his grandson would do the same. So he'd
smashed whoever was in his path to prevent it.

'Arturo told Rico that his mother didn't care for
him,' Anna resumed. 'As he grew older, I tried to
make him see what had really happened, and now I
think he does justice to Maria's memory. But it's not
the same as having her when he needed her.'

'No, of course not. But at least he had you.'

Anna smiled fondly. 'He used to cling to me and
say, "Nonna, do you love me? Promise that you love
me." Such a sad, beautiful little boy. Wait here. I
show you something.'

She waddled back into the kitchen but returned at
once, carrying a small leather photo album with a
worn, well-thumbed look. Anna handed it to Julie. She
opened it, and her heart nearly stopped.

Gary's face looked out at her.

'Rico was seven years old there,' Anna said, pointing. 'I took that picture. He had to show me how to
work his camera, and I kept pressing the wrong buttons. We laughed so much.'

'He—he was delightful,' Julie stammered.

She'd known Gary was like his father, but seeing
Rico at Gary's age showed her how close the likeness
was. How they would have loved each other! How
much they'd both missed!

Anna's shrewd eyes were on her. Hastily Julie began to leaf through the other pictures: Rico in his early
teens, his late teens, and then one that almost made
her cry out. There was the boy she'd loved—twenty-
three, eager for life, for love. And it had betrayed him.

'Oh, yes,' she whispered to herself. 'That was how
he smiled.'

Anna didn't answer, but her eyes saw everything.

There was only one more picture, obviously taken recently. This was Rico as she'd seen him when she first arrived—stern, unsmiling.

'I used to hope he'd find some girl who'd love him truly and make him happy,' Anna sighed.

'And—and did he ever find her?' Julie asked, concentrating on her food.

'Once…long ago. He thought she was an angel. When he told me about her, his face shone with joy. He couldn't stop talking about her, how perfect she was, how she was going to have his baby. He'd known so little love and he was so grateful to her for loving him. Once he said to me, "I would lay down my life for her." But…' Anna shrugged sadly. 'She abandoned him. Since then, he's never been the same. His heart withered. That is what she did to him.'

The bright good humour had faded from the old woman's face, leaving behind the unforgiving judgement of a mother figure for someone who had wounded her young.

'But perhaps it wasn't her fault,' Julie urged. 'Don't forget what you know about Arturo. Maybe he forced her to abandon him.'

Anna shrugged. '*Sì*. It would be like him. But she gave away Rico's child. How can she have loved him and do that? I tell you, that was when he knew that her love was a sham. And if such a thing could happen with her, then every woman's love was a sham.

'I don't know all that happened. Even with me, there is much he keeps to himself. But I know this. He was once a boy with a warm, loving heart. He became a man who loves nobody.' Her eyes glinted with sudden shrewdness. 'But perhaps you can make him love again.'

'Me…I…' She was dismayed to find herself blushing.

'I see the pictures of you two together in all the papers.'

'Anna, you can't believe what you see in the papers. People like to believe that Rico and I—I mean, it's good for business.'

'Business! Hah!' Anna snorted. 'And what about you? You don't love him?'

'I…' Julie floundered. But the next moment, Anna came to her rescue.

'*Idiota*!' she said, striking herself on the forehead. 'Where are my manners to ask you such a thing? Mind your own business, Anna. You are *cretina*!'

Julie dissolved into laughter, relieved to have been let off the hook. 'I don't think you are,' she said. 'But I can't talk about him—not just now.'

'Of course. And your plate is empty. I bring more food.

'No, please…'

But she was talking to empty air. Anna had vanished into the kitchen, bawling instructions as she went.

Julie was glad of the respite. It was true that she couldn't speak openly about Rico, but neither could she dissimulate with this earthy, honest woman. Although they'd only met a short time ago, she already knew that Anna's shrewd eyes would see through any pretence.

Obviously she didn't know the truth. If she did, she would judge Julie harshly. And Julie instinctively cared about her opinion.

Anna came roaring back with a plate piled high,

which she set down in front of Julie. 'Eat, eat, eat!' she commanded. 'You are too thin.'

'I need to be thin,' she protested. 'I have to wear glamorous dresses that show every extra ounce. If I can't get into them, I shall tell Rico it's your fault.'

Anna screamed with laughter. It was so infectious that Julie joined in, which made Anna laugh even more. She reached out and took Julie's face between her hands. They were warm, steady hands and they gave her a strange jolt of happiness. She, too, had lacked the steady love of a mother and she suddenly understood exactly why Anna was so important to Rico.

Then Anna's face brightened still more. A look of utter delight swept over it, and the next moment she'd bounded out of her seat, arms flung wide in ecstatic greeting. 'Rico!'

Julie looked round to find the two of them locked in a fierce embrace. Rico hugged Anna robustly, then looked into her face. His own face was transformed. All the cynical sophistication that marred it had vanished, to be replaced by heartfelt joy.

'I was afraid you don't come,' Anna told him at the top of her voice.

'You know I can't stay away from you,' he said with a grin.

'See who's here.' Anna nodded towards Julie.

Julie wondered if he would be annoyed at finding her here, but Rico said mildly, 'Yes, I saw. You two seem to be getting on well.'

'She's a nice girl,' Anna hissed. 'You sit down with her while I get food.'

She bustled away. A waiter indicated that he was

ready to take his order, but Rico waved him away. 'Anna will serve me,' he said.

From deep in the kitchen, they could hear Anna making her presence felt to the accompaniment of crashing plates.

'She's certainly putting herself out to please you,' Julie observed.

'She always does. She likes it.'

'But how old is she?'

'I don't know. Probably over sixty.'

'Over sixty? And what time will she finish working here?'

Rico stared at her. 'What are you saying?'

'She won't finish until after midnight, will she?'

'Much later. The festival is on.'

His calm tone galled her and she snapped, 'I expect she started at midday?'

'Earlier, probably. She buys food in the market first.'

'You have the nerve to say that you love her and yet you let her live like this?' Julie said indignantly. 'She's an old woman. She ought to be putting her feet up, not working herself to death because you're too mean to give her a decent pension.'

He looked at her curiously. 'I see. So that's what you're mad about.'

'I'll say I am. If you could hear the way she talks about you. Everything is "my Rico". She thinks you're wonderful. Why are you staring at me?'

'I—was I?'

'You looked as if you'd seen a ghost. Never mind that. Let's talk about Anna and the way you're treating her.'

For the next few minutes, her words washed over

him. His mind was filled with pictures of Miko the horse, the nameless dog in the pub, and a young girl who only ever became angry when she was defending the vulnerable. The memories made a spring of happiness well up in him.

Over her shoulder, he saw Anna bearing down on them, armed with laden plates. He leaned back out of Julie's line of sight and gave Anna a huge wink before barking out, 'Hurry up. I'm hungry.'

Julie stared, outraged at his tone.

'*Scusi, scusi,*' Anna mumbled, hurriedly setting down the plates before them.

'I should think so,' Rico said curtly. 'And get some salt, fast. There's none on this table.'

'I've been in such a hurry,' Anna said humbly.

'Always excuses,' Rico sneered. 'If it happens again, I'll complain to your employer. *Hey!*'

The shout was the result of having a plate of spaghetti tossed over him. Julie rose to her feet, eyes flashing. 'You ought to be ashamed of yourself,' she seethed. 'How dare you talk to Anna like that after all she's done for you! It's bad enough that you let her slave here till all hours at everyone's beck and call— what's so funny?'

Rico and Anna had collapsed with laughter. They clung together and rocked back and forth, helpless with mirth. Julie sat down and looked uncertainly from one to the other.

'You bad boy!' Anna chided him, starting to clean him up. 'Why do you make fun of this nice girl?' She patted Julie's hand. 'This restaurant is mine.'

'Yours?'

'My Rico has bought it for me. Also two others.'

'Oh,' Julie said in a hollow voice.

'I bought them as an investment so that Anna could retire on the proceeds,' Rico said. 'I meant her to take it easy, but she won't.'

'I like to cook and be with people,' Anna said. 'Who wants to put their feet up and be alone?'

'But everyone was yelling at you,' Julie protested.

Anna shrugged. 'So? That idiot over there is my brother. The two younger idiots are his sons. They yell at me, I yell at them. So what?'

Right on cue, an unseen presence inside bawled, 'Anna!'

'I go,' she declared, heaving her bulk up from the chair and waddling away.

'I must go and get cleaned up,' Rico said. He laid a hand on her arm. 'You won't leave?'

'No.'

'Promise,' he said urgently.

'I promise.'

He was gone barely five minutes, and when he returned he was wearing a clean white shirt. 'I keep a room and some clothes here,' he explained.

'Then this is your real home? Not the villa.'

'I suppose that's true. Yes, it is true. I come here when I want to be made a fuss of.'

'What a fool I was,' Julie said sheepishly. 'I should have known you wouldn't keep her slaving away.'

'How should you know? It's my fault if you think the worst of me. But I'm so glad you two like each other.'

'I think she's wonderful.'

'What made you come here?'

'I was eavesdropping when you were on the phone to her, and I was curious.'

'Curious? Does that mean jealous?'

She considered. 'Yes,' she said at last. 'It does.'

'I'm glad. I should hate to think all the jealousy was on my side.' He looked at her with meaning.

'Beppe?' she asked hilariously.

'Don't be fooled by his age or his waistline. Women fall for him in droves.'

'And I understand why.'

'Oh, you do?'

'I love his sense of humour.'

'I never had very much of that,' he said wryly.

'No.' She smiled. 'But you had a lot of other things that I remember very well.'

'Were you really jealous of Anna?'

'You'll never know how much.'

She had to raise her voice to be heard over the sound of a trombone. A band was passing along the street, making unskilled but vigorous noises.

'It's Noiantri,' Rico shouted.

'What is?' she shouted back.

When the band had gone by, he said, 'In Trastevere, we celebrate the festival of Noiantri every year. The word means. ''We Others'' in Romagnolo, the Roman dialect. That's how we think of ourselves here. We're different. We believe that we're the only true descendants of the ancient Romans.'

'We? You talk as though you were one of them.'

'I feel like one of them. Like you said, this is my real home.'

All around them, couples were dancing in the piazza while fireworks whizzed and roared overhead. Rico held out his hand and swept her away into the noisy, jostling crowd.

They danced any old way, bouncing here and there, clinging to each other and laughing joyously. A man stood up to sing in a hoarse, unpolished voice, and everyone cheered him wildly. The band blared. Rico swung her round and round until she was giddy, and then there were only his lips on hers.

'Come with me,' he whispered.

'Yes, anywhere.'

Together they climbed the narrow stairs to the little room in the apartment over the café. Plainly furnished, it held only a wardrobe and a bed just big enough for lovers.

At first they just stood in silence their arms around each other, feeling at last a deep peace in each other's presence.

'Are you really here?' he whispered.

'Yes, my darling, I'm here…I'm here.'

'And you won't go away again?'

She couldn't answer because his mouth had already covered hers, his lips caressing her gently, eagerly. He kissed her mouth, her eyes, her forehead, touching her with reverence.

When they were undressed and lying on the bed, he didn't try to claim her at once, but held her body against the length of his own. The passion was growing between them, but tonight, something was even more important. They had come home to each other's arms.

They lay together, watching the sky light up as fireworks streaked up into the sky and fell in glittering showers. Their eyes met, and they shared a smile full of mystery and understanding. Rico began to kiss her gently and caress her body with tender, loving movements. The old joy came flooding back. Julie felt her heart flower again as her body responded to his desire with an ardour of its own.

She had been made for him, and him only. She returned his kisses, delighted at his instant reaction.

'You're beautiful,' he murmured. 'How have I lived so long without you?'

She couldn't speak. His skilful hands were moving over her, escalating desire wherever they lingered. She wanted him so much, and the feel of his face between her breasts was inexpressibly sweet.

He loved her gently, as though he feared that she might break in his arms. And she felt safe with him, as she had thought never to feel again. It was wonderful to be able to shower her gifts on him again and sense the passionate gratitude in his response.

That gratitude had always been there, she recognized. As a boy, his loneliness had made him imbue her every caress with significance so that he had almost worshipped her when she'd nursed him through a minor illness.

The lonely boy had grown into a lonely man who needed her love now more than ever. And she had grown into a woman of depth and profound tenderness, who could instil in him desire, but also something else, infinitely more precious.

She showed him in actions, enfolding him in her arms in a gesture of protection, silently promising to keep him enclosed for ever in the haven of her love.

It was he who slept first and she who lay awake, watching over him, keeping vigil against the world.

CHAPTER TWELVE

THEY slept with their arms around each other. Julie awoke feeling relaxed and happy. Rico was just opening his eyes and stretching like a contented cat. She kissed him, slipped out of the narrow bed and went to the window.

Outside, the street lights were beginning to fade, as the first gleam of dawn appeared. As the doors closed on the last of the night's revellers, the early stallholders were throwing open their windows, yawning and rubbing their eyes.

'Doesn't this place ever go completely to sleep?' Julie asked contentedly.

'Never quite,' Rico replied, coming close and slipping his arms around her from behind. 'There's always some activity or other going on.'

'I used to dream of this,' she murmured, leaning back against him. 'Long ago, when you first told me about Trastevere and I saw us living here, I thought of it just like this. It was such a lovely dream.'

'Is it a lovely dream to be poor?'

'I've always been poor. The thought didn't scare me. And I had you—or thought I had. That was riches enough.'

'You had me,' he assured her. 'You never knew how much I loved you. I couldn't find the words to tell you. I tried, but what came out was a pale shadow of the truth.'

She knew what he meant. It had been the same with

her. She'd offered him heartfelt words, but they hadn't seemed enough. She consoled herself with the thought that she would give him a baby and show her feelings in actions.

But she couldn't tell him this now. So she remained silent, only turning her head to feel his lips on her forehead.

'It was a dream,' she mused. 'People aren't allowed to be as happy as we were, or not for long. One brief glimpse of heaven, just enough to torment you all your life. Perhaps it would be better not to see heaven at all.'

'Hush, you don't really believe that.'

'No, I don't believe it. I can never forget what we had or how beautiful it was. We'll always have those memories.'

'You speak as if everything was over for us, as though there could never be any future. But there has to be. We can't lose each other again.

'I want to tell you something. I realize now that I was wrong to blame you. It took me too long to face that it was my fault. I should have told you the truth about myself all those years ago. At first it was a game, pretending to be poor and knowing that you loved me as a poor man, for myself alone. I almost worshipped you for that.

'I pictured myself returning from Italy, telling you the truth, showering you with luxuries. But I never though of what I'd done to you—leaving you vulnerable. It's true I didn't dream what my grandfather would do, but that's no excuse. I knew him. I should have thought. But I didn't, and when the crisis came, you were defenceless. How could I do that to you?

And how could I blame you afterwards when I'd left you to face it alone?'

He took her face between his hands. 'Do you understand? I blame you for nothing, nothing. The blame is all mine.'

It was the declaration of perfect love and trust that she had longed for. He was Rico again, as she'd always longed to find him. And now, at last, it was safe to tell him everything.

'Rico, there's something—'

Her words were cut off by a knock on the door, and Anna's voice saying urgently, 'Rico, Rico!'

'What is it, Nonna,' he called back.

'There's a phone call from Milan. Quickly.'

'They call you here?' Julie asked.

'Only if it's something very urgent,' he said. 'Damn. I'm coming, Nonna.'

He pulled on his clothes in a hurry and the next moment he was gone.

She could have cried out at the ruin of her perfect moment. But underlying dismay, there was still happiness. What had just happened between them could never be taken away. The moment would come again.

She dressed and went along to the little kitchen. Anna, vast and impressive in dressing-gown and curlers, was at the stove. She grinned at Julie, thrust a coffee into her hand and pointed to the next room from where they could hear Rico's voice.

Julie took him the coffee. He was talking in angry, urgent tones.

'We had an agreement...he can't go back on it now...tell them to do nothing until I get there...yes, I'll be there today.'

He hung up, drank his coffee and gave her a brief kiss.

'Will you be away long?' she asked.

'A few days. There's a meeting I must get to.' He touched her face gently. 'Why did it have to happen now, when we have found each other again?'

'When you return—'

'Yes, it will be soon. Suddenly his face darkened and he held her tightly. 'Will you be here? Shall I return to find you gone again?'

'Never, my love.'

'Promise me.'

'I promise. Rico, don't be afraid. Things are different now.'

'For years I had this nightmare. Always in dreams, I returned home calling your name, and you were never there. Don't let me fall into that nightmare again.'

'The nightmare is over,' she vowed. 'Trust me, Rico. Can't you trust me?'

'Yes,' he said with a slight effort. 'Of course I trust you. What were you going to say before Nonna called me?'

'It can wait until you get back.'

'I'll call you.'

'Use this number,' she said, scribbling her mobile number. 'Then you'll find me anywhere. Goodbye, my love. Come back to me.'

Strangely enough, his absence was one of the happiest times Julie had ever known. She visited Gary daily, performed to rapturous audiences and dreamed about the future.

She visited Anna, who asked no questions but seemed to understand without words. She even let Julie into Rico's room where she could sit and feel his presence. That was how she discovered that he had kept the note she'd written him long ago. Its brutality distressed her and she crumpled it up, praying for the chance to make it up to him for all he'd suffered.

Rico returned from Milan in a glad state of mind. He'd taken care of his enemies, imposed his authority and was eagerly anticipating a reunion with the woman he loved. He planned to call Julie as soon as he reached the villa.

But a surprise awaited him at his home. A stream of servants ferrying suitcases packed to bulging came down the stairs and out to a waiting van. His steward informed him that Mariella had been there for the past hour. He found her in the room that had been hers. Wardrobe doors stood open, revealing that nothing was left inside. Drawers were empty. The room had been stripped as bare as if a plague of locusts had swarm over it.

It was the first time they'd seen each other since the night at the club when he'd floored Barono.

'I came for my things,' she said. 'Salvatore has implored me to leave you and live with him. He says I deserve a man who understands women.'

'I hope you haven't left anything behind,' Rico said, regarding her looting with tolerant cynicism.

Mariella shrugged. 'If I have, Salvatore will buy whatever I need.'

'I hear you're going to be in his next film. I hope you'll be very happy together.'

'He says I'm the love of his life,' Mariella declaimed in throbbing accents.

'How nice.'

'I have even persuaded him not to sue you for assaulting him.'

'So I expected,' Rico said. 'It would spoil the story if my real reason was aired in court, wouldn't it?' She scowled, and he added hastily, 'But it's very kind of you.'

'Yes, I think it is, too, after the way you treated me.'

'I don't think you did so badly out of me. We were always honest with each other, Mariella. There was no pretence of love on either side.'

'And you think you're going to find love with your stupid English girl?'

'Leave her out of it,' Rico said quietly.

'She's really played you for a sucker. Those demure manners, butter wouldn't melt in her mouth. And all the time she's making a fool of you.'

'*That's enough*!' Rico snapped. 'You know nothing about her.'

'Don't I? Ask her to tell you who Gary is—if you dare.'

Rico's shrug was a masterpiece of indifference. 'Gary is a friend. I know all about him.'

'Do you know how often she visits him when your back is turned?'

Rico turned very pale. 'What the devil are you talking about?'

'He's here in Italy because she couldn't bear to be apart from him. While you were away, she spent every day with him.'

Suddenly the nightmare was there again—the absence, the return to find everything different, love gone, only emptiness left. The details were a little changed, but the pain was the same.

Julie had tried to tell him something before his departure. What was it?

He'd telephoned her. She'd always been there. But that was her mobile phone. She'd made a point of giving him the number. She might have been anywhere.

What had she wanted to tell him?

With a supreme effort, he assumed an air of confidence in front of Mariella. Hell could freeze over before he'd let her suspect his agony.

'You're lying,' he said. 'Don't try to make trouble between Julie and me.'

Mariella gave a catlike smile. 'All right, darling. I'll just leave you to find out for yourself. I hope your disillusion isn't too painful.'

'Hope it is, you mean,' Rico said, eyeing her coldly.

She shrugged. 'Whatever.'

'I've made a mess of everything,' Rico groaned.

'Hah! You only just find that out?' Anna snorted. She slapped down a plate of spaghetti carbonara in front of him. 'Eat!'

'How can I eat when everything is over?'

'Eat. Then it won't be over.'

'Thanks, Nonna.'

'Don't call me Nonna. You think I want anyone knowing I helped raise an idiot?'

Rico managed a faint grin, not at all offended by this blunt talk. If anything, it pleased him, for it brought back the days when he'd sat in the grandiose kitchen at the villa, talking over his troubles with the only person who understood.

The kitchen of Anna's little apartment was far from grandiose, but it had the same smells of garlic, tomatoes and pepper, all of which he associated with comfort. There was comfort, too, in the sound of her bustling about, yelling at him with the disrespect of a grandmother in pungent Romagnolo. He answered in the same dialect.

'It seemed so simple when I planned it,' he mused between mouthfuls. 'But things went wrong from the moment I saw her again.'

'Of course. Things never work out as you plan them.'

'They did for the old man.'

'That's because he had no heart. He was ruthless, so he could forget about people. You're not like that.'

'I'd forgotten how she could affect me—after all those years. I got confused and I made mistakes. That night we went out in the *carrozza*—it seemed such a good idea. Change tactics, romance her until she lost her head and told me what I wanted to know—about my son—because she's the girl who—'

'You think I don't know who she is? I knew from the moment she walked in.'

'Yes, I suppose you did. But I was the one who lost my head. Suddenly it was like being boy and girl again, and I wanted the night to go on forever—just to be with her. I'd forgotten that my spies were watching. And she noticed them—'

Anna said an extremely rude word. Romagnolo has some of the best rude words in the world, and this one cast serious doubt on Rico's paternity, his intelligence and even his sanity. But he seemed to find it fair, for he responded with a wry face.

'She was very angry—'

'*You don't say!*' Anna bawled sarcastically. 'Well, well! She was angry. Fancy that! What was she supposed to do when she discovered her lover was spying on her? Kiss your feet?'

'She wasn't supposed to know. I was going to call them off after that, but she discovered them first and walked out on me. So then I got angry, too, and I made her sing at my home that night—and Mariella was there on my arm—'

'So Julie thought you didn't care about her because you got Mariella? Give me patience!'

'And it got worse, and then…I don't know. Every time I thought I was finding the way—things went wrong.'

'You mean you did something stupid?'

'I did many things that were stupid.'

'But this was ages ago,' Anna said. 'Since then, the two of you came here and you made it up. So she forgave you.'

'I thought she had. Now I'm not so sure. There's this other man. His name is Gary. I've heard her talk to him on the phone with such a note in her voice— the note that used to be there only for me. I thought she loved me, Nonna,' he went on wretchedly. 'But she's been stringing me along—and it's my own fault.'

Anna sighed. 'Oh, Rico! What hope is there for you when you go about with blinkers? She loves you. I could see that at once.'

'Then why isn't she frank with me?'

'Perhaps she's afraid of you. You've become a harsh man who judges easily. But with this woman, you're different. She's your best hope unless you throw her away. Do something quickly.'

'What can I do, Nonna? It's too late. I told you, she's got someone else.'

Anna snorted her contempt for all men. She set coffee before him, then picked up her handbag. After rummaging through it, she took out a piece of paper and gave it to him.

Rico studied it, puzzled. It bore an address in Fregene.

'My niece has a villa at Fregene. She recognized Julie from her picture in the paper and called me to boast about her famous neighbour.'

'Has she seen this man?' Rico asked.

'She has seen Gary. Now stop asking questions and go to Fregene!'

Julie knew that Rico was due home at any moment. He said he'd call her when he arrived, but the hours passed with no word from him.

She finally called the villa and learned from the steward that Rico had arrived back three hours ago but had gone out again at once.

The afternoon wore on into the evening. As always, she put her feet up for an hour in the hotel. But she couldn't doze off. She was waiting for Rico to call. And he didn't.

Then it was time for the evening's performance. He would be there waiting for her. But he wasn't.

She tried to be reasonable. He must have a lot to see to on his return. But the silence was unnerving. It took all her professionalism to give of her best that night. Both her mind and her heart were in turmoil.

She slept badly and awoke to the sound of the phone. It was Cassie, and she sounded agitated. 'I'm sorry to call you so early, but I'm worried. I think we're being watched.'

Instantly Julie sat up straight in bed, every nerve screaming. 'Has anyone approached you?'

'No, but there's this car. I can see it from the window. It was there yesterday. Then it drove away, but last night it came back and it hasn't moved.'

'Lock all the doors,' Julie said urgently. 'Don't answer to anyone except me. I'm on my way.'

She was downstairs in a few minutes and hired one of the hotel cars. Soon she was on the road to Fregene, driving as fast as she dared, her mind seething with questions and fears.

Rico had been watching the house all night. She had no doubt that it was him. Somehow he'd found her hideaway and was waiting his moment to pounce. That was why he hadn't told her he was back. He planned to spirit Gary away while she was unaware. Oh, why had she been so careless as to bring Gary here? How could she stop Rico from snatching him?

She feared the worst as she drew up by the beach at Fregene, but Rico's car was still there. The doors were closed and the windows rolled up, and at first she thought it was empty.

She began to run to the house but stopped when she thought she heard someone call her name. She turned. Rico was getting out of his car.

'Julie…' he said. He sounded hesitant.

'Stay here,' she cried, flinging out a hand to ward him off. She ran towards him, keeping between him and the house. 'Rico, please, listen to me.'

His face was ravaged. 'Will it help—talking? Will it change anything?'

'Nothing can change the past, but if I could make you understand—'

'Why did you lie to me? Why couldn't you have told me the truth all this time?'

She'd come close to him. 'I was afraid of what you'd do.'

'I'd never do anything to hurt you, Julie. I love you too much. When you first came here, I was crazy with pain—I'd have done anything. But it was no good. I still loved you, and it was too much for me. I thought—' he drew a ragged breath '—I thought we'd found each other again.'

'So did I. Rico, I love you.'

'Don't lie to me. Julie, I know. Don't you understand? I know you're in love with another man. I know he's in that house.'

'You know…?' she whispered.

'Everything. You've been visiting him while I was away. I ought to hate you for that, but I can't. I can't hate you for anything. Why did you do it? Was it your idea of revenge? Did I deserve it?'

She searched his face. Some part of the truth was beginning to dawn on her, but it was too wonderful to be easily believed. 'How can you believe such a thing of me?' she breathed.

'I came here yesterday, determined to confront your lover. But I couldn't do it. I sat here for hours, then I drove away again.

'I came back last night, but I still couldn't make myself knock on that door. If I don't see his face, maybe he isn't real.' He gave a mirthless laugh. 'I was afraid. Can you imagine that? I've never been afraid of anything, and yet—'

'Rico—'

'Does he truly love you, Julie? Love you as much as I do? I don't believe it. After all we've meant to each other, can't you forgive me and start again? Does this man—this Gary—really mean so much to you?'

'Yes,' she said steadily. 'Gary means all the world to me. We've loved each other for almost eight years, and I can't do without him.'

Rico's shoulders sagged. 'In that case, there's nothing for me to do but leave.'

'No, I want you to meet him.'

'What would be the use of that? Let it go, Julie. I was wrong. I bear you no ill will. You did what you had to do. But eight years! You turned to him very soon after me, didn't you?'

'A few months,' she said with a little smile. 'Rico, I promise you, when you meet Gary, you will understand everything.'

Something in her voice made him go very quiet. Had the first hint of the truth begun to reach him? Julie took his hand and led him across the sand towards the villa. She opened the front door. On the threshold, Rico paused, still uncertain.

'Gary,' Julie called. 'Come here, my darling.'

He usually came dashing towards her, but today the child seemed to know something was different. He pushed open the kitchen door and stood there, black-haired, dark-eyed, the image of the man facing him.

Julie put a hand on his shoulder and smiled down at him in reassurance. He returned the smile, and Rico's heart nearly stopped. For in that smile the child was like his mother, too.

'I've brought someone for you to meet,' Julie said.

Man and boy looked at each other in silence. At last, Rico drew a long, slow breath. 'Are you…Gary?'

The child nodded. 'Who are you?'

'I'm…' The words wouldn't come. It had been eight long years. Rico dropped down to one knee in front of his son and looked into the eyes that were so like his own. He tried again. 'I'm your—'

'This is your father,' Julie told the child gently.

Gary's expression became intent. He studied Rico's face, meeting his eyes candidly, unafraid. He was a son any man would be proud of. The sight broke Rico and he reached out blindly, drawing the little boy hard against him and hiding his face. Julie saw his shoulders shaking and covered her eyes, which had blurred suddenly.

'All this time,' Rico said huskily. 'All this time…'

He pulled back and discovered that his son was regarding him curiously. The child put out a tentative hand and touched the tears on his father's face. His Italian side was very strong in him, and even at seven he wasn't afraid of emotion.

'Why are you crying?' he asked.

'Because I'm happy,' Rico managed to say.

'Is that why Mommy's crying, too?'

'I think so—I hope so.'

The little boy looked from one to the other. Julie's heart was overflowing and she was beyond speech. Rico got to his feet.

'Julie,' he whispered, 'why didn't you—'

'I didn't dare tell you. All those years when Arturo was alive, I was afraid for you. But I took his money only to help me raise Gary. Then, when I came here, I was afraid *of* you. I've been waiting, hoping for the moment when I could tell you the truth. How could you believe I would give away our son—all I had left of you?'

'I think in my heart I never could really believe it. That you seemed able to do such a thing left me bewildered. It was so unlike you. And all this time you have been as good and true as I remembered from our happy days. You have been…you.'

He gathered her into his arms, not kissing her, but holding her against his heart, his cheek against her hair, while his tears flowed unrestrained.

There was no need for words in the passing away of all sadness between them. She lifted her head and he looked into her face, clearly seeing the truth and beauty that had always been there if he'd only known how to recognize it.

'Mine,' he said huskily.

'Always yours. My heart is yours, my son is yours, and my life is yours.'

He spoke solemnly. 'I tell you that my heart has never belonged to another woman, no matter what—'

'Hush,' she silenced him. 'We need no explanations. Only the future matters.'

'You'll stay here now, with me. We'll be married.' The words were half a command, half a plea.

'Yes, we'll be married. Gary and I will never leave you again.'

'And we'll be a true family at last. Oh, my dearest…'

His mouth was on hers in the first kiss of their new love. They clung together like castaways who had finally found a safe haven.

A tall, elderly woman had slipped into the room. Gary turned to her, puzzled. 'Aunt Cassie, why are they crying *and* kissing?'

'Let's leave them alone,' she said drawing him away. 'And I'll try to explain.…'

Diana Hamilton is a true romantic and fell in love with her husband at first sight. They still live in the fairytale Tudor house where they raised their three children. Now the idyll is shared with eight rescued cats and a puppy. But despite an often chaotic lifestyle, ever since she learned to read and write Diana has had her nose in a book – either reading or writing one – and plans to go on doing just that for a very long time to come.

Look out for HIS CONVENIENT WIFE, another wonderful story by Diana Hamilton. On sale December, in Modern Romance™!

THE UNEXPECTED BABY
by
Diana Hamilton

CHAPTER ONE

'WHAT took you so long?' Jed's eyes gleamed with sultry promise beneath heavy half-closed lids, his gorgeous mouth curving sensually as he invited, 'Come back to bed, Mrs Nolan. And take that thing off. Pretty it may be, but your body's a darn sight prettier.'

Elena couldn't meet his eye. She felt sick. She told herself it was shock, or auto-suggestion. She stuffed her hands in the side pockets of the silk wrap she'd dragged on before leaving the bathroom so he wouldn't see how much they were trembling.

Her mouth went dry just looking at him. He was her love, her life, everything. He made her feel special, secure, treasured.

The sheet tangled around his lean hips was the only thing between him and total nakedness. Six foot three of superbly honed masculinity, with a sizzling, white-hot sexual magnetism that jumped out and hit her. For a thirty-six-year-old business man—a shopkeeper, Sam had once half mockingly described him—he had the body of an athlete and a face that only just missed classical perfection, courtesy of a slight bump at the bridge of his nose—broken on the rugby field—and a tough, pugnacious jaw.

Sam's name in her mind made her want to scream. How could she have been so reckless? She had thought she'd known what she was doing, when in reality she'd known nothing at all, just gone ahead in her usual pig-headed fashion, wanting it all. Everything.

And how could she bring herself to break the news to Jed? Put something like that into the pure beauty of their marriage? The short answer was she couldn't. Not yet, anyway. Not while the irrefutable evidence was a scant ten minutes old, burning holes in her brain.

Her heart punched savagely at her breastbone as with a whimper of distress she discarded her wrap, flew impulsively to the bed and flung herself down beside him. Wrapping her body around him, she whispered with soft ferocity, 'I love you... I love you...'

'Still? After a whole week of marriage?'

Teasing silver lights danced deep in his lazily hooded eyes as he smoothed the long golden silk of her hair away from her face, and Elena said, her voice tight with anguish, 'Don't mock me, Jed. Don't!'

'As if!' His smile was soft, melting her, as he eased her onto her back, propping himself up on one elbow, his beautifully proportioned body half covering hers. Thick dark hair tumbled over his forehead, the curve of his mouth a sinful seduction as he gently rubbed his thumb over her full lips.

Tears misted her eyes. She had never believed she could love someone so much it hurt. Or that she could ever be this afraid. For ten years she had been afraid of no one, and nothing. She'd known what she wanted and sweated blood to get it. And now, because of a moment of reckless, arrogant folly, she had turned herself into a frightened wreck, full of dread.

'Something's wrong,' he said gently, a slight frown

pulling dark brows together now. 'Tell me, my darling.'

She couldn't! Not yet, not until she could get her own head around it. And even then it would be almost impossible. Hating having to lie to him, even by omission, despising the way her voice shook, she muttered, 'Not really—its just that what we have frightens me, Jed.' And that, at least, was the truth.

It hadn't frightened her before; she had joyfully accepted the gift of their love for each other with both eager hands. But it frightened her now because she was afraid they were going to lose it, that his love for her wouldn't be strong enough to cope with what she was going to have to tell him.

The unbelievably precious gift of their love had come so quickly, so easily. She'd been too deliriously happy to imagine that it could be taken from her just as suddenly.

She swallowed the knot of aching tears in her throat and said thickly, trying to lighten the sombre darkness she could see in his eyes, 'You see, I still can't believe you could have fallen in love with a thirty-year-old divorcee when you could have had just about anyone!' She tried to smile, and failed, and closed her eyes instead. Her heart threatened to burst as she felt his lips kiss the tears away from her spangled lashes.

'I didn't want just anyone,' he assured her, his voice huskily tender. 'But I wanted you from the first moment I saw you. The circumstances couldn't have been more dire, but I already felt I knew you from what Sam had told me, and I took one look at you and knew I wanted to be with you for the rest of my life.'

That had been six short weeks ago, when she'd travelled from her home here in Spain to England for Sam's funeral. And despite the terrible, numbing sadness of the occasion, with the raw early-April wind that had scoured the small Hertfordshire graveyard adding to the misery, she had taken one look at Sam's elder brother and known she had found the only man who could make her break her vow never to become emotionally dependent on any man ever again.

Just one look and her life had changed; she had changed.

Jed eased himself down beside her and drew her bright head into the angle of his shoulder, holding her as if she were the most precious thing in the world. 'I didn't want one of the glossy harpies that crowd the social scene with monotonous regularity—shallow and superficial, the sort of woman whose main interest in a man is the size of his bank balance. I wanted *you*. Talented, successful, a self-made woman—heart-wrenchingly beautiful. And scorchingly sexy is the icing on the cake, the ribbon on the package! And from what you've told me, you're well rid of the man you married when you were little more than a child. What was it? Barely nineteen years of age? Sweetheart, everyone's allowed to make one mistake, and he was yours!'

One mistake? What about this latest one? Would he dismiss it with such compassionate understanding?

If only they hadn't rushed into marriage; if only she hadn't believed there would be no consequences after what she and Sam had done—hadn't believed she was right in dismissing the possible repercussions of that one last night, when wine, the heady promise of the beginning of the early Spanish spring, the feeling that something was missing in her successful life and an overdose of sentimentality had led to something that could poison her whole relationship with the man who had taught her to recognise the depths and strengths of a love she had never before even guessed she was capable of.

She turned her head and feverishly kissed his warm, hair-roughened skin, searching for the flat male nipples, the palms of her hands splayed against the heat of his skin, her fingers digging into the suddenly taut muscles of his stomach. She heard the passionate inhalation of his breath, felt the responsive surge of his body and swallowed hot, salt tears. She would not cry. She would not!

There could be few such precious moments left to them.

When his mouth took hers it was a statement of passionate possession, and she answered it with the fire of her need, her adoration, curling her legs around him, opening for him, accepting him eagerly, answering the fevered stroke of his hands as they caressed her body with a feverish exploration of her own.

She felt the intensity of his rapture as he possessed her, and she lost herself in their loving, fear forgotten, just for now, just for the slow, exquisitely languorous time of his loving, just while they drove each other to the outer limits of ecstasy. She rained wild kisses on the hot skin of his throat, felt the wild beat of his heart and clung to this, this perfection, because maybe it would be the very last time for them.

* * *

'I could get used to this!'

Despite her bare feet, Jed must have heard her walk out of the whitewashed stone house onto the patio. Or felt her presence, she decided with a shiver of recognition, just as she always sensed his nearness before she actually saw him.

The black T-shirt he was wearing was tucked into the pleated waistband of a pair of stone-grey tough cotton trousers. The way he looked—lithe, lean and dangerously male—rocked her senses as he turned from the low wall that divided the patio from the sun-drenched, steeply sloping gardens below. 'And just in case you think I'm a cheapskate, saving on honeymoon expenses by using my bride's home as a hotel, I've made breakfast.'

Coffee, a bowl of fresh fruit, crispy rolls and a dish of olives. Half her brain approved his efforts while the other half gloried in the warmth of his smile, in the unashamed, naked hunger in his eyes. 'Though I might do without,' he added. 'Food, that is. You look good enough to eat. You satisfy each and every one of what I've discovered to be amazingly huge appetites!'

Did she? Elena's aquamarine eyes locked onto his, warm colour flaring briefly over her high cheekbones. Every moment was doubly precious now, every word spoken with love to be treasured, because very soon now it would end.

After her shower she'd pulled on a pair of frayed-edged denim shorts and an old white T-shirt, not taking any trouble because half an hour ago, when he'd slid out of bed, she'd feigned sleep, needing just a little time on her own to decide what to do. And she'd faced the awful knowledge that it was no use waiting until the time was right before she introduced the serpent into their corner of paradise.

The time would never be right for what she had to tell him, and keeping the truth from him would only make him think more badly of her.

But the way he was looking at her, the way his eyes slid over every last one of her five-foot-six slender inches and endless, elegant, lightly tanned legs, paralysed her with physical awareness. So, despising her weakness but unable to do anything about it, she took his former remark and clung to it as to a reprieve. Just a few more hours. Surely she could give herself that?

Striving for lightness as she poured coffee for them both, she told him, 'Stop fishing for compliments—there's nothing cheapskate about you! I practically forced you to agree to spend our honeymoon here.'

She was justifiably proud of her home. She'd bought the former Andalucian farmhouse with part of the proceeds from the sale of the film rights of her first runaway bestseller. And she and Jed had already decided to keep it as a holiday home, to come here as often as they could—a welcome respite from the pressure of his position at the head of the family-owned business. Based in London, Amsterdam, New York and Rome, it had a two-hundred-year-old tradition of supplying sumptuous gems and exquisitely wrought precious metals to the seriously wealthy.

Sam had considered the business arcane, refused to have anything to do with it, making his mark in the highly competitive world of photo-journalism.

She pushed his name roughly out of her head, but,

almost as if he'd known what she'd done, Jed pushed it straight back in again. 'I can understand why Sam came here so often between assignments. Life travels at a different pace, the views are endless and the sun is generous. He told me once that it was the only place he could find peace.'

He refilled his coffee cup and tipped the pot towards her, one dark brow lifting. Elena shook her head. She had barely taken a sip. Listening to him talking of his brother was screwing up her nerves and shredding them. Why should he decide to talk about him now? She couldn't meet his eyes.

Jed replaced the pot, selected an orange from the blue earthenware bowl and began to strip away the peel, his voice strangely clipped as he remarked, 'Over the last couple of years, particularly, he was always getting sent to the world's worst trouble spots. Though I think he thrived on the edge of danger, he must have been grateful for the relaxation he knew he could find here. With you. He seemed to know so much about you; you must have been extremely close.'

Elena's throat closed up. He had rarely mentioned Sam's name since the day of his funeral, but now the very real grief showed through. The brothers had had very little in common but they had loved each other. And now she could detect something else. Something wildly out of character. A skein of jealousy, envy, even?

'He was a good friend,' she responded, hating the breathless catch in her voice. She watched the long, hard fingers strip the peel from the fruit. Suddenly there seemed something ruthless about the movements. She wondered if she knew him as thoroughly as she'd thought she did.

She shivered, and heard him say, 'In a way, I think he deplored the fact that I did my duty, as he called it—knuckled down and joined the family business and took the responsibility of heading it after Father died—despised me a little, even.'

'No!' She couldn't let him think that. 'He admired you, and respected you—maybe grudgingly—for doing your duty, and doing it so well. He once told me that your business brain scared the you-know-what out of him, and that he preferred to go off and do his own thing rather than live in your shadow, a pale second-best.'

Jed gave her a long, searching look, as if he was turning her words over in his mind, weighing the truth of them, before at last admitting, 'I didn't know that. Maybe I wouldn't have envied him his freedom to do as he pleased and to hell with everyone else if I had.' Regret tightened his mouth. 'I guess there's a whole raft of things I didn't know about my kid brother. Except, of course, how fond he was of you. When he came home on those flying visits of his the conversation always came round to you. He gave me one of your books and told me to be impressed. I was; I didn't need telling,' he complimented coolly. 'You handle horror with a sophistication, intelligence and subtlety that makes a refreshing change from the usual crude blood and gore of the genre.'

'Thank you.' I think, she added to herself. There was something in his voice she had never heard before. Something dark and condemning. She left her seat swiftly and went to lean against the wall, looking at the endless view which always soothed her spirits but signally failed to do anything of the sort this morning.

Perched on a limestone ridge, high above a tiny white-walled village, her home benefited from the pine-scented salt breezes crossing western Andalucia from the Atlantic, moderating the heat of the burning May sun.

Elena closed her eyes and tried to close her mind to everything but the cooling sensation of the light wind on her face. Just a few moments of respite before she had to face the truth, brace herself to break the news to Jed before the day ended. Could she use her gift for words to make him understand just why she had acted as she had? It didn't seem possible, she thought defeatedly.

Since the ending of her first disastrous marriage, she had refused to let anything defeat her, get in the way of her fight for successful independence. But this—this was something else...

'You haven't eaten a thing.' He'd come to stand behind her, not touching but very close. The heat of his body scorched her, yet she shivered. 'Not hungry? Suddenly lost your appetite?'

His cool tones terrified her. He hadn't already guessed, had he? No, of course he hadn't. How could he? Despising herself for the way she seemed to be heading—spoiling the morning and the few hours' respite she'd promised herself—she turned and forced a smile to the mouth she had always considered far too wide.

'No, just lazy, I guess.' She walked back to the table. She would have to force something into a stomach that felt as if it would reject anything she tried to feed it. 'I thought we might go down to the coast today.' She plucked a few grapes from the dewy bunch nestling in the fruit bowl. 'Cadiz, perhaps, or Vejer de la Frontera if you fancy somewhere quieter. We haven't set foot outside the property all week.'

Edgy, acutely aware of the way he was watching her, she popped a grape into her mouth and felt her throat close up as he answered, 'So far, we haven't felt the need to, remember?'

She bit on the grape and forced it down, because she could hardly spit the wretched thing out. His words had been idly spoken, yet the underlining accusation came through loud and clear. They hadn't needed to leave the property; they'd had all they needed in each other. Simple expeditions through the gardens and into the pine woods, eating on the patio or in the rose-covered arbour, their lives attuned to the wonderful solitude, the rhythm of their lovemaking, the deep rapture of simply being. Together.

'Of course I do.' Her voice was thick, everything inside her panicking. The incredible feeling of closeness, of being made for each other, was slipping away. She knew it would happen once she'd broken her news, but the frightening distance between them had no right to be happening now. It hadn't been there before he'd begun to talk of Sam. 'Pilar, who helps me around the house, was instructed to keep well clear after stocking the fridge on the morning we arrived.' She spoke as lightly as she could, desperate to recreate all that wonderful closeness for just a little longer. 'We're starting to run low on provisions, so I thought we could combine shopping with sightseeing, that's all.'

'Is it?' He prowled back to the chair opposite hers and sat, his hands clenched in the side pockets of his trousers. Steel-grey eyes searched her face. His voice was low, sombre, as he imparted, 'Sam and I had our differences, but he was my brother and I loved him. His death rocked me. Until coming here, to where he was happy, where he found peace and comfort, I haven't been able to open up about what I feel. Yet it seems to me that you don't want to talk about him. Get edgy when I mention his name. Why is that?' he wanted to know.

What to say? She couldn't deny it. She picked up her cup of now cold coffee and swallowed half of it down a throat that was aching with tension, and Jed asked tightly, 'Were you lovers? Is that the reason?'

Dread tore at her heart, knotted her stomach, perspiration dewing her forehead. For the first time since meeting him she deeply regretted his uncanny ability to see right into her soul. She twisted her hands in her lap and tried to smile.

'Why do you ask? Don't tell me you're trying to pick a fight!' Did her prevarication come out sounding as jokey as she'd intended? Or had she merely sounded as if she were being strangled?

'I ask because my talking about him appears to disturb you. It's something I never considered before, but from what I can gather Sam spent a fair amount of time here. He was a handsome son-of-a-gun. Add the spice of a dangerous occupation—no mere *shop-keeper*, our Sam—and an extremely beautiful woman with a talent he greatly admired, and what do you get?' He lifted one brow. 'I repeat the question.'

Elena felt everything inside her start to shake. Although Jed was doing his best to look relaxed and in control, his hands were still making fists in his side pockets, and that tough, shadowed jaw was tight. There was more to this than she could fully understand.

The fact that she'd been married before hadn't mattered to him. He hadn't wanted her to talk about it, had assimilated her, 'It was a dreadful mistake; he turned out to be completely rotten,' then refused to let her go on with the complete explanation she'd intended to make.

He'd dismissed her marriage to Liam Forrester as a total irrelevance, and had never once asked if there had been any other man in her life in the intervening years. He had acted as though their future was the only thing that was important to him.

Yet couple her name with Sam's and something suspiciously resembling jealousy and anger stared out of the eyes that had, thus far, only looked at her with love, warmth and hungry desire.

Because Sam had been his brother? Was there a twist of bitterness on that sensual mouth now? The sardonic stress he'd laid on the word 'shopkeeper' told her that Sam must have tossed that taunt at him at some time, told her that it still rankled.

And had Sam been handsome? Looking back, she supposed so. Not as tall as his brother, nothing like as powerfully built. Smooth, nut-brown hair and light blue eyes, with elegant features. He would have been a wow as an old-style matinée idol. Handsome he might have been, but he couldn't hold a candle to his older brother... Sam had had none of Jed's dangerous masculinity, none of that forbidding sexual excitement.

'Elena. I need to know.' There was a raw edge to his voice she had never heard before, and a few short hours ago she could have reassured him. But now, knowing what she knew, the task seemed impossible. Nevertheless, she had to try.

'I first met your brother at a party I threw to celebrate my second movie deal.' She concentrated on the facts because that was the only way she could handle this. 'I've made a lot of friends in this area—ex-pats as well as Spaniards. Sam came along with Cynthia and Ed Parry. He was staying with them for a few days—apparently he'd known Ed since university.'

She saw the way his brows pulled together, the way his mouth went tight, and knew he was turning over every word she said, impatient because she wasn't telling him what he wanted to know. But she had to do this her way, or not at all.

'That had to be about a couple of years ago,' she went on, needing him to see the whole thing from her perspective, needing to get it right. 'And, as you know, he often visited this corner of Spain when he needed to unwind. Usually he stayed with the Parrys—'

'But not always?'

'No,' she agreed, doing her best to stay calm, to ignore the churning, burning sensation in her tummy.

'We got to know each other well, enjoyed each other's company. He'd wander up here in the evenings and we'd talk, and sometimes, if it got very late, I'd offer him the use of one of the spare roms. You asked if we were lovers...' She lifted slender shoulders in a light shrug. 'He once admitted he had a low sex drive—something to do with using all his emotional and physical energy in his work. He knew the dangers of getting news out of the world's worst trouble spots. He talked a lot about you, your mother, your home. He was proud of his family. He told me he'd never marry, that such a commitment wouldn't be wise, or fair, because of the way he earned his living. But he said you would. Some woman to give you children because you wouldn't want the business to die out with you. Said that women flung themselves at you, couldn't keep away. But that you were picky. And discreet.'

Too late, she realised exactly what she was doing. And loathed herself for it. She had side-stepped his question and was trying to turn the situation round and become his accuser, letting the implication that he was a calculating user of women hang contentiously on the air between them, pushing them further apart.

And the bleak, most scornful look on his face told her he knew exactly what she was trying to do. And why.

Suddenly, the nausea that had been threatening all morning became an unwelcome, undeniable fact. She shot to her feet, one hand against her mouth, and lurched through the house to the bathroom.

Knowing he had followed her didn't help a scrap,

and when it was over she leant weakly against the tiled wall, the futile wish that she could turn the clock back three months uppermost in her mind.

'Sweetheart—come here.' He pulled her into his arms and she rested her throbbing head against the hard, soft-cotton-covered wall of his chest, wishing she could hold onto this moment for ever and knowing that she couldn't.

The look of compassion, of caring, on his face didn't help. It made things worse because she didn't deserve it. And when he said softly, 'What brought that on? Something you ate? I'll drive you to the nearest surgery if the sickness carries on,' she knew she had to tell him now.

Waking before him early this morning, she'd been rooting round at the back of the bathroom cabinet, looking for a fresh tube of toothpaste, when she'd found the pregnancy testing kit she'd bought.

Over the last few days she'd felt strangely nauseous on waking, had suffered one or two inexplicable dizzy spells. Common sense had told her that there were no repercussions from what she and Sam had done, but she'd run the test all the same, just to put her mind at rest.

And now she was going to have to face the consequences.

She pulled out of Jed's arms, her face white as she told him, 'I'm pregnant, Jed.'

Despite her ashen face, the dark torment in her eyes, he smiled at her, slowly shaking his head, one brow drifting up towards his hairline. He pulled her back against his body and enfolded her with loving arms.

The unresolved question of whether she and his brother had been more than good friends could wait.

'How can you possibly be sure of that, sweetheart? After only one week! It's a nice thought, but I'm afraid it's got to be something you ate!'

For a time she allowed herself the luxury of being held, waiting for her heartbeats to slow down to normal, for her aching head to stop whirling with stupid regrets. They'd discussed starting a family and decided there was no reason to wait. They both wanted children. Which was going to make what she had to tell him so much worse.

When she finally placed her hands against the powerful muscles of his chest and eased herself away from the haven of his embrace, she felt calm. Empty. She was about to tell him something he probably wouldn't want to live with, to kill his love, which was the most precious thing she had. She had to do it quickly and cleanly. The agony was too great to be prolonged.

'It's true, Jed. I did the test this morning.' She saw the look of disbelief on his face and knew he was about to tell her she'd got it wrong, misread the instructions. She forestalled him quickly, her voice thin because of the effort it took to control it. 'By my calculations, almost three months.'

And then she watched as his eyes froze over. 'Three months ago I hadn't met you, and the first time we had sex was on our wedding night,' he stated grimly, his lips thin and bloodless. 'So perhaps you'd like to tell me, my dear wife, who it was who fathered the child you're carrying?'

His cold sarcasm hurt her more than anything that

had ever happened to her in her entire life. She could have handled anger, insults, even physical violence—anything that sprang from powerful emotional trauma. This icy sarcasm, almost amounting to cynical indifference, was worse than if he'd stabbed a rusty blade into her heart.

What she had feared had happened. He had already gone away from her emotionally, relegating the magic of their lovemaking to mere having sex.

And he was waiting for her answer, his eyes dark and bleak, his mouth tight against his teeth. She gathered up the last vestiges of her strength, exhaled a shuddering sigh.

'Sam.'

CHAPTER TWO

HE STRODE away, his shoulders hard and high and rigid. Elena couldn't move. Her feet felt as if they'd been welded to the cool marble floor tiles, and her arms were wrapped tightly around her quivering body.

Only when she heard the sound of the car he'd hired to bring them from the airport was she shocked into movement. Her flying feet scattered rugs as she ran to the front of the house, tugging open the sturdy front door, racing through the courtyard and out onto the stony track.

He couldn't leave her like this, run out on her, with nothing said, nothing explained—never mind resolved! But the cloud of dust, the noise of the rapidly receding engine told her that he could. And had.

Her first instinct was to get her own car out of the barn and follow him. But he would hate that. Even if she caught up with him nothing would be achieved. He had taken what he obviously felt he needed; time alone to sort his head out.

If only he had given her enough time to explain, to tell him the whole truth. He would still be hurting... But not this much.

Pushing her fist against her teeth, to stop herself throwing her head back and howling her pain to the burning bowl of the sky, she ran to a rocky outcrop, uncaring of the sharp edges cutting into the soles of her bare feet, and watched until the cloud of dust disappeared on the valley floor. Then walked slowly back to the house, defeated, wretched.

Jed would come back in his own good time, and all she could do was wait. But for the first time ever she could find no comfort in her beautiful home, the symbol of her fabulous success. Lovingly recreated from what had been little more than a near derelict shell, her home, her gardens, her slice of Andalucian mountainside, had previously reinforced her belief in herself, in the financial and emotional independence she'd made for herself.

As she'd confided in Sam, on what had turned out to be his last night in Spain, 'When I left my husband ten years ago and came out to Cadiz, I had nothing—not even my self-respect, because Liam had taken that away. I worked in bars and lived in a miserable one-room flat and took to writing in what spare time I had as a way of forgetting. Luckily, it paid off, and what had begun as therapy became my whole existence.'

The wine had been flowing freely on that dark February evening, and she'd lighted a fire in the great stone-hooded hearth, because the evenings were chilly in the hills. Sam's mood had been strangely reflective, almost sombre, the atmosphere—that of long-standing easy friendship—conducive to soul-baring.

'And now, because my books took off in a big way, I have everything. A successful career and pride in my work, a beautiful home in a lovely part of the world, a wonderful circle of friends—more financial security than I ever dreamed of having. Everything except a child, and sometimes that hurts. I guess I hear my biological clock chiming out yet another passing hour. But as I have no intention of ever marrying again...'

She shrugged wryly, sipping her wine to deaden the ache of her empty womb, her empty arms. Liam had adamantly refused to contemplate fatherhood. He'd wanted a glamorous wife on his arm, not a worn-out rag of a woman, stuck at home tied to a bunch of grizzling kids.

'We have a lot in common, you and I.' Sam levered himself out of the comfy leather-upholstered armchair on the opposite side of the crackling log fire and opened the last of the three bottles of wine he'd brought when he'd invited himself for supper earlier. 'You want a child, but you can't stomach the idea of a husband to go with it—once badly bitten and all that.' He withdrew the cork with a satisfying plop, and although Elena knew she'd already had more than was wise, she allowed him to refill her glass.

Over the two years he'd been coming to this corner of Spain, to snatch a few days' relaxation between assignments for one of the more erudite broadsheets, he had become her dear friend. There was something driven about him that she could relate to, and nothing remotely sexual so she was doubly comfortable with him.

She smiled at him with affection. Too right, she didn't want or need a husband. Never again—the one she'd had had turned out to be a disaster.

Sam kicked a log back into place with a booted foot and stood staring into the flames, his glass loosely held in his hands. 'I'm dead against marriage, too, but for different reasons. With my dodgy lifestyle, it's not on. Besides—and I wouldn't admit this to just anyone— I've a fairly low sex drive. Unlike my brother.'

Jed. Sam often talked about him. He lived in the

family home, somewhere old and impressive in the shires, and headed the family business—gobbling up any opposition, sitting on a fat portfolio. And now, it appeared, he was a womaniser too.

But Sam was telling her, 'Since his late teens he's always had women making a play for him—nubile, dewy-eyed daughters of the landed gentry, women who lunch, tough career cookies, the lot. But, to give him his due, he's picky and very discreet. Mind you, he'll marry some day, to get an heir. He wouldn't want the family business to die out with him. But not me. All my emotional, mental and physical energies go into my job. I only feel properly alive when facing danger, grabbing photographs and copy from volatile situations.'

Elena hated it when he talked like that; it made her feel edgy. She watched him drain his glass, heard him say, 'Like you, the only regret I have is knowing how unlikely I am to ever have a child of my own. To my way of thinking, passing on one's genes is the only type of immortality any of us can ever hope for.' He turned to watch her then, his lean, wiry frame tense. 'There is an answer, though, for both of us. I'd be more than happy to offer myself as a donor. I can think of no other woman better to carry my child. I'd make no demands, other than the right to visit with you both when possible. Never interfere. Think about it.'

He put his empty glass on a side table and bent to kiss her lightly on the forehead. 'You would never have to lose your freedom and independence to a husband; you wouldn't have to go through the messy business of sleeping around to get the child you're beginning to crave. No risk of nasty diseases! And I'd get my single claim to immortality.' He smiled into her shell-shocked eyes. 'Sleep on it, why don't you? I'll call you in the morning. If you want to go for it, we can get straight back to London and start things moving. There's a private clinic headed by a professor of gynaecology who owes me a favour—it's useful, sometimes, to have friends in high places! Night, Elena—I'll let myself out.'

At first she'd dismissed his idea as utterly preposterous, but the longer she'd sat over the dying embers the more deeply she'd thought about it, and the less outlandish it had become.

He'd talked about her craving for a child, and he was right. Sometimes, the need to hold her own baby in her arms was an actual physical pain, a deep, regretful sorrow that wouldn't go away. And when that happened—with increasing regularity—everything she had achieved for herself seemed suddenly worthless.

She would never marry again, and the thought of sleeping around in order to get pregnant was deeply repugnant. And she liked and respected Sam Nolan, didn't she? Admired him. The child who carried his genes would be blessed.

When he called the following morning her answer was an affirmative.

She'd made the necessary trip to the London clinic with Sam, never once imagining that almost six weeks later she would be at his funeral. Deeply saddened by the loss of a talented young life to a stray sniper's bullet in a war-torn East African state, and more than devastated because only that morning after a month of hope, she'd discovered that his idea hadn't worked.

Sam hadn't achieved his claim to immortality and she would never have a child to hold and love.

She'd met Jed at that simple, heart-wrenching ceremony, and from that moment on everything had changed. For both of them.

It was dark when Jed finally returned. Elena, pacing the courtyard, heard the sound of the approaching car and panicked.

Would he view her pregnancy differently when he learned how the baby had been conceived? Would he believe she and his younger brother had never been lovers? Accept the fact that they had been merely good friends who'd found themselves in a similar frustrating situation and had gone for a rational solution?

The dim outside lights were on—soft golden light reflecting from the surrounding whitened stone walls of her sprawling home, tendrils of soft mist trailing gently around terracotta planters burgeoning with foliage and sweetly scented flowers.

The silence when the engine cut out was immense, the night air sultry. Perspiration beaded her face as she waited, tension tying her in knots. She had to make him listen to her, believe her. Surely their love for each other entitled her to a fair hearing?

He appeared at last in the arched doorway to the courtyard, his big body taut, very still. The softly diffused lights, black shadows and trails of mist made him look desperately forbidding. Elena grasped the back of one of the cast-iron two-seaters that flanked the outdoor table. Her spine felt as if it had turned to water; she needed some support.

'Where were you?' she asked thickly as the minutes

of fraught silence ticked away. He didn't appear to be in any hurry to break the ice. Someone had to do it.

'Seville.' The short answer was clipped. But at least he began to walk over the cobbles towards her. 'As you know, Nolan's are to acquire a retail outlet in Seville. I was due to meet our architect in a fortnight's time, to decide which of two suitable properties to go for.' He stopped, feet away from her, almost as if, she thought hysterically, the air surrounding her might contaminate him. 'For reasons I'm sure you'll understand, I thought today might be as good as any to get back in harness.'

Elena flinched. They'd planned on a three-week honeymoon, here at her home, Las Rocas, then to spend a week in Seville together to meet with the architect and explore the lovely city. Plainly, the honeymoon was over. But after her bombshell what else could she have expected?

She made a small, one-handed gesture towards him, her throat thick with sudden tears. But if he noticed the way she reached out to him he didn't respond, and she let her hand drop defeatedly back to her side and said raggedly, 'Can we talk?'

'Of course.' The dip of his head was coldly polite. 'But inside. It's been a long day.'

He moved towards the house and Elena followed, pushing her long straight hair back from her face with a decidedly shaky hand. She could have borne his rage, his recriminations, far more easily. At least then she would have known what was going on inside his head, could have reassured him, told it as it was, asked him to try to understand.

She hadn't met him, much less fallen in love with

him, when she'd made the decision to be artificially
impregnated—for reasons that had seemed right and
sane and reasonable then. He was an intelligent, compassionate man. Surely he would understand how she
had felt at the time?

Striding straight to the kitchen, Jed reached for the
bottle of Scotch tucked away in one of the cupboards,
unscrewed the cap and poured a more than generous
measure for himself.

'In view of your condition, I won't ask you to join
me.' He swallowed half the golden liquid, then pulled
a chair away from the chunky pine table and sat, long
legs outstretched, the fingertips of one hand drumming
against the grainy wooden top, his dark head tilted
slightly in insolent enquiry. 'So talk. I'm listening. Or
would you rather I set the conversational ball rolling?'

His voice was so cold, almost as cold as his eyes.
They reached deep inside her and froze her soul.
Shakily she pulled a chair out for herself and sat on
the edge, not opposite him, but further down the table
so he would have to turn to look at her.

He didn't, and she was as glad as she could be under
these impossibly hateful circumstances. She didn't
want to see the frozen indifference of his eyes, not
when they had once looked at her with so much love.

She shuddered suddenly, convulsively, knotting her
hands together in her lap. Briefly, her eyes flicked
round the farmhouse kitchen—heavy copper pans
gleaming against the white-painted stone walls, the
great stone chimney breast, gleaming terracotta floor
tiles and carved, polished wood dressers, the pots of
scented geraniums on the broad windowsills.

She'd always loved this room, and this last week,

in Pilar's absence, she and Jed had made their meals here together. Chopping vegetables and fresh herbs from the garden, washing fruit. Talking, laughing together, sometimes catching each other's eyes, understanding the need, the love, reaching for each other, the meal in the making forgotten...

It didn't seem possible that all the love and laughter, that magical feeling of closeness had gone. She wouldn't let herself even think that it would never come back. Yet his attitude had erected a mountain between them. She didn't know if she was strong enough to climb it.

She had to try, though. It was imperative. She flicked her tongue over her dry lips as she struggled to find the words. The right words. Words that would help him understand. But he said impatiently, 'As you seem to have been struck dumb, I'll do the talking.' He swallowed what was left of his whisky and swung round on his chair, looking at her now from narrowed, unforgiving eyes. 'I've thought about our distasteful situation and reached certain non-negotiable decisions. We stay married,' he stated grimly, then reached for the bottle and poured another shot into his glass.

Something tore at Elena's heart, a savage little pain. 'You considered divorce?' After what they'd been to each other she could hardly believe it. Would he hate himself for even thinking about it once he knew the truth? Would she be able to forget how he'd considered cutting her right out of his life without giving her the opportunity to explain herself?

'Naturally. What else did you expect?' He wasn't looking at her now, but staring at his glass as he twisted it around between his fingers, watching the way the liquid caught the light and fractured it. 'Under the circumstances it was the first thing I thought of. However, for two reasons, I decided against it. The first Catherine, my mother. She likes you.' The very tone of his voice told her he couldn't now imagine why. 'Our marriage was the only thing that lightened her grief over Sam's death. A divorce, so soon, would be rather more than she could be expected to bear.

'The second reason for keeping the marriage going is my brother's unborn child. I don't blame Sam for any of this. He died without knowing he'd made you pregnant. So, for my brother's sake, we stay married. I intend to take a full part in his child's upbringing. Call it a duty of care. Sam tended to mock me for being the dutiful son, but perhaps, wherever he is, he'll be thankful for it now.'

For a moment his eyes were drenched with the pain of grief, and Elena's heart bled for him. She wanted to reach out to him, to comfort him, to tell him that everything could be all right if he'd let it be, if he'd listen to her and try to understand.

She was halfway out of her seat, on her way to him, but the quelling darkness of his expression put her back again, his voice cutting as he told her, 'We will put up a good front, for the sake of my mother and the child when he or she arrives. But, that apart, I want as little as possible to do with you. We'll return to the UK in three weeks' time, as arranged, and I'll get out of your hair as much as I can—visit the overseas branches. You can make the excuse that travelling doesn't agree with pregnancy.'

He pushed away from the table and rinsed his glass

out at the deep stone sink, upturning it on the drainer, and Elena choked back a sob.

Every word he'd uttered had strengthened the wall between them, making it impossible to breach. Whatever she said to him now, whether he believed her or not, those words—the brutal ending of their marriage in all but name—would never be forgotten.

'And if I don't agree to this—this farce!' She struggled to her feet, but had to support herself against the table. 'I want you to listen to my point of view. I want you to hear what really happened. I have that right.'

'You have no rights!' He flung down the towel he'd been drying his hands on, the first sign of a real emotion directed at her since his return showing through. 'And you brought this ''farce'' on yourself. You married me while knowing you could be pregnant by my brother,' he castigated harshly. 'Why? Because you didn't fancy single parenthood? One brother was lost to you so you might as well settle on the other? He might not live such a dangerously fascinating, swashbuckling type of life, might not be as pretty to look at, but he'd do? Marry me and hope fantastic sex would make me overlook everything else.'

He turned away, as if he couldn't bear to look at her. 'Well, you were wrong. It didn't. You're good in bed, I'll give you that. But not that good. In any case, I can get fantastic sex whenever I want. No strings, no messy secrets, no regrets.'

That hurt. If he'd ripped her heart out of her body with his bare hands it couldn't have hurt more.

Pain took her by the throat and shook her, making speech impossible. But she had, somehow, to make him understand, to begin the process of partially exonerating herself, for both their sakes. Distrust of her was turning him into a man she didn't know.

'When we first met, I truly believed...' Her voice, difficult to push past the constriction in her throat, faltered and died as she remembered the way he'd approached her after the graveside ceremony. 'You must be Elena Keele; Sam often spoke about you. Don't go away.' He had touched her black-gloved hand briefly, and warmth had momentarily displaced the aching sorrow in his eyes. 'Come back to the house. I think your company would be a comfort to my mother. And to me. Through Sam, I already feel I know you.'

And so it had begun.

Aware that he was watching her struggle for words, the straight line of his mouth twisted to one side, sardonically interested in her fumbling attempts to excuse the inexcusable, she went scarlet and told him roughly, 'I thought I wasn't pregnant. I started a period on the morning of Sam's funeral.' It had been sketchy, and of very short duration, but she'd put that down to the shock of learning of her friend's death, the rush to get a flight to London, hire a car and drive out to his home village to pay her last respects.

The next had been equally slight, but it hadn't crossed her mind that she might be carrying Sam's child. She'd been back in Spain for two weeks then, regretfully leaving Jed in England. They'd spent two weeks getting to know each other, learning to accept the unbelievable fact of love at first sight. But she'd had a deadline to meet, and if they were to be married as soon as possible—which they had both known almost from that first moment of meeting—Jed had a lot of business ends to tie up, too.

The love, the magic, the precious feeling of being born for each other couldn't have disappeared so completely. Surely it couldn't?

She approached him with more determination. He had to hear her out. 'Jed—Sam and I—'

'Spare me!' he cut across her, his eyes derisive. 'I don't want to hear the sordid details.' He headed for the door, his footsteps ringing firmly on the tiled floor. 'And I'm sure you'll understand if I don't believe a word you say. Why keep a testing kit around if you were so certain your affair with my brother hadn't left you with any music to face? Why use it at all?'

'Because I'd begun to feel nauseous in the morning! I believed pregnancy was out of the question, but did the test just to make doubly sure!' she shot back at him, her temper rising. How could a man who'd said he'd love her till the day he died refuse to properly hear her side of the story, refuse point-blank to believe a word she said?

Her shoulders rigid, she bunched her hands into fists at her sides and told him, her voice grinding out the slow words, 'Sam and I were *never* lovers.'

'No? One-night stand, was it? Don't try to tell me he forced himself on you. Sam wasn't like that. It was more likely to be the other way around. From my experience during this last week your appetite for sex is pretty well insatiable.'

Bitterness was stamped all over his harsh features, and it held his spine in a rigid line as he walked out of the room. In that moment she hated him.

She had never hated anyone before, not even Liam. She had despised him, but never hated him. The savage emotion consumed her. She paced the terracotta

tiles, her arms wrapped around her slender body, holding herself together in case she should explode with
the hot rage that flared and flamed inside her.

How dared he treat her as if she were trash? Accuse
her of such monstrous things? And where had the man
she loved more than her life disappeared to? Had he
ever really existed, or had he been mere wish-
fulfilment, a figment of her imagination? The man who
had just walked out on her was a cold-hearted, arrogant, egotistical monster!

He could forget his 'non-negotiable' decision of a
sham marriage. She would accept no part of it. Did he
think he had a God-given right to dish out orders, arrogantly decide how she would live out the rest of her
life?

Did he really think she would stay legally tied to a
man who thought so badly of her? Did he imagine,
for one moment, that she'd unquestioningly suffer the
misery such a vile arrangement would bring her?

As far as she was concerned their marriage was over
in every way there was. She had no intention of returning to England with him, living a lie. She was
perfectly capable of looking after her child on her
own—that had been the original intention, after all.

Her child did not need a father figure, especially one
as all-fired intransigent, bloody-minded and arrogant
as Jed Nolan!

First thing in the morning she would tell him to
pack his bags, get out of her home. She never wanted
to have to see him again.

CHAPTER THREE

She didn't get the opportunity to ask him to leave. He'd already done it.

The sun had only just begun to gild the flanks of the rugged hills with new-day light when she left her solitary bed and dragged herself downstairs after a monumentally miserable and sleepless night.

Which bedroom Jed had used she had no idea, and didn't care, she told herself as she secured the belt of the robe she'd thrown on more tightly around her narrow waist. As soon as he surfaced she would ask him to leave, announce that she'd be in touch, through her solicitor, some time in the future. Let him know that he wasn't the only one who could make decisions and hurl them around like concrete slabs.

If he wasn't prepared to listen to her, to believe her, then their relationship wasn't worth keeping—certainly not the acrimonious, desolately empty relationship he had in mind. Better by far to make a clean break.

Making for the kitchen for the coffee she suddenly dramatically needed, she saw his note the moment she pushed open the door. A scrap of paper on the polished pine table top. It didn't say a lot, just a scrawl of distinctive black handwriting. 'I'll be in Seville for the next three weeks. I'll collect you for our return journey.'

The hell you will! Elena scrunched the paper up and

37

hurled it at the wall. Frustrated by his disappearance, before she could tell him she had no intention of meekly tugging her forelock and submitting to his orders, she felt her blood pressure hit the roof.

She didn't even know which hotel he'd be using in Seville. She couldn't get in touch and remind him that she was perfectly capable of making the decisions that would affect the rest of her life, that no way would she be returning to England, simpering and smiling and pretending to be deliriously happy. No way!

Hot tears flooded her eyes. Had she been secretly hoping that Jed would have come to his senses this morning, found enough trust in her to believe her story? If so, she'd been a fool. Well, no more.

She'd just have to sit out the next three weeks with the rage festering away inside her, and— Suddenly the now all too familiar morning sickness struck, and twenty wretched minutes later she was standing under a warm shower, patting her still flat tummy and murmuring wryly, 'You're certainly giving Mummy a hard time, Troublebunch!'

Even as the tender smile curved her lips her eyes filled with tears again. Tears for Sam, who would never know he'd left a child behind, for herself, and for Jed, who had lost something wonderful that could never be retrieved.

Warm needles of water washed the tears away, and she dried herself, wrapped her long hair in a towel, dressed in cotton shorts and a halter-neck top and told herself they were the last tears she would shed for any of them.

Life went on.

She had her child to look forward to, and she would

love it to distraction and give him or her the happiest life any child could want. Now that she was marginally calmer she could see that, in a way, it was a blessing that Jed had taken off. That action alone told her that he'd never truly loved her. If he had, he'd have trusted her, believed her, asked for more details. It had also saved her from a demeaning slanging match, from allowing all her hurt to pour out and hit him right between the eyes.

When she next saw Jed she would be able to tell him of her own decisions, calmly and rationally. She was intelligent enough to know that no amount of rage could alter anything. He despised her now; all the love had gone and nothing she could do or say would bring it back. That was a fact. Hard to face, but not impossible.

She could handle the hurt; she'd managed before and would manage again. Certainly the way Liam had hurt her had been a mere pinprick compared to this. But then she'd had nothing, just a mother who'd wrung her hands and wailed, prophesied heaven alone knew what horrors if she insisted on skipping the country with little more than the clothes she stood up in.

But from having nothing and no one she'd made a good life for herself. At least this time round she had a successful career to fall back on, and was carrying the child she'd begun to need so desperately.

So, on the whole, she reasoned, wondering if she could manage a glass of water and a slice of dry toast without upsetting her unborn baby, everything balanced out and she could hack it.

She wasn't at all sure about that one week later, when Jed arrived with his mother.

She hadn't been able to think about starting a new book, and hadn't responded to the faxes from her agent which had come chattering through over the last couple of days—apologising for interrupting her honeymoon, but apparently excited over some awards ceremony to be held in London. She hadn't been interested. One day she'd have to read through them properly, absorb what her agent was trying to tell her and respond. But not now. Not yet.

She'd driven down to the village and told Pilar to take two more weeks' leave, and then had sought the solitude she so desperately needed in the hot few acres of Spanish earth that was her garden.

She was weeding amongst the massed clumps of sweet-smelling carnations that bordered one of the twisting paved paths when she heard the car. Brushing her hands down the sides of her cotton skirt, she stood up and walked towards the house, resenting the intrusion. Resenting it to the point of internal explosion when she saw Jed handing his mother from the car.

She couldn't imagine what either of them was doing here, or what she could possibly say to them—especially Catherine Nolan, who was one of the nicest women to draw breath.

Wearing a pale blue linen suit, the older woman looked less stressed out than the grieving mother she'd come to know during the two weeks she'd stayed in Netherhaye, the family home in rural Hertfordshire. Though she had perked up enormously for the quiet wedding, bossing the caterers and florists around, mak-

ing sure the small reception back at Netherhaye was
as perfect as it could possibly be.

'Elena!' Catherine beamed as she became aware of
her daughter-in-law's approach. 'How good of you to
agree to let me come—only for a few days, I promise.
I won't intrude longer than that!'

So Jed hadn't told his mother of the complications
that had rendered their marriage null and void.
Catherine wouldn't be looking like a plump, slightly
flustered, happy mother hen if he had. But then he
wouldn't, of course, she reminded herself, doing her
best to find a smile of sorts. Hadn't duping his parent
into believing everything was blissful been one of his
two main priorities?

'It's lovely to see you.' She bent to receive
Catherine's kiss and didn't look at Jed. He was removing luggage from the boot, just a shadowy presence in the background, and that was the way he had
to stay if she was to hold onto her sanity, swallow
back the scalding renewal of the pain and rage she'd
talked herself into believing was over and done with.
'I'm sure you're ready for a drink.'

'Oh, I'd love one. It's quite a drive from Jerez airport, isn't it? But such lovely countryside—oh, what
a gorgeous courtyard—all those lilies! And will you
just look at those geraniums? They never get that huge
at home!'

Barely hearing the spate of compliments on her
home, Elena led the older woman into the cool, airy
sitting room and watched her plop down into a deep
comfy armchair with an audible sigh of relief.

'Bliss! Now I can take my shoes off.'

'And I can fetch you that drink.'

Elena escaped into the kitchen. She saw Jed toting luggage up the stairs, clenched her jaw and ignored him, closing the kitchen door behind her firmly. She could have gone after him and demanded to know what the hell he thought he was doing, bringing his mother here when their marriage, so recently begun, was well and truly over, leading the poor deluded woman to believe that she, Elena, had agreed to this visit.

But she didn't. She simply wanted to hide. During the past week she had talked herself into believing she could handle the irretrievable shocking breakdown, that when she saw him again it wouldn't hurt because sensibly, being an intelligent adult and not a soppy child, and because she'd done it once before, she knew how to cut her losses and go on.

But it did hurt. It hurt like hell.

She reached for two wine glasses and a bottle of white Rioja from the fridge; she needed the stiffening, even if Catherine didn't.

Catherine did. 'How deliciously cold. It hits the spot! Isn't Jed joining us?'

'He's taking your cases up.' And taking an inordinate amount of time about it, she thought edgily, doing her best to sound relaxed—though why should she bother, when Catherine would learn, sooner rather than later, that her new daughter-in-law was shortly to become an ex?

While Catherine chattered about her flight out, Elena, wine in hand, perched on the arm of one of the chairs and wondered whether to break the news now. Catherine would have to know, because following Jed's orders and pretending the marriage was fine when it wasn't was something she was not prepared to do.

She was trying to decide whether she should dress it up some way, and how, or whether she should come straight out with it when Catherine stopped her thought processes stone-dead.

'I have to tell you—your marriage to my son was one of the happiest occasions of my life, Elena. It didn't make up for losing Sam, nothing could ever do that, but it helped enormously—helped ease the dreadful grief and gave me something good to think about. Since I lost their father, all I've ever wanted is happiness for my boys.'

She looked so earnest, her eyes rather too moist, tears not far away, because she was still trying to come to terms with the worst thing that could happen to a woman: the loss of her child. Elena felt her stomach give a sickening lurch. She didn't want to hear any more, but short of walking out of the room she couldn't avoid it.

'Like any mother, I wanted my boys settled with a good woman, happily married with children of their own. I'd begun to despair of it ever happening.' She gave Elena a soft, shaky smile. 'Sam—well, he was like a will o' the wisp, impossible to pin down or keep in a settled place, and Jed—well, he was too settled, too much a workaholic bachelor, wedded to the business. But when Jed invited you to stay at Netherhaye, after the funeral, it was like a blessing. Just to watch the two of you gave me joy—and hope for the future. I could see what had happened, any fool could. I watched the pair of you holding your feelings back—not only because to hurl yourselves into each other's

arms might have seemed crass, in view of the circumstances, but because you were obviously making sure
you got to know each other before you made any commitment. Though of course Jed and I already felt we
knew you very well, through what Sam had told us.

'Knowing that my one remaining son had found the
perfect love at last was the only thing that kept me
going through those dark days. So when he phoned a
few days ago, to check I was all right on my own, I
asked if I could come on a short visit. I hadn't meant
to,' she said earnestly, 'it just came out. I know you're
on your honeymoon, but I suppose I needed to see you
both to restore my faith in God, to remind myself He
can dish out the good as well as the hard to bear.'

Her smile was now so loving and peaceful it made
Elena's heart bleed. How could she spill out the truth
and ruin this good woman's precarious contentment?
Plunge her back into the dark abyss of grief where
there was no glimmer of consolation to be found?

Jed had decided on the pretence of marital bliss because he had known what the truth would do to his
grieving parent, and Elena could understand that, sympathise. His harsh dictates, so coldly spelled out for
her, became more the reasoned decisions of a man
who knew his duty.

He would hate the idea of putting on a front as
much as she did, but felt, because of the tragic circumstances, that it was the only right thing to do.

She didn't want to understand, and heaven knew she
didn't want to sympathise. She wanted to cut Jed right
out of her life, never see or hear of him again, carry
on with the long haul of forgetting the pain, the terrible
slicing pain of seeing his precious love turn to hatred.

Not knowing what to say, she refilled Catherine's glass and took a gulp of her own as yet untouched wine, and Jed said from the doorway, 'Should you be drinking that?'

The sound of that cool voice with undertones of condemnation made her heart clench, especially when the penny dropped and she realised why he had asked that question. Alcohol and pregnancy didn't mix. Sam's baby was another of his priorities, another duty of care.

'Don't be so stuffy! It's almost suppertime. We're not hitting the sauce before breakfast! Come and join us.' Not knowing his reason for the criticism, Catherine turned to her son, raising her glass, proud maternal love in her eyes.

Putting her own glass down on a side table, aware that her hands were shaking, that every darn thing inside her was shaking, Elena risked an under-lash look at her husband.

He sauntered casually into the room, with a smile for his mother, hands stuffed into the pockets of his close-fitting dark trousers, the silk of his white shirt falling in fluid folds from his wide shoulders.

Yet there was strain there, there in the deepening of the lines that bracketed his beautiful, passionate male mouth, the tell-tale pallor beneath the olive tones of his skin. The past week had been tough on him, too.

But it was all entirely his own fault. She quelled the momentary surge of compassion. If he had given her the basic human right of being heard. If he'd given her the opportunity to tell him about the clinic treatment then he would have believed her when she'd told him that she and Sam had never been lovers.

'Now, you two…' Catherine beamed at them both indiscriminately, and Elena wondered if her mother-in-law was so blinded by what she wanted to believe that she couldn't sense something was wrong. 'I didn't invite myself here just to play gooseberry. There's something I need to discuss with you both. I could have said it on the phone, or written, but I wanted to see you…'

As the older woman's voice trailed uncertainly away Elena knew her present contentment was a fragile thing, with dark grief lurking beneath the surface of her courage, waiting for the opportunity to reclaim her.

'We're delighted you came,' Jed put in swiftly, briefly squeezing his mother's plump shoulder as he walked past to stand by Elena. 'We haven't done any sightseeing at all, so your being here gives us the ideal opportunity—we can do it together. I know Elena's anxious to show us her favourite places.'

Elena knew no such thing! Playing the devoted ecstatic wife for an audience of one while they trotted round the countryside would kill her! And when Jed went on to ask, 'So, what was it you wanted to discuss, Ma?' Elena shot to her feet and grabbed the first excuse to get out of there she could find.

'It's time I made a start on supper. You must be hungry, Catherine. You can tell us what's on your mind while we eat.'

She took her wine and fled, closing the kitchen door behind her, her heart punching against her breastbone. Catherine had mentioned staying a few days. Not long. But it would be purgatory. How could she pretend she and Jed were devoted newlyweds? Yet how could she do anything other? She couldn't heap more misery on that poor woman's head!

She and Jed would have to find a way out. She didn't know how, but she'd come up with something. She'd have to. The present situation couldn't be borne.

Tiredly, she carried her glass to the sink and tipped the wine away. Jed had been right, of course. Pregnancy and alcohol didn't mix.

His cool voice slid over her. 'I'm glad you agree I'm right.' He took the empty glass from her nerveless fingers and watched the last of the wine drain away.

Elena shuddered. She hadn't heard him follow her, and the coldness of his voice made her feel as if a wave of icy water had washed over her. How could he have forgotten everything they'd been to each other so completely and so callously?

Yet hadn't she, over this last endless week, been trying to do the same?

It was probably the only way, she conceded now, and turned away from him. 'Of course you were right. But you're not always, and you'd do well to remember that.' And he could ponder that, or not, as he chose. He had refused to hear her side of the story, walked all over her attempts to explain. She wasn't going to put herself in the position of being humiliated all over again. 'Why don't you go and entertain Catherine? Leave me to make supper.'

There were things she needed to say to him, but they would have to wait. Right now she wanted him and his icy voice and his tight-boned face well away from where she was. Her emotions had been in a mess ever since she'd discovered she was pregnant, and his return—with Catherine—had sent them skittering around, completely out of control.

She couldn't handle it, and didn't even want to have to try.

But Jed had other ideas. 'She's on the patio, soaking up the sun and the rest of the wine. She's not as young as she was and travelling tires her.'

'Then she shouldn't have come!' Elena bit out as she swung round to face him. 'What do you think I felt like when I saw you arriving together? The least you could have done was phone and warn me!' The moment the words were out she wished she could swallow them back. The poor woman had only made the journey to reassure herself, remind herself that there were things to be happy about. This situation with Jed had got her so she didn't know what she was saying or thinking.

'I didn't know you were so selfish.' Cold eyes raked her with glittering dislike. 'But then there were other things you made sure I didn't know.' His mouth twisted bitterly, his eyes continuing a brutal assessment. 'You look a mess. Freshen up while I make a meal. And behave yourself in front of Catherine. If you upset her I'll make you wish you'd never been born.'

Elena stalked out before she exploded. By the time she reached the relative sanctuary of her room her heart felt big enough to belong to an elephant, big enough to burst. How dared he treat her as if she were scum? How dared he?

She kicked her shoes into a corner, dragged the faded old cotton skirt and gardening shirt from her quivering body and stamped into the bathroom. Ten minutes later, wrapped in a towel, she knew what she had to do. For her unborn child's sake she had to stay calm. And to have any hope of achieving that she had to be careful not to sink to Jed's level, not to say vile and hurtful things, and not—most definitely not—rant and rave and throw things!

She chose a fitted silk sheath that ended a couple of inches above her knees and left her lightly tanned arms bare. The colour matched her eyes and the fabric clung to every curve. Soon now she'd start to bulge, and have to wear tents, and after the birth she'd probably turn matronly—so if she wanted to look on the cool side of sexy while she still could, who was there to stop her? Certainly not her pig of a husband.

To counteract the sexy length of leg on view, the way the silk of her dress lovingly caressed the curve of breast, tummy and thigh, she pulled her hair back from her face in a elegant upswept style and touched her wrists with old-fashioned lavender water.

Cool and sexy, both. And if the enigma annoyed the man she wished she'd been sensible enough not to fall in love with, tough.

'My goodness—you do look lovely!' Catherine said as Elena joined her on the patio, where Jed was putting a selection of salads down on the table.

'Thank you.' Elena managed a smile as she sank into the padded seat next to her mother-in-law. She knew Jed had turned from what he'd been doing to look at her, but refused to meet his eyes. She'd been on the receiving end of too many contemptuous looks coming from him to go looking for more.

'Believe it or not, I used to have a shape! Then the boys arrived, and that was that!' Catherine's eyes twinkled at her, and Elena thought, My God, one day she's going to have to know she's going to be a grand-mother. Sam's child.

She pressed the tips of her fingers to her temples. How would the older woman take the news? It seemed that every time she took a breath another problem popped up. The decision she and poor dead Sam had taken was creating unbelievable ripples—

'I nodded off for a few minutes, I'm afraid, what with the sun and the wine and the worry of flying on my own for the very first time,' Catherine was con-fessing, unaware of Elena's boiling thoughts. 'Or I would have changed for supper. Should I trot along and tidy up now?'

'No.' She didn't want to be left alone with Jed. She still felt too raw to cope with any more of his hurtful comments. He'd disappeared back into the kitchen, but he could be back at any moment. The negative had come out too quickly, too harshly. Making a conscious effort, Elena smiled. 'You're fine as you are, really. I'd much prefer you to stay and chat!'

And chat she did, and was still at it when Jed finally appeared with a dish of pasta dressed with olive oil and garlic. 'We seem to be running low on provisions,' he commented mildly, not making it sound like a crit-icism for his mother's benefit. 'So we'll make do with pasta and salads, OK?'

It would have to be. Elena hadn't bothered to shop, hadn't felt like eating during the last nightmare week, and his lumping them together, making them a 'we' made her disproportionally annoyed.

'Scandalous, isn't it, Catherine?' Her smile was as cool as the way she was wearing her hair, as cool as her cologne. 'We couldn't bring ourselves to venture out into the real world, even for food.'

She did look at Jed then, saw that her taunt had rubbed salt into an open wound, watched his mouth tighten, his jaw clench, saw raw pain in his eyes and told herself she didn't care. He could dish out hurt but he couldn't take it. At least he *could* take it, she amended as she watched him hand dishes to Catherine, but he sure as hell didn't like it.

'Well, now,' his mother commented comfortably, blissfully unaware of undertones. 'That discussion I told you I needed.' She dabbed olive oil from her mouth with a soft paper napkin. 'As you know, Elena, your mother helped me organise your wedding reception, and I persuaded her to stay with me at Netherhaye while you were working back here before the wedding and Jed was tying up loose ends, as he called it, all over the place. And, to cut a long story short, we grew very friendly in a very short space of time. Now…' She glanced at her son. 'I don't know whether I'm jumping the gun, but I rather hope you two will make Netherhaye your home, bring up your children there as your father and I did. It's been in the family such a very long time.'

Elena caught the warning glint of steel in Jed's smoky eyes and bit down hard on her lower lip, dragging it back between her teeth, holding back a cry of denial as Catherine went on, 'I certainly don't want to rattle around there on my own, and, despite intruding on you here for a few days, I'm of the opinion that newly weds don't want to find a parent lurking around every corner, cramping their style. So, either way, I'll be moving to somewhere very much smaller.'

Elena registered Jed's harsh inhalation and wondered if he was inwardly applauding his mother's decision. It would make things easier for him, wouldn't it? They wouldn't have to play at happy couples very often; he could trot her out on social occasions then pop her back in her box and forget all about her.

Over her dead body!

'Are you sure about that, Ma?' Jed asked, leaning forward slightly, the better to judge his parent's true feelings in the dwindling evening light. 'I don't want you to think you have to make a snap decision, or that Elena and I wouldn't be happy to have you live with us.'

Elena watched him narrowly. He looked and sounded totally sincere. On the one hand, having his mother remove herself from their immediate orbit would make life a lot easier for him. But, on the other, he was deeply fond of Catherine, cared about her. The whole idea of pretending their marriage was normal had stemmed from his desire to keep the older woman happily deluded, spare her any further grief.

'You know how you love the old place; all your memories are there—and you're besotted by your garden!'

'And having seen something of Elena's, and her beautiful home, I know Netherhaye will be in good hands.' Catherine smiled gently and put her hand over her son's. 'Sam's gone now, and in any case he wouldn't have wanted the responsibility. Netherhaye is yours.'

'Even so,' Jed said gruffly, 'I don't like to think of your being on your own. Not yet, not until...' His voice tailed off, and despite herself Elena had to admire his understanding and compassion. If only he had extended a tenth of it in her direction!

'You really mustn't worry about me!' Catherine smiled at both of them. 'What I was about to tell you is I won't be alone! I can't remember who got the idea first, but Susan and I are going to set up home together. There's a cottage for sale in the village—you remember the Fletchers, Jed? Well, they're moving to the south coast, to be nearer their married daughter and grandchildren, and while I'm here breaking the news Susan is doing the business with the agent and putting her own home up for sale. There! What do you think of that?'

Elena didn't know what to think. Jed was saying something, but her head was buzzing so loudly she couldn't hear a word. Her mother hadn't mentioned anything about selling the small house in Birmingham where Elena had been born. The fact that she hadn't taken her into her confidence hurt.

'As soon as this house was habitable, I asked her to live with me,' Elena stated numbly. 'She said she was too long in the tooth to uproot herself. Several years on, she's obviously changed her mind.'

She pulled herself to her feet. The stars were bright now, in the dark velvet sky, and the scent of mountain herbs was released in the soft warm breeze. She couldn't stand it, any of it! The night was so beautiful while her emotions were so painful, twisted and ugly. 'If you'll excuse me, Catherine, I'll clear away.' She balanced dishes and plates one on top of another and forced a thin smile. 'Ask Jed if you need anything.'

'Did you have to be so bloody curt?'

The bedroom door closed quietly behind him and

Elena pulled the soft linen sheet up to her chin, swallowing the hot hard lump in her throat.

Contempt blazed from his narrowed eyes and she really couldn't taken any more.

Her mother had never forgiven her for the failure of her marriage to Liam. She had thought the sun rose with her handsome young son-in-law. Even when she'd learned the truth she had tentatively suggested, 'Perhaps you drove him to it, dear?'

Her own marriage had been a miserable thing. Elena's father had had one affair after another, finally disappearing off the scene altogether when Elena was fifteen. Naturally Susan had wanted her only child's marriage to be perfect. She would be even more unforgiving now, when she learned that her second attempt at matrimonial happy-ever-after had been even less successful than the first!

'Go away,' she said wearily. 'I'm in no mood to talk right now.' Though there were things that needed to be said, of course there were—decisions of her own he had to hear about. And she had to make another attempt to break through his stubborn refusal to listen to her story. She should have told him about the treatment she'd undergone as soon as they'd realised they were falling in love. But Sam's death had been so recent, and Jed's grief so raw—a grief she hadn't wanted to exacerbate. She had decided it would be better to wait. And the treatment had been a failure—or so she'd truly believed at the time. She deeply regretted her decision to wait until time had softened the edges of Jed's grief.

Yes, there were things that had to be said, but the

stress and trauma of the past week had finally caught up with her, draining her of every last ounce of energy.

'You're ''in no mood''—that figures.' He advanced slowly, unbuttoning his shirt. 'Your ego's too big to see round, isn't it? *Your* needs are the only things that matter. You agree to marry me, conveniently forgetting to mention that you and Sam were lovers, that there was a distinct possibility you might be carrying his child, then get all hurt and bewildered when I understandably say I want out.'

He pulled his shirt from the waistband of his trousers, the tanned skin of his tautly muscled torso gleaming in the soft diffused light, the line of his mouth condemning as he continued, 'And then you blank Catherine—who doesn't deserve it—because, *amazingly*,' he stressed insultingly, 'your own mother appears to prefer her company to yours.'

Elena closed her eyes, fighting to hold back a feeble sob. Never before had she felt this useless, unable to take one more brickbat. She had been barely nineteen when Liam Forrester—he of the sharp suits, fast cars and dazzling smile—had swept her off her feet. And only a year later her world had come crashing down when she'd discovered she was married to a common criminal. But she'd picked herself up, because she was basically a fighter, and made a new life for herself from the ashes of the old.

But now, it seemed, she'd lost it. Lost the ability to pick herself up and carry on and—'What are you doing?' she asked thickly, her eyes opening wide as the rustle of clothing sounded ominously close.

'What do you think?' His trousers joined his discarded shirt on the carved blanket box at the foot of the bed. Naked, apart from brief boxer shorts, his male magnificence made her throat clench.

'You can't sleep here!' She panicked, despising herself for not being able to invest the words with more authority. 'Our marriage, for what it was worth, is over.'

'So it is,' he agreed coolly. 'But don't worry, I've no intention of making demands on the delectable body you went to so much trouble to display this evening. What were you trying to do? Remind me of what I was missing? If so, it didn't work. Move over.'

'No.' She kept her eyes firmly closed as he removed his shorts, hugging the sheet more tightly under her chin because she was naked, too. And she hadn't done her best to look sexy to remind him. Or had she?

She felt the mattress dip and began to shake. Having him share her bed would be sheer, unmitigated torture.

'I'm not overjoyed about this, either,' he admitted drily as he extinguished the bedside light. 'But Catherine's always been an early riser. Crack of dawn and she's up and doing.' She felt him slide his legs beneath the sheet, punch the pillow. 'If she sees us coming from separate rooms in the morning she'll know something's wrong.'

'And that's all that matters, is it?' Elena snapped, stung. Didn't he consider her feelings at all?

'At the moment, yes,' he said, his voice cleaving the soft warm darkness. 'She's going through a tough time at the moment; I won't add to it. Sam was always head and shoulders her favourite. Naturally she wouldn't have wanted to lose either one of us. But she did, and I'm the one that's left. I feel guilty enough about that without adding to her grief. Just go to sleep, will you?'

He turned his back on her, carefully leaving a yawning space between them, and Elena lay rigidly, staring into the darkness.

What he'd said about feeling guilty was crazy. Wasn't it? Or was there something about his relationship with his brother that she didn't know about? Something that might explain the brutal transformation from a warm and loving husband, partner, friend and companion, the soul-mate she'd believed him to be, into a hard, uncaring, bitter adversary?

She didn't know, and if she asked he wouldn't tell her. He had refused to believe her when she'd truthfully said that she and Sam had never made love, closed his mind when she'd tried to explain, cut her out of his life and his heart.

Whatever it was that had troubled his relationship with Sam had risen up and cut out his love for her as surely and completely as a surgeon expertly wielding a very sharp knife.

CHAPTER FOUR

THE smooth rhythm of his breathing agitated her beyond bearing, set every nerve-end tingling. Lying as
far from him as she could get, practically on the edge
of the big double bed, she held her body stiffly, every
muscle aching with tension.

How could he instantly fall into a healing, untrou-
bled sleep? she thought resentfully. Why couldn't she?
Why was she the one to lie awake, body aching, mind
burning, every inch of her flesh craving his?

Why couldn't she write him off and calmly get on
with her life as he obviously had?

If he'd truly loved her he'd have listened to her,
trusted her. But he hadn't. He hadn't even loved her
enough to do her the courtesy of at least listening to
her explanations of what had happened between her
and Sam. So why couldn't she stop loving him?

Unanswerable questions made jagged circuits of her
brain, tormenting her, but just as she decided she'd be
better off downstairs in her study, reading through
those neglected faxes from her agent, she slid abruptly
into exhausted sleep, and woke to find herself cuddled
into Jed's naked body.

Hardly daring to breathe, Elena gingerly opened her
eyes. Grey pre-dawn light was filtering through the
partly closed louvres, and at some time during the
night they had unconsciously moved together.

Who had first reached out for the other was not the

issue. It had happened. The only question was what to do about it.

Jed's arm was curled around her shoulder, his hand splayed against her back; one of her arms circled his taut waist while the other was tucked against his hard-muscled chest. Her fingers were touching the softly vulnerable hollow at the base of his throat, and their legs seemed to be inextricably twined together.

Her heart punched, heat crawling through her veins as the flood of desire she had no control over pooled heavily, sweetly, inside her.

He was deeply asleep, the rise and fall of his chest slow and steady, the motion lazily brushing the hardening globes of her breasts. She struggled to control the instinctive response and failed, holding her breath until she thought her lungs would burst.

She knew she should try to extricate herself, gently and carefully, so as not to wake him, end the bitter-sweet torment of this stolen intimacy, put an end to the frightening immediacy of this terrible aching need.

But her body seemed to be growing heavier, sinking deeper into the soft mattress, pressing more closely into his, electrical currents sparking from the contact of flesh against flesh, setting up convulsive shudders low down inside her. And his skin was damp, slicked with perspiration; it felt like warm sleek satin.

She ached to run both her hands over his body, re-claim all that had been hers until that terrible day just over a week ago. But she couldn't do that, she mustn't do that, mustn't give in to the intolerable temptation.

Physically, he was wrapped around her, but mentally and emotionally he had gone away, far away…

She knew the moment he woke, heard the deeper

tug of his breath, the muted, feral sound he made at the back of his throat as his hand slid down from her shoulder to spread across the curve of her buttocks, pulling her onto his immediate arousal.

Too late now to creep away without waking him. Much, much too late. Elena scarcely dared breathe, her eyes filling with sudden emotional tears.

There was no denying his urgent physical need. Or hers. But would he make love to her? And if he did would it be lust, a loveless using of her body, or would it signal a change of heart, a desire to cast out the havoc of contempt and distrust, to start again with a willingness to listen, to understand?

But shouldn't she signal her willingness to make a fresh start, let him know that for her love hadn't ended with his cruel words?

A heartbeat away from lifting her head to find his lips, whisper the words of love against them, she felt his body go rigid, heard the low-voiced self-deprecating profanity as he twisted off the bed, then padded around pulling garments from drawers before heading for the *en suite* bathroom.

She felt like dirt, and scrambled up against the pillows, wrapping her arms tightly around her body to contain the pain. The moment he'd reached full consciousness, realised what he was doing and who he was doing it with, he'd acted as if he'd found himself in bed with his arms round a bundle of evil-smelling slime!

Pushing the pain of that as far out of sight as it would go, she blinked the moisture from her eyes, controlled her breathing and swung her long legs out of bed, reaching for her wrap.

She tied the belt tightly about her small waist, the full-length mirror throwing back a wanton reflection. Rumpled blonde hair, the filmy robe doing nothing to hide her nakedness. She didn't care. There was no room for false modesty in this hateful situation. Much as she'd tried during the past long, lonely week, she hadn't been able to stop loving him. She'd been fooling herself if she'd thought for one moment that she had. But that didn't mean she'd lost all her pride.

Jed was under the shower, a cold one by the looks of things. She averted her eyes from his perfect male body, raised her voice above the sound of pounding water. 'This situation's impossible.'

'I'm not over the moon about it, either.' The gush of water stopped, and after a split second Elena steeled herself to look at him. He was wrapping a towel around his lean hips, his mouth taut, water plastering his hair to his skull, droplets gleaming on his fantastic body.

Elena clenched her hands at her sides, forbidding the instinctive, self-destructive need to touch. 'Then do something about it,' she ordered around the lump in her throat. 'Or I will.'

The towel he'd been using to rough dry his hair dropped to his side, narrowed grey eyes lacerating her. 'And what's that supposed to mean?'

She lifted her chin. He didn't frighten her. After the loss of his love, nothing could ever frighten her again. 'You could listen to me, for a start. Let me tell you exactly what happened between me and Sam.'

'No.' Angry emotion darkened his eyes. 'I don't want to hear what happened, listen to you trying to justify yourself. It sickens me.'

She couldn't reach him, she recognised hopelessly. Even if she went down on her knees and begged him to hear her out it would make no difference.

Trying to control the frustration that churned inside her, the pain of it all, she said flatly, 'If that's the way you want it. If you want to be this stubborn you can never have really loved me. And I'm not going to plead with you. But I warn you, I'm not prepared to pretend we're a loving couple when we're not. I refuse to go back to Netherhaye with you and live my life that way. So Catherine has to be told, sooner or later.'

His eyes glittered sharply. 'Later. Very much later. And you know damned well why! Or are you so wrapped up in what you want you don't care about anyone else?'

The rasped barb found its target. Her heart twisted painfully inside her. Of course she didn't want to cause Catherine any further emotional suffering, and it was an indictment of his so-called former love for her that he would so easily believe her capable of doing anything of the sort.

She closed her eyes, hiding the despised weak glitter of tears, and Jed said coldly, 'While she's here you'll act the part of a besotted wife. You managed it in bed this morning, so carrying on the act in the light of day shouldn't give you too much of a problem.'

Her eyelids batted open at that, revealing sea-blue glittery diamonds. How dared he? She hadn't consciously instigated that close embrace, and, initially at least, he'd loved every second. Wanted her—

As he wanted her now! She recognised the slight flare of his nostrils, the tightening of his jaw, the slow burn of colour across his prominent cheekbones, the drift of narrowed scorching eyes over her as-good-as-naked body. Something curled, dark and sharp, inside her. He might not love her now, but he sure as hell still desired her, she thought in bitter triumph. Something that elemental would take a long time dying.

'It's all yours.' He scooped up the clothes he'd brought in with him. 'I'll dress in the bedroom.' He brushed past, colour still darkening his face. He couldn't get away from her fast enough, she thought, untying her belt. He might hate himself for wanting her but there was nothing he could do about it.

It must have been an unconscious desire to pay him back for the pain and humiliation he'd dished out that had been behind her decision to dress the way she had. Elena walked out of the living room onto the patio, where Jed and Catherine were eating breakfast, and saw fury darken his eyes and pull his mouth into a straight, hard line, and was wickedly glad she'd clothed herself in tiny lemon-yellow silk shorts and a matching cropped halter-necked top.

'You look like a ray of morning sunshine!' Catherine beamed, clearly having forgotten and forgiven Elena's abrupt departure the evening before.

'Thank you.' She returned the older woman's smile wholeheartedly. For the duration of Catherine's stay she would play it Jed's way—with an added twist of her own! A game she would play for all she was worth, because it would be a way of showing him, and, more importantly, herself, that she was far from beaten.

She pulled a chair out from the table and sat, angling herself towards her husband, her long, shapely legs stretched out. Triumphantly she watched a muscle jerk at the side of his tough jaw as his unwilling eyes travelled the lightly tanned length of them, fastened for a millisecond on the juncture of her thighs, swept up over her naked midriff, then lingered on her breasts, lovingly cradled in sexy sheer lemon silk.

She felt her nipples peak beneath his sultry eyes, and knew he'd noticed when he abruptly pushed himself to his feet and disappeared in the direction of the kitchen, telling them tersely, 'I'll make fresh coffee.'

'My, I never thought I'd see the day when Jed got all domesticated! You're obviously very good for him!'

Not so you'd notice, Elena thought drily as Catherine laid down her cutlery and patted her round tummy. 'He insisted on making me scrambled eggs, even though everyone knows I should go on a crash diet. What are you having?'

'Just juice.' She poured some from the frosted glass jug and lay back in the sun, trying to look relaxed. Thankfully, this morning's session of feeling nauseous had only lasted a few minutes, and she'd managed to keep a glass of water down. At her mother-in-law's mock frown she added, 'I don't eat much in the morning, but, boy, do I make up for it at lunchtime!'

She buried her nose in her glass to hide the sudden onslaught of misgivings. Some time in the not too distant future Catherine would have to be told about the pregnancy. Was Jed aiming to pass Sam's child off as his own, forestalling the type of scandal he would hate? If so, he was in for an unpleasant surprise, because if there was no hope of saving their marriage she was sticking to her intention of making a clean break, the timing of which was dependent on how long it took Catherine to get back on an even keel.

Jed walked out with the fresh coffee, speaking to his mother. 'Would you like to stay here and rest up while Elena and I go down to the village for provisions?'

Elena accepted the fresh coffee he poured her and knew what he was up to. Suddenly he wasn't so sure about his own ability to act the part of a loving bridegroom in front of his parent, and in any case he probably wanted privacy to read her another riot act.

'Don't be silly, darling,' she drawled, before her mother-in-law could reply. 'Catherine hasn't come all this way to sit on her own on my patio. Why don't we go down to Cadiz, shop, have lunch, sit by the sea?' She turned her wide smile on her mother-in-law. 'You'd like that?'

'Oh, it sounds lovely, dear! Cadiz—so romantic— Francis Drake and Trafalgar—and wasn't it there that the King of Spain got his beard singed?'

'Out in the bay.' Elena smiled. 'If you extend your stay, and I hope you will, we could cross it on the ferry—the locals call it the *vapor*—and visit Puerto de Santa María. It's well worth the effort.'

Catherine beamed. Elena could see the earlier flicker of uncertainty wiped from her face. She had invited herself here, and Jed's suggestion that she spend the morning alone must have made her feel like an intruder. Jed wasn't normally insensitive where his bereaved mother was concerned. His suggestion that they leave her behind clearly showed that she was getting to him.

Elena turned a sultry smile on her stony-faced husband. 'Then that's settled, darling.' She watched his eyes go black as she lounged back in her chair, stretching her arms above her head provocatively. She hid a smile. If he accused her of flaunting herself, he'd be right. It was the only way she could think of to get her own back!

'Then perhaps you should get ready to leave?' He'd turned his back on her, staring out across the rumpled mountains. His voice was as smooth as cream, with an underlying strand of steel only she could detect.

She got lazily to her feet to obey his order. She could afford to be magnanimous; she was winning, wasn't she? Yes, the hard line of his shoulders was rigid beneath the fluid folds of the grey-green shirt he wore tucked into the waistband of his narrow-fitting stone-coloured trousers. She was really getting to him!

Swinging round to Catherine, she advised, 'Wear flatties; there'll be quite a lot of walking. And a shady hat. If you haven't brought one with you I can lend you one of mine.'

She wandered back to her room, not letting herself think beyond the trip to the capital of the province. If she was to get through the rest of Catherine's stay without going to pieces, she couldn't afford to think.

A toning button-through gauzy cotton skirt and matching short-sleeved jacket made her look decent. But she left all of the skirt buttons undone, apart from the top two, just to provocative. She pushed her feet into thonged sandals, crammed a floppy-brimmed straw hat on her head, found another for Catherine and was ready to face Jed again.

She found him blandly urbane, excessively polite as

he drove them down the mountain, following Elena's directions as they skirted the tiny red-roofed, white-walled village that clung to the lower hillside and spilled down into the valley.

He was showing her that two could play games. His features had lost their earlier tension, and she couldn't see his eyes behind the wrap-round dark glasses he was wearing. Thankfully, Catherine's non-stop commentary on all she was seeing made any conversational efforts on her own part redundant, and her 'Oh! I could stay here for hours!' when they were in the crowded, exotic market made Elena want to hug her.

'I have a better idea.' Jed's mouth quirked humorously as he regarded the flushed, happy face of his parent. As his arms were full of bundles and carriers of fresh produce, he dipped his head to indicate a pavement café on the edge of the colourful, bustling market square. 'Wait for me there while I go back to the car and put this lot in the cool-boxes. Then we'll find somewhere nice for lunch.'

He treats her as if she were a child, Elena thought, a traumatised child who has to be handled with great care. And she was guilty of that, too, she realised, as she found herself tucking Catherine's arm through the crook of her own and murmuring cajolingly, 'We'll have coffee, shall we? It's nothing like the weak apology for the stuff you get back home!'

She registered Jed's nod of approval just before he turned away, shouldering his way through the noisy crowd of vendors and shoppers. So he approved the way she was doing as she was told, treating Catherine with kid gloves. His second order, that she act like a besotted new wife—which she had every intention of obeying to the letter when his mother was around—would, she vowed with a tight little smile, be something he was going to regret. She was sure he already was!

As soon as she and Catherine were settled with their *café solo* Catherine cast her eyes around the shimmering heat of the square, the shady orange trees and the golden stone of the high, balconied buildings. 'It's all so beautiful and vibrant, isn't it? I can understand why you choose to live here—I hope you won't miss it too much when you go back to Netherhaye. But I'm sure you and Jed will spend as much time as possible at Las Rocas.'

As things stood, she wouldn't be going back to Netherhaye, and Jed would certainly not be spending time with her at Las Rocas. But of course Catherine couldn't know that; she would only be allowed to learn the truth once she was more settled herself.

So Elena merely smiled and sipped her coffee, and tried not to think of the way her marriage had foundered, the emptiness of the loss of love, and Sam's shadow reaching from beyond the grave, casting a blight over what had once been so bright and beautiful.

Yet it wasn't Sam's fault, and it wasn't hers. They had done what they'd done for what had seemed to be sane and rational reasons at that time, and she'd truly, truly believed that they'd failed.

No, the fault was Jed's for refusing to listen, for thinking foul things about her, for not loving her enough—

'Try not to be upset over your mother's decision to make her home with me.' Catherine interrupted the desolate drift of Elena's thoughts, thoughts she told herself to put on the back burner for the time being, obviously mistaking her moment of solemn silence for something else.

'I could see it came as a shock to you last night. I know Susan intended writing to you about it, but she obviously hasn't got around to it.' She patted Elena's hand comfortingly. 'She was grateful and touched when you offered her a home here with you several years ago—she told me so. But, as she said, Spain seemed a long way away, and you'd flown the nest, made a huge success of your life, and she didn't want to cramp your style! She and I both agree that the younger generation don't want an old mother sitting up in a corner, probably getting in the way. Which is why I decided to move out of Netherhaye. Less responsibility for me—and lots of privacy and leeway for young lovers! And Susan and I get on famously, so I shan't be in the least bit lonely.'

How long would Catherine and her mother remain bosom friends? Elena brooded uncomfortably. When the marriage breakdown became public knowledge they would be bound to take sides—

'Why the long faces?' Jed had appeared from nowhere. He was smiling, but his tone had been tough, as if, Elena thought, he suspected her of taking this opportunity to come out with all the nasty facts of one hideously wrecked marriage.

'Girl-talk!' Catherine said brightly, standing up and tucking her handbag under her arm. 'Let's find somewhere to eat—I'm starving! And don't look so quelling.' She prodded Jed's broad chest with a forefinger. 'We girls are entitled to have our secrets!'

The wrong thing to have said, Elena thought. Jed

smiled for his mother, but his eyes, when they glanced her way, were full of contempt. He was thinking about the child she was carrying. Sam's child.

Suddenly she wanted this day to be over. Wanted Catherine safely back in England. Wanted Jed to love her again, wanted to turn the clock back...

But what she wanted she couldn't have. She followed the other two into a shady warren of narrow cobbled streets. Her spine felt like wet string and her heart felt like a lump of sludge, low down in the pit of her stomach. She didn't know how she was going to get through the rest of the day because she was hurting so much.

She had two options, she decided bleakly. One, she could drag along, looking and feeling like a wet weekend, making Catherine suspect something was very wrong, because she wasn't a teenager in a sulk but a mature woman on her honeymoon. Or, two, she could act the part of the besotted new bride, just as Jed had told her to!

Pride made her decide on the latter. Taking a deep breath, blinking away the threat of tears, she caught up with the other two, slipped between them and took Jed's arm, leaning against his shoulder, her hip and thigh brushing his as they walked.

She felt a shudder rake through his body, noted the way he tensed, and turned her grin of satisfaction into, 'There's a gorgeous restaurant overlooking the sea. We could eat outside, catch the breeze.'

Jed grunted and Catherine cried, 'Sounds good to me! Lead the way!'

Elena did, keeping up the body pressure, reminding herself that she was punishing him, repeatedly reminding herself of just why she was having to stoop to that—to take her mind off the effect the closeness of him was having on her.

When they'd seated themselves at an open-air table in a discreetly secluded corner—deliberately chosen because if she was going to make an exhibition of herself she didn't want it to be public—shaded by an awning of clambering vines, cooled by the breezes from the Atlantic, Elena could see that Jed was having a hard time controlling his temper.

The look he gave her as she slid into the seat beside his, allowing the unbuttoned edges of her skirt to fall apart to display every last inch of her long tanned legs, told her he was bitterly regretting having ordered her to pretend to be a loving wife!

Good! She gave him a brilliant smile and did her best to convince herself that she was enjoying this, getting under his skin, making him want her and despising himself for doing it, livid with her for doing it to him.

She put her hand on his arm and trailed her fingers down his skin. She felt his muscles tense and knew he wanted to brush her hand away, but he couldn't do anything of the sort under Catherine's fond maternal eye.

'Perhaps I should order, darling?' Elena murmured. 'Very few people here speak any English at all—Cadiz isn't one of those heaving internationally orientated tourist spots.'

'Whatever.' He dipped his head in seeming compliance, but she knew he didn't like her taking charge. He liked making his own decisions—witness the way he'd issued those directives on the way their future was to be conducted.

Tough! Elena consulted the menu and opted for roast vegetable salad—red peppers, tomatoes and aubergines—and clams cooked with sherry and garlic. 'Does that sound OK to you guys?'

She beckoned one of the white-coated waiters over and ordered in fluent Spanish. When she'd come out here all those years ago learning the language had been a priority, and now Catherine said admiringly, 'Is there no end to your talents?'

Smiling enigmatically, Elena plucked the shady hat from her head and ran her fingers through her hair, looking at Jed through her long, tangled lashes, her mouth pouting. 'I think you should ask my husband that!'

Recklessly flirting with him throughout the meal, Elena caught Catherine's doting, satisfied smile and guilt pushed itself right into her heart.

She was creating a fool's paradise for this nice woman. She felt ashamed of herself. The true situation, stripped of pretence and game-playing, crashed down on her then, swamping her with misery, making her feel wretched.

And she felt worse than wretched—she felt terrified—when, after Catherine had excused herself to visit the washroom, Jed took her chin in cruel fingers and told her, 'I know what you're doing and why you're doing it.'

His eyes raked her face and her heart quailed at the dark, brooding intensity of his eyes as they rested on her lips. 'Our marriage may be over in all but name, but be careful I don't grab what's so enticingly on offer. There's only so much a man can take before he forgets his scruples.'

And then his mouth was on hers, savagely parting her lips to gain admittance to the soft, sweet moisture within. She fought against the punishment—her hands balled into fists, pushing against his shoulders—fought against the flames of desire inside her, until the pressure of his lips altered, became utterly, shatteringly sensual, deeply erotic, as incredible as it had ever been when he'd loved her as much as he'd needed her, and then she opened willingly for him, fists unclenching, fingers gripping the wide span of his shoulders, blood pounding through her veins.

There was no room in her head for thought, misgivings. Her whole body had exploded with need, with wanting him, loving him. Her brain had suffered meltdown, couldn't cope with reality, wallowed in fantasy...

Until he smoothly put her away from him, advising coldly, 'Think before you play games with me. Teasing can be a two-edged sword. So watch your step, sweet wife, or you might find you've bitten off rather more than you want to chew.'

EMMA RICHMOND

But he appeared on time for a meal, composed,
controlled as fresh, and attentive as though he'd asked
herself to marry him and she had said no. Catherine
didn't seem to notice any undercurrents, but you

CHAPTER FIVE

ELENA put herself in the back of the car and let the
conversation between mother and son up front wash
right over her.

Jed had declared sexual war. That was what his kiss,
his steel-edged remark had amounted to.

Men could make love without love having a look-
in, he'd as good as warned her. For her it would be
different, because she couldn't stop loving him, no
matter how she tried, but she'd despise herself if she
allowed him to use her that way.

Why had she been so stupid? Why couldn't she
have acted normally, smiled and looked pleasant
whenever he spoke, for Catherine's peace of mind, but
kept her distance? In acting the way she had she'd
pushed him to the limit of his endurance.

The way she'd behaved had been cheap and childish, and under normal circumstances she was very far
from being either. But these weren't normal circumstances, she thought miserably. She'd found herself in
the terrible situation of feeling hatred for the only man
she'd ever really loved. Hatred, love, pain and despair
were a mind-shattering combination, and had made her
act in a way that made her despise herself.

She spent what was left of the afternoon showing
Catherine around the property with a smile pinned on
her face. Jed had said he had a raft of business telephone calls to make and had shut himself away in her

study. As far as Elena was concerned he could stay there. The less she saw of him the better.

But he appeared in time for a light supper, herb omelette and fresh fruit, and afterwards Elena excused herself. 'I've got masses of watering to do, Catherine. So why don't you put your feet up and let Jed tell you about the new premises he's opening in Seville?'

And she escaped to the peace of her garden.

She'd changed into soft worn denims and a workmanlike cotton shirt, and tied her hair back with a leather thong. The everyday, pleasant chore of wandering up and down the winding paved paths, turning the hose on the stands of stately white lilies, hedges of dwarf lavender, fat pink roses and the silvery eucalyptus trees which looked wraith-like in the dusky light calmed her troubled spirits just a little.

Trying to retaliate had been an unworthy idea, serving only to inflict further hurt on both of them. Jed no longer loved her, so it was better to let it go with as much dignity as possible. The way she'd flirted and flaunted hadn't been dignified at all.

A sound at the head of the path she was working from brought her head round, her colour coming and going, her heart racing as Jed walked down the short flight of stone steps.

His face wore the closed look she had come to dread, but as he drew nearer she could see the pain in his eyes, pain he was trying to hide.

As her heart flooded with sudden compassion she despised herself anew for what she had set out to do today, and wondered if she had enough courage to tell him so. She felt as if she'd reached an important crossroads in their relationship. If she could apologise and make him believe her sincerity—

'Catherine says to say goodnight. And while I was in your study I found these.' He spoke tonelessly, cutting through her thoughts, and for the first time she noted the papers he held in his hands. 'Another came through today. Your agent is beginning to sound hysterical. Perhaps you should deal with them.'

Those neglected faxes. She shrugged, pulling in a long breath. 'I guess,' she agreed listlessly. 'Whatever it is she needs to discuss just hasn't seemed important.'

He gave her a level look. 'No? Not even something that could set the final seal of approval on your work?'

Twilight deepened the lines at either side of his mouth, shadowed his eyes, making them an enigma. She shrugged his question away. 'Look—can we talk?'

She might have imagined it, but suddenly he seemed slightly more approachable. There was so much she wanted to say to him, so much to explain. She didn't know where to begin. She could understand why he was so bitter, so angry. Putting herself in his position, she knew she would have felt the same. But it needn't be this bad for him. If only he'd allow a chink in that rock-solid armour of pride and listen to the truth!

'That's what I had in mind.' He closed the space between them. 'Shall we find somewhere to sit?' Reaching round her, he tucked the folded faxes into the back pocket of her jeans. The brush of the backs of his fingers against her buttock sent fragments of fire skittering through her veins, and all she could do was try to ignore them, rein in this helpless, hopeless yearning and follow him blindly, her sandalled feet scuffing the path, until they reached the secret rose-covered arbour, tucked away behind a bank of oleanders.

Her heart tightened in pain. She could understand his need to get well away from the house. He was probably expecting their conversation to get heated, involve raised voices. He wouldn't want Catherine to overhear. But here? Didn't he remember the evenings when they'd chosen to wander down to this lovely secluded place, sitting close together, the scent of roses perfuming the air, sharing a bottle of wine, murmuring words of love, unable to keep their hands off each other?

Or had he wiped those memories from his mind because, like her, they no longer had any meaningful place in his life?

Elena wanted to turn and head straight back for the house, to avoid hurting any more than she already was. But they had to talk, and this was the first time he'd displayed any willingness to properly discuss their situation instead of issuing untenable orders and walking away.

'I want to apologise for the way I behaved today,' she told him breathlessly, getting the words out before her courage deserted her. She sat on the far corner of the bench, knowing before he actually did it that he would sit as far away from her as he could. She knotted her hands in her lap. He wasn't making this easy. 'What I did was childish.'

'Hardly that. You came on to me like a totally adult woman. A woman who wanted sex. Like the woman who would have lapped it up early this morning, even though she knew she was carrying another man's child.'

Elena closed her eyes, locking her jaws together, taking the insult that had been delivered in a cold, hard voice. From where he stood, she deserved that. She leaned her head against the supporting pillar, her voice barely audible. 'It's not as simple as that.' How could she begin to explain the complexities of what she felt?

'No? You surprise me. But don't waste your breath apologising. The damage is done.'

She wasn't going to ask what he meant by that bald statement. She just hoped and prayed he didn't mean he was intending to give her what he believed she'd been practically begging for.

'Talking of sex,' he remarked, almost conversationally, 'and what I have reason to know is your huge appetite for it, I can't understand why you didn't invite me into your bed shortly after we met. Heaven knows, twenty-four hours after meeting you I was besotted. All I could think of was making love to you. We even discussed it,' he said drily. 'Remember? And decided the circumstances weren't right. Sam's death was still very recent. Then you had to come back here to work, because you had a deadline to meet, and I had a lot on my plate back home.

'And the days we both spent back at Netherhaye again, prior to the wedding, were hectic. So, all in all, we decided to wait until our wedding night. So romantic.' His voice levelled out with scorn. 'It would have been a damn sight more practical from your point of view if you'd dragged your willing victim into bed. That way you could have fooled me into thinking the child was mine—due to be born a little prematurely, perhaps, but nothing to get my knickers in a twist about. But perhaps you simply didn't care? After all, I was a poor second choice.'

God, but he hated her! Could love die as quickly and completely as his had, be born again in the guise of implacable, unbending hatred? She balled her hands into fists and pressed her knuckles against her temples, her head falling forwards.

If she told him what had really happened, and he actually believed she was telling the truth, would it make a scrap of difference? She didn't know, but she had to try.

She looked at him with stark appeal, took a shaky breath and told him, 'I want to tell you how Sam's baby was conceived—'

'You think I actually want to hear the sordid details?' His voice was harsh enough to raise goose-bumps on every inch of her skin. He thrust himself to his feet. 'Lady, you are unreal!'

'Jed! Wait!'

But he was already striding back towards the house, finding his way through the narrow, winding paths, and much as she would have liked to stay out here, nursing wounds, she knew she had to follow.

It was almost fully dark now, the only signposts the darker undersides of the crowded plants where they encroached on the edges of the paths. Angry frustration beat through her veins, making her temples throb. It wasn't the fact that she was carrying another man's child that was responsible for this unholy mess, it was his own damned intransigence, his refusal to listen, his uncompromising hostility!

She caught up with him in the kitchen. He was pouring whisky into a tumbler. He had his back to her, and when he turned she could see he was calmer, back in control of himself and his emotions.

Well, bully for him! She wasn't. No way! Flooded with adrenalin, she stared at him, rigid with strain, sea-green eyes clashing with the cool, slightly contemptuous grey of his.

'Instead of trying to bend my ear with the details of your affair with my brother, why don't you tell me something about your first husband?'

'Liam?' Her brows pulled down in a frown. 'Why? You never wanted me to talk about him before.'

'His existence in your life wasn't important when I believed you were perfection on two legs. The past didn't matter—only our present and our future. But now we don't have a future worth the name.' He pulled a chair out from the central table and straddled it, arms leaning across the back-rest, beautifully crafted hands holding his glass loosely. He looked set for an hour or two of relaxed conversation.

Elena knew better. She brushed past him to get to the fridge to pour orange juice, to ease the tense muscles of her parched throat. She wanted to scream and shout, but knew she couldn't risk waking Catherine.

He took a mouthful of whisky. 'Well? Given the drastic alteration in my opinion of you, I'm asking now. You divorced him, you said. Why was that? Didn't he look right? Wasn't he good enough in bed? Rich enough?'

She wanted to toss her juice in his face, but her hands were shaking so badly with reined-in temper she could barely hold the glass. She slid it onto a work surface and Jed lobbed at her. 'Or was it the other way around? Did *he* divorce *you* because he, too, found out you weren't what you seemed?'

She felt her face flare with redoubled anger. Perhaps he wanted to discuss Liam because he couldn't bear to hear about her relationship with Sam. Suddenly she was too enraged to care. And what had possessed her to fall in love with someone so bitter and twisted she would never know!

He wanted a run-down on her relationship with Liam. So she'd give him one. And if it wasn't what he wanted to hear he had only himself to blame. She forced her mouth into a defiant parody of a smile. 'Liam was very good to look at.' Slightly brash, though, she could see now, from her vantage point of maturity, but she wasn't telling Jed that. 'All the girls were crazy about him and Mum thought he was God's gift—and for a woman who's as embittered as she is about the whole male sex, that's some accolade!' Her mouth gave another defiant twist. 'One of my friends threw a birthday party at some fancy club and that's where we met. He swept me off my feet, as the saying goes.'

Because she'd been desperate to be loved. Her parents had given her little of that precious commodity. Her father's job had taken him away a lot, and, in any case, he'd been too busy chasing anything in skirts to have time for his daughter. And her mother had been too busy wallowing in self-pity over the miserable state of her marriage to have time to think of her child's very real needs.

Unconsciously, she placed a hand over her tummy.

Her child wouldn't suffer because of its mother's wrecked marriage!

'And I had no complaints about his performance in bed, either,' she told him toughly. She'd been a virgin when she'd met Liam, so she'd had no experience to draw on. Only when making love with Jed had she discovered the ecstasy, the almost terrifying rapture. But she wouldn't think about that. If she did it would remind her of the love they'd found together, and lost, and she'd start crying again.

She saw his hard mouth twist, and knew she'd pierced the veneer of calm indifference. She ignored it because she couldn't afford to feel any empathy with him and stated bluntly, 'There was plenty of money, too. I kept my job on as a dogsbody in a local newspaper office, and he managed one of the city's betting shops. He drove a fast Japanese car and we spent our evenings in the best clubs. He liked me to look glamorous for him. He spent money like there was a bottomless pit of the stuff. I found out where that pit was when I came down with flu one day and left work early. I discovered his lucrative sideline in criminal activities by chance—he cloned credit cards.' She lifted her chin. 'Believe it, or not, I despise dishonesty. I despised him for the web of deceit he'd spun around me. I left him.'

'Is this true?' Jed demanded, any pretence of indifference sliding away.

'You think I'd make it up?' she asked scornfully. 'I can put grim storylines down on paper, but, whether you like it or not, I'm straightforward in my personal life.' So think on that, she tacked on silently, meeting the sudden brooding gaze with a hard, challenging stare.

'So what did you do?' he asked.

'Do?' She shook her head slowly, a slight frown pulling her brows together. It had been years since she'd thought of any of this, of Liam. She'd put it all behind her and got on with her life. She'd seen what dwelling miserably on the past had done to her mother and had wanted no part of it. 'I went to the police, of course.'

And if that made her sound hard, so be it. By then their marriage had been on the rocks. She'd been sick of the round of nightclubs, fancy restaurants, the fast crowd he belonged to, suspicious of where the stream of money was coming from, worried when he told her he'd hit a lucky gambling streak because luck didn't last.

'Mum was dead against it. She said I should simply leave him and let him get on with it. She said dirt stuck. No one would believe I hadn't been a part of it.'

'And did they?' His eyes probed her, carefully assessing her expression.

Elena lifted her shoulders wearily, reclaiming her glass of juice and swallowing it thirstily. The fire of anger had burned out and now she felt fit for nothing, mentally capitulating beneath the weight of the present situation, which was even more traumatic than the one she'd had to endure all those years ago.

She said flatly, 'After some tough questioning, yes. After the trial I came out to Spain, with little more than the clothes I stood up in—no way would I touch any of the things bought with stolen money—reverted to my maiden name and divorced him when he was two years into his prison sentence.'

It was impossible to tell what he was thinking. They'd been so in love, so close until recently, they'd been able to read each other's minds.

Not now. Not any more.

Only by the merest flicker of those darkly shadowed eyes as they touched her now wilting body did he indicate that he was aware of her presence at all.

He was probably weighing every word she'd said and deciding that her former husband had taken to crime to satisfy her ever increasing demands, that she'd coolly handed him over to the authorities before they caught up with him, foreseeing a humiliating end to the glitzy roller-coaster ride. He'd be grouping himself with Liam as the injured party. He believed that badly of her.

And he confirmed it when he said drily, 'How moral you make yourself sound. But then you're good with words. You have to be, the job you do. But there's one thing even you can't lie about, or gloss over—the fact that you married me in the full knowledge that you could be pregnant by another man.'

Anger blistered her. 'Stop this!' Her hands flew up to her head, as if to hold it on her shoulders before frustrated rage blew it away. 'Listen to yourself! I'm carrying Sam's child—nothing as vague as another man's! Sam's! Why can't you bring yourself to say his name?'

From the odd comments he'd made she was beginning to think she knew. She wasn't sure, but if she was right it would answer a whole heap of questions about his total and absolute refusal to listen to her.

'Because the thought of you and him together infuriates me,' he came back quickly, rawly.

'Infuriates?' She questioned his choice of word sharply. 'Until just now you weren't interested in my first marriage. As far as you were concerned it was unimportant. And you didn't ask if there'd been any other men in my life since my divorce. You appeared not to have a jealous bone in your body.'

Carefully, she kept her voice calm, refusing to believe there was nothing but hatred behind that stony façade, hoping, almost against hope, that she could find a way to get through to him. 'Just as I didn't want, or need, to know who you might have shared a bed with before we met. I believed our future was all that mattered, not what might or might not have happened in the past. I'm sure you felt that way, too.'

He shrugged, impatience highlighting his eyes now. 'I see no point in rehashing this.'

'Probably not,' she conceded, 'but there is one. Ask yourself if you'd have felt so badly—so betrayed,' she granted him, 'if this baby had been an accident, fathered by any other man. Some man, say, I'd had a brief and meaningless affair with before I met you. And then ask yourself why you categorically refuse to let me tell you what really happened between me and Sam.'

'I would have thought that was glaringly obvious.' He spoke drily but there was a frown-line between his eyes now. Was he thinking about what she'd said? Really thinking instead of letting his emotions get in the way of logic?

'This tortured conversation is getting us nowhere.' He put his empty glass down on the drainer, and she knew that if she let him go she would have lost this last opportunity to get through to him. He would never again stand still long enough to have a meaningful discussion about anything.

As he walked to the door she said firmly, 'Sam wasn't my lover. He was my friend, nothing more. I wanted a child; Sam donated the sperm. A completely clinical happening. Check with the clinic in London if you don't believe me!'

He went very still, as if her words had frozen him. And then he turned, slowly. Something like ridicule looked out of his eyes. 'I applaud your inventive imagination. It gets you into the bestseller lists but it won't get you anywhere with me.'

Although the hope of finally getting through to him had been slender almost to the point of invisibility, it hurt like hell now she'd lost it. She pushed past him, out of the room, before he could see the desolation on her face, went to her room and closed the door.

Sleepless hours later she heard him go into the second guest room, and something hard and dark clawed at her heart. Not even for the look of things where Catherine was concerned could he bring himself to share the air she breathed, let alone this bed.

Finally she'd been able to tell him the truth about her baby's conception. But he didn't believe her.

She turned her face to the pillow. It didn't matter. Nothing mattered, did it?

CHAPTER SIX

'CONGRATULATIONS, Elena! What a clever little duck you are!' Catherine cried as Elena ventured out onto the terrace at ten-thirty the next morning. 'Jed's been telling me all about it.'

Elena pushed her hands into the deep pockets of her common or garden cotton skirt and tried to look as if she knew what her mother-in-law was talking about. She'd overslept, woken feeling queasy as usual, and dressed down, dowdily even.

She glanced across the terrace to where Jed was sprawled out on a lounger, yesterday's newspaper over his face to protect it from the fierce rays of the sun, wearing frayed denim shorts and nothing else.

Elena swallowed a constriction in her throat. He had a beautiful body, tanned all over, a smooth, slick skin, not too hairy, and not bulging with muscles, either, but honed and hard, superbly fit.

Almost as if he'd sensed her eyes on him, Jed explained lazily, 'I was telling her about the frantic faxes from your agent about the awards ceremony and your latest book being short-listed.' He plucked the paper from his face and swung his bare feet to the floor, pushing a hand through his hair, making it stick up in soft spikes which invited the touch of her fingers.

Firmly, she pulled her dark glasses from a capacious skirt pocket and put them on. She didn't dare let him look at her eyes because he'd surely see the starkness of unwilling need there. She wouldn't let him know that every time she looked at the man who thought she was a deceitful little liar, totally devoid of morals, her body stirred with that desperate, consuming need. She still had her pride, if little else in the way of self-defence. She'd do her damnedest to hang onto it.

'And as we'll have to return to London to attend, I've booked us on the same flight back as Ma. Luckily there were spare seats.'

Catherine was saying something about enjoying the flight home so much more if she wasn't going to be on her own. Elena wasn't listening properly. She wasn't in the mood to concentrate on the older woman's happy chatter.

He was doing it again, mapping her life out for her, telling her what to do and when to do it, regardless of her feelings, not even asking her what she wanted. No doubt he'd decided she didn't merit that courtesy.

And possibly the worst thing—the almost unbearably frustrating thing—was her complete inability to do anything about it. Not in front of Catherine, anyway.

She swung away, her shoulders tight with tension, walking to the edge of the terrace, feeling the hot Andalucian breeze mould her cotton top to her body, lifting her head to inhale the spiritually healing scent of her garden flowers, the more astringent perfume of mountain herbs.

Life had been so uncomplicated once. She'd had it all—her home in a country she'd come to love for its vibrancy and passion, this spectacular view, a highly successful career. The only thing to mar it had been the growing and savagely compelling need to hold her own child in her arms.

It was ironic that the child that was now growing inside her was the reason for her present ejection from the paradise she'd found in Jed's love.

'Why don't you finalise the details with your agent, darling?' He'd come to stand beside her. He put a hand on her shoulder. His touch branded her. She wanted to swipe his hand away, tell him not to call her darling because he didn't mean it, tell him to stop torturing her!

She turned her head sharply, her breath catching explosively in her throat, her hair flying around her shoulders. His slight warning frown told her *Not in front of Catherine*, but he sounded totally laid back when he added, 'We've only a couple more days here, so Ma and I will get out from under your feet. We'll go and explore the village, potter around, give you time to pack and make arrangements for closing the house up.'

He was giving her a breathing space. That, at least, was something to be grateful for. Somehow she managed to make all the right noises, to smile, even, telling them about another village, further down the valley, where there were the ruins of a castle and a thirteenth-century church, expressing rather vague and insincere regrets that she was unable to accompany them, escaping at last to the privacy of her study, feeling the blessed silence of her home settle around her.

She sat at her desk and sank her head into her hands. She had a few precious hours alone, no need to play-act for Catherine's benefit. Thoughtfully, Jed had given her that time. But probably not for her benefit, she decided with a shuddery sigh. He must have realised the strain she was under and hadn't wanted her to explode in front of his mother and ruin the poor woman's illusions.

And he could escape, too, just for a few hours. Get away from the woman he'd once loved and now regarded with contempt and distrust.

She lifted her head, pushed her hair away from her face with one hand, reached for the phone with the other and began to dial her agent's London number.

Netherhaye was as lovely as Elena remembered it. A sprawling edifice of golden stone, drowsing in the late afternoon sun, the lovely house managed to insert a sharp finger of sadness into her heart. Had her marriage still been strong, beautiful and true, she would have looked forward to their sharing their time between here and Las Rocas.

But she mustn't think like that, she told herself. And made herself concentrate on the housekeeper's effusive greetings. Edith Simms was a fixture, Catherine had told her. Efficient, willing, very likeable—almost part of the family.

She pushed the unwelcome feeling of sadness out of the way. She'd coped well these last few days, but only because she'd known she had to, and the hundred and one things she'd had to do—and a few dozen more that had been pure invention—before she could leave Las Rocas had helped more than anyone would ever know.

But she wouldn't be away from Spain for too long, she assured herself. The only way into the future was to smother all her emotions and go forward, get on with her life. But that would have to wait until after the ceremony.

'I've made the master suite ready for you and Mrs Nolan,' Edith said to Jed, smiling comfortably, convinced she'd done the right thing. Elena wondered what she'd think if she knew the truth, that Jed couldn't bear the sight of his new bride, that the thought of sharing a bedroom with her made him shudder.

'Thank you, Edith.' Jed's features were impassive. 'I'll take the cases up—no need to get your husband in from the gardens. Is he still managing?'

'Oh, yes, very well. It's the winter when his arthritis plays up and makes things difficult. Come the warm weather and he's right as ninepence.'

'Good.' Jed smiled down into the housekeeper's homely face. 'I'll have a word with him about getting a lad in to do the heavier work—and don't worry about him starting to feel old and redundant. I'll make sure he knows he's the gaffer and that we need his valuable experience and know-how.'

'Thank you, Mr Nolan, sir!' Edith breathed, her faded brown eyes like an adoring spaniel's as Jed strode away to fetch the cases from the car. Elena told herself not to go soft and start admiring his understanding and compassion. He'd shown not a scrap where she was concerned.

'And Susan Keele asked you to phone just as soon as you had a moment.' The housekeeper had turned to Catherine, and Catherine's eyes went round and wide, like an excited child's.

'She must have some definite news about the cottage! How wonderful! I'll phone right away. You'll want to speak to her, too, Elena. Let's go through to the little sitting room.'

Of all the many rooms at Netherhaye this was one of Elena's favourites. Comfy armchairs, slightly the worse for wear, were grouped around a stone hearth where apple logs burned brightly in the colder weather. Chunky little oak tables were piled with gardening books and magazines, and Marjory Allingham prints hung on the faded ochre walls, and there was a view of the mysteriously inviting edges of Catherine's water garden from the mullioned window.

'Here—' Catherine held out the receiver. 'It's ringing out. You speak to her first.'

Elena took it and began to explain why she and Jed had returned from Spain much sooner than expected.

'Well, it's nice to be on the short-list, I suppose, but a pity to spoil your honeymoon,' Susan dismissed, not to Elena's very great surprise. Her mother had never been much interested in what her daughter did—apart from her marriages. Susan wanted her settled so she could cross her off her list of things to worry about. Elena shuddered to think what her mother's reaction would be when she learned the truth.

'The sale's going through that end, and I've put this house on the market.' Now she was all enthusiasm, practically buzzing with it. 'I should have made a move years and years ago—got away from bad memories—but I never could seem to be able to face it. I'm really looking forward to sharing that cottage with Catherine. I do admire her. The way she coped with Sam's death made me see that life goes on.'

After five more minutes in the same vein, Elena handed over to Catherine and went to see what Jed had done about their sleeping arrangements, wondering if her mother could be right and Catherine was far stronger than they'd thought.

It was worth thinking about. Maybe they didn't need to pussyfoot around her quite so much. Maybe she could take the news of the breakdown of their marriage without going to pieces.

Maybe she could tell her the truth without feeling too guilty...

She found Jed in the beautifully furnished, elegantly decorated master suite. He was staring out of one of the tall windows and didn't turn, much less greet her when she closed the panelled door behind her. Well, what else had she expected?

She said tonelessly, detachedly pleased she was at last winning the battle with her emotions, pushing them down, grinding them out of sight with a metaphorical heel, 'I can use the room I had when I stayed here before.' And refused to let herself remember how extraordinarily wonderful that time of falling so deeply in love had been.

'No.' Still he didn't turn to face her, seeming to find the view of the gardens and the rolling countryside beyond irresistible. 'Not until Catherine's settled into the cottage. And by then I'll be making myself scarce. I told you I would, remember? Then you can have the whole damned place to yourself!'

She heard the note of angry exasperation but didn't let herself take any pleasure from the fact that she could still provoke some emotion. She told herself she was now completely indifferent. It was over. Over and finished. And because it was it had to be tidied away, put neatly out of sight, and then it could be forgotten.

'I'm sorry, but I won't go along with that,' she told

him in a clear, cool voice. 'You decided we'd play at being the ideal happy couple. I wasn't consulted. So you can play-act on your own, because after that wretched awards ceremony I'm out of here.'

'No.' He did turn then. Abruptly, almost clumsily. She saw the harsh lines of strain on his tough features and refused to betray her hard-won indifference by feeling any compassion for him at all. He had brought it on himself by refusing to believe that there had been nothing more than a clinical arrangement between her and his brother. 'Have you no consideration for Catherine's feelings? And what about the child? Doesn't he or she deserve the care of two parents? I know Sam would have wanted that.'

Pallor spread beneath his tan, and intuitively she knew what it had cost him to mention his brother in this context. She said, more gently than she'd intended, 'I'm sorry, but I can't agree with you on that, either. Sam wouldn't have wanted his child brought up by parents who loathed each other.' She spread her hands in a gesture that said how hopeless the situation was. 'You say we could be polite and pleasant to each other in the company of others. But think about it. Life would become intolerable and the cracks would start to show—Sam wouldn't have wanted us to suffer that way.'

She probed the hard grey eyes, wondering if she was getting through to him. Impossible to tell. He seemed to have blanked off, the earlier flare of emotion under tight control. 'I'm perfectly capable of caring for my child on my own. I don't need support, financial or otherwise. And remember, I'm not a silly little girl; I've been making my own decisions for

many years now. And as for Catherine, I think she
deserves to be told. Not brutally, of course, but gently.
I'm beginning to believe she's stronger than you
think.'

He turned back to his contemplation of the view,
hands thrust into the pockets of his trousers. 'You're
getting good at doing this, aren't you?'

'Doing what?' She didn't understand.

'Saying goodbye and moving on.' Hard shoulders
lifted in a shrug. 'Liam, Sam, me.'

'This is different,' she said quickly, without thinking, her feelings for this man fighting to surface.

'Is it?' It was his turn to display utter, drawling
indifference. 'Now why is that?'

'Because I love you.'

She tried to bite back the words but they'd already
escaped her. Why the purple petunias had she used the
present tense?

Because her emotions were stronger than her will
to control them.

She left the room as quickly and quietly as she
could, knowing that the stand she'd so decisively
made had been fatally undermined by those four un-
thinking words.

She was going to have to try harder. Much, much
harder.

The oak-panelled breakfast room was filled with morning sunlight when Elena walked in, feeling groggy.
Not so much morning sickness but the aftermath of a
hatefully restless night.

Jed had refused to hear of her moving out of the
master suite. He'd pointed her at the huge double bed,

tossed one of the pillows and a light blanket onto the Edwardian chaise longue beneath one of the windows and spent the night there, sleeping like a baby as far as she could tell, while she'd lain in the big lonely bed, stiff as a board, not letting herself toss and turn because he might wake and guess the reason for her restlessness.

And now he was at the breakfast table, finishing off with toast and marmalade, unfairly hunky in a soft white T-shirt and narrow, scuffed black denims.

He laid aside his newspaper and remarked blandly, 'I told Edith you wouldn't want a cooked breakfast. Help yourself to juice and toast—if you're ready for it. Should I ring for fresh coffee?'

She shook her head, sitting opposite him, smoothing out the full skirts of the tan-coloured cotton dress she was wearing, pleating the fabric between her fingers as he filled a glass with orange juice and pushed it towards her with the tip of his finger.

If he was going to act like a polite stranger, pretend nothing had happened to turn lovers into enemies, then she'd go along with it. For now. Frankly, she didn't feel up to fighting, restating her decision to leave him and make a clean break. It would have to wait until she felt better able to handle it. Once the awards ceremony was out of the way she could concentrate on organising the rest of her life.

He'd picked up his paper again, but after a few minutes of intolerable silence, when the only sound appeared to be the bumping of her heart against her ribcage, he lowered it and told her, 'Catherine's taken herself down to the cottage. Apparently the Fletchers moved out a couple of days ago. Contracts won't be exchanged for another six weeks or so, but she couldn't wait to look round the garden and make plans for transforming it.'

Six weeks of pretending to be the ecstatic new bride, then Lord knew how much longer staying meekly here, playing the role of the understanding wife, while he made himself scarce, immersed himself in business.

That was his decision. It wasn't, and never could be, hers. Her stomach lurched, an uneasy prelude to ejecting the few sips of juice she'd swallowed. She pushed the glass away.

'I'll be in the garden if you want me.' He folded the paper and put it to one side, his tone telling her he knew she wouldn't. 'I'll be helping Simms trim the yew hedges and breaking the news that he's to have permanent help.' He stood up, looked at his watch. 'I suggest you register with the local GP. Edith will let you have the surgery's number. Make an appointment to have a check-up. It's past time you did.'

And he left the room.

She hadn't said a word, Elena realised as deep silence settled around her. Not a single one. Was this how Jed saw their future? He dictating, she accepting, turning into a mouse?

Pushing herself to her feet, she knew she couldn't let that happen. She went to find Edith.

Two hours later she followed the sound of the electric hedge-cutter and found Jed on a step-ladder, neatening off the top of the ten-foot high ancient yew hedges that surrounded Catherine's formal rose garden.

Simms said, 'Nice to see you again, Mrs Nolan—

grand day isn't it?' He smiled at her and wheeled a barrow of trimmings away, and Jed came down the steps, switching off the noisy implement, a slight frown lowering his straight black brows.

He looked gorgeous. All man and touchable. Very, very touchable. Heat, hard work, sweat and hedge-dust had left smudges on his face, rumpled up his hair and created damp and grubby patches on his old T-shirt.

Elena swallowed convulsively but kept her head high, her face serene. And of course he was looking puzzled, wondering why she was so glossy, so packaged.

She'd arranged her pale hair at the nape of her neck, in a smooth, cool style, fixed tiny gold studs into the lobes of her ears and was wearing a suit he hadn't seen before—straw-coloured linen, with a short-sleeved, nipped-waist, collarless jacket over a straight skirt that ended two inches above her knees—and plain, slightly darker-toned high heels.

She said, as if reciting from a list, 'I've registered with Greenway and I've arranged for a check-up in four days' time.' The morning of the awards ceremony. And before he could give her a verbal pat on the head for being a good girl and doing as she'd been told, she said, in the same breath, 'Edith said it was all right for me to borrow the Astra. So I'll head for London now. I managed to get a room at my usual hotel—a lucky late cancellation—and I'll see you back here in three days' time.'

She heard him pull in his breath as she turned to go, and a second later his voice made her pause. 'Running away, Elena?'

She swung back. Never let it be said she hadn't the

courage to look him in the eye. 'No. Shopping. I'd like something extra special to wear for the ceremony. You never know, I might win. And if I don't, I'll want to go down with all flags flying. Besides—' she did what he'd done to her at breakfast: looked pointedly at her watch, and wondered if he felt as she had done—surplus to requirements '—I need to see my editor and my agent. I'm sure you can square my flit with Catherine. She at least understands that I have a life.' She lobbed him a flinty smile. 'You should be grateful. I'm sparing you my noxious company for three whole days. And nights.'

She turned again and walked down the path. Her spine was as straight as it could possibly go, but, boy, was it tingling! She half expected him to bounce up behind her and grab her, lock her in the attic, if that was what it took, and keep her there until a situation arose that demanded she be brought out and paraded— a new bride doll with a painted smile and a puppet master to pull her strings.

But he did no such thing. Of course he didn't. He let her go.

The hotel she always used when she flew into London to see her publisher was comfortable and unpretentious. It suited her. Or had done.

Tonight she couldn't settle. Jed haunted her mind and filled her heart. Memories of the good times, those special, wonderful, loving times, kept coming back, resurfacing seconds after she'd thought she'd pushed them back into oblivion. The bad times, too, were ever present, tormenting her.

Since arriving she'd made an appointment to meet

with her editor tomorrow, and another to have lunch with her agent the day after that. The rest of the time would be spent shopping for that perfect dress, shoes to wear with it, maybe a new perfume.

She'd get her hair trimmed. And what about a facial? Manicure? Browse through the bookshops. Why not? Anything to fill the hours, occupy her mind.

But the nights—what was she to do about the nights? She frowned at the television set, talking to itself in a corner of the room, picked up the remote control and zapped it off. She took herself to bed and tried to read, but the words didn't make any sense at all.

She had shown Jed that she had a mind of her own, that she wasn't prepared to dance to his mournful tune, live a lie into the foreseeable future. She'd made her stand and escaped an intolerable situation.

This trip to London hadn't been about buying new clothes, it had been about escape. But she could never escape, no matter how far she ran, not while he was still firmly in her heart.

CHAPTER SEVEN

ELENA fixed the diamond ear-studs with steady fingers. Set in ornate, chunky gold, they matched the bracelet around her slender wrist. Jed's wedding gift to her. She'd leave these lovely things behind at Netherhaye when all this was over. She had only decided to wear them tonight because they were the perfect complement to her dress.

She stood back, looking at her reflection in the full-length mirror. She'd do. No ballooning bulge in the tummy region yet, although during her check-up Greenway had assured her it wouldn't be long before it appeared!

But for now the champagne-coloured satin sheath lovingly caressed every softly rounded curve. Ending a few inches above her knees, it made her look very leggy, and the deeply scooped top, suspended only by the thinnest of shoestring straps, made her breasts look fuller than they were. Or maybe that was down to her condition?

She'd left her hair loose tonight, a shimmering golden sweep curving down to her shoulders, and for once her make-up couldn't be faulted. She looked, she decided dispassionately, like a sophisticated, sexy, mature professional woman. It was the look she had deliberately set out to achieve.

And, thankfully, not a butterfly in sight.

Jed was to accompany her to the awards ceremony.

Even she had had to admit that it would look odd if
he didn't. There'd been a few qualms, though, when
he'd told her that he'd booked a suite for the night in
the up-market hotel where the ceremony was to be
held, but he'd told her glacially, 'I don't suppose
you'd want to travel up to town in your glad rags, or
face the drive back in the small hours. The suite has
two bedrooms and a sitting room, so we should be
able to share it without coming to blows.'

So she'd handle being here with him without the
buffer of Catherine's company and Edith's to-ings and
fro-ings. She felt calm enough right now to be sure of
that.

His perfunctory tap on the door of her bedroom told
her it was time to go. She pushed her feet into pale
bronze-coloured high heels and straightened her shoulders. She wasn't looking forward to this evening, but
she'd grit her teeth and get through it in style.

He was ready and waiting in the ultra-modern, elegantly furnished but impersonal sitting room, and as
his eyes swept over her body then back to her face
she saw his hard jaw tighten.

'You look very beautiful, Elena.'

'Thank you.' She took the clipped compliment as
calmly as she could. He was simply being polite. And
she could have said the same of him, but she'd bite
her tongue out before she'd repay the compliment.

He looked better than good whatever he wore, but
in his black dinner suit he looked spectacular.
Sizzlingly handsome yet challengingly remote. He
could shatter her senses but she wouldn't let him.

Deftly, she swept up her evening purse from the
side table where she'd left it earlier. She caught the

glimmer of gold from her wide wedding band and misery welled up inside her.

For a moment it swamped her, but she resolutely stamped it down. And then Jed said, in a rough, tough voice she barely recognised, 'Believe it or not, whichever way it goes tonight, I'm proud of your achievements.'

Dipping her head in brief acknowledgement, she blinked furiously. It would be easier on her if he kept his mouth shut. She didn't want his compliments or his praise. In this hateful situation they hurt far too much.

And she would not cry! Wouldn't let herself be that weak! He certainly knew how to get to her, twist the knife and bring her pain. Though, to give him his due, he probably hadn't meant to.

He didn't realise how much he could hurt her, how desperately she wanted things to be as they had been, or how desperately she was trying not to want it.

She bit her lip as she preceded him into the lift. And Jed chided gently, 'Do that much longer and you won't have any lipstick left.' He took her hand as the lift settled to a well-bred halt and the doors slid open. 'There's no need to be nervous. I'm rooting for you— whatever the panel of judges have decided. I admit I don't read the genre, but I *have* read your work, and for my money I fail to see how anyone else can come near you!'

If things had been different she'd have squeezed his hand, smiled up into his eyes and told him he was biased. And kissed him for his kindness.

As it was her fingers lay coldly within his, any reply she might have made stuck in her throat. He had only taken her hand because they were now on public show and the pretence had to go on.

She wasn't nervous about tonight, but he thought she was and so had put his negative feelings for her behind him, trying to make her feel better, calm her down. But he was only making it worse, reminding her that at heart he was a good man, caring and com-passionate.

She had lost all that, and the loss was once again sharpening its claws on her heart. She was finding it impossible to bear.

But tonight—whichever way the award went—she was on show. She couldn't turn tail and head back to her room, no matter how desperately she wanted to do just that. She couldn't let him down. The effort of getting through the evening was probably the last thing she would ever be able to do for him.

'You look a star!' Trish, her agent, cried excitedly.

Paula, her more down-to-earth editor, stated, 'Don't worry about the competition, El. None of them hold a candle, I promise.'

'That's exactly what I've been telling her!' Jed slipped an arm around her waist and tugged her against his side.

Elena wanted to scream. Didn't he know what he was doing to her? No, of course he didn't. He thought he was giving her reassurance, and the way he was holding her was nothing but playing to the gallery.

Straightening out her brain, she made the introduc-tions, noticed the way the two women—and every other woman in the room—ate him up with their eyes, and wondered again how he could ever believe he could come second-best to any man.

A lavish, pre-ceremony dinner was to be served in this glittering room, and the four of them were sharing a table. The food, so everyone said, was superb, and there seemed to be an endless supply of champagne. And Jed was being ultra-supportive, acting the part of the adoring husband, making her insides quiver with longing for the impossible, making it impossible for her to eat a thing.

'I think, under the circumstances, one small glass of champagne would be permissible,' he said softly, while their dinner companions had their heads together discussing publishing trends. He poured for her, and put the cool stem of the glass between her fingers.

She didn't want it. She'd stuck to spring water all evening, and wasn't in a champagne mood in any case. He probably thought she needed the Dutch courage, because all attention was beginning to turn to the small raised dais where the guest speaker was taking up his place to present the awards.

Elena didn't listen to a word. At any other time during her writing career she would have been ecstatic to have had a work of hers short-listed for the prestigious Golden Gargoyle Award, given for the best horror novel published in the preceding year.

Now it seemed monumentally unimportant. She had only agreed to attend tonight because to have stayed away would have been a snub. In the future she would need her career. She was determined that her fatherless child would have every possible advantage.

Tumultuous applause forced her into an awareness that the evening was coming to its end, at least as far as the awards were concerned. And then Jed put his hands on either side of her waist and helped her to her feet. Smiling into her bemused eyes, he murmured, 'Congratulations! Go get it, sweetheart. I hope you rehearsed your speech!'

Only then did it sink in that *At the Rising of the Moon* had won her the coveted award. Walking towards the dais, she wondered why she couldn't feel even the tiniest flicker of elation, the smallest smidgen of professional pride. And then she told herself she knew damn well why she didn't, and hoped to goodness the bleak knowledge didn't show in her face. Professional achievement was nothing compared to Jed's love.

She had one, but she had lost the other.

Somehow she managed to smile and say a few words. Weaving her way back through the body of the room, she was waylaid by people who wanted to congratulate her so often she was beginning to think she'd never make it back to their table before breakfast!

When she finally made it Jed was waiting, watching her with pride. She had to admit it looked genuine, but then he'd been putting on a remarkably polished performance all evening.

Trisha and Paula gave her enormous hugs, and Paula said, 'Trish and I are now going to circulate—give you two some time on your own. You are still on your honeymoon, after all!'

They melted away, glasses firmly in hand, and Jed said tonelessly, 'Shall we do the rounds? I'm sure there are still people who'd like to congratulate you.'

Mutely, Elena shook her head. She wanted out. Wanted the whole charade over and done with. Tears suddenly misted her eyes. She stared down at the glittering trophy clasped in her hands so that he wouldn't see how emotional she had suddenly and infuriatingly become.

There had been times, just recently, when she'd believed she had come to terms with losing this man. This wasn't one of them. The evening had taken its toll, and heaven only knew what would happen if they stayed on, proud, adoring husband, ecstatically happy wife, on display for public consumption. She'd probably go to pieces and make an utter fool of herself. She'd had as much of this cruel fantasy as she could take.

'I'd rather go to bed,' she confessed wearily, not meeting his eyes. 'Pull the sheets over my head and wake up feeling halfway normal.'

'Fine.' He put a hand under her elbow and led her from the room. He'd sounded drained, too.

They rode the lift in silence, the tension almost strident as they entered the suite. The distance across the pale sage-green carpeting to her bedroom suddenly seemed immense. Elena didn't know if her shaky legs would carry her that far. Lack of food, she supposed, and thrust her fingers through her hair.

The trophy fell to the floor and bounced on the carpet, and Jed turned, frowning darkly. 'Are you all right?'

The last thing she wanted was him fussing over her, pretending to care. There'd been enough pretence this evening to last her several lifetimes.

She looked at him through tangled dark lashes, her lids too heavy to open wide, and tried to tell him she was fine. But she couldn't get the words out. She swallowed hard, then moistened her glossy lips to see if that would help, and watched him watch the convul-

sive movement of her throat, then lift narrowed eyes
to her mouth and fasten them on her own.

She saw the slow burn begin deep in the smoky
irises and drew in her breath sharply, totally and sting-
ingly aware of him, of this silent seclusion. He wanted
her. It was there in his eyes, in the tightness of the
line of his mouth. He wanted her and she needed
him...

'Get to bed,' he said roughly. 'You look done in.'
He turned, retrieved the trophy and put it down on a
coffee table. Elena swayed on her feet.

The split second of danger was over. He'd success-
fully fought it off. But she could still feel the dark
sting of it pulsing through her veins. All the wanting,
all the need, had practically solidified into something
she could reach out and touch. Emotion powered
through her as she faced the acres of carpet, the bedroom door that seemed to shimmer and shift, recede
even further into the distance.

She swayed dizzily, and strong hands grasped her
shoulders, steadying her, holding her. 'You're ill?' he
demanded, using one hand to lift her chin and read
the truth in her eyes.

'No,' she whispered threadily, deploring the weak
rush of tears to her eyes, the way her lips parted helplessly as he gently brushed the moisture away with the
ball of his thumb.

'Don't! I can't bear to see you cry,' he said rawly.
'Tonight you looked so beautiful, so assured. I want
you to stay that way. Believe it or not, I don't want
you to be unhappy.' He folded his arms around her,
holding her just a little away from him, as if he wanted
to make sure that their bodies didn't actually touch. 'I

thought I did, but now I know I can't hate you that much.'

A primitive spurt of anger made her pull in a ragged breath. She felt humiliated. His emotions where she was concerned weren't powerful enough to even let him hate her properly! Had his former so-called love for her been similarly lukewarm? Was that the reason he'd been able to shut her out of his heart so damned easily? Had refusing to believe the truth about her baby's conception been the easy way out for him?

She felt weak and shaken, but she balled her hands into fists and pushed feebly at his chest. He ignored her childishly ineffectual blows and scooped her up off her feet. 'You're physically and emotionally exhausted,' he told her in a matter-of-fact near monotone as he carried her towards the door to her bedroom. 'I'll see you into bed and ask Room Service for warm milk and toast. That should help you sleep. You were far too hyped up to eat anything at dinner.'

She didn't want his spurious kindness, his warm milk, or his dratted attention to what he would see as his precious duty! She wanted... She needed...

A fierce rush of adrenalin pushed all caution to the winds. She squirmed hectically against him, struggling to get back on her own two feet, shrieking, 'Let go of me! Stop being such an odious holier than thou, pompous, prattish little gentleman!'

She squirmed more furiously, wriggling and pushing against him, her narrow skirt riding high on her thighs, her face scarlet with temper, outrage and frustration, her breath coming in short, sharp gasps, unaware until it was too late—far too late—of the fine tremors that shook his lean, hard frame, of the dangerous glitter of fiery intent in eyes that were suddenly narrowed, black with savage emotion.

'I can be as ungentlemanly as you like, sweetheart, believe me!'

His hands tightened on her body as he shouldered open the bedroom door and strode to the bed. He tumbled her onto the covers, one hand fastening her wrists together above her head, his darkly glittering eyes making a quick inventory of her body, sweeping up the length of her silk panty-hose-clad legs to the scrumple of champagne satin around her hips and on to the rapid rise and fall of her breasts, their swollen peaks thrusting against the slithery satin that barely contained them now.

And back down again, more slowly. Much more slowly. Caressing her. Elena shuddered helplessly as desire made a pool of liquid heat inside her. She stopped breathing as she followed the journey his eyes were making, her flesh quivering in mindless anticipation because each slow stroke of his eyes was like the physical touch of his lean, sensual fingers.

She could feel the tension in him, almost feel the tremors that shook his taut frame, smell the raw, hot male scent of him. Slowly he released her wrists, and her body conquered what was left of her mind and moved luxuriously, sensuously, beneath the burning drift of his eyes, drugged eyes, that swept slowly up to lock with hers.

'Yes,' he said softly. 'Now.' He removed his jacket and tossed it carelessly aside, ripping away his shirt to reveal muscles clenched with need, a need that raged tempestuously through her, too. A need she understood, found impossible to deny, a need she answered as she lifted her arms to him in silent invitation.

With boneless grace he joined her, taking her hands and winding them around his neck, groaning deeply as her fingers stroked his nape. Lovingly, they feathered down his throat, down to the hectic pulse-beat at the base.

She loved him, always would. Her body craved him with a hunger that was out of control. With a tiny mew of rapture she wriggled closer, pressing her breasts against his naked chest, feeling the race of his heartbeats as he slid one tiny strap away from her shoulder and then the other.

Yes! She needed skin to skin, flesh to burning flesh. And, as ever, he knew what she wanted because that was what he wanted, too.

He closed the tiny gap between their mouths and she opened for him, inviting the raging hunger of his kiss, shuddering all over. Her fingers were digging into his back as he slid a hand up the length of her thigh and tugged impatiently at the waist of her panty-hose, sliding the silk away from her body, his breath catching as his touch revealed she was wearing nothing else beneath her dress.

She hadn't dressed for seduction. The lines of a bra and panties showing beneath the clinging satin would have spoiled the svelte impression. Yet seduction was happening here, she thought muzzily. But who was seducing whom?

It didn't matter. Nothing mattered now but this, this togetherness. He reached behind her to find the concealed zipper of her dress, turned her over and stripped the fabric from her heated body.

She endured the slow stroke of his hands as they moulded her from her shoulders down to her thighs for as long as she could bear the deliriously rising excitement inside her, then turned with a sign of frustrated need, arching her body into his.

He kissed her slowly, her mouth, her eyelids, the hollow of her neck, taking his time, making her take hers, just as he had done so many times before, not rushing things in spite of the urgency of his body's response.

A wild coupling to assuage an urgent need had never been his way with her. He was finding the most circuitous route to heaven, making sure the arrival would be as sublime for her as it was for him, just as he had done in the days when he had loved her.

'Sweetheart,' he murmured throatily as he lifted his head from her breasts, his eyes hazed with desire. 'This is so unbelievable. What you do to me...'

Even the words were the same, almost incoherent endearments, words that told her of the depth of his love. Only this wasn't love.

A tiny icy shiver froze her veins. It congealed her blood, shocked her into recognition of what was actually happening here.

She still loved him, couldn't stop no matter how she tried. Physically and emotionally she would always be his. But he hated her—not enough to wish her harm, he'd said—but implacably, eternally.

This, this happening, was simply sex. Perhaps, right now, he believed they could use each other and survive the encounter unscathed.

But she knew differently. Tonight, for all sorts of reasons, she'd pushed him beyond endurance. Lots of men lost sight of their scruples as soon as they dropped their trousers. But not Jed. He would despise himself. And she would despise *herself* for letting it happen, actively encouraging him.

They would despise each other and fatally spoil the memories that were left of how they had loved each other once.

As his fingers found the sweet moistness that told him she was more than ready for him she knew she had to stop this, for both their sakes.

Wriggling away from him was the hardest thing she'd ever do, but she had to do it. Pushing herself back against the heaped pillows, reaching for her discarded dress, she held the satin against her breasts and lied recklessly, 'If you want sex, just go ahead. I won't stop you. But I'm warning you, there'll be a difference. You see, I don't love you any more. How can I love a man who thinks I'm a liar? It will be just like scratching an itch.'

Being cruel to be kind just wasn't in it, she conceded bleakly as she watched his features display at first blank incredulity, followed by black anger, then cold contempt.

And then he swung himself to his feet, and she watched him walk away and ached to call him back, retract those hateful, hateful words, and pushed her knuckles against her teeth to stop the anguished cry escaping.

CHAPTER EIGHT

GETTING out of bed the following morning took a monumental effort of will. After what had happened last night Elena didn't know how she was going to face Jed; she only knew she had to.

They couldn't go on like this. Somehow she had to make him understand that she couldn't and wouldn't play her part in the painful charade he had so arbitrarily decided on, and this morning, before they set out for Netherhaye, was the perfect opportunity.

She dressed in the cotton trousers and top she'd travelled down in, stuffed the award trophy and the satin designer gown any old how into her overnight bag, and forced herself to walk through into the sitting room.

Jed was bent over the table beneath the window, clipping sheets of paper together. Her eyes flicked to the briefcase propped against the table-leg. He must have fetched it in from the car. Very early this morning, or late last night? Hadn't he been able to sleep, either?

She loved him so much, her heart felt as if it would burst with the aching pressure of it. And there could be no relief from the awful pain. Her love for him had to be her sad secret.

'There's breakfast if you want it,' he said coolly, pushing the papers into the briefcase and snapping it shut. 'Help yourself.'

Striving for a semblance of normality, she walked over to the heated trolley. Beneath the covered dishes Room Service had provided enough to feed a small army. From the untouched state of everything, Jed obviously wasn't hungry.

Neither was she.

He turned to face her then. Dressed in narrow dark grey trousers, crisp white shirt and a sober blue silk tie, he looked remote and totally unreachable. His face could have been carved from stone, his mouth compressed in a hard, tight line.

She had never seen him look so drained, so utterly world-weary. She upturned the two cups briskly and poured coffee for them both. He needed something.

But he accepted the china cup and saucer with a slight frown, as if he wasn't too sure what it was, put it down on the table-top and told her, 'I'll go down and settle the bill, then I'll pick up a cab on the street. The suite's yours until midday, and be sure you eat something before you drive back to Netherhaye. You're happy about handling the Jag?'

And if she said she wasn't, would that make any difference to the plans he'd obviously made? She wouldn't put bets on it. She put her own untouched coffee back on the trolley. Ignoring his question, she asked, 'Where are you going?'

'Head office. I'll put in a few days' work and stay at my club.'

He dropped a set of car keys on the table and glanced at his watch. He was leaving. He couldn't wait to get away from her. Was he remembering what she'd said last night? Was he disgusted with himself for allowing things to get that far? The gulf between herself and the man she knew she would always love had never seemed so wide.

She couldn't let him walk away like this. They had to talk, discuss the situation properly. The problem of their ruined marriage and far from happy future had to be resolved. They couldn't continue in this painful limbo.

'Do you think that's wise?'

He gave her a bored look.

'What will Catherine think when I return from my glitzy night of triumph on my own and tell her you've cut our supposed honeymoon short so you can get back to work? She'll expect to see us together, looking deliriously happy, you know she will. It was your idea to keep her fooled.'

That did get his attention. She saw his straight brows pull down in a frown and knew he'd registered the implications of what she'd said. She picked up her cup and carried it over to one of the white leather-upholstered armchairs.

'You didn't find your own bunking off a problem,' he reminded her tersely.

'That was entirely different. Even you must see that.' She crossed her long legs at the ankles, took a sip of coffee and tried to keep calm. His bag was already packed, she noticed, ready and waiting by the main door to the suite. 'She's a woman. She knew how important it was—shopping for the perfect dress. She couldn't wait to see every last purchase I'd made. She won't see your ''bunking off'' in quite the same light.'

'Then what do you suggest?' he snapped through his teeth, and pushed his hands into his trouser pockets, his feet planted apart. He looked about as moveable as a mountain, and she narrowed her eyes at him. Why did she love him so very much? He was arrogant, intransigent, stubborn…!

'Nothing at all.' Elena held his coldly bitter eyes. 'I'm not suggesting anything, just demonstrating how impossible this situation is. For both of us. You made a stupid decision and forced it on me. There's no way we can play happy couples for Catherine's benefit and still stay sane.'

He seemed to be weighing up her words. Long seconds passed before he spoke, and then he said slowly, almost silkily, 'You appeared to be happy enough with my proud, adoring husband act yesterday evening, in front of all those people.'

Elena closed her eyes briefly as that taunt sank in. She knew he'd been putting on an act, of course she did, so why did his admission that he was neither proud nor adoring hurt this badly?

Because she was a fool! A fool for hoping in her heart of hearts that he might still feel something for her, just a small echo of his former love.

'And ecstatic, I would imagine,' he went on coldly, 'to discover you could still bring me to my knees with wanting you.'

He gave her a hard look as her face crawled with colour. 'Don't fret about it. I deserved the lesson. I should have known better. A few days ago you "let slip"—' his mouth curled derisively '—that you still loved me. At the time I wondered what your twisted mind was plotting. I stopped believing in your love when I learned of your pregnancy. And last night you let me have the truth right between the eyes. You don't love me, and you never did.' He shot another impatient look at his watch. 'I have to go. And before you start accusing me of cowardice, I do have an important meeting in half an hour.'

At her quick frown he drawled, 'Check with my secretary if you don't believe me. I phoned in yesterday afternoon and heard that a gem dealer from Amsterdam is in town. I got her to set up a meeting. A deal with him, provided the terms are right, would be important enough to convince even Catherine that I needed to break into my wonderful honeymoon. I'll get in touch with Simms and he can pick me up when I'm ready to go back to Netherhaye.'

He was already at the door, on his way, but he told her in the same breath, 'As you appear to be—amazingly—worried about living a lie, I'll give you something to think about. I refuse to lie to Catherine about the true parentage of her coming grandchild. Sam was her whole world, so she'll be delighted to know she'll be able to hold his child one day. So who's going to break the news? And how do we square that within the framework of our blissful marriage? Because that is what it will appear to be on the surface—not for your sake, and God knows not for mine. But for hers, and the child's.'

He looked at her with withering scorn. 'A tough one, isn't it? I think I'll leave it all to you. With your devious mind you should be able to come up with something to convince her!'

She'd had enough—taken too much! She knew her pregnancy had hurt him, and her heart bled for him. But, dammit, he wouldn't believe her side of the story—just closed his mind to everything but hatred!

Colour flamed on her face, and he was part-way out

of the door when she grated at him, 'I'll tell her the truth. It will be a relief to speak to someone who'll do me the courtesy of really listening and believing me, because you darn well won't. If you had ever loved me you would!'

And she fled into her room, locking the door, flinging herself face-down on the bed, taking her rage, frustration and pain out on the pillows. She heard him knocking but shrieked at him to go away, and eventually he must have done, because when she finally pulled herself together the suite was achingly silent.

Drained of all emotion now, she sluiced her face in the bathroom and tied back her hair. She looked at herself in the mirror and saw defeat.

He had the truth, but he couldn't or wouldn't believe it. Her pregnancy meant he didn't want to.

Quickly, before she could sink herself in a mire of misery, she checked her room. Time to go.

She wasn't looking forward to the drive. City streets were a nightmare, the roads out of town would probably be crowded, and she'd never driven anything so powerful as that Jaguar.

And the thought of having to act all bright-eyed and bushy-tailed for her mother-in-law's benefit when she finally made it back to Netherhaye made her feel positively ill.

Her mouth firmed. She had to get a grip. Stop being such a wimp. It wasn't like her to get hysterical, throw childish tantrums, lose all her backbone. She thought of Jed, sitting in that meeting, negotiating yet another dazzling deal, putting her out of his mind quite easily because why think about his devious tramp of a wife when he didn't actually have to?

It helped. If he could block her out and get on with his life then she could do the same.

Picking up her bag, she went through to the sitting room to collect the car keys, and Jed, sprawled out in one of the armchairs, drawled, 'Tantrum over?'

Elena felt as if she was coming unstitched. Just when she thought she'd got herself together again, he popped up and undid all her work. She swallowed thickly. 'You'll be late for your precious meeting.'

'I've rescheduled it for this evening—a working dinner.' He shrugged impressively broad shoulders and hauled himself to his feet. He took her overnight bag and told her, 'I never knew you could get hysterical if you didn't get your own way. One of the joys of being newly wed? Learning something different about one's partner every day?'

She hated it when he was sarcastic. It made her hurt so badly she couldn't think of a snappy come-back, and simply stared at him when he said, 'I'll take you home, then drive back in for that meeting. Shall we go?'

'There's no need. I'm—'

'The state you're in, do you think I'd have a moment's peace if you were behind the wheel of a potentially lethal weapon?'

He held the door open for her and all she could do was follow. She'd been perfectly capable of driving—if not exactly looking forward to the city traffic—before he'd popped up where she hadn't expected him to be and ruined everything.

She didn't suppose he'd altered his arrangement out of concern for her well-being. He wouldn't have a moment's peace if he thought she was likely to put a dent in his prestigious car!

As he held the passenger door open for her five minutes later he gave her a narrow-eyed stare. 'When we've cleared the traffic you can tell me more about this story you've concocted to convince Catherine that you and I can live happily ever after, despite the little hiccup of your being pregnant with my brother's child. Fasten your seat belt.'

He closed the door and paced round the front of the gleaming silver car. She closed her eyes defeatedly.

Of course he didn't believe her. Had she really expected he would? There was too much going on inside his head as far as Sam was concerned to let him accept the truth.

The silence between them was intense, building up to scary proportions as the sleek car edged forward in the inevitable traffic snarl-ups. Jed's long fingers drummed impotently on the steering wheel, his profile grim. Despite the warmth of the early summer day Elena shivered. She couldn't wait until they got out of this and hit the open road. Maybe then this twisting tension would ease off just a little, allow her racing heartbeats to settle down.

But when they did she wished they hadn't, because he said, 'Congratulations. When you came up with this fairy tale—nothing between you and Sam but a clinical procedure—I thought it was to placate me. But it wasn't, was it? It was a way of getting Catherine on your side. Our marriage ends in divorce—which is what you want—you come out of it smelling of roses and I'm the big, bad ogre. Bully for you! Who else but you could have come up with such a story? It's too incredible not to be believed.'

'Except by you, of course,' she said through her teeth, staring out of the window at her side, uninterestedly watching the stockbroker belt slip by.

'Of course,' he concurred, uncharacteristically slowing down a touch to keep within the speed limit. Elena gave a mental shrug. She had expected him to really put his foot down, deliver her back to Netherhaye in record time, not prolong the agony of being cocooned here together, physically close but mentally and emotionally at opposite ends of the galaxy.

'Whether you believe it or not, it's the truth,' she told him bitterly.

Jed gave a derisive snort. 'Lady, you slay me! Do you actually believe I'm green enough to fall for such an unlikely story? For starters,' he bit out, when her only answer was a weary shrug, 'if it had been the truth you'd have told me about it.'

Stung into speech by the unfairness of that, she retorted, 'I tried to, remember? Several times. You flatly refused to listen. Then, when you had no option but to listen, you decided I was telling lies. You decided Sam and I had been having an affair and I'd married you knowing I was carrying his child.'

'I mean *before* we married. You didn't think to warn me we might be expecting the patter of tiny feet rather sooner than I might have expected.'

She let her head sag back against the smooth leather upholstery. She felt too wretched to speak. And what was the point in telling him anything? He would only accuse her of lying, whatever she said.

'Well?' he prompted coolly. 'I do need to know, if

you intend to spin this yarn for Catherine. We need to get our stories straight.'

Elena's stomach knotted painfully. How could something that had been so beautiful have come to this? The death of love was a terrible, terrible thing. Couldn't he see what tying them together with lies created for public consumption would do to them?

Outside the car the rolling countryside shimmered in the early summer heat; inside the air-conditioning made her shiver—or perhaps it was the icy wash of his voice. 'If anyone asks I take it you intend to say I was fully aware of the situation all along? The truth—that I was completely in the dark until circumstances forced you to come clean—would point to a certain lack of common decency on your part.'

'Accuse me of anything you like,' she said thickly, pain tearing through her, 'but not a lack of decency.'

She had made her decision not to tell him of what she and Sam had arranged until Jed had done his grieving for his brother. It might have been the wrong decision, but it had been made with the best of intentions.

She turned wretched eyes in his direction, then quickly looked away. The grim contempt on his hard profile was unbearable. 'On the day of Sam's funeral I started what I thought was a period and truly believed the treatment hadn't worked,' she whispered threadily. 'Somehow, it made the sadness even worse. Over the years of our friendship he and I discussed many things—marriage and children amongst them. I longed for a child,' she confessed. 'But I'd had one taste of marriage and didn't want a second. Sam said he wouldn't marry because of the nature of his work, but he regretted not having a child because he believed that having a child was the only claim to immortality the human race could hope for.'

Talking about it now, she couldn't hold the words back. They tumbled over each other, urgent, low, probably too low for him to hear everything she said. That wasn't really important now, because he wouldn't believe her in any case, but verbalising her memories gave her a tiny measure of reassurance.

'We decided, for our own separate reasons, to try to make a baby. Sam had a friend in London—head of a private clinic—and pulled in a favour. But, like I said, I thought the treatment hadn't worked. Looking at his grave that day, I knew he'd lost his claim to immortality, as he'd seen it. It added a heavier burden of sadness. I wasn't prepared to put that on you at that time. I truly thought it best to wait.'

She leaned her head sideways on the back of the seat, staring through the window. Jed's silence was like a heavy weight. Had he heard what she'd said? Was he sifting through it, looking for something he could use to prove she lied? Or did he consider the whole unlikely story unworthy of comment?

The latter, most probably, she decided with a wretchedly miserable mental shrug. There seemed no point in asking him. She was too emotionally drained to counter any further scornful accusations.

Another fifteen minutes would see them back at Netherhaye. Would the gods be kind? Would Catherine be in the cottage garden, making plans to transform it when she and Susan took up residence? Or would she be home, waiting to hear every last detail of last night's ceremony, fully expecting her to be bubbling with happiness and excitement?

The thought of being plunged into pretending life was a ball, without a breathing space to get herself together, drained her already meagre supply of energy.

To take her mind off the prospect, and Jed's continuing telling silence, she forced herself to concentrate on the passing scenery.

The lanes were narrower now, the verges a tangle of Queen Anne's Lace, wild roses and honeysuckle, the overhanging trees heavy with new leaf. And every time her eyes dropped to the wing mirror she saw the dusty blue Escort that she was sure she'd seen close behind them way back in the city streets.

It was unlikely to be the same car, of course. That make was very common. But watching it, sometimes left behind as the Jaguar swept round a bend, sometimes coming up close, then dropping back to a safe distance, gave her something other than misery to occupy her mind.

When the Jaguar turned off into Netherhaye's long, tree-lined drive the blue car went straight on towards the village, and all Elena's dread of having to face Catherine and pretend came flooding back. But Jed cut the engine well before the house came into sight.

He turned to her in the green silence and softly put his hand over hers. She lifted bewildered eyes to him, his touch riveting her to her seat. She was incapable of movement. Whatever she'd expected, it wasn't tenderness. It altered everything. Instinctively, her fingers wound around his, his touch making her breathless.

He'd been looking at their entwined hands, and now he raised his eyes to lock with hers. She thought she saw a longing there in the smoky depths, some deep emotion that echoed the longing in her heart.

She trembled, tears shimmering in her eyes, and he held her hand more tightly, just for a moment, then pulled away, gripping the steering wheel, his knuckles showing white.

'Elena—can we cool it?' he asked flatly. 'Give it more time—give me more time?' His eyes swept her troubled face. 'I'd like to think I did—do—mean something to you. It's tough knowing what to believe, given the circumstances, but I'm working on it. The whole situation's done my head in, and believe me, that's not something I'm happy with. Will you give me more time to get to grips with this before you go along a path we'd both find difficult to retrace?'

She dipped her head in silent acknowledgement of his words, biting down hard on her lower lip, sucking it between her teeth, holding back dredging disappointment.

Stupid to have hoped he was ready to say he believed what she'd told him, was willing to go forward, build on the rebirth of trust and understanding.

Had he asked for more time just to stop her walking away? Making the breakdown of their marriage public, shattering Catherine's happy illusions and making it difficult for him to have a say in his brother's child's future welfare—much less be the constant presence in his or her life he had always insisted on?

Or had he really had a change of heart? Had he been telling the truth when he'd implied he was trying to come to terms with everything that had happened, that he wanted to be able to believe she loved him?

She didn't know. But she had to take the chance because it was the only one she had.

'I'll go along with that. Take all the time you need. I want you to believe me because, God knows, it's the truth,' she told him falteringly, and hoped to heaven she was doing the right thing in letting herself hope, not storing up more pain for the future, handing him a sharpened stake to thrust through her already bleeding heart.

CHAPTER NINE

RELUCTANTLY, Elena left the rustic seat at the far end of the garden, the one with the view over miles of open countryside, and began to amble slowly back towards the house.

She treasured these early-morning walks and the solitude she found; it was her way of escaping for just a little while. During the three days of Jed's absence his mother had done nothing but chatter. She'd wanted to know every last detail of the ceremony, had clipped out every newspaper report she could find and was proudly sticking them in a scrapbook. And when that subject was temporarily exhausted she chattered excitedly about the cottage, the changes she and Susan would make after they moved in.

It was perfectly understandable. Talking non-stop about everything and anything took her mind off the recent loss of her son, and Elena was more than happy to listen, but she did need a few quiet times of her own in which to do some thinking.

Jed had phoned each evening. Until last night they'd been duty calls, largely made, Elena suspected, for his mother's benefit, nothing personal.

But that had changed last night, when he'd said, 'I've thought a lot about what you told me and there's more I want to ask. But I'm beginning to think we can work this out—if you want that. I'll be home tomorrow evening, hopefully around dinner time?

Perhaps we should go back to Las Rocas. What do you think? We need to talk some more, and we can do it more easily on our own.'

Hope had lapped her body with warmth as she'd agreed shakily, a little breathlessly. 'That sounds fine.' And it had. It couldn't get much finer. At least now he was willing to talk, perhaps to believe her and begin to understand the desperate, gnawing need that had driven her to accept Sam's offer. 'Shall I book the flights?'

'No, leave it to me. I'll arrange it for Friday, if I can.'

She had said, because it had been bothering her, 'I really do think Catherine should be told about the baby before we leave. I couldn't fasten my jeans this morning, so by the time we come back from Spain—' fingers crossed they would be coming back together '—it might be obvious. I've no idea how quickly these things happen.'

His ensuing silence had alarmed her. Had it been too soon, taking too much for granted, to talk about her pregnancy with such apparent ease? It was a subject he couldn't be happy with, and she could understand that. But the need to tell Catherine the truth had been playing on her mind.

'You're quite right,' he'd agreed at last. 'Whatever happens, she has to know the truth. Would you prefer to break the news on your own, or would you rather wait until I can be there?'

'On my own, I think.' The way he'd said 'whatever happens' meant he wasn't sure about their future at all, she'd recognised dispiritedly. She didn't want any bad vibes coming from him to spoil whatever pleasure

Catherine could take in knowing her beloved Sam had left a child.

And now she was going back to the house to find Catherine and have that talk. Elena's mouth went dry at the prospect. Unconsciously she straightened her shoulders, and tucked her workmanlike blue and white striped shirt more firmly beneath the waistband of her loosely styled white cotton chinos.

She ran Catherine to earth in the morning room, making designs for her new garden on graph paper. 'Darling! You were quick—did you get everything you needed?'

'I haven't been to the village yet.' Elena wandered over to the window seat where Catherine was working. 'I've been having a lazy walk around the garden.' And thinking about what I have to tell you, and how I'll tell it, and wondering how you're going to take it, she added silently.

'Oh—if I'd known!' Catherine transferred the block of graph paper from her knees to a small coffee table at her side. 'When he phoned I couldn't find you, and Edith said she hadn't seen you, so we thought you'd already gone to the village.'

'Who phoned?' Elena sat on the other end of the window seat, trying not to let her sudden panic show.

Jed? Had he changed his mind about coming home this evening? About Spain? Had he decided they had nothing to talk about after all?

'A journalist from one of the women's magazines— I quite forget which one. They want to do an interview with you,' Catherine answered excitedly. 'About your books, and the award, and whether you'll be making your home here or dividing your time between here and Las Rocas. He seemed really keen for information. If I'd known you were only in the garden I would have come to fetch you. Anyway, he said he'd phone back later on to arrange an appointment, so I'm sure he will—as I said, he seemed very keen—so many questions!'

Elena's smile was one of relief. Her panic attack had been for nothing, except, of course, to show her how very much she was hoping she and Jed could find a way through this mess.

She dismissed the journalist and his interview easily from her mind. She supposed she should be flattered, or interested, but she wasn't. There were far more important things in life. 'Catherine,' she said gently. 'I have something to tell you.'

Choosing her words with care, she began at the beginning, watching Catherine's eyes grow wider with every word she said, then filming with tears as she whispered, 'Sam's baby—I can't tell you how much that means to me. To hold a child of his in my arms, a living part of him. And I can understand why you agreed to it at that time. I don't think men can properly understand the primeval instinct to mother—I guess you felt your biological clock ticking away and panicked.

'And typical of Sam, too, bless him! He always said life was too short to miss out on the things you really wanted, and if the opportunity arose you upped and grabbed it. Much as I loved him, I'm afraid that the words "duty" and "responsibility" were a foreign language to him. Though what he lacked in that department, Jed more than made up for. And—' Her teeth worried at her lower lip. 'What was Jed's reaction?'

'He wasn't exactly ecstatic,' Elena understated. 'But I promise you, he's working on it.' It was as much as she could offer. It would be cruel to paint a rosy picture when everything could still go badly wrong.

'Yes,' Catherine remarked softly. 'Jed would work hard to accept it. He's such a strong character and I know how very much he loves you. He told me he found the missing half of himself when he found you.' She put her fingertips to her suddenly trembling mouth. 'I do hope the poor boy doesn't feel he's lost out to Sam again. That would be unbearable for him.'

'Lost out again?' Elena questioned gently, her pulses quickening. Was Catherine about to confirm what she already suspected—that for some unfathomable reason Jed felt he came a poor second-best to his matinée-idol-handsome younger brother? 'How could that possibly be?'

'It's entirely my fault; I know that.' Catherine answered the question in her inimitable, round-about-the-houses way, her eyes anxious. 'I feel so guilty when I think about it all. At the time we thought we were doing the right thing. Park House is such an excellent prep school, and it had been arranged that Jed should go there when he was eight.

'Sam was just a tiny baby then—a sickly baby, demanding all my attention. I absolutely refused to hire a nanny; I needed to care for him myself. From one or two things Jed let slip when he was in his early teens I'm sure, with hindsight, he must have felt he'd been pushed out—especially when Sam wasn't sent away to school but was tutored privately at home. He was still a frail little boy, and wayward and wilful, too. We knew he wouldn't fit in with school discipline.'

She was twisting her fingers together so frenziedly that Elena thought her mother-in-law's hands might fall apart at any moment. She took one of them in hers and held it gently. She couldn't believe this warm and loving woman would ever knowingly hurt anyone. 'I'm sure you did what you thought best.'

'I didn't think about it deeply enough!' Catherine castigated herself, her fingers gripping Elena's now. 'Because Jed was always stronger and tougher than his brother, in every possible way, it was Sam who got the lion's share of encouragement and cosseting. And because we knew the family business would be safe in Jed's hands it was Sam who got to do what he wanted in life.

'Jed was never asked what he wanted; we just took it for granted he'd do his duty and shoulder the responsibility. And after his father died Jed was always here for me—strong, supportive, clear-headed and caring. While Sam—well, we often didn't know where he was for weeks and months at a time.

'So when he did come home for a few days between assignments what did I do? The prodigal son and fatted calf wasn't in it! The silly thing is, I think—no, I *know*—that I made much more fuss of Sam to make up for secretly loving Jed the best.'

Elena gently released her hand from Catherine's clutching fingers. What she'd said explained so much, why the fact that it was Sam's child she was carrying had been so hard for Jed to face, for starters. Hadn't she asked him to try to imagine if his reaction would have been the same if she'd had a brief affair with any other man and fallen pregnant, well before she'd even met him?

He wouldn't have been delighted, but because he was a highly intelligent, compassionate man, without, until recently, a jealous bone in his body, he would have understood that mistakes can happen. And, because they'd loved each other, he would have found a way to accept it.

But because *Sam* was her child's father he simply couldn't take it. Even if the baby's conception had been the result of clinical treatment.

She said quietly, 'Thank you for telling me this. I think you should tell Jed, too. Explain it, as you've just explained it to me. It would wipe away his misconceptions about coming a poor second-best to his brother.'

She stood up, finding a reassuring smile. 'I'll make some coffee; we could both do with some. And don't worry. You did a fine job of bringing up both your boys. Sam was clever, charming, a great friend to many people, and he excelled in the work he did; he took it very seriously. And Jed—' She spread her hands expressively. 'Jed is simply the best.'

Elena got back from her delayed trip to the village at a little after three o'clock that afternoon, just as the phone rang. She put the packages and carriers she'd brought in from the car down on the parquet floor of the hall and lifted the receiver, pushing her hair out of her eyes with her free hand.

If it was the journalist who'd called earlier he'd be wasting his time. She and Jed would be on their way back to Spain by this time tomorrow.

It wasn't. It was Liam. Elena took the instrument from her ear and stared at it, frowning. She couldn't believe it. Why would her ex-husband be calling her? How did he know she was here?

His insistent voice on the other end of the line had her reluctantly listening again, her soft mouth pulled down in distaste.

'What do you want?' she asked him frigidly, wondering if he'd bother to phone again if she simply put the receiver down and cut him off.

'I just told you.'

'And I wasn't listening,' she told him back.

'Then you'd better listen this time,' he said toughly. 'I want money. Big fat bunches of the stuff. And I want it now. Because of you I was banged up. You turned me in. I always treated you right, showed you a good time,' he said resentfully. 'Now I've paid my debt to society,' he sneered. 'So it's your turn to clear your debt to me.'

'I don't owe you a single thing.' She couldn't believe she was hearing this. It was surreal.

'Ten years at Her Majesty's pleasure. You call that nothing? You set me up. You owe me. And don't tell me you can't afford it. I know better. And don't say you won't, because if you do I'll make big, big trouble. For you and your nice new husband.'

Elena's eyes flicked round the hall. The house felt empty, but she knew it wasn't. At any minute Catherine might wander through and want to know if she was talking to that nice journalist who had phoned earlier.

How could she explain that she wasn't, that she was

speaking to her ex-husband, the ex-convict, who was now demanding money with menaces?

She really could do without this on top of everything else!

Dealing with it firmly, she said, 'Get lost. You're talking nonsense.'

'OK. If that's the way you want it. You just sit back and wait till the rubbish hits the fan. You and hubby will be covered with it.'

Her stomach contracted and goosebumps peaked on her skin. He sounded as if he really meant it, as if he had some dirt he was waiting to fling over her and Jed.

She couldn't think what. He was the one who had plenty to hide. Nevertheless, it had to be dealt with. She didn't want him even trying to make trouble. She and Jed already had enough of that on their hands.

'We can't talk here,' she said with sharp aggravation. Talking to him at all was the last thing she wanted, but she had to find out what was on his sneaky mind so she could do something about it.

'Now you're being sensible, babe.'

There'd been a time when his slight cockney accent had fascinated her. Now she felt nothing. 'So give me your number and I'll call you back,' she instructed coldly. She'd have to drive back to the village and use the public call box. She could make the excuse that she'd forgotten something. It was a damned nuisance, because she'd meant to spend what was left of the afternoon making herself look good for Jed, planning what she'd say to him.

She scrabbled around in the drawer of the table for paper and something to write with, but he derided,

'You think I'm stupid, or something? Meet me at the end of hubby's fancy drive in fifteen minutes.'

So he was close. That close?

For the first time she felt scared. When she'd married him all those years ago she'd thought she knew him. One year on she'd discovered she hadn't known him at all. Who knew what evil retaliation he had in his mind?

She glanced at her watch. No way would she let him know he was beginning to worry her. 'Make it an hour,' she said firmly, and tried not to shake.

'Why? So you can call in the cavalry?'

'No, because it suits me.'

She replaced the receiver decisively and leant against the table, waiting for her heartbeats to steady. In one hour's time Catherine would be resting in her room, something she always did because, as she said, she was sixty years old and entitled to pamper herself.

And Edith would have come over from the converted stable-block she and her husband had occupied for years to begin preparing the special dinner they'd planned to welcome Jed home.

Dinner was always at eight at Netherhaye, so Jed was unlikely to be arriving before seven. 'Around dinner time,' he'd said.

That gave her plenty of time to get rid of Liam and make sure he didn't come back.

Exactly one hour later her confidence had haemorrhaged away, and the winding, tree-lined drive seemed endless, her legs feeling uncomfortably shaky, as if they might give way under her at any moment.

Liam Forrester's pleasure was Liam Forrester's

main preoccupation. He liked to have a good time, liked fast cars, high living, was happy to cheat and steal to get what he wanted. Being behind bars would not have made him a happy man.

And her evidence had put him there.

As Liam stepped out from beneath the trees she suppressed a cry of alarm. She refused to let him see any sign of fear.

He swept his eyes over her casually clothed body, making her skin crawl. 'You could do with a bit of glitz, and I'd never let you wear trousers—you've got fabulous legs. But you look good. Success suits you.'

Prison hadn't suited him. It was almost a shock to see how he'd altered. His blond hair had dulled to an ashy brown and looked unkempt, he'd grown a paunch, and the once sharp dresser was now wearing stained, shabby black trousers and a cheap imitation leather jacket.

'How did you know where I was?'

The question was forced from her. Her life when she'd been married to him seemed so long ago. He was the part of her past she'd wanted to expunge from her memory; she had almost forgotten his existence.

'Easy. I've been following your career with interest. Not much else to do in the nick but read the papers. And plan how I'd catch up with you one day and see you shared your success with me—like I shared mine with you once upon a time. Trouble was, I read you lived somewhere in Spain, so when I got out I couldn't get my hands on you.'

He stepped closer. He'd put on weight and looked big and threatening. The lane that passed the end of the drive was rarely used. Anything could happen.

He saw the fear in her eyes and smiled. 'Don't worry, I'm not daft enough to wring the neck of the golden goose! I reckon fate's on my side for once. It was a stroke of luck seeing that piece in the paper about you winning that award. I just needed to hang around, follow you down here, book into the village pub and ask a few questions.'

The blue Escort, she thought tiredly. And questions. 'You phoned earlier pretending to be a journalist,' she stated.

He grinned, and for the first time she caught a fleeting echo of the good-looking, easy-on-the-eye charmer he had been when she'd first met him.

All her girlfriends had been deeply envious of the way he'd pursued her so single-mindedly. If only they had known what he really was they would have pitied her instead. If only she hadn't been so flattered, so dazzled, naively incapable of seeing the real man behind the façade.

'Talkative woman, your mother-in-law. I even got the address of your Spanish home,' he boasted. 'I quite fancy lazing around on a Costa, drinking sangria in the sun, but for the time being ten thou will do. In cash. Tomorrow. Same time, same place. Or else.'

She glared at him, appalled. There had to be a way out of this nightmare, she thought wildly. The police? If she took out an injunction to make him stay away from her would that apply in Spain, or would she also have to go through the Spanish courts?

Jed, she thought weakly. Oh, if only he were here! He would know what to do.

She swung on her heels, heading back for the house. Liam was out of his head if he thought she'd hand over that kind of money and then sit back and wait until he came and asked for more!

If he'd shown some remorse for his crimes, said he was on his uppers and trying to go straight, then she would have gladly given him something to help him get on his feet again and find honest work. But this— this was extortion with menaces! He would never change.

'Don't walk away from me!' His hand grabbed her arm before she'd gone two paces. There was brutal violence in his voice now and she stood very still, hardly daring to breathe. She couldn't bear him touching her, wanted to shake him off, but didn't dare provoke him.

'That's better.' He sounded calmer now, and he said with a honeyed sweetness that sent shivers down her spine, 'I can spin a good yarn, too, honeybunch. You don't have a monopoly. It would be a real cracker in the hands of a top journalist. Given the type of publicity you get, the tabloids would pay well for the skeleton in your cupboard. Married to a common criminal, enjoying all the goodies—which of your readers is going to believe you didn't have a part in it? Or at the very least know what was going on, where all that extra money was coming from, and fully condone it?

'Dirt sticks, sweetie-pie. It would cause a small sensation, but just imagine what it could do if the more sober broadsheets picked it up.' His fingers tightened on her arm as he bent and whispered in her ear. 'Your husband's an establishment guy; he heads an awesome establishment-type business. The customers for his fabulous gems come from the very top social drawer. There's many a royal lady wearing something fabulous from Nolan's. Bit of a slur on the revered family name to have it coupled with a woman with that kind of past, wouldn't you say?

'The nobs just might start buying their platinum and diamond knick-knacks from one or other of his high-falutin' rivals.' He jerked her closer. 'So pay up, or, as I said—take the consequences.'

He pulled her even closer, intimately close. And she could do nothing about it. All the stuffing had been knocked out of her. He meant it, all of it. He'd get the money one way or another.

In the light of the publicity surrounding her recent acceptance of that prestigious award the seamier tabloids would pay top dollar for his story, his warped allegations, disregarding the fact that there might not be any truth in them because stuff like that sold papers.

People liked to see other people get to the top, but they liked it better when they saw them knocked right back down again!

She could handle it for herself, but she couldn't let Jed and the Nolan gem empire be smothered in that kind of slimy publicity. She couldn't let that happen to him.

'You can have your money,' she said bitterly, hating having to give way but having no choice. 'I don't have that amount in my UK account. But we're going back to Spain tomorrow. I can get my hands on it there and send—'

'I'll give you three days.' He stuck his face inches from hers. 'And I'll come to Spain and pick it up in person. No cheques in the post, nothing traceable. Cash. I know where to find you, remember.' He pushed his face closer. 'Is your phone unlisted?'

She shook her head, trying to draw back. He wouldn't let her.

'Good. I'll call you. Tell you when and where to meet me.'

The scrunch of tyres on the gravelled surface of the drive had Liam pulling his face out of hers, turning his head. Elena felt weak with relief. Being so close to him had made her feel nauseous and dizzy. But she would rather collapse in a heap than cling onto the foul blackmailer. Only when she heard the expensive clunk of the Jaguar's door did she fully understand what was happening.

Frantically forcing her brain to function, she turned. Jed had returned hours earlier than expected. She didn't know whether to be glad or sorry.

Sorry, she supposed sinkingly, as she looked into his hard, expressionless face. Wearing the dark grey trousers of a business suit, his white shirt tie-less, open at the neck, sleeves rolled up to the elbow, he looked gorgeous. But quelling.

'I guess you must be husband Mark Two.' It was Liam who broke the heavy silence. He advanced, cast an appreciative eye over the gleaming car, extended his hand, which Jed ignored, and aimed for a clipped public school accent but failed. 'I'm Mark One. For your sake, old boy, I hope she doesn't do the dirty on you like she did on me. But don't put money on it.'

His hand dropped back to his side. 'Well, if you're not going to invite me in for drinkies, I'll be on my way.' He shrugged, stuffed both hands in the pockets of his disreputable trousers and swaggered away. Then he turned, his smile malicious. 'Take a tip from me, old boy. With that woman around you'd better learn to watch your back.'

CHAPTER TEN

'WHAT was he doing here?'

Jed looked at her with narrowed eyes. The afternoon sun was hot, but Elena shivered. He was looking at her with cold suspicion when she'd wanted to see the beginnings of the trust and understanding he'd hinted at in last night's telephone conversation.

Liam had ruined his homecoming.

'Asking for hand-outs,' she told him, setting her jaw, because if she let herself relax her teeth would start to rattle with nervous tension. She knew she couldn't tell him the whole truth about her ex-husband's successful blackmail attempt because Jed would insist on calling his bluff, contacting the police, and then those smears and allegations would end up in the tabloids. She couldn't let that happen.

It might, as Liam had threatened, actually harm his business, not to mention his reputation, and even if it didn't, seeing his wife's name smeared in the gutter press would hurt his pride. He'd take it on the chin, but he'd find it deeply distasteful.

'What for?' he asked tightly. 'The price of a pint? New clothes—he looked as if he could use them! Or more? Was it more, Elena?'

'Of course.' She hadn't been able to keep the bitterness out of her voice. She could have said, Just something to tide him over while he looks for work— something to take the steam out of the situation. But she hated having to lie to Jed, even by leaving things unsaid.

He caught her tone. Of course he did. 'And did you give it to him? The way you were folded round each other when I turned into the drive suggests you might have done. He looked remarkably pleased with himself, and you looked as if you weren't averse to reliving old times.'

From his viewpoint it could have looked that way. She had to give him that, she conceded miserably. Yet she couldn't tell him what had really been happening. She shuffled her feet in the gravel, realised what she was doing, how guilty and embarrassed the childish action would make her look, and stopped, pushed her hands into the pockets of her trousers and shrugged.

'Hardly that. Old times with Liam are something I'd prefer to forget. I certainly wouldn't want to relive a second of them. And how could I give him anything, even if I'd wanted to? I've only got pin money with me, and I couldn't write a cheque because my UK account is as good as empty.'

She'd only kept it going because it had been handy to have something to draw on when she visited the UK for meetings with her agent and publisher. Since coming over for Sam's funeral and her wedding, and now the awards, she'd practically cleaned it out.

He seemed to accept that, but probed ruthlessly, 'Did you tell him where to find you?'

'Of course not!' Did he think she'd kept in touch with Liam, perhaps even met up with him after his release from prison? That made her very angry. How could he think she'd do that and, worse, keep it from him?

He acknowledged her flare of anger with a dip of his head, his narrowed eyes not leaving her face, as if he was looking for the truth and couldn't find it. 'Then I'm to take it that his appearance at Netherhaye was a wondrous coincidence, an unlooked-for opportunity on his part to ask you for money,' he said, with a dryness that set her teeth on edge.

By the way her skin was burning she knew her face had turned brick-red. Fury, frustration and resentment coiled her insides into a tight knot. Just when she and Jed might have had a chance to work through their problems and find each other again, when he might have learned to love and trust her once more, Liam had swaggered along and driven an even bigger wedge between them.

'Can't we forget the creep?' she asked impulsively. 'I had nothing at all to do with him being here. He followed us down, apparently. He'd read about the award ceremony and thought I'd be a soft touch. He phoned earlier and suggested we meet. Believe me, I didn't want to, but I agreed because I didn't want him hanging around, making a nuisance of himself.'

She couldn't tell him any more. She hoped to heaven what she had told him would be enough, that he'd put the whole nasty episode out of his mind. And it seemed her prayers had been answered, because he opened the car on the passenger side and held the door for her. 'Get in. You might as well ride up to the house with me.'

And when he joined her and turned on the ignition his tone was the same, cool and distant. 'I take it Catherine's having her afternoon nap? Ask Edith to bring a tray of tea out onto the terrace, would you? I could do with a reviver before I shower.'

That careful politeness set the tone for the remainder of the afternoon and evening. It was as if, she thought as she tried to do justice to Edith's delicious marinated salmon steaks, served with baby new potatoes fresh from the garden and spicy ratatouille, his mind was functioning smoothly on the surface while sorting through the ramifications of the scene he'd come upon with her and Liam.

She risked a look at him as she sipped her iced spring water. He looked so darned controlled. Too controlled? Would his emotions burst through, blowing them both away?

'Now, neither of you must worry about me,' Catherine said when Edith had cleared the used plates and dishes. Jed had already told her they'd be leaving early next morning to catch the flight to Jerez—told her in that same calm, dispassionate voice. 'I expect Susan to arrive any day. Apparently she's a knock-out on the sewing machine—so we'll measure up for curtains, take a trip into town and choose the fabric. We're going to be so busy! So make the most of the rest of your honeymoon and don't give me a second thought.'

'Talking of which, I'll go and sort out the documents dealing with the lease on the property in Seville.' Jed turned his soulless smile on Catherine. 'And, no, I won't spend most of the time working.' He declined the fresh strawberries and helped himself to coffee, taking it with him, and Elena knew it was an excuse to leave them, to do his thinking without having to make polite conversation.

'I haven't had a chance to say anything to him about the baby,' Catherine confessed mournfully, helping herself to the berries. 'I did try to start a conversation before you came down for dinner, lead up to it gently, but he put on that remote face and froze me off.' She put down her spoon. 'I'm worried about him, Elena.'

'Don't be.' Said with more confidence than she felt. 'I get the feeling Jed can cope with anything life throws at him.' Her certainty of that went bone-deep. But after the scene with Liam would his form of coping revert to what it had been? The total blanking off, cutting her out of his heart with surgical precision?

She didn't think she could bear that, not after being so sure he was on the point of breaking through to an understanding of the events that had led to her pregnancy, and through that understanding learning to forgive her—and Sam.

Liam had done more harm than he would ever know.

'I can't help worrying, it being Sam's baby—'

'Try not to,' Elena soothed. Suddenly the stresses of the day caught up with her, draining her energy. She wanted to crawl into a hole and hide, and only come out when all the bad things had gone away. 'You'll have your chance to talk to him—about the baby, and his and his brother's childhood—soon enough. Right now he's working things out for himself. He needs space.' She finished her coffee and pushed herself tiredly to her feet. 'If you don't mind, I think I'll go and pack. I might see you later, if I don't fall asleep first! And if you see Edith before I do, tell her from me the meal was perfect.'

Packing for them both took next to no time. Elena

looked at the big double bed and wondered if Jed would join her. Pointless wondering when in her heart she knew he wouldn't.

If Liam hadn't done so much damage he might have done. Maybe they would have talked far into the night. Or maybe he would have simply held her. Or maybe simply slept at her side, not touching, not talking. That would have been enough.

She put a couple of soft down pillows and a light blanket on the chaise longue and got ready to occupy the bed in solitary state.

It was more of the same the next day. Not until they were in the hire car leaving Jerez airport did a hint of a thaw creep in.

They had the windows down, and she was sure she could smell the sherry on the hot air, the scent so evocative of this wealthy, productive corner of Andalucia. She watched Jed fill his lungs, certain he was beginning to look more approachable, and asked, 'Do you mind if we detour through Cadiz?'

'Sure.' He eased the car into the traffic and headed south. 'We're going to need provisions, I guess. I don't suppose you got around to getting in touch with Pilar to let her know we were coming?'

She hadn't even thought of it. All her mental energies had been focused on him. But his mention of the provisions she had overlooked handed her the excuse she'd been racking her tired brain to find.

'I'll need to go to the bank for cash, and then I thought we could stop by the market.' She clutched at the excuse he had given her gratefully. 'We could either eat out—early-supper-cum-late-lunch—or head straight back to Las Rocas.'

'Head back,' he said. 'I fancy a quiet night in the mountains.' He stamped on the brakes as a yellow Seat, covered in the white dust of the local Albariza soil, cut across them with long, strident blasts of its horn. Jed grinned, his teeth very white against his sun-darkened skin. 'Spanish maniac! Still, I could get used to it!'

She left him parking the car while she went into the Banco de Andalucia. She couldn't have felt more guilty if she'd been wearing a stocking on her head and carrying a sawn-off shotgun. She felt sneaky and devious, doing this behind Jed's back.

But he would have refused to allow her to give in to blackmail demands, and then he would have had to suffer the hateful consequences, she knew that, so even though she felt awful about it she was doing this for his sake, because she loved him. For herself, Liam could have gone ahead and done his worst.

Thankfully, because she was a valued customer and well known at this branch, the transaction was completed swiftly. And she walked out onto the hot pavement with the pay-off for Liam stuffed at the bottom of her handbag and the bunch of pesetas for household expenses innocently folded in her purse.

Jed was strolling towards her, the breeze from the ocean ruffling his soft dark hair. Her heart flipped. He was so special, so very much loved.

She waited for him, watching the way he moved. She loved his grace, his elegant strength. It made her heart hurt; it always had and always would. And the way his eyes lit with warmth when he saw her made her give him a lilting smile. Perhaps she could let herself believe that he'd done his thinking and their time here together would be special and important, a time of coming to terms with what had happened, accepting it and going on together.

And Liam, hopefully, completely out of the frame.

'I should have thought to ask you to wait.' His eyes went to the open doors of the bank. 'I could have changed a few traveller's cheques. Want to come back in with me while I do it?'

Stopping him from going into the bank with her had been precisely why she'd asked him to drop her off while he found somewhere to park. 'No need,' she told him blithely. 'Let's hit the market! I withdrew plenty.' And wasn't that the truth!

'OK. Shopping, if you say so—I'll just try to get used to being a kept man. I keep forgetting I'm married to a wealthy woman!'

His relaxed smile gave her the courage to tuck her arm through his, just companionably, nothing to make him think she was about to repeat the flaunty, flirty behaviour she'd so misguidedly produced when they'd spent the day here with Catherine.

Born out of pain, a primitive need to hurt him back, it hadn't been one of her better ideas.

She was aiming for friendly, not flirty. Friends exploring the busy, colourful market, heads together as they examined the piles of fresh produce for the best bargains, having mild arguments over the choice of swordfish steaks, giant prawns or clams, amicably resolving the difficulty by buying some of each.

When they were overburdened with bags almost bursting with irresistible fruit and vegetables they looked at each other and grinned.

'Whose army are we aiming to feed?' Jed's eyes

were warm, soft silver, his sexy mouth relaxed, smiling for her, and Elena felt herself sliding effortlessly back into the safe haven of his love.

At least, that was what she felt here and now, in the bustle and noise of the exotic outdoor market, with the Spanish sun beating down, and she was going to hang onto the feeling and hope nothing happened to take it away.

'I guess we should make tracks for home and start chomping our way through it.' Aquamarine eyes sparkled for him. 'But how about grabbing an orange juice first?'

'Not only beautiful, but bright too.' He took her share of the bulging carriers and added them to his own. 'Lead on. The rabbit warren of narrow streets confuses me.'

Nothing confused him, Elena thought, keeping up with his long, effortless stride. Present him with a problem and he'd work it out, calmly, intelligently and logically. Which was what he'd done regarding the problem their marriage had faced.

The fire and fury bit at first had been natural. His emotions had got in the way of logic. But he'd had his thinking time and—her heart lifted, spinning wildly—everything was going to be all right! Suddenly she was deliriously sure of it.

They found a restaurant on the Plaza Topete, and, sitting at a table on the *terraza*, surrounded by urns brimming with perfumed flowers, sipping huge glasses of freshly squeezed orange juice, Jed remarked, 'I take it the creep was trying to twist your arm, using bully-boy tactics?'

She nodded. There was no need to say a thing. He'd

been reviewing the scene in his mind, remembering body language, and had arrived at the right conclusion. She didn't want to talk about her ex-husband, not now, not ever. She was feeling far too guilty because of what she had agreed to do to want him inside her head.

But Jed didn't want to let it go. 'Speaking objectively, and having seen him, I can't understand why you ever married the man. You're an intelligent woman, Elena. Independent, fastidious.'

Knowing what she knew, that she was deceiving him over the payment of Liam's blackmailing demands, she wished he'd leave it, forget the other man had ever existed. But if there were things he wanted to know she'd tell him, because she owed him that. And his tone hadn't been censorious, just calmly, objectively questioning.

She traced a line in the condensation on the outside of her glass, amazed to find her hand was steady when her heart was punching her breastbone. 'He didn't always look like that, or act like a lout. He had a silver tongue, was very easy on the eye. He had the type of charm that could dazzle. I was gullible, easily flattered, overwhelmed by his lavish gifts—glitzy designer gowns, shoes made in heaven, jewellery. A bit flashy, not the sort of thing Nolan's would touch with a sanitised bargepole, but expensive nevertheless.' Her fingers worried at the corner of her mouth, and the way Jed fastened on that nervous betrayal, one brow drifting upwards, told her he knew how upset this conversation was making her.

She *was* upset—her deceit over those blackmail demands was doing her head in—but if she weren't careful he might think she was mourning the man her first husband had been.

She clamped both hands round her glass and forced herself on. 'After a time, it all began to pall—the fancy restaurants, the nightclubs, the feeling of being dressed up and paraded. And I came out from under his spell for long enough to question where all the money was coming from.

'Gambling, he told me. And that I wasn't happy about. Poor but honest—that was the way Mum had brought me up. And that was why I was so shocked when I discovered his criminal activities, why I went to the police. Why I divorced him. Now—' she looked at him from between her lashes, her eyes unconsciously pleading '—can we forget him?'

'With pleasure.' He was on his feet, collecting their belongings. 'Consider the subject permanently closed. Shall we head for the hills?'

She dragged in a shuddery breath, relief smoothing down her prickly nerve-ends. Whatever test he'd been setting for her, it seemed she'd passed with flying colours.

They'd reached Las Rocas in the late afternoon, Jed flinging the windows wide while Elena dealt with the shopping. They'd taken turns to shower and change, both careful not to force an intimacy too soon, not before the problems within their marriage had been resolved.

They'd been down that road on the night of the award ceremony and it had ended in unmitigated disaster.

And now, after a quickly prepared meal of garlicky

prawns, vegetable medley and masses of fruit, they were sprawled out on Siamese-twinned loungers, gazing out over the terrace at the vast starlit velvet night, the perfume from her pots of lilies and sweet-scented jasmine drugging the senses.

She'd felt so swelteringly hot and sticky when they'd arrived she'd thankfully exchanged the clothes she'd travelled in for cotton shorts and a loose, cropped and sleeveless top. Jed, too, had dressed lightly. The fine cotton, collarless black shirt hung from his rangy shoulders in soft folds, the sleeves pushed up above his elbows, his brief white shorts making those long, elegantly muscular legs look deeply tanned and unbelievably sexy in the mellow glow from the outside wall-lamps.

Quickly, Elena fixed her attention on the stars. The temptation to reach out and touch that bronzed skin was deeply compelling. Pictures of their former hedonistic lovemaking banded her brain, making her heart flutter, her mouth go dry.

'Do you mind if we talk?' From the corner of her eye she saw him turn onto his side, supporting his head with his hand. 'Look at me, Elena.'

She turned her head, obeying his soft command, her bright hair spread out on the reclining back-rest of the lounger. Starlight glimmered in his eyes, deep shadows emphasising the harsh hollows and planes of his face, making the line of his mouth tantalisingly sensual.

'OK?'

'Of course.' Her soft mouth quivered. This was the breakthrough; she knew it was. She was willing to tell him anything he wanted to know.

'I believe your story of artificial insemination. And, no, I didn't check with the clinic. They wouldn't have told me anything in any case. It would have been a gross breach of patient confidentiality. But the more I thought about it the more it made sense, fitted in with what I knew of Sam. Did you really want a child that badly?'

He hadn't taken his eyes off her face for a second, and she returned his steady gaze unflinchingly. 'Yes, I did,' she breathed. 'It was a physical ache that wouldn't go away. It got so bad it made everything I'd achieved in my life seem worthless.

'After my divorce I made a solemn vow never to marry again. I'd make my own life and make it good. That,' she whispered, 'was before I met you and knew how wrong I'd been. Sam wanted a child, too, but for him it was different, a kind of stake in the future, his sole claim to immortality. It was a cerebral need. Not, as mine was, a deep emotional hunger. It was almost as if he knew he didn't have long to live.'

Unconsciously, her hand covered her unborn child, the protective gesture as old as time. And Jed rolled closer and slid his hand beneath hers, moving it gently over her rounded tummy.

'Is this little bulge the result of gorging yourself at supper? Or is it what I think it is?' His voice was husky, heavy velvet, his dark head close to her bright one, his clean breath feathering over her face.

Elena pulled in a raggedy breath and moved, making enough space for him, just, on her lounger. If he'd a mind to avail himself of it.

He had, and, so close to him now she was sure he must hear the race of her heart as it pushed the blood wildly through her veins, she murmured, 'It's what you think it is.' She held her breath, because his re- action would tell her what their future was more plainly than any words. If he showed any sign of dis- taste then she'd know that he would always resent Sam's child, and the future wouldn't look hopeful.

He didn't say a word, simply undid the button at the top of the waistband of the shorts that were now just that little bit too tight, allowing his hand the free- dom to dip lower.

Relief made her giddy for long seconds, and then desire pooled at the juncture of her thighs, sweet and sharp and urgent. Would his hand slide lower, touch her there? Did he want her half as much a she wanted him?

Would he let her into his heart again? Would he love her, let her love him?

'Jed—' she croaked, wanting to ask him, but he wouldn't let her finish, his voice sliding over hers.

'Once, at Netherhaye, you let slip that you still loved me. Then that night at the hotel you told me, most emphatically, that you didn't. Which version of the state of your emotions am I to believe?'

'The first.' She turned her head, resting her cheek against the angle of his shoulder, burning for him, lov- ing him, loving him… 'We were so close to making love. I knew you'd despise yourself if you did. And despise me for letting you. You hated me, closed me out, wouldn't believe me! I had to do—say—some- thing to stop us!'

She was rapidly losing her ability to control herself. The need to feel his hands on her body, his lips on hers, to curl herself round the hard male length of him, to feel him deep inside her, hear words of love on his lips again, was pushing her to the limits of her endurance.

The hand that had been softly stroking her tummy stilled. She held her breath, the fear of rejection surging back, a sour taste in her mouth, a cold stone in her heart. But he said thickly, 'Will you forgive me for that? Can you ever forgive me for that? For refusing to listen, and, when you forced me to listen, telling you you were a liar? For refusing to trust? I think I went half out of my mind at that time.'

'Oh, darling...' In answer, she wound her arm around his neck, her lips feathering his mouth as she told him, 'Of course I do! I understand how you must have felt. Had the positions been reversed I'd have behaved ten thousand times as badly!'

'I don't think I deserve you.' His voice was rough, but his hand was gentle as it moved on her tummy again, protectively gentle. 'But I promise you this. I will love this child as if it were my own. Not for Sam's sake, and not because I love its mother. But for its own sake.'

Emotional tears streaked her face and he kissed them lovingly away. She could feel the fine tremors that shook his taut body as he found her lips and parted them with his, and the last coherent thought she had was that Catherine had not been given the opportunity to wipe away those misconceptions of his about coming a poor second-best to his brightly burning, will o' the wisp brother.

He had put those aside himself. Dismissed ancient sibling jealousy and reclaimed his own.

This much loved—adored—husband of hers was an honourable man.

'You are so beautiful,' he told her, his voice raw with need. 'Let me show you how I love you.' He took her hands and lifted them, turned them, placed fervent kisses in the centre of each curled palm. Then he lifted his head. The lamplight gilded the skin that was pulled tightly over his bones, his smoky eyes locking intently with hers. 'Show me you forgive me.'

Emotion shook her; she couldn't speak. She wound her arms around his neck again and kissed him fiercely, and he returned her frenzy as, hands trembling, they tore the clothes from each other's bodies until flesh met burning flesh.

She heard him groan and curled her legs around his body, inviting him to enter her. She heard the slow, inward drag of his breath, saw his tough jaw tighten and knew a second's terrible fear that this was all going wrong, before he said raggedly, 'I'm wild for you, afraid of hurting you and the baby. Help me to love you gently.'

She melted against him and thought she was in paradise. Nothing else could have spelled out his love for her more perfectly.

'We'll make it as slow and long and lingering as you like, my darling,' she promised as he slid gently, slowly within her, and she wrapped her arms more tightly around him and *knew* she was in paradise.

CHAPTER ELEVEN

THE evening sun was low, spreading misty purple shadows in the valleys. Elena moved around the kitchen preparing supper. Sautéed clams with garlic and lemon, and parsley from her garden. Her eyes were inevitably drawn from the task in hand over the terrace, to where Jed was dragging the hose around the garden, dressed only in worn denim cut-offs and espadrilles.

A sensation that was near to pain clutched at her heart. Oh, dear heaven, how she loved this man! Over the two days they'd spent here the new intensity of their love had revealed itself in every touch, every caress, every look and every word. Their love for each other doubly precious because they had so nearly lost each other.

'Would you prefer it if we stayed here until the baby's born?' he'd asked her this morning as they'd stood on the terrace contemplating what needed to be done today in the rioting garden, not wanting to set foot outside their secluded paradise. His arms had come around her, pulling her into his body, his hands softly cradling her breasts through the gauzy aqua cotton of the loose sundress she'd been wearing over nothing at all.

'Would you mind?' She'd tipped her head back, nuzzling her lips against his throat, feeling the beat of his pulse, feeling her breasts swell invitingly beneath his tormenting hands.

'I'd prefer it. This place suits you, and it's certainly grabbed my affection. We could visit Netherhaye once in a while, just to keep the old place aired, and have Christmas there every year and invite the Mums. Because I've been thinking; I can just as easily keep an eye on the business from here. We could spend the bulk of our time here, making babies.' His voice had teased, taking every last one of her senses and giving them delight. 'Would you like that?'

She'd turned in his arms then, pushing herself against him, holding him to her heart, closing her eyes on a ragged breath as she'd felt his body stir with desire. 'I want to give you babies,' she'd told him, her voice ferocious with love. 'Dozens of them!'

And now this big-hearted man of hers was winding the hose back on its reel, and the play of muscles across his powerful back and shoulders mesmerised her, making her throat tighten with emotion. He was so beautiful.

And he would be hungry. He'd worked hard in the garden all afternoon, wanting her with him but not allowing her to do more than idly dead-head the blossoms. He was very determinedly taking care of her.

She finished tossing the salad as he straightened up from his task. He'd be with her in a matter of seconds. All the ingredients were ready; she could cook the clams while he had his shower.

The phone rang. She dried her hands and took the receiver from the wall-mount, and Liam said aggressively, 'You got it?'

Her heart stopped, then punched at her savagely.

'Where are you?' She'd gone cold all over, shaking. Everything had been so wonderful, Jed had been so perfect, so understanding, and she had put Liam and his demands to the back of her mind.

Now he was filling her head with panic. She wanted to put the receiver down, go on pretending he didn't exist.

'Close.' He answered her question. 'I'm looking at the front of your property right now. Nice place. Must be worth a bomb. So when and where do we meet?'

Her stomach was churning sickly, her brain in a tumult. But she had to think. And quickly. Jed would walk in at any moment.

She cast a wide-eyed, frantic glance at the door and said tightly, 'Then you will be able to see the big door in the wall. The package will be outside it tomorrow at dawn.' And she hooked the receiver back just as Jed walked through, and felt her face flood with guilty colour.

'You OK?' His eyes narrowed with concern. 'Who was on the phone—not bad news?'

She had to get herself together. Stop shaking. Look normal. She pulled in a deep breath, willed herself to carry this off.

'No, of course not. Just my agent reminding me I'm due to give my publishers a synopsis of my next book any time now,' she invented, hating having to do this, reminding herself that she was doing it for his sake, trying to feel better about it and failing miserably.

'Sweetheart...' He came closer, his easy smile making her want to weep. 'Don't let them pressure you.' He folded his arms around her and her head dropped gratefully against the wide span of his chest. His skin was warm, slick with sweat. She parted her lips, tasting him.

'You never need write another word,' he said firmly. 'Not unless you want to. And if you do, then you tell them you do it on your own time, at your own pace. That clear?'

He was making a stand for her, taking her side as she knew he always would. That it was inappropriate didn't matter a damn. He would shoulder her problems, deal with them fairly and firmly, always on her side.

She wound her arms around his neck and said fiercely, 'I love you!'

'Hey! You think I don't know that? That's why I'm here. That's why I married you, remember.' He was smiling as his lips took hers.

Very gently, Elena moved Jed's arm, holding her breath, afraid he would wake.

She hadn't slept, increasingly edgy as the hours of night slipped past her. Constantly reminding herself that she was doing this for his sake alone was the only way she could stop herself from breaking down and confessing everything.

He had slept, wrapped around her. His conscience hadn't been stinging, keeping him awake. Tomorrow—today, actually—they were going to Seville.

Over supper Jed had told her he was due to meet the designer he'd contracted to gut the present building and turn it into something discreetly impressive, glamorous yet restrained, the international hallmark of a Nolan's showroom.

'I'd like you to be involved—if only to give your opinions. Besides—' his eyes had glinted at her '—I want you with me. I can't bear to be away from you for a second, let alone the best part of a day.'

'You think I'd let you go without me!' She'd smiled for him, hanging onto the thought of the trip to Seville. By then the business with Liam would be over. He'd have taken his bundle of crisp notes and run. And she could put him out of her mind and get on with her wonderful life with Jed.

Gingerly sliding out of bed, she wondered if she'd be too sleepy to make any contribution to today's business meeting. And then told herself of course she wouldn't. Relief that this was all over would carry her through, make her bubble and bounce with sheer happiness.

The louvres were open, and she found her silk robe by the grey pre-dawn light, slipped it on, the fine fabric cool against her naked skin, and tied the belt with shaky fingers.

She was hardly daring to breathe, and her heart felt as if it had swollen to twice its normal size, bumping about inside her chest. But Jed was still sleeping. She slipped like a shadow from the room.

It would take no longer than three minutes—four at the most—to slip out with the package and get back into bed. And if he did wake during that time, find her missing, he'd assume she'd gone to the bathroom.

She'd deliberately left her handbag on top of the counter just inside the kitchen door, so she didn't need to put a light on to find it. Quickly, she reached for it, and knocked the salt and pepper grinders to the tiled floor. She cursed herself for forgetting they were there.

The noise sounded horrendous. Her fingers clutched the soft leather of her bag and her heart stopped beating, then thundered on as quietness settled around her.

He hadn't woken. She delved for the package and padded through the house, taking care not to bump into furniture. The main door was heavy, wide and ancient. Jed had shot the bolts home before going to bed. She reached for the top one, remembering the grinding noise it made. They both needed oiling.

She was sweating, rivers of panic rushing through her veins, when she finally pulled the door open and stepped outside into the enclosed courtyard at the front of the house.

All she had to do now was put the package outside the big arched doorway.

In contrast, those doors swung open easily, and she was on the stony track, the rosy fingers of dawn already touching the tops of the crumpled mountains. She bent to put the package down—and Liam stepped out of the shadows.

She slapped her hand across her mouth to push back her cry of fright, and dropped the package. Liam picked it up, weighing it in his hands. She hadn't expected him to be waiting. She hadn't wanted him to be waiting. She had never wanted to see him or speak to him again.

'Thanks, doll.' He grinned at her. 'You know it makes sense.'

He looked more respectable than when he'd appeared at Netherhaye. The dark grey denims and matching battle jacket looked new. And she could see a fancy truck parked a little way down the track. Had he borrowed it? Or stolen it? Either way, she didn't care. She wanted him off her property.

'Just go,' she hissed through her teeth, shivering now in the chilly dawn air.

'Only when I've checked this isn't a wad of newspaper.' He opened the package, pulling out the crisp notes. He leered at her. 'I'm not *au fait* with the exchange rate, but it looks about right to me. I don't think you'd be stupid enough to do the dirty on me again. It will do nicely, for starters.'

'There won't be any seconds,' she told him decisively, refusing to give in to the desire to have hysterics. 'So take it and go, and just be thankful I didn't go to the police and have you put behind bars again!'

She heard the opening of the door in the wall behind her and went weak with a totally unexpected surge of relief. She had tried, for his sake, to keep him ignorant of this vile business, but he had woken and followed her out so she had failed.

But this failure was sweetly welcome. She no longer had the need to deceive him. If Liam did go to the tabloids when she refused to make more payments—and Jed would insist she did nothing of the kind—then at least he would be forewarned, prepared when those smears against her character—and, by association, his—came to light.

'Get off this property, Forrester.' Jed's voice was hard and flat. 'If I see your face around here again I'll personally rearrange it for you.' The lack of emotion in his tone made the threat very real. Even Liam blinked as he hurriedly stuffed the paper money back into the package, as if he was afraid the other man would take it from him.

Turning swiftly, Elena hurried to Jed's side. He hadn't bothered to dress, just pulled on the cut-offs he'd worn the day before. She reached out a hand, her fingers light and cool on the firm, warm skin of his arm. 'Thank you,' she said huskily, and really, really meant it.

'Get back inside before you get a chill.' His eyes swept the inadequate silk that skimmed her naked body. He turned and walked through the arched doorway, waiting for her, then re-secured the double doors. He strode back to the house, straight to the bathroom. She stood outside the door, listening to the gushing of hot water, her heart quailing.

Surely he didn't think…

She pushed open the door just as he turned the shower head off. He reached for a towel, his eyes flat. 'I suggest you go back to bed. From the look of you, your furtive assignation obviously took it out of you. Funny thing is, if I hadn't cared I would never have known you'd told him where you'd be, arranged for him to come to you. What did you do? Promise to give him that hand-out because you felt sorry for him? Or because you like to keep men dangling? Can't you let him go?'

He was still using that flat, emotionless tone. That made it all so much worse. It couldn't all be going so wrong, not for a second time!

He finished with the towel and tossed it in a corner. 'As I said, if I hadn't cared I wouldn't have known. I heard noises, heard the bolts being drawn. I thought you couldn't sleep. So I followed. I didn't want you to be sleepless and alone. But you weren't alone.'

She knew how it must look. But she wasn't going

to stand by and see their lives ruined, their future to-gether blown out of the water. 'Jed,' she said firmly as he walked past her into the bedroom, careful not to touch her, 'will you please listen to me?'

'No, thanks, I've done more than my fair share of that.' He was dressing. A pale grey suit in a light-weight fabric, pale grey silk shirt and a dark tie. 'Trou-ble is, you're too good with make-believe. I suddenly find I don't know what's truth and what's fantasy.' He settled his jacket on his shoulders and glanced at his watch. 'I may get back from Seville tonight. And, there again, I may not.'

Elena sat on the edge of the bed and watched him walk out, her eyes defeated, brimming with a sudden rush of unstoppable tears.

This couldn't be happening all over again. Surely it couldn't? Hadn't he learned from his earlier refusal to listen to what she had to say?

Yet he had worked it out in his own good time, weighing what seemed bad, very bad indeed, against what he knew of her, the love they shared, and had reached the truth.

On the other hand, perhaps seeing her with Liam again had completely turned his opinion of her around. That first meeting had been explained away, and he'd come to accept it. But the second—the wad of money that could only have come from her. The indisputable fact that she had arranged to sneak out and meet her ex-husband. Would he now see everything she'd said as a tissue of deceitful lies? Even the way Sam's baby had been conceived?

She spent the day alternating between faint hope and bleak despair. He didn't come that night, nor in the morning. But Pilar did.

CHAPTER TWELVE

ELENA knew she had to make herself eat something for her baby's sake. She was uninterestedly slicing fruit when she heard the unmistakable sound of a noisy two-stroke engine pull into the courtyard.

Pilar on her moped, come to check on the practically invisible irrigation system that kept the pot plants alive. It saved having to drag the hose or watering cans up to the terrace that overlooked the garden and the courtyard at the front.

Pilar always came to check the system was working properly at least once a week when Elena was away. Now the Spanish woman would know she was back in residence, and would expect to take up her normal household duties.

But Elena didn't want to see anyone. Only Jed. And Jed, it seemed, was in no hurry to come back.

Sighing, she resigned herself to the inevitable as the heavy slap of Pilar's sandalled feet heralded her arrival in the kitchen. A huge woman, she was full of good humour and energy. Elena liked her very much, and vowed not to let her know how desperately she wanted to be left alone.

'So you are having the baby—that is good! The little one will bring you much joy! I speak as I know from the five of my own!' Pilar said in her exuberant, heavily accented English.

Her eyes widening, Elena glanced down at the front

of her sundress. Another five months to go—was her pregnancy so obvious?

Pilar, taking a gaudy spotted pinafore from a plastic bag, tied it round her huge middle and disabused her. 'Señor Nolan called to tell me the good news and say you are back here now and I am needed.'

'When did he call? This morning?' Had he been in the village below, that close to her, and not bothered to come up here? Was he coldly and unemotionally cutting her out of his life again?

'No, no.' Pilar gave her a look that suggested she doubted her sanity. 'While I was making lunch yesterday. He asked in the village for the house of Pilar Casals. Now you see I was right to make you talk to me in English all these years! Señor Nolan has no Spanish, but we were able to understand each other.'

Which was more than Elena did at this moment. Jed should have been in Seville by yesterday lunchtime. But Pilar gave her no time to ponder why he hadn't been, telling her, 'And Tomás is to come and water the garden and do other heavy work. That is good for all of us. He is on his way now, on his bicycle. I tell him my old motorbike won't take my weight and his. Are you going to eat that fruit, or shall I make the good *tortilla*?'

'Fruit,' Elena said weakly, resuming her slicing before Pilar could make good her threat.

She could understand Pilar's elation very well. Her husband, Tomás, only worked when Pilar forced him to, and would happily sit around all day at one of the pavement cafés down in the village, drinking strong coffee and smoking his evil-smelling cigarillos under the shade of an orange tree, reading the papers and talking to his friends, perfectly content to let his wife work to put food on the table for the family. She would be delighted to know he would be bringing in extra income.

When Pilar began clattering round with the mop and bucket Elena took her fruit to eat in the garden under the shade of a giant fig tree. Pilar would fetch her if Jed phoned. Though she had by now stopped hoping that he would.

Responsibly, he had arranged for her to have all the help around the house and garden she needed, and had probably told Pilar to see she ate properly. He had done his duty by her and his brother's unborn child. He would want little or no further contact.

By the end of the afternoon the ache in her heart had become permanent, the feeling of loss so acute it was difficult to contain. Surely his business in Seville wasn't keeping him away this long? If he'd meant to return he would have done so by now. She had a thumping headache from listening for the sound of his car.

Tomás had set off back to the village on his rusty old bicycle, and Pilar was heading through the courtyard, pushing her moped, on her way home, turning to call over her shoulder, 'I have made you Pollo con Tomate; be sure you eat it.'

Standing in the doorway, Elena made herself smile and promise to eat the chicken in tomato sauce. She didn't want the Spanish woman to guess how despairingly unhappy she was.

Then she heard the sound of an approaching engine and her smile turned to one of wobbly relief. He had come back!

Her legs turned to something resembling water vapour and she sagged back against the doorframe, her stomach full of nervous flutters as she saw him appear in the arched doorway in the outer wall. Even though her eyes were misted with emotion she could see how drawn he looked, how tired. He stopped and exchanged a few words with Pilar, then walked towards her, the severity of his expression enclosing her rapidly beating heart in ice.

Nothing had changed in the last thirty-six hours.

He walked past her, into the coolness of the hall. She followed. At the entrance to the sitting room he made a curt after-you gesture with one hand. 'Shall we talk?'

It was what she wanted, but her heart was somewhere under the soles of her feet, heavy and aching. The coldness of his voice, his eyes, everything about him, told her he was about to say something she couldn't bear to hear.

She clung to the back of a chair for support. Her legs were shaking so badly. He put his briefcase down on a table and told her, 'As you'll have gathered, the Casalses will give you all the help you need around here. And I spoke to Catherine last night and told her you'd decided to wait here until the birth. It is your home, the place you'll feel most comfortable in.'

He pushed his hands in his pockets and turned to stare out of the open windows, as if he'd seen enough of her. 'I'll be flying out to New York tomorrow and staying for four weeks, maybe five. I'll let you know. After that I'll check up on you from time to time, and nearer the birth I'll be with you. We'll book into a hotel in Cadiz. I've checked out a private maternity unit on the outskirts, and booked you in. I'm sure,' he said coldly, 'you went into the logistics of getting proper prenatal care when you first decided you wanted a child.'

She'd listened to him outlining his plans for their sterile future, the unemotional delivery of the words stunning her into silence. But now she blurted anguishedly, 'Jed! Don't do this to us!'

He turned then. Slowly. His eyes were empty, as if no one lived behind them. 'My dear,' he drawled, 'I don't believe I'm the one doing anything to ''us.'''

He shifted his attention to the briefcase on the table, opening it, pulling out an all too familiar package. 'This is yours. I hope you'll dispose of it more sensibly next time. When I left here yesterday morning,' he said in a terse explanation, when he met her puzzled stare, 'I scoured the village and found his vehicle outside that run-down-looking *pension*. Considering the earliness of your assignation, I thought he might be staying nearby. I persuaded him to hand this back.' He dropped the package on the table with a look of mild distaste. 'And I hope it won't come as too much of a disappointment, but you won't be seeing or hearing from him again. I got the message over to him in a way that not even he could misunderstand.'

He snapped the briefcase shut. 'I'll phone you from New York.' And he walked out.

Elena let him go. There was no point in following him, arguing, pleading. Jed Nolan had made up his mind and there was nothing she could do or say that would alter it.

He phoned from New York, faithfully each week. Elena's despair turned to hopelessness, and then to dull apathy. His questions were bluntly to the point, and it was all she could do to drag out her responses.

She was well. She had regular appointments with her gynaecologist in Cadiz. Yes, she had visited the maternity unit. And that was it; that was all.

If his phone calls depressed her then his first visit did more than that. He arrived at noon, cool in a loose white cotton shirt, lightweight oyster-coloured trousers. The heat of the summer made her sweat, her hair flop lankily around her face. She felt fat and ugly and didn't want to see him.

He left when Pilar did, and she curled up on the sofa and cried until she felt sick. She felt as if someone had dug a deep, dark pit, thrown her in and covered her up. She didn't think she would ever climb out of it again, didn't think she wanted to.

On his second visit, exactly a month later, he left well before Pilar. The Spanish woman was beside herself with excitement. 'Señor Nolan is such a good man! See how he cares about you!' Her black eyes rolled expressively. 'Sadly, his business takes him so much away. But—' she could hardly contain herself '—last time he say to us he is buying a car. For us. Yesterday it came. A new car, not an old thing. For our own. But for Tomás to drive you wherever you need to go. First he needed to satisfy himself Tomás is safe. That one, I told him, is very safe for driving. Too lazy to drive faster than a snail! One car we had once, in our early days. Then it fell to bits and now the hens live in it in the back yard.'

He was doing his duty. He was good at that. She dreaded his next visit. Next month she would be huger than ever. She hated him seeing her like this. Fat. Dull. Lifeless. Dreaded the polite questions on the state of her health. Was she eating enough? Eating the right things, getting plenty of rest?

He'd brought little snippets of news—very little about what *he* was doing and where he was doing it, mainly about how well Catherine and Susan were settling in their cottage, digging up the entire garden, apparently, and replanting, haunting sale rooms and antiques shops for just the right pieces of furniture. So he had to have visited Netherhaye, spent some time there.

The two ladies had threatened to fly out to visit her, but, Jed had told her, he had dissuaded them, telling them she was busy on a new book. Was she writing?

Mutely, she had shaken her head. She was doing nothing but managing to get through each day. Sometimes even that seemed too much to cope with.

She knew now, without him having to tell her, that after the birth he would go for divorce. Catherine was back on her feet, had a new life to make in a new home, plenty to keep her occupied. There was no need now to stay married.

Oddly enough, she accepted it, had come to understand him better.

He was nothing if not an honourable man, a man who took duty and responsibility seriously—she only had to witness the care he had extended to her, albeit from a distance, to know that.

A man of his word. He would have nothing but contempt for a wife who consistently presented him with what he could only view as deceit.

He might have loved her once. She knew he had. But he couldn't stay with her.

Not even for great sex.

Not even for a true and loving heart?

The parcel of tiny baby clothes arrived from England when the winds of early October carried the first hint of autumn chill through the mountains. Elena's heart came out of deep-freeze.

The parcel had come from Catherine and her mother, and she dialled the number Jed had given her and spoke to them both. It was Catherine who said, 'I'm glad to hear you're sounding better. You got me worried, you sounded so flat when we phoned last. I even suggested to Jed when he was over here a few weeks ago that Susan and I might visit and cheer you up. You must be missing him so—I can't think why he doesn't make someone else do all these foreign trips.'

'These lovely things have cheered me up,' Elena said, and meant it. So far she had done nothing to prepare for her baby.

'And you remember what we talked about back in early summer? About the way I tended to spoil Sam and why? Well, I did get to have that talk with Jed.' Catherine gave a fluttery half-laugh. 'And do you know what he said? He said he'd worked that out for himself, and that it had helped in a certain situation. I can't think what he meant, and he wouldn't tell me. Anyway, I'm glad I got it said.'

She knew what he'd meant, Elena thought sadly, after ending the conversation five minutes later. Jed had thought things through. He'd believed what she'd

told him about her baby's conception, accepted that
he didn't come second-best to his brother, accepted
that he had no reason to doubt that he came first with
her, and always would.

Until what had happened with Liam had changed
all that, made him question her integrity all over again,
question his own judgement of her character, weigh
up the facts as they were known to him and find her
wanting.

It was the worst thing that had happened to her, but
she had to accept that he would never change his opinion back again. So she had Pilar and Tomás help her
turn the bedroom with the south-facing windows into
a nursery, decorating it in soft shades of cream and
primrose-yellow. Then she organised a day out for
them all.

They did it in style, all dressed in their best. She
and Pilar in the back of the car—Pilar gave a great
shout of laughter. 'You and I together, we will break
the springs!'—and Tomás proudly in front, dressed in
a shiny blue suit, driving, Elena was sure, with the
brakes on most of the time.

By the time they'd toured the stores and baby bou-
tiques, ordered everything from a crib to a fluffy bear,
they were flagging. Elena treated them to lunch, surprised to find herself hungry, enjoying herself.

So life went on, and it was early November, the
nights cold enough now for huge fires made from the
logs Tomás split daily.

Soon, she supposed, Jed would put in an appearance, and, nearer the time of the birth, whisk them off
to wait in one of the hotels in Cadiz, to be near the
maternity unit. He had given his word and he would

keep it. No matter how difficult it would be for both of them; no matter if seeing him again resurrected the awful, keening pain in her heart.

He came on a black night of torrential rain. She heard him call her name and willed her heart to keep beating calmly, not to panic, not to ache, and most of all not to fruitlessly yearn for what could never be again.

She hauled herself out of the chair where she'd been watching the dancing flames and listening to the wind howling in the chimneys, and smoothed down the smothering smock she was wearing over maternity leggings. She resolutely refused to let herself feel embarrassed by the way she looked.

Her hands rested on the shelf that had once been her waist. This was her baby, her life. He wanted no part in either. She had to remember that. When he walked into the cosy, comfy room, the heavy curtains closed to shut out the wild night, she said, 'I think you should turn round and go straight back before the road gets impassable.'

Although he had visited occasionally since he'd discovered her with Liam he had never stayed overnight. She doubted he would want to, even if she suggested it. 'In weather like this there can be rock falls, and the road down to the village turns into a river.' He looked haunted, she saw, hollow-eyed with weight loss. She didn't dare show she cared. 'There's no need for you to be here.'

'I see the need,' he said harshly, as if that was all that mattered. He strode further into the room, shrugged off his rain-darkened soft suede coat and dropped it on the floor. His black cashmere sweater clung to the wide bones of his shoulders. His eyes raked her, eyes that burned with the emotion that had been missing for months.

'One.' He came closer. 'You shouldn't be alone here in weather like this. Two.' He came close enough to touch her if he'd wanted to. 'I need to be here. With you. I can't stay away. Don't ask me to.'

Elena's brow wrinkled, her eyes searching his face. What she saw was fierce intent and something else, something soft and lost that looked like pleading. Did he mean his sense of responsibility, the duty of care he felt towards her and Sam's unborn child, wouldn't let him rest when he knew she'd be alone at night after Pilar and Tomás had left?

Or did he mean something else?

'I don't understand.' Her mouth felt unmanageable. The niggling backache she'd had all day suddenly became a ferocious spasm. She swallowed a gasp, waited until it had passed, then sank down again onto her chair.

Immediately he hunkered down in front of her. 'Are you all right?'

'Perfectly.' His hair was wet, rumpled. She wanted to run her fingers through it—wouldn't let herself, of course.

He gave her a searching look and then, as if satisfied, stood upright, fed more logs onto the fire, then began to pace.

'I put you on a pedestal,' he told her with almost savage self-contempt. 'I had no right to do that. No one's perfect.' He swung round and smiled thinly. 'Not even me. Especially not me. I believed what you told me about the baby. Not because I checked your story, because I didn't. But when I'd cooled down my heart told me you were telling the truth. Then that business with Forrester cropped up and muddied the waters, and I didn't know what to believe.'

He was staring into the fire again, one arm draped across the stone mantel, when the next contraction came. Elena sucked in her breath and ignored it. This was more important.

'I had no damned right to let that happen,' he said rawly. 'If you felt sorry for him—you had been his wife and you must have loved him once—and wanted to help him get back on his feet, then I had no right to prevent you, to get violently jealous because you still had a residue to feeling left for him.'

Silently, Elena got to her feet, her hands pressed into the small of her back. The contractions were coming strongly now, quickly. But before she said anything about it, did anything about it, she had to know. 'Are you suggesting we try again—to make this marriage work?'

'Not try.' He turned to her, his eyes burning. 'It *will* work—if you can forgive me.'

'Why now?' she asked thickly, not daring to let herself believe in this sudden change of heart. 'It's been almost four months. You stayed away. And even when you made those duty visits we might as well have been on different planets.'

'You think I don't know that. You think it didn't tear me apart?' His eyes were tortured. He spread his hands. 'Do you think I don't know what a fool I've been? I can't bear life without you, Elena. I need to be with you, I love you, dammit!'

This was Jed, her Jed. Showing the emotions he'd

battened down. His flaws were all too human, as were hers. His strengths were what mattered, and she would match them with her own. She would find the courage to accept what he was saying. She moved towards him and put her hands on his shoulders.

'I love you. I never stopped. Loving you hurt, but it never stopped.'

The hands that reached for her, held her, were unsteady, his kiss tender, infinitely loving. 'I want to hold you for ever,' he said thickly. 'I've always regarded myself as being ultra-sensible, but with you my emotions rule my head. I'd have said all of this much sooner—months ago—but I was afraid I'd blown it, that you'd tell me I'd had my chance and wouldn't get another. I want you to promise that the next time I behave like a cretin you'll hit me with something heavy.'

'Promise,' she concurred breathlessly. 'If you'll do something for me.'

'Anything.'

She couldn't doubt his fervour. 'Phone Tomás and ask him to bring Pilar up right away. She's had five babies, and helped deliver dozens more.'

A tiny moment of shock, then he said quickly, 'The baby's coming?'

She nodded. 'A couple of weeks early.'

'Get your things. I'll drive you,' he told her firmly, taking charge. But she knew better.

'There won't be time.' She touched his arm. 'Phone Pilar.' She rode the next contraction, sweat dewing her face. She hadn't thought it would happen so quickly.

He gave her a brief but searching look and strode out of the room. He was back in moments.

'They're on their way. Also a doctor and midwife from the maternity unit.' He took her hand. 'Everything's going to be fine. You're not to worry.'

She clung tightly to his fingers. The doctor and midwife wouldn't be here in time, but everything *would* be fine as long as Jed was with her. 'You do love me?' she gasped, her eyes darkening with the ferocity of the contractions that were coming so close together now. 'That's the only thing that might worry me.'

'More than my life!' He cupped her face with his hands. 'I've never stopped. Whatever happens, I'll always love you. You have to believe that.'

She did, oh, she did! She smiled for him radiantly. 'That goes for me, too. So the only problem we have is how to get me to the bedroom.'

'Easy.' His face soft with loving concern, he lifted her in his arms and carried her there, and laid her gently on the bed.

'And not even out of breath,' she teased. 'A man who can carry something the size of a baby elephant has to be hero material!' She heaved herself to her feet again. 'It's better that I keep walking. Help me into a robe, would you, Jed?'

He did, loving care in everything he did, and she caught the tiny flicker of relief in his eyes when Pilar stumped into the room, carrying an armful of towels. She lifted her hand and touched the side of his face. 'Everything's going to be fine.'

'Naturally!' Pilar said firmly. 'It happens all time! Tomás is boiling water.' Her eyes didn't leave Elena; she was timing contractions. She nodded her head briskly. 'I collect things we need. Soon you will want to push. I will be back.'

Soon, very soon now. Elena knew it. 'There's something you should know, my darling. About Liam—'

'Shush.' He laid a finger across her lips, his eyes soft. 'He doesn't matter. If you're concerned about him, and want to help him get back on his feet, I'll track him down and return the money. I had no right to take it from him in the first place.'

'No,' she huffed. 'Will you listen to me for once?' Physical pain didn't make her feel sorry for herself; it made her cross. 'I didn't give him the equivalent of ten thousand pounds because I wanted to, dammit! It was what he demanded. Blackmail. Hand it over—' she panted '—or he'd blacken my name through the tabloids. And by—association—yours—and Nolan's. I knew you'd say let—let him do his worst. I didn't want that. Didn't mind about me. Did about you. Kept it from you. Hated it. Oh, my God!'

Her baby was very anxious to be born. Pilar was there. She took over. Helped her to the bed. It was all happening. Jed held her hand, stroked her forehead, murmured reassurances and loving words of praise.

Then he said, with a catch in his voice, 'This baby is like its father. Impatient. Sam's child. Sam could never contain himself, even when he was very young. If he wanted to do something he wanted to do it *now*. Wanted to climb a particular tree, then he'd hare right up it. Wanted to see if he could climb up on the roof to see if the chimneys were wide enough for Santa to climb down, then off he'd set. My parents had to watch him all the time; that's why he wasn't sent away to school.' He refreshed the cloth he'd been using to cool her brow in a bowl of lavender water. 'Physically, he was a weak child. But he had enough spirit for ten. Left to his own devices he'd have burned himself out.'

'You didn't mind?' she managed, hanging onto his hand, sure she was mangling it.

'For a time, yes, I did mind. I believed I'd been pushed out in favour of the new baby. Frankly, I resented him. Right up until I was around fifteen or sixteen. By that time I was able to understand more. And you were right. When I knew you were carrying Sam's child the old resentment did come back. But not for long. I was wrong—about him, about Liam,' he said quickly. 'If I'd known the creep was blackmailing you I'd have done a damn sight more than get your money back and threaten him.'

Elena didn't hear any more. Jed loved her, truly loved her, and all was right with her world. And she had a job to do, a great big whopping one by the feel of it.

And fifteen minutes later her baby daughter lay in her arms. Nine lusty pounds, with blue eyes and a mass of fine blonde hair.

'She looks exactly like you. She even has your stubborn chin!' Jed uncurled the tiny fingers. 'And before you ask, no, I don't give a damn if she isn't biologically mine. In every other way she is, and always will be. Yours and mine.'

Samantha Nolan's sturdy legs were working like pistons as she climbed the last of the steps up from the garden. She'd been helping Tomás water the flowers and her dungarees were soaked.

And she'd got mud in her hair. She liked Tomás, and Pilar. She liked everything except spinach.

Mummy said she'd like that when she was grown up. Samantha didn't think so. When it got to nearly winter she'd be four, and quite grown up.

She stopped to stick her bright head in a pot of scarlet geraniums. The spicy smell made her sneeze. She liked that, too.

She stumped up the final steps. Now she was going to teach her twin brothers to talk. They were nearly one year old, so it was time they did. Then she'd teach them to read, and draw proper pictures.

They were crawling all over the terrace, blue-clad rumps in the air, under the watchful eye of Mummy and Daddy. Mummy and Daddy were lying on the loungers that they always pushed together, and holding hands again.

They were always holding hands and cuddling. Samantha didn't mind that, so long as she got her share. She loved them very, very much. Ignoring her babbling, wriggling little brothers, she flew over the terrace and hurled herself into two pairs of loving arms.

MILLS & BOON

Winter
weddings

Three brand new Christmas novels

Penny Jordan   Gail Whitiker   Judy Christenberry

Published 18th October 2002

Available at most branches of WH Smith,
Tesco, Martins, Borders, Eason, Sainsbury's
and all good paperback bookshops.

1102/59/SH39

CHRISTMAS
SECRETS

Three Festive Romances

CAROLE MORTIMER   CATHERINE SPENCER
DIANA HAMILTON

Available from 15th November 2002

Available at most branches of WH Smith,
Tesco, Martins, Borders, Eason, Sainsbury's
and all good paperback bookshops.

1202/59/MB50

MILLS & B

THE

Regency

RAKES

A wonderful 6 book
Regency series

2 Glittering Romances
in each volume

**Volume 3 on sale from
6th December 2002**

*Three brand-new,
sinfully scandalous short stories*

Regency
BRIDES

Anne Gracie, Gayle Wilson, Nicola Cornick

Available from 20th September 2002

*Available at most branches of WH Smith,
Tesco, Martins, Borders, Eason, Sainsbury's
and most good paperback bookshops.*

1002/29/MB46

Do you think you can write a Mills & Boon novel?

Then this is your chance!

We're looking for sensational new authors to write for the Modern Romance™ series!

Could you transport readers into a world of provocative, tantalizing romantic excitement? These compelling modern fantasies capture the drama and intensity of a powerful, sensual love affair. The stories portray spirited, independent heroines and irresistible heroes in international settings. The conflict between these characters should be balanced by a developing romance that may include explicit lovemaking.

What should you do next?

To submit a manuscript [complete manuscript 55,000 words]
OR
For more information on writing novels for Modern Romance™

Please write to :-
Editorial Department, Harlequin Mills & Boon Ltd, Eton House, 18-24 Paradise Road, Richmond, Surrey, TW9 1SR or visit our website at **www.millsandboon.co.uk**

Modern Romance...
"seduction and passion guaranteed"

Submissions to:
Harlequin Mills & Boon Editorial Department,
Eton House, 18-24 Paradise Road, Richmond, Surrey, TW9 1SR,
United Kingdom.